ARCTIC WILL

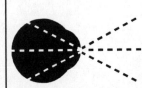

This Large Print Book carries the
Seal of Approval of N.A.V.H.

WATCH EYES TRILOGY, BOOK 3

ARCTIC WILL

JOANNE SUNDELL

WHEELER PUBLISHING
A part of Gale, a Cengage Company

Farmington Hills, Mich • San Francisco • New York • Waterville, Maine
Meriden, Conn • Mason, Ohio • Chicago

LIBRARY OF CONGRESS CATALOGING-IN-PUBLICATION DATA

Names: Sundell, Joanne, author.
Title: Arctic will / by Joanne Sundell.
Description: Large print edition. | Waterville, Maine : Wheeler Publishing, a part of Gale, Cengage Learning, 2017. | Series: Watch eyes trilogy ; #3 | Summary: As the 1910 Alaska sled dog race approaches, Anya and Rune must prevail over dark spirits bent on killing every Chukchi dog on Native Earth.
Identifiers: LCCN 2017016665| ISBN 9781432842253 (hardcover) | ISBN 1432842250 (hardcover)
Subjects: LCSH: Large type books. | CYAC: Supernatural—Fiction. | Shamans—Fiction. | Adventure and adventurers—Fiction. | Survival—Fiction. | Chukchi—Fiction. | Siberian husky—Fiction. | Dogs—Fiction. | Ghosts—Fiction. | Arctic regions—History—20th century—Fiction. | Large type books.
Classification: LCC PZ7.S954645 Au 2017 | DDC [Fic]—dc23
LC record available at https://lccn.loc.gov/2017016665

Published in 2017 by arrangement with Joanne Sundell

Printed in the United States of America
1 2 3 4 5 6 7 21 20 19 18 17

To the great dog driver,
Leonhard Seppala
∼ without whom this tale could not be told

Always ∼
To my beloved Siberian huskies
∼ without whom this tale would not be told

AUTHOR'S NOTE

The Chukchi people of northeast Siberia, over thousands of years, wisely bred and developed the Siberian husky we know today. This work of fiction is set in the context of real events that took place in northeast Siberia and on the Alaskan frontier in the early decades of the twentieth century.

PREFACE

"The Chukchi believed that their dogs guarded the gates of heaven, and that the way you treated a dog in this life determined your place in heaven. If this is so then surely when time comes for us to pass, we will be assured of a place of great honor. It is said that your dogs wait for you, asleep until you come across, then they pull your sled through and into heaven."
(National Sanjankah Dog Association)

Only the Gatekeepers in the heavens stood guard over Anya's dogs. The great Siberian pair turned their lofty heads to Nome and away from other layers in time in other worlds known to the Chukchi. The past had caught up with the present on Native Earth and foretold the terrible future. The years would go fast from here on. The human spirit must prevail on Native Earth — in

9

this time and in this place — for the Chuk-chi dog to have any chance. The young guardians summoned to the Alaska frontier by the gods of the Chukchi and the Vikings, destined for such a task, had accomplished much, but they paid a heavy price. Their spirit, their will to continue the fight, had been crushed. The golem, the great enemy of the People, had been beaten back, but not for long. The final battle had yet to be fought.

The Gatekeepers fixed their watch-blue eyes on the danger ahead, calling across the arctic winds in mournful chorus with all of the ancestors.

CHAPTER ONE

"The short summer was over, and dark times of trials, snowstorms, and piercing cold loomed ahead."
Yuri Rytkheu, *A Dream in Polar Fog*

An Eskimo village outside Nome ~ late winter, 1909

The Chukchi pup fought his tie. He bit repeatedly at the worn hide that kept him from his mother. His cries went unanswered, but still he whimpered. He needed comfort.

They all did.

Held an unreachable distance apart, each tethered to their own post in the snow-covered dog yard, the husky pack could not curl up in close circles to help brace for the coming storm. The scant straw on which they lay easily scattered in the stiff breeze. Temperatures dropped. The day turned dark.

The same instinct charged through each of the seven surviving dogs. They were alone, forgotten by their guardians. The pack had suffered the loss of their leader, Zellie, then one of their team dogs, Mushroom, and now their strength and wheel dog, Xander. To also lose their guardians, the human hands that guided them in this new wild, threw off any sense of well-being.

One guardian had left and the other stayed, but didn't come close. The dogs sensed that the guardian who had left, *Rune,* would not return to the pack. Still, on some level deep inside them, they would wait for him. Their instincts stopped at this sensation and didn't cross any line of life or death. He was just gone. *Anya* was not gone, but her rejection of them hurt and left their spirits dampened. Youthful, loyal dogs, they missed her touch, the sound of her quiet commands, the kindness she gave them, and the safety of her presence.

Life without their guardians near left them agitated, stirred. They relied on the unconditional affection and companionship of Anya and Rune. The affection was mutual, their devotion strong. This kept them going. This gave them direction. They were a pack. To survive, the pack must stay together. Their watch-blue eyes hazed over in grief for the ones gone, especially Xander. His loss marked their freshest wound. His strength had been counted on and his position in the pack relied upon. Little Wolf bemoaned his absence and appeared the most upset. The gray and white runt had dropped weight, and was now down to little more than thirty pounds. He grew weaker by the day.

Physically, the rest of the dogs were all right. The exception might be the female dogs, Magic and Midday. Their ability to breed remained in question. Otherwise, old injuries had not reopened on either of them. Raw paw pads had toughened. New illness had not struck. Predators from the wild surround had not attacked. Punishing human hands had not dragged them away. No whips came after them. The dogs ate and drank what they were given by the steady-handed human who fed them. They felt akin to the human but any relation ended there. He was not a guardian. He did not bring the song of the ancestors to their ears. He did not quicken their hearts to beat in time with the drums of the ancients. He did not bring Spirit.

Spirit lived in the air over tundra and ice, always close, always with them. No more. The dogs didn't sense her presence, not since Anya abandoned them. The same keen instinct that signaled the connection between Anya and Rune told the dogs Anya and Spirit had a connection, a binding tie to each other and, in turn, to them. The dogs didn't see Spirit or hear her call across the open, but they felt her blanket them in the cold, incorporate energy into their tired legs, and bleed with them when they hurt. Centuries of Chukchi-bred heritage made Spirit a part of them, and this fact sparked their awareness of the time before they lived, when spirits were born to their breed. Spirit was a reflex, an impulse, an urge to run, to hunt, and to endure . . . and she'd abandoned them.

Wolves howled across the wide. Dogs howled as if in answer. Then silence. Then the calls would begin again. The arctic cries didn't penetrate the dismal atmosphere in which Magic, Midday, Midnight, Flowers, Frost, and Little Wolf found them. Only five-month-old Thor yowled and whined in return, exercising his lungs and practicing his call to the wild. His actions went unnoticed by the rest of the pack, even his mother, Flowers. Thor didn't understand this, which made the spotted pup yelp and toss his head back farther to try again. Born on the Alaska frontier, a part of him naturally tuned to the unknown wild more than the others.

His first weeks of life should have killed the Chukchi spirit and arctic will inherent in him. Abandoned, alone, in the dark, and torn away from his mother, he had shut down. His watch-blue eyes saw only death until tender human hands saved him. Anya gave him life. She gave him back his spirit. Once gained, his instincts would not let go of such a gift. This sense was reflexive and immediate in the young pup. Gentle by nature, Thor was already fierce about holding onto life. This strong will coursed through his young limbs and set him barking and jumping, anxious for the day. He was a solid match for any larger mix of husky pups born in the North, whether malamute, coastal, or village dog.

He would need to be strong. The ice storm was coming.

Thor circled down in the snow to shield against the wind and cold. He bit one last time at the tie that bound him before momentarily giving up on his task. He wanted to run. The urge overwhelmed him. The tundra beckoned. The frozen sea lured. His claws pawed and relaxed repeatedly at his urge to run, to hunt, to mush. The winds called to him. The winds called *Anya*. He missed the hand of the guardian who helped give him life. He did not understand why she never came near. He did not understand why she had him tied. These sensations left him lost, confused, tired. Thor finally closed his droopy blue eyes and gave in to sleep.

Anya stared blankly into the cookfire of the shelter she shared with Vitya. She barely noticed him. Winter had come, and their summer lodge had been reinforced with boarding and more hides, this time caribou and not walrus, as was custom back in her home village. She didn't question the difference, nor had she noticed when Vitya helped Chinook fortify their Eskimo housing, only vaguely aware of what went on around her.

Shut in already, deep in troubled thought, boards and hide walls made little difference to her. Zellie and Xander's deaths did, and sent her into a melancholy from which she might not recover. Her memories were clouded. A part of her acknowledged that Rune had left her. The world around her was cold, despite the cookfire that burned brightly beneath her outstretched fingers. She shuddered at the chill of death and the isolation of abandonment.

Old fears nagged and dragged her down. Visions of ice floes crashed into one another in her confused state of mind, and she imagined her dogs slipping off their icy edges into the Great Crag — all lost to the dark spirits hiding there, waiting to strike. Why did she imagine dark spirits? What was the Great Crag? Had Zellie died there? Had Xander? No, Rune pulled Xander from the jowls of death in the great sea, didn't he? Could Rune be with Xander? No. She didn't think so. Rune left her, and had walked away. Like everyone always had. She was, after all, *possessed.*

Anya's head throbbed. Sharp pain darted across each and every one of her mixed-up thoughts. She jerked her hands from over the cookfire as if burned. Only moments ago she was freezing, and now she burned. Too hot, she had to get outside, to the cool of the arctic winds. The winds would soothe away her troubled thoughts. The winds would calm her. In the next instant she shot up and rushed through the door flap of the Eskimo lodge.

"Anya!" Vitya roared, but he didn't get up and go after her. Sitting across from her at the same fire, he'd been watching her and saw the sudden upset on her pretty face, his *gitengev* — his pretty girl. The time would come, when he got her back home to their village in Siberia, when she would want to stay by him inside their own yaranga — the home they would build together. They would marry first in Chukchi custom. Time was the answer. He must give her more time to get over the seafaring interloper, *Rune Johansson.*

"Rune Johansson," Vitya hissed out and then spat at the ground. He put his hand to the spot and smashed the dirt there as if Rune were beneath. Feeling every bit the Chukchi warrior, Vitya longed to vanquish his enemy. Rune was his enemy, no matter that Rune had been the very one to help reunite him with Anya by bringing him across the great sea. Rune wanted Anya. Vitya knew it. Vitya could tell the moment he saw Rune and Anya together. He could also tell Anya had feelings for Rune, *mistaken* feelings, Vitya believed. Still, it made him afraid. This whole year apart from her, Vitya felt she loved him and missed him. Now he was afraid she did not and had not.

Rune might have left them together in the Eskimo village of Chinook, but Rune wanted Anya the same way he did. If Rune returned to Nome before Vitya got Anya back across the great sea, he might spirit Anya away from him again, this time for good. Vitya couldn't let that happen. He couldn't take that chance. He took one more stab at the dirt and then got up. Anya was his. She would never belong to Rune Johansson. She belonged to him, only him.

Vitya blew out a hard breath. He thought of his challenge ahead — to win Anya back. Anya was in a bad place in her mind and in her heart. Some of her dogs had died. This was a great loss to her. Her strange behavior alarmed him, and he couldn't seem to bring her out of her dark trance. She was shaman. She was special. Maybe this sad trance was part of a ritual she had to go through. Maybe she only spoke to spirits, and not to him, for good reason. That's what Vitya guessed, since she'd stopped talking to him — that she must be communicating with the spirit world. He wasn't a part of Chukchi magic. She was. The sooner he got her back to Siberia and to the people, the sooner his *gitengev* would return to him. This Alaska frontier was no place for her or for him, Vitya had already decided.

He and Anya shared the same dwelling, but he felt worlds apart from her, as if she were tied to an unreachable post like the dogs outside. She ignored them, too. Never in all their growing up together had Vitya seen her turn cold against any Chukchi dog. Her father, Grisha, had given her an important job when he assigned her to cull, raise, and train his huskies. Women in their home village would help select pups to keep for breeding, but were not assigned to train and work them. Anya had been. Grisha must have known Anya was special. Vitya's insides gave a turn. Then why did Grisha trade his daughter away at Markova, if she'd been so special! At least Vitya suspicioned that's what happened. Grisha never said a word about her when he returned from Anadyr.

What Anya did — releasing Grisha's dogs to run away so they wouldn't be split up and traded at the next fair — was wrong, and she should have been punished. But what did Grisha do? First he threatened her with a harpoon, aiming to kill her, and then he changed his mind and took her with him and the dogs for trade. Vitya had watched Anya leave their village. He remembered how Grisha stood in between him and Anya to keep them apart. Grisha wouldn't allow Vitya to follow. Vitya's insides clenched. He should have gone with Anya anyway. Why hadn't he? All he did was give her the necklace he'd carved for her. Vitya regretted not standing up to Grisha, no matter how important Grisha was to their village.

Vitya didn't deserve to have Anya's affection, he realized. He'd abandoned her when he should have gone with her a year ago.

That she still wore the husky carving around her neck was a surprise, a good one. It gave him hope he could win her back. It was a connection between them. He'd wanted her to think of him. She must have, or else she would have tossed the necklace away. Vitya gained satisfaction from this, since Anya wore his gift in front of Rune Johansson. Not anymore. *Rune was gone.* This also gave Vitya satisfaction. Anya would forget Rune, and Vitya would make sure she did. He and Anya were alone. He, Vitya, would be the one to take care of her as before. Then he thought of their kiss and remembered her soft lips. Anya was his *gitengev,* his.

Given enough time, Anya would come back to him in body and spirit. In the meanwhile, he would watch over her and her dogs. Since she seemed to discard her dogs as if culled, he wasn't sure what he should do with them. What was best? To keep them tied to posts as they were now, or find work for them in front of a sled so they might hunt and pull loads, or would it be best to release them to fend for themselves? They could run free, but Chukchi dogs did this only in summer. In winter, dogs were tied to posts when they weren't working. Vitya wanted to talk to Chinook about this. The wise Eskimo would know what was best in this *Alaz-kah,* he thought. The problem was they didn't speak the same language. Anya had been Vitya's translator until she shut down all conversation with him. With no other choice, Vitya had to try to talk to the Eskimo on his own.

Rune had carefully captained the *Nordic* back to Seattle's busy harbor. In all his years at sea, traveling and working with his father, he'd never liked returning to land. Always restless to leave on another trade venture, to chart arctic waters, to be shipboard and not land-bound, he used to badger his father to let him sign on to any ship that might be heading out of the harbor, to any destination north. His father would lecture him about the movement of the ice pack and the dangers the Arctic presented during the coldest months of the year. "Few trade ports stay open in winter," he would tell Rune. "There's plenty of work to keep us here, son." Yeah, paperwork, Rune resentfully concluded. He flatly refused to shuffle papers and push a pen around all day. That's when Rune would charge out of his father's shipping office, determined to think of some way to get his father to change his mind.

Not this time. Not after this trip.

Rune didn't have an opinion one way or the other about arriving back in Seattle, as he steered the *Nordic* with exact precision to its docking berth; not one move or one turn of his steerage was wasted. A collision with another ship in the crowded wharf could bring disaster. Intent on his task and trusting his crew to see to theirs, Rune deliberately kept his focus on the *Nordic* and away from the ache at the back of his neck. He refused to remember why he had that particular pain.

His neck had bothered him from Nome to Seattle this trip. So what? Sailors had to endure discomfort. Aches and pains were just part of the bargain for seafarers. So were storms and ice pack giving chase, and seas too high to cross with food and fresh water nowhere to be found! He was alive, wasn't he? He'd no reason to complain. Besides, his father had finally let him captain one of his *skepps* . . . two times now.

This thought sneaked in when Rune's careful guard was down. The scar at the back of his neck singed. He didn't try to swat the mystic pain away, but he tried hard to keep his thoughts at bay. Rune didn't want to remember anything that had happened during the past year. When he did, it

23

was all maze and blur with no faces clear and no places distinct. Left confused, all that Rune knew is that he hurt, not just the scar at his neck, but in his heart, in his soul. He didn't know why. Deep down, he didn't want to know. His scar marked him with the sign of the Viking gods — the sign of the runes — an ancient symbol, that's all it was. It didn't have anything to do with anything. Rune was his name and no more than that.

One more memory, a sensation really, did unnerve him and did force his attention: he'd known fear over the past year. He'd never had that sensation in his bones before, at least not to this extent. He didn't like the feeling. Sailors couldn't afford such emotions. They could get a man killed. They could sink a ship and its entire crew. No, he couldn't afford to be afraid . . . *or in love.*

No quicker than this unlikely thought hit, Rune swatted it away and refused to wonder why he should think such a thing. Love wasn't any part of his life; it never had been and never would be. Rune pulled the corded bell rope down sharp to signal their safe docking; the sound deafened in his wheelhouse. He pulled the rope sharp again to help drum out the turn of his thoughts. His agitation, no doubt, was due to his mother and his sister being on board the *Nordic.* He didn't love them and they didn't love him. So be it, and so what?

The outside world could question his family's loyalty and affection for one another and with good reason. He didn't come from a caring family. His father was the exception. On a level Rune had trouble understanding, he did care for his father, but not for Margret or Inga. Rune never felt his mother welcomed him into this world and he never believed his sister wanted him here, either. Maybe this was the way in families with a lot of money. Rune had no idea. No matter; he charted his own way.

Seventeen years old now, he would keep on doing his own charting. Besides, time came in life for a man to be a man and not dwell on things over which he had no control. Rune had no control over the cold, hard fact that his mother and his sister were empty-headed and empty-hearted. There, he said it. His father had said the same thing, but maybe in a different way, before he watched Rune set sail on the *Nordic* with Margret and Inga, headed back to Seattle.

Rune felt a twinge in his chest at this recall, at the thought of setting sail back to Seattle. He tried to ignore the unwelcome feeling, but he couldn't shake it. Why should

25

the idea of leaving for Seattle bother him? His mind was a blank on why. His next thought turned back to Nome and this rattled him. His neck pinched. There was no one and nothing in Nome that should bother him or that he should worry over leaving behind. He couldn't remember and he didn't have time to worry over unimportant things like feelings.

Duty-bound, Rune did his father's bidding and shepherded his mother and his sister out of Nome. His father didn't need to ask him. Rune would have seen them safely home anyway. He supposed that a part of him forgave them for their transgressions. Rune couldn't help but think they'd wronged him beyond cutting family ties, with all of their coldness and greed. But as for what other transgressions they'd committed, he couldn't remember. *Dammit.* His confusion and lack of memory agitated him. Why should he care anymore? *I shouldn't.* The truth went down hard. Rune didn't care much about anything anymore. He couldn't remember a time when things mattered. Something must! But for the life of him, he couldn't come up with even one thing.

Work was important. Shipping was important. His father let him captain the *Nordic.*

His father at least trusted him that much. Rune didn't question his good fortune. For too long, all he'd wanted was his father's trust in him. This was the first time, right? Yes, he'd never captained any of the Johansson fleet before. At least he didn't think so. The scar at his neck burned to the point of pain. Rune didn't have time for this. He had to help off-load everything on the *skepp,* including his so-called family. This wasn't anything he looked forward to — escorting his own mother and sister off the ship and out of his life. This was his intention, however. He just wanted to be alone. He didn't need family. He didn't need friends. He needed to work, that's all.

Straightening his spine, getting ready to leave the wheelhouse of the *Nordic* and see to his passengers, crew, and freight, he tried to turn a deaf ear to the stray dogs he heard barking as they ran up and down the harbor, doubtless excited over the return of yet another ship. Maybe they thought they'd get a handout, or maybe a friendly pat. Rune had no idea. Why he even noticed the dogs, he had no idea. He'd never worried over them before. He did now. Were they hungry? Were they scared? Did they have shelter? Were they safe? Agitated all over again, Rune raced down the steps to the

27

main deck. He didn't like these uncertain feelings. There was that damned word again! He didn't want to *feel,* period.

The arctic winds were persistent. They didn't soothe Anya after all. They followed her and made it impossible for her to avoid their whispers — their haunting cries for help. She couldn't imagine why the winds spoke to her and why she could understand them. *Is it because I'm possessed?* Why else would she receive such ghostly messages on the winds across tundra and ice? She needed answers. Anya wanted her memory to return, all of it. She wanted to know why she understood spirits and why they asked *her* for help.

She'd lost Zellie and Xander. This memory was fixed in her head and heart. This memory cut her up and down, jabbing and stabbing like a hundred harpoons killing her over and over, day in and day out. This memory made her long to end her own life, to sacrifice her life on Native Earth and reunite with Zellie and Xander so they might help pull her sled across into heaven. She knew she was Chukchi and not Eskimo and she sensed spirits, good spirits and bad.

Anya put her hands to her temples and tried to quiet the pounding in her head. She kept on walking through the Eskimo village in the snow, despite the cold and despite Inuit villagers trying to get her attention. Dogs barked. Yes, but *not* Zellie and Xander. She needed to get away from the village, and out in the open where she could think. She was desperate to get her memory back, enough to know why she understood voices from the spirit world and why she remembered Rune enough to hurt so from his leaving. She'd lost him, too, but so many details blurred. His handsome face, she remembered, but little else at the moment.

Anya had on her kerker, her seal-fur coverall. Her body was warm, but any trail to clear thinking had turned cold. She clutched her fingers into fists and then released them, much as a husky might relax and then draw in its claws, itching to run. Slowed down by confusion and blurred recollection, Anya kept on her way out of Chinook's village with no direction in mind, as she might have if her full memory returned. Then she might remember she was a true Chukchi shaman, a medium able to travel between worlds who followed the guide of the Directions across arctic winds. For now, frustrated at her lack of recall she decided she must have been mistaken about any ghostly spirits trying to talk to her. Her

29

imagination had gotten the better of her, that's all.

Anya stomped through the deepening snow. Her boots and hide-leggings, *mukluks* to Alaska frontiersmen, protected and helped pave her way. She didn't wear *siwash* or *dutch* socks, as many on the frontier did — trappers, traders, travelers, and miners alike — who needed to pull them on before stepping into their heavy boots. Anya's Chukchi mukluks served her well and she didn't need any blanket or wool socks. *Gasp!* She realized she wore *necessaries* — under-clothes of the white man. The heavy cotton drawers and top scratched under her kerker. When had she adopted the ways of the white man . . . and the English words of the white man?

Then she heard the whispers again. They wouldn't stop! Anya slammed her hands over her ears and tried to shut out the cries for help. It didn't work. She took down her hands and stopped. She'd no choice but to listen. This couldn't be her imagination. The howling winds that surrounded her and held her to the spot were spirits from another world. She knew it. Her stomach churned. Heavy snow blew past. Anya faced into the weather on hard-taken steps. Forced to listen to the winds and whispers, she did.

She understood their haunting cries.

It is time. It begins again.

Some will live. Many will die.

Only human hands can save us.

Anya swallowed hard and clutched her fingers into fists again. She didn't wear her hide mittens and hadn't thought to bring them with her. *Only human hands can save us.* Anya held her bare hands up to the sky as if the winds spoke of *her* human hands. She spread her fingers wide and stared at all ten of them. The oddest sensation suddenly struck her, and she felt her fingers begin to tingle. Then both hands started to tremble and shake ever so slightly. More curious than afraid, she watched the bizarre vision of her hands fading in and out of sight. She stayed calm yet she felt anything but. She could swear her hands vanished and reappeared, but that couldn't be. I am no ghost!

The moment Anya thought *ghost,* her stomach pained so badly, the ache sent her to her knees. She knew this feeling. It was familiar. Memory forced her to stand back up. In a time before, in a world gone past, she spoke to spirits — *to the dead* — to the ghosts of her ancestors. Managing to stay on her feet, she listened to the spirits, husky and human, telling her she was right to think what she did — that she was a part of two worlds — that she was part husky and part human. Anya dropped to her knees again, this time out of cold fear.

She was possessed after all.

One Chukchi dog escaped him; only one out of nine so far that stole away from Mother Russia's shores. The golem rubbed his whiskered face. Agitated, he needed a shave, and he needed to get out of his prison. The revolution neared. For now, dark spirits did his bidding in the world beyond and had marked the Chukchi and their dogs, but it wasn't enough. Some dogs and some breeders still lived. All *kulaks* must die. Chukchi breeders were kulaks. Their dogs brought them riches. Their dogs allowed them to live well . . . too well. The Chukchi dog must not be allowed to breed, especially outside of Russia. He, the golem, would stop them. He was in charge, in this world and in the world beyond!

He hadn't realized his full power yet, but when he broke from his prison, he would set in motion his final plan to liquidate the Chukchi and their stunted dogs. The dogs were weak. The new Russia would need more superior dogs to power the industrial times to come. The golem meant to breed a greater dog. The Chukchi dog had no place in Russia's future. *None!* The golem's anger seethed. His insides sparked with the main reason he wanted to stamp out the Chukchi breed. The purebred dogs would give the Chukchi power and the will to stand up against his future communist rule, in the same way they'd pushed back the Cossacks' and the Czar's forces in times past. This, the golem could not allow.

Once he wiped out their dogs, the Chukchi would lose their arctic will to survive and their means to do it, in this world or any other. The breed would be dead, period. The golem blew out a smoky breath, then stamped out his cigarette. Restless, he paced back and forth across the cold cement of his cell. The gray walls closed in and made him think of a stone coffin.

"Aaaaarrrrrrggggg!" he roared against the image of his own death. He had power and might. Death could not touch him. This prison was not his grave. Soon it would crumble just like all of his enemies, just like anyone who tried to stand in his way. All would live collectively and all would obey him. He stopped his pacing and flopped onto his cot, and then settled his back against the hard stone. Cracks ran along the wall behind him, as if signaling the breach he'd already caused in this world. The golem leaned his head against the crack and shut his eyes, to better recall his beginning.

Born into this world in human shape, he remembered his creation at the hands of dark spirits molding and shaping his form from molten clay — red clay. He burned hot but the nurturing touch of dark spirits soothed him as a babe, he distinctly recollected. His mother was embers and his father, ash. Together these fiery spirits brought him life. There were others like him, he understood even at his infant age. Others came before him and others would follow, born in the same way. His mother told him as much in her rasped whispers to him:

You are not the first of your kind, but you are the only one of your kind born to this world at this time. You will have dominion in two worlds, the same as others before you. You are a golem gifted with the demon spark. This spark gives you power. This spark lets you breach worlds and reign in both. You will achieve greatness. You will have dominion and all will yield to you. You are one of us. You are a dark spirit who can bring worlds to your feet. Fear is your weapon. Use it, my child. Make your mark for all time.

The golem fumbled in his shirt pocket for

another cigarette. Out of matches, he was about to toss his unlit smoke to the floor when he spotted an unused matchstick there. He calmly got up off his cot, then snatched the needed match. Remembering his mother's words had quelled his anger. He must never lose sight of his powers and the reason he was born — *to make his mark for all time.* He'd made a good start, he thought. He had begun to make his mark on Russia by issuing commands in the world of dark spirits, to destroy those who would try to stop him in the world of humans. Born into both worlds, he had power in both and meant to use it, just as his mother had commanded him.

The golem struck the match against the skin of his hand and watched its flint flare to a burn. He lit his cigarette and took a satisfied draw. In that moment, he didn't have to wonder if there were others like him, with the same purpose, the same intent he had. Others had made their mark since the beginning of time and so they would until the end of time. Human civilizations had been destroyed with such marks in many places on earth. The golem had his territory planned out and marked. To create his new Russia, he must destroy its old civilization. Fear was his greatest weapon. His greatest enemy — the one that troubled him the most — was the Chukchi and their dogs in far-northeast Siberia. He'd decided this over a year ago, fixed in his demonic thinking . . . *for all time.*

Yet, one Chukchi dog had escaped him.

Already done with the smoke just lit, the golem smashed it under his boot. The idea of any dog or dog breeder getting away from him stoked his fury and sent him pacing back and forth in his cell; this action had become routine. He'd let down his guard and let the one Siberian husky get away, one from the original team stolen from his Russia and escaped to the Alaska frontier. The animal was dead, he thought, but he didn't get a sense of where or when the death occurred. With the leader dog, *Zellie,* he knew exactly. With the copper-red and white swing dog, he knew exactly. But with the black and white wheel dog, he couldn't be certain. This threatened the golem's power — losing sight of any of the Chukchi dogs that fled across the Bering Sea. He needed to find the one dog.

An even greater threat loomed over him which he had to take care of first. Teams of Chukchi dogs — *all stunted in growth and weak in will* — were going to race outside of Russia in the spring, in Nome. Many would

36

see the race. If the dogs chanced to run well, many would mistakenly applaud the speed of the Siberian dogs. Many on the Alaska frontier would want to breed their dogs with the Chukchi dogs to gain speed. This fact did not upset the golem — that some might breed the Chukchi dogs with Eskimo dogs or wolves or mixes from the Outside — but the fact that an intent breeder might keep the Siberian bloodlines pure infuriated the golem. No *kulaks* can live!

The Midgard serpent had failed him. The Viking boy had made it across the Bering Sea with the new Siberian teams. The serpent had attacked, but had been struck down by the sword of the ancient Viking gods. This could not happen again. The sword that cut down the serpent was finally in the golem's hands, resting in the deep and waiting to strike against the boy when given the opportunity. The golem must strengthen his control over the gods of the Vikings and the gods of the Chukchi he'd been able to commandeer to his side. The fires of *Hel* and the Raven god would know his full wrath if they failed him again!

The golem's chest pumped with renewed energy; his black heart was fueled by the distinctive odor of fear that sparked electric in the air around his enemies, spirit and hu-

37

man alike. They all knew he was coming for them. They all knew they could not stop the ice storm. He'd dashed their spirits and confused their purpose, and all but crushed any arctic will to endure. Revenge tasted sweet so far, but he wasn't done. The breeders must die. The Chukchi dogs must die. No more could escape him.

One had.

The golem's teeth clenched and his jaw set in a hard snarl. His yellow eyes beaded over. Saliva dripped down his chin. If he discovered the lone Chukchi dog alive, he would rip it to shreds. It was inevitable that he would since he was master of this time . . . *for all time.*

CHAPTER TWO

"... And when, on the still cold nights, he pointed his nose at a star and howled long and wolflike, it was his ancestors, dead and dust, pointing nose at star and howling down through the centuries and through him."
Jack London, *The Call of the Wild*

Xander's wounds were killing wounds. His strong instinct for life had kept his heart beating and his lungs working air in and out in strained huffs during his struggle to crawl away and flee his guardian's hand. The moment *Anya* left him for the last time and disappeared outside their cover, he'd opened his bleary watch-blue eyes and sensed he'd escaped the gentle hand of death. He couldn't see anything but shades of shadow. Already hurt badly from the ring of killing dogs and the battle just fought, Anya's *Spirit* saved him from death, but he knew he was dying. He was ready and expected his guardian's knife to come and end his pain. He was ready to join his ancestors in the sleep of death. His guardian was not. He must help her. He owed it to her: his life and his death.

This awareness came from ingrained impulse and intuition and not from any human process of thought. His guardian wanted to help him, not hurt him. This awareness gave him the will to crawl away from her to die on his own. He wanted to help her, not hurt her. His loyalty and affection for Anya ran deep. His memory of her had not faded. Of others, yes.

He had no memory of others in the time before dying — that's how Xander sensed his time and place on Native Earth since he'd separated from his trusted guardian. He did feel dead inside, at least the part of him where conscious awareness and instinct intersect and battle for control. Xander was aware of Anya and the closeness, the companionship, and the loyalty he felt toward her human shape in his mindfulness, but instinctively he turned away from her when he heard howls from the wild. The howling lulled and drew him in. Anya's image began to fade.

So did any hope for other memories. He

had no memory of any other call to heed but the wild; he had no memory of his old life as a gentled Chukchi dog. He had no sense of the Gatekeepers or any connection to Zellie that might alert him to his husky beginnings. The impulse to scan the horizon and wait for her return, as he'd done every day since her death, did not prick his senses on this side of his recollection. Zellie was gone from him, forgotten. So were the others, human and husky, he'd known in the time before dying.

The Gatekeepers trained their watch eyes on Xander, overcome with sadness for his loss to the wild. The aurora borealis could light the heavens in continual swirls and motion, but this would not bring illumination — *spirit* — back to Xander. The Chukchi spirit in him had been taken by the golem, and because of this they laid no blame at Xander's feet for parting from his husky pack. The golem meant to wipe out their breed and had succeeded in snuffing out the human spirit in Anya and Rune and the Chukchi spirit in Xander.

Time marked in painful pauses, stopping then picking up again only to pass by more quickly than before. The atmosphere clouded, thick with tension.

Awakened unnaturally from her eternal sleep, Zellie's unearthly being had been roused and stirred by the upset cries of the Gatekeepers. Instead of waking to help pull the sled of loved ones across to heaven — her husky task in death — the agonizing cries of the Gatekeepers alarmed her misted presence enough for her to take shape in the outline of her canine ancestors. Once formed so, she understood the cries of the Gatekeepers.

Her companion and friend unto eternity had been lost to her.

Xander didn't know her memory.

How could she help him cross to heaven, if he didn't know her and the ancestors?

To the extent of Zellie's ability to experience any sensation of any kind in death, she was afraid for Xander and for all the Chukchi. What if they were all lost? Upset especially over Xander, what if she could not help pull his sled through to heaven when the time came? Then she would surely be alone unto the end, for if all became lost, there would be no more Chukchi heaven. These sensations came to Zellie across generations of reflexive behavior and instinctive pack mentality of life and death, much as humans process thought and go into survival mode when met with suffering and loss.

Such is the force of life even in death.

Such is the power of love.

Zellie had never been afraid to be alone until this dark awareness penetrated the boundaries of her amorphous self. She fought to keep the outline of her husky shape intact when the howls began to erupt from her barely defined throat. She involuntarily called over the wild to Xander, and would keep on for as long as it took for him to hear her, determined to hold her shape and his, in the world of the Chukchi . . . *for all time.*

"Lassie, will you *nee* help me with my *dugs*?" Fox Ramsey implored of Anya.

She sat cross-legged on the ground by the cookfire in her tented shelter and barely looked up when the stranger entered through the heavy door flap. The center pole of the Eskimo lodge vibrated slightly. Snow had blown in behind the man. His face was familiar to Anya, but no other memory stirred. Stripped down to a thin-hide dress, which she wore over long underwear, her body felt cold inside and out. She stretched her hands to the fire and not to the man just come in, in any sign of greeting. The boiled meat in the pot over the fire bubbled in the oil. The food didn't entice. She'd never liked bear. She wished the meat was fresh-killed walrus so the bite would be rich in nourishing blood. How she would savor such a taste . . . if she were hungry.

The man was talking. She didn't listen.

"I *ken* you've been through a lot and are a wee bit *doon,* but I need you, lassie. I know the lad, Rune, is gone, but Vitya refuses to help me *oot.*" Fox pled on, but then hesitated when he noticed something was wrong with the lassie. He hadn't seen her for weeks, and she appeared changed. Still a pretty lassie and still too thin, her look was faraway. Her straight brown eyes held no sparkle. Suspicious of the change in her, Fox immediately thought of her dogs and his heart went out to her. Had any more of them died? He shook off his parka and took a seat opposite her on the ground, on the other side of the fire.

Anya noticed the man again and shrugged her shoulders. He wasn't very old. It wasn't Vitya this time. She wanted to be alone. She wanted the man to go away and Vitya to stay away. She just wanted to be by herself with no spirits and no humans prodding and poking at her and disturbing her solitude. She'd stopped talking to Vitya to shut him from her and make him go away.

Humph! She'd do the same with this stranger. Her gaze stayed fixed on the fire.

"Lassie . . . Anya." Fox tried again to get through to her, this time using her name. If she would just look at him, maybe she would recognize him and talk to him, and he could find out what this was all about. He needed to start with her dogs.

"Anya, are your *dugs braw*? Are they good?"

She darted a look right through him at his words.

Fox swallowed hard. *Damn!* It *was* about her dogs.

"Anya, are they —"

"Dead?" she interrupted. "Yes, Zellie and Xander are dead! And so is Mushroom!" She whispered this last, not meaning to, and not remembering what Mushroom even looked like. Sobs welled up inside her and she fought to choke them back.

"Are-are you satisfied?" she barely got out before tears cut off her words.

"Lassie, I'm that sorry," Fox said, and wished he had a way to comfort her. Seeing her at this time so overcome with grief, he understood the reason. He'd heard about Xander and knew he'd been seriously wounded, but he'd hoped the proud black and white wheel dog would live. He'd hoped wrong. Mushroom must be the dog killed in the mines. What a loss to the lassie and such a shocker. When Fox thought about it, losing even one of the unique Siberian huskies was sad, indeed. Hadn't he traveled across the Bering Sea, all the way to the Markova Fair in Anadyr, to bring back teams of Chukchi dogs? Yes, all to race in the next sweepstakes.

This is why he needed Anya's help, but right now she needed his.

Vitya saw the Scot enter the Inuit village and followed him. He knew the dog driver would come looking for his Anya. She wasn't up to any talk about anything, much less with *Fawks.* She didn't talk to Vitya, and she wouldn't talk to the Scot because Vitya wouldn't allow it. He was tired of letting anybody keep him from Anya. Grisha had. Rune had. No more. Vitya would watch over and protect Anya, and no one would stand in his way ever again.

Why he got so angry so easily these days puzzled Vitya. Rune was gone and Vitya didn't have to worry about any rivalry with him anymore. As for Fox, he wasn't a bad person. He was a good man who only wanted to train and race Chukchi dogs. Vitya had helped him care for the teams traded for on the journey here. It was a way for Vitya to get across the great sea and to find Anya. That was then. This is now. Vitya had found Anya and wouldn't leave her again, not even to help in a neighboring dog yard. When Fox had asked him for his continued help, Vitya shook his head in a firm no.

Dogs were dogs. Dog drivers were dog drivers. If Vitya didn't help Fox, there were plenty of others who could. With so many dogs around, there had to be other trainers and dog drivers. Vitya had seen scores of dogs since his arrival in this new country, some huskies, some mixes, and some he couldn't identify. Around Chinook's village there were many native dogs, village and coastal. There were Inuit men who could help Fox, and there must be men in the white man's village trained to work with sled teams.

Now Fox sought out his Anya. He must want Anya to help him.

Vitya broke into a run. Anya was in no shape to work with dogs, period, and much less three other Chukchi teams of them. Who was he kidding? Even if she did come out of her sad trance, Vitya didn't want her to leave Chinook's village. He wanted her to stay where he could keep an eye on her and keep her safe. He didn't want to take any chances Rune Johansson might return without Vitya knowing, and spirit Anya away. No, Vitya would make sure Anya didn't wander too far from him.

She wore his necklace.

She was *his*.

A lawyer by trade and a dog driver at heart, Albert Fink passed the modest gavel back and forth in his hands before setting it down to stay, on the same table where he usually sat when he came inside the Board of Trade Saloon. It wasn't time to call a meeting of the Nome Kennel Club, of which he was president, but he kept the gavel with him all the same. For luck, he thought. Without thinking about it, he lowered a hand to his gun belt, and rested his fingers over his trusted Smith & Wesson pistol. For luck, he instantly thought. The contact with the cold steel brought a feeling of security to him. He'd need his gun and more to help keep the peace when time came for the next sweepstakes. More *Siberian wolves* had been imported to Nome, and Albert didn't doubt the reason: to race against the Alaska frontier's own.

This could spell big trouble among bettors in the next All Alaska Sweepstakes and turn friendly competition into a battle royal. Things could get ugly real fast if hardworking miners and frontiersmen lost all their earnings to the Siberian husky teams. The last race proved that to Albert, when bettors reacted to the Johansson boy and his "Siberian rats," as they were called by many, competing in the race and then finishing in third place. Eleven teams had had to drop out due to the sudden blizzard, which caused the first near riot. Bets had been placed and money already lost. Then, when fear spread through the waiting crowd that Scotty Allan might get beat by the two teams left in the sweepstakes, the next wave of upset hit. Their winnings waited for them in the Bank of Nome, and their bets were on Allan, and, "By damn, no other dog driver and no upstart kid could cross the finish ahead of Scotty!"

Albert had to pull out his pistol and shoot at the ceiling to break up the bad mood and get everyone's attention; he had to shoot first before others did. Their guns wouldn't be pointed at the ceiling but at each other. Albert couldn't afford to wait for men to go at each other or at him, each one upset over money. It was always about money in Nome, about the gold. If men didn't see it in their gold pans, they'd better see it in their pockets after a race win. Desperation came easy to men in the North. Money didn't, at least not to most.

Gold fever spread fast, but dog racing fever, even faster, Albert realized. How to stop it before it started; that was the problem he faced. Too late to stop the word-of-mouth fact that everyone in Nome and out on the frontier knew about the Siberian dogs' arrival, Albert had to hope that was as far as any thought or talk about the dogs went.

Albert had found out right away about the new arrivals the moment he sat down to supper at the Board of Trade Saloon, the very evening the small huskies off-loaded onto Nome's shores. Conversations drifted his way. Most men laughed about the *funny-looking-foreigners* and had already concluded they were meant for the mines. Common sense should have told them otherwise. Common sense should have stirred their memories over the race they'd all witnessed the past winter. Not once did Albert hear talk of the little dogs from Siberia racing against their own dogs, which led Albert to conclude that locals still didn't think much of the team that placed third in the last sweepstakes — only an hour behind the winner.

For his part, Albert did.

The Siberian dogs were fast as lightning. They might have won. In the back of his mind, Albert had wondered if something might have happened to prevent their win. It was just a flash across his thoughts, but it nagged at him. Now, with more Siberian dogs arrived, the thought gave him a big headache. While most residents in the area and out on the surrounding Alaska frontier were likely to think Fox Maule Ramsey was plum crazy to bring more "Siberian rats" to Nome, since he needed much larger, freight dogs to successfully work his mines, Albert's thinking didn't take any such turn. He didn't think the Scot was crazy, and he didn't think the dogs were intended to work the mines.

Fox Ramsey meant to race them, Albert was convinced.

So long as he was the only one who had reached this conclusion, things in and around Nome should stay calm, at least among bettors on the next sweepstakes. Well into the most difficult part of winter, with isolation set firm in the bones of miners and frontiersmen alike, Albert hoped they all kept their focus on their work in the mines and hunting and trapping, and joined in the friendly ski competitions held throughout the cold months. Nobody bet on skiers and jumpers, and the rivalry was always good clean fun. Usually, Albert told himself when he remembered one fist fight between two very competent yet very competitive Norwegians last season. Smaller dogsled races were run, too. All in fun, Albert mentally repeated as he tightened his grasp on the handle of his Smith & Wesson. He meant to keep the next All Alaska Sweepstakes that way — all in fun.

Satisfied with his demonic handiwork, the golem had to give some praise to the dark spirits under his command for carrying out his wishes and instilling fear in his enemies. It was his greatest weapon — fear — and it had worked on the girl and the boy so far. They were afraid, hurt, and alone. He savored such a win in this battle to the death. He'd robbed them of their spirit and taken their memories to the place where they knew only fear, hurt, confusion, and despair. Victory was sweet.

Keep them afraid and keep them apart.

This he must do. The human guardians of the Chukchi dogs had too much power when they joined forces against him. Their spirits could outwit his, if given the chance. They would have no more chances. They were without hope and helpless now, and he meant to keep them that way — their human spirits would not prevail over him. He, the golem, held dominion over all in the world of spirits and the world of humans. The End was coming.

I bring the ice storm.

Out of cigarettes, the golem shouted for his jailors to give him more. His jailors were afraid of him and he knew it. He was the one behind bars, yet they feared him. Fear was ever his greatest weapon. Smiling to himself over this, he kept up his shouts. His jailors knew he was a powerful man despite this prison. They knew he would be out soon and free to crush them like a dead cigarette if he wanted.

Snatching the smokes from the shaky hand of his guard, the golem ripped open the pack right away and lit the welcome tobacco. He took a deep inhale, then blew it out. It didn't satisfy. Something was wrong. The one husky, the one Chukchi dog he couldn't account for, had somehow gotten away. The dog should be dead and probably was, but the golem didn't know for sure. He liked being sure. It was the only way to gain and keep power, being sure of every action and reaction.

Dead or alive, the dog hid from him.

Not for long, the golem promised; he would find the escaped dog.

"No *kulaks* can live," he spat out, then crushed the cigarette stub beneath his boot and imagined it was the unaccounted-for Chukchi dog.

Xander had instinctively crawled away from Anya, blind and in pain, barely able to walk a few steps before stumbling in the snow, to die alone in the open. No one had to take him there to die; he knew to travel his last steps on his own. It was the Chukchi way. He was Chukchi. It would be his way. The guiding hand of the ancestors replaced the guiding hand of his guardian, and helped shepherd him out of the Eskimo village toward the wild, to his sacrificial resting place. The song of generations of enduring, determined, steadfast Chukchi dogs drove his weakened bones and failing heart to help him make his last journey. This howling song came on the winds and helped raise his tired body to stand and to break away from his human companion and friend, *Anya*.

Xander knew the sound of her name as she knew his. To his instincts, her name naturally meant trust, loyalty, and affection. To his instincts, her touch brought comfort, guidance, and protection. These instincts he would carry with him across the hard ground he must cover to get to the open; he would hold onto his stamped memories of Anya and not let go. Human or husky, such is the power of love, even in death.

A quiet calm had set in around Xander. He'd made it to a place that was a safe distance from Anya where she would not witness his death. Able to finally, he stopped his hard-fought sojourn. He would die alone. A faint memory of Zellie stirred in him, and he whimpered for her — he waited for her to pull his sled across to heaven. Generations of breeding built this last impulse into his canine being. He didn't fear in any human terms Zellie might not be there, but even so, a slight nudging at him kept him from his death. Hurt, alone, and afraid, Xander's discomfort forced him to stay in this life when he begged to leave.

Odin's wolves had found him. The pair of great gray wolves had left their master of the Viking gods, to do his bidding: to save Xander if they could. And so had the Gatekeepers of the Chukchi gods summoned them. The *spirit of the wolf* was called upon. The wolves would help, if they could. They would heed the call to battle, the call to the wild.

The wolf and the dog battle as one on Native Earth and in the ancient heavens.

It is time. It begins again.

The great wolves sensed their powers were limited on Native Earth, and they must rely on the spirit of the wolf, the strength of the wolf, and the intelligence of the wolf . . . and not mist and magic, as exists in the worlds beyond. The only sign brought from the domain of their gods was their watch-blue eyes. This marked their difference from other wolves on Native Earth. The spitting snarl of the yellow-eyed wolf that would stalk them pricked their ears and alerted them to the danger ahead.

Both wolves nudged at the lifeless Chukchi dog, one at Xander's head and the other at his side. The dog lay still and dying, but if any life could be stirred in him, they meant to find it. They'd been summoned by the gods and they would obey. Their feral instincts told them what to do, to heal, and to try and bring life back into the fallen husky. Its wounds were savage, but so were they, as savage as the wild that surrounded them. The husky would die unless the wolves nursed Xander's arctic will back to life. Quickly, they set to work, licking and healing the tears and rips across Xander's body, covering him with their feral touch and rasped tongues that carried the medicine of the ancients. When done, they nestled in close to the still-lifeless husky to watch over and protect him, each taking a side.

Wolves from the wild howled across arctic winds. Odin's wolves heard but did not answer the calls. *The wolf and the dog battle as one.* Others would help them, other savage wolves they could count on for help. The ice storm was coming. The smell of death polluted the otherwise clean arctic air. Odin's wolves sniffed at it, then scanned the horizon, each on their side of the fallen Chukchi dog, to keep a full watch for what was to come. The enemy would be among their friends. They must stay alert to stay alive.

"Lassie, I'm sorry about your Xander," Fox said, seeing how upset Anya was, and knowing he ran the risk of causing more upset with his attempt to give her any comfort. "About Mushroom, too," he added in a faded-away tone. Fox didn't like the idea of carrying on a conversation with her about her dead dogs but it seemed like the only way he could get through to her and maybe help her. She was crying, but at least she didn't look dead inside herself.

"Xander," Fox reluctantly pressed on, "was a *braw dug,* he was. Where is he laid to rest?"

Anya whispered something to Fox, but he couldn't hear her.

"Lassie, what did you say?" Never in all his years had Fox seen such torment on anyone's face as was on Anya's. He realized in that moment he should leave her alone in her grief. He shouldn't have come to ask for her help, and he shouldn't force her to think on such loss. She'd suffered enough. He started to get up, to leave.

"I said, I don't know," Anya repeated, this time in a clear voice.

Fox immediately settled back down to his spot on the other side of the cookfire, opposite her. He would stay. He would listen. He would help her, if he could.

"When I came back inside here to Xander, he wasn't here," Anya told him, her voice dropped to a whisper. She realized it and made an effort to speak in a clear voice again. This effort kept her from crying. She looked at Fox now and not at the fire. Her memory pained her, but it hurt worse to hold so much inside. "Xander was dying and I meant to help ease his pain and help him die. This is why I rushed back inside to him and this is what I do not know, Fox. I do not know what happened to him. He was too sick to even move, and blinded, too." Anya had to stop and get a breath. Her chest ached from loving Xander and missing him and worrying over where his body lay.

Fox listened and watched her. He had a hard time believing her words, but the girl wouldn't lie to him; he knew that much about her. Grief could be playing tricks with her mind, but he didn't think so. This was something more and something he didn't understand, either.

"Xander is dead, for I feel nothing of his life; no sign of his spirit alive on Native Earth," Anya managed to get out, past her sore throat. "He must have somehow crawled away to die in the Chukchi way. He must have . . ." Her words drifted away. She didn't look at Fox anymore but at the cook-fire again.

"Is this why your spirit is gone, too, lassie?" Fox gently questioned.

Anya looked at Fox again. She remembered him. He was kind. He was to be trusted.

"Yes," she quietly answered, though the mention of *spirit* upset her. She didn't know why.

Vitya entered the Eskimo lodge in time to

hear Anya. That she was talking to the Scot fueled his anger. She didn't talk to him anymore, and he couldn't understand why she would talk to Fox and not him! Vitya had known Anya all her life, and Fox was almost a stranger to her. Hurt was what fueled Vitya's anger, hurt and jealousy.

"Get out of here!" Vitya shouted at Fox in his native Chukchi tongue. "Go now and do not return!"

Anya said nothing nor did she get up, but she gave Vitya such a look, it made him be quiet. Still, she would not speak to him and she would not say to Fox what Vitya had roared. Vitya was the one she wanted to leave. Vitya brought memories of a home she would never know again. Her memory had begun to return in flashes and did nothing but upset her. She couldn't put people and faces together with the right names. She couldn't remember times and places, at least not exactly. When did she leave her home? Why didn't Vitya come with her? It was all a blur, an upsetting confusion and blur!

"Anya!" Vitya found his voice and roared, wishing she would roar back at him. Anything was better than her silent treatment.

Fox stayed put. He wasn't about to stir the pot any more than it already was. Obviously the lassie didn't take too kindly to Vitya. He didn't understand Vitya's words, but he got the meaning, all right. And what was the lad doing yelling at *him*? Fox wished he spoke Vitya's native tongue. He should be yelling at Vitya for refusing to help with his three Chukchi sled teams. Why didn't Vitya want to help? Fox didn't understand this any more than why Vitya got angry at him, since Vitya was such a help with the dogs on their crossing to Nome.

Anya got up from off the ground and glared at Vitya.

Vitya understood her look and knew she wanted him to leave. He refused. They were communicating at least. His anger at the Scot died down. Then, when Vitya noticed Anya didn't wear the necklace he'd given her, an altogether different emotion hit: *fear,* fear he'd lost her for good. The husky carving around her neck signified to Vitya she had feelings for him. She didn't wear it now, so she must not have feelings for him anymore. He didn't want to get mad at her, but he was. Better anger than fear. He didn't want to hit her but he wanted to hit something or someone.

Then he thought of *Rune Johansson*!

Had he come back for Anya?

Afraid Rune had done just that, Vitya

glared at Anya accusingly, as if it were her fault. Upset and thinking irrationally, he gestured toward her neck. She didn't wear his gift! Where was it? He wouldn't use words, either. Let her guess what he was thinking. Let her see how it feels to shut someone out and hurt them. Sad trance or not, Vitya wanted Anya to hurt, just as he hurt.

Fox didn't make a move, but watched them both. Uncomfortable, since this should be private between the lad and lassie, he couldn't figure a way to slip out without notice. In truth Fox didn't want to slip away. Anya might need him, and so he would stay.

As it was, neither Anya nor Vitya appeared to notice Fox.

Anya shook her head to help bring clarity and bring back her memory. She put her fingers to her neck and touched her smooth, bare skin. Why should Vitya point at her so? Why should he point to her neck of all places? Her fingers skimmed the top of her dress; the thin-hide garment was as smooth as her skin. The beads on its rim tickled the tips of her fingers. The colorful embroidery in and around the beads was so pretty; she felt pretty wearing such a beautiful dress. *Like Nana-tasha's.* She remembered her grandmother, able to put her name with her face, and able to put together the reality that her grandmother was dead.

Anya fell to her knees and clasped her hands, then let new tears fall.

"Nana-tasha," she whispered. "Nana-tasha."

Vitya heard her and knew she spoke of her grandmother. He could see how Anya still grieved and realized he should leave her alone in her grief. This was not the time to hold a grudge against her for not loving him. When she was well and herself again, then he would speak to her of his feelings. He would use words to tell her how much it hurt him that she'd tossed away the necklace he'd given her. That's exactly how Vitya felt at the moment — tossed away.

"I go, Anya," he said in a flat Chukchi voice.

Vitya left so quickly, he didn't notice her nod of acknowledgment, nor did he notice that his necklace adorned the entrance of the hide lodge, honorably placed just above the door flap and almost out of sight. In fact, once outside, Vitya forgot about Fox still inside with Anya, his mind was so set on Rune Johansson. He needed to find out if Rune had come back to Nome for Anya. His heart hardened against Rune. The

Chukchi warrior in him was ready for battle. Anya was his, no matter if she'd taken off his necklace, and no matter that she'd tossed him away from her. Vitya would win her back as soon as he took care of Rune Johansson!

Anya sat back down across from Fox but said nothing. She'd heard Vitya stomp away and supposed he'd come back. Right now she didn't care. Nana-tasha was gone. Zellie was gone. Xander was gone. Rune was gone. She was alone.

Thinking of Rune disturbed her. She shifted her position and drew up her knees and hugged them. Then she darted a look at Fox to see if he'd noticed her discomfort. No. Fox stared into the fire and not at her. She did the same. Why did thinking about Rune disturb her? She reflexively put a hand to her bare skin and let her fingers drift down to the neckline of her beautiful, soft hide dress.

Gasp!

The dress was a gift from Rune.

CHAPTER THREE

Fox tramped back through the snow to his family mining operation and to his three teams of Chukchi dogs gathered there. He hadn't been able to bring himself to ask the lassie to help him care for and train his huskies. She needed more time to get over the loss of her dogs. He wouldn't ask Vitya for help again; he'd get a no again. A lot was riding on Fox's success in the next All Alaska Sweepstakes. For a reason beyond getting a win with one of the teams, he felt a strong connection to this particular race, as if it were his destiny to participate in the important event. Why he felt this way, he'd no idea. The sweepstakes were important to everybody who ran dogs or bet on them on the Alaska frontier, not just him.

The idea of getting his own Siberian dogs to race seemed obvious to him once he saw how well the smaller huskies ran against the much larger teams, coming in third and only an hour behind the winner, Scotty Allan. Allan was an expert dog driver. There were others. Fox thought of Coke Hill, Charles Johnson, Percy Blatchford, John Hegnes, Fay Delzene, and John Johnson, to name a few of the best.

Fox knew John Johnson well and already had him in mind to drive one of his Siberian teams. John was a good guy and a good driver, tough as they came. He might ask Charles Johnson to dog drive, too. *Aye,* Fox would ask John Johnson and Charles Johnson to dog drive for him. Fox would take the third team. Fox fixed these pairings in his mind and imagined them all crossing the finish first, second, and third, ahead of all the rest. When time came, he would enter the teams in the sweepstakes in honor of his uncles. Fox felt good about his choices and good about their chances to do well in April.

Yet something bothered him. In the back of his mind, he could swear he'd heard a voice whispering threats. Fox didn't have an enemy in any of the gold camps or among dog drivers, at least that he knew of. He wasn't the type to go around stirring up trouble or getting into any. He certainly wasn't the type to imagine anybody after him. Still, he could swear he'd heard whispers that, "Someone is coming; something is there." Well, he didn't have time to dream up trouble. He had three teams of Chukchi dogs to see to, and by damn, he would! As for their training, he meant to keep a low profile. It was no secret he'd brought the Siberian dogs to Nome, but maybe he could keep secret that he meant to race them in the next sweepstakes.

There it was again, the same voice. *Someone is coming. Something is there.* Fox looked over his shoulder, convinced he was being followed. He stopped and turned around fully, no matter that he didn't see anyone or anything amiss. The trail to his mining operation and other gold camps carried the same sledges, the same wagons, the same stream of men and dogs and horses working their way through the hard winter. Eskimos, miners, and frontiersmen alike passed by and no one said anything out of the ordinary. Some would nod in greeting, then keep on their way. Fox exhaled sharply and wondered if the cold had finally gotten to him, after all this time away from his native Scotland. The Highlands could be fierce but Alaska proved a harder test. It must, or else his thinking wouldn't be so rattled.

Maybe he needed a nip of good Scotch whiskey to chase away whispers nagging from the dark recesses of his mind. "Speak o' the devil," Fox muttered aloud. He just might be. "Aye, right," he spat. "Naw," he didn't believe any devil chased after him. He needed to keep his head. The idea of a wee bit of whiskey appealed and quickened his step back to the Ramsey mines. He had enough to do, getting his dogs and his dog drivers set to train, without worrying over someone coming after any of them. He wouldn't tell anyone about what he heard over the arctic winds. They would think him crazy. If anyone told him the same thing he'd think they were crazy or at the very least, *"mad wi' it"* drunk!

Fox turned his thoughts back to the lassie. He meant to check on Anya from time to time, the poor thing. Upset over her dogs, she was. *Aye,* the lassie had a ways to go before she would be set right again. She was not alone. She had Vitya to help her. But so far, Fox didn't think the Chukchi lad had done much but upset the lassie. The same could be said for himself, Fox thought. Vitya had refused to help him, which still puzzled him. Why?

Cold to the bone, Fox hastened his step and thought only of how easy that nip of scotch whiskey would go down.

"Rune, come here," Margret Johansson

demanded of her son. "My big trunk is not here with my things. Didn't you get all of my things properly loaded when we boarded in Nome? Tsk. Tsk, son; such a bother you can be sometimes."

Rune didn't mind his mother's glare or her nagging. She darned well knew her trunk was fine and had safely made the trip to Seattle, and she just wanted to give him a hard time. He was in no mood for one of her spoiled rants and knew his sister would likely be next. Soon as he thought it, Inga was there.

"My best coat is ruined! It's your fault, Rune!" his sister wailed and flopped down on the nearest shipping crate she could find. "Just look at this sleeve; it's torn to bits. *Mor,* tell Rune to do something about it," Inga whined to her mother.

Margret rushed to her daughter and sat down next to her.

"There, there," she crooned and put her arms around Inga. "It's just a tear, dear. We will have a seamstress sew it good as new. Better yet, we will get you a new one, *won't we,* Rune?" Margret turned her disagreeable tone onto her son.

Rune glared at both of them.

"Why, *Mor*?"

"Why, what?" Margret shot back at Rune.

Her once-lovely looks turned sour.

"Why did you have me in the first place?"

"Humph," she bristled. "Such a silly question doesn't deserve an answer." Margret squirmed in her seat next to her daughter and looked away from Rune.

"You can't look at me, can you? And you can't answer my question," he said in a flat, quiet voice — flat to match his feelings. "It's all right, *Mor*," he said. "This is *farval*. I say goodbye to you and to Inga. *Farval* to you both," he gritted out, then turned his back and walked away. He'd already given his crewmen instructions to assist his mother and sister off the *Nordic*.

"Rune Johansson, you come back here!" This time his sister yelled after him. "You can't just walk away from us. You haven't gotten me a new coat yet!"

Rune heard Inga but he kept on his way. Sea birds squawked over his sister's shouts, but couldn't drown out her shrill demands. Even the stray dogs barking couldn't drown her out.

"You stop and you come back, Rune! Now! I should have done more to your precious Anya and her stupid dogs!" Inga blurted.

"Inga, hush!" Margret put her hand over her daughter's mouth. She knew the danger of loose lips, in this case, Inga's. "Hush and say no more," Margret counseled. Maybe her son hadn't heard the truth come out.

Too late — Rune heard every word.

Anya. The name pierced through him, kindling his senses and his memory to brutal awareness.

My God, Anya, forgive me for leaving you!

He suddenly remembered what the other transgressions were that his mother and his sister had committed against him; the transgressions he'd struggled to recall. *They'd hurt Anya and her dogs.* What had Inga just said? "I should have done more to your precious Anya and her stupid dogs!" Any love Rune might have been able to magically conjure for his mother and his sister was forever killed in that moment. He turned around and reapproached them. Both had stayed seated on the loading crate.

"You are dead to me. When you leave this ship, know that I never wish to set eyes on you again. What you did to Anya and to her dogs cannot be forgiven. You both have dark hearts and no souls. Get off my ship," Rune commanded.

"*Your* ship?" Margret yelled and then got up. "I am Margret Johansson and the Johansson shipping line is more mine than yours. The money in this family is mine.

71

The ships in this family are mine. You are my son and that is all you are," she fumed. "You are upset over some silly half-native girl with dogs, and that's ridiculous. It is certainly not enough to warrant your poor treatment of me and your sister."

Rune struggled to hold his temper and to keep his fists at his sides. His family had hurt him, and he wanted to hurt them back, for Anya's sake. She was the one who'd been hit the hardest by his mother and his sister. His crew had started to gather and he understood their concern. A ship was no place for this kind of trouble. Rune was captain. He needed to fix this. He turned about to his men and gave new orders.

"Karl, Josef, Sven, take these trunks and these persons off the ship. Leave them at the train station. You don't need to accompany them any farther than that."

"*Ja,* Captain," the three sailors answered in near unison before approaching Margret and Inga and their stacked trunks.

"You'll pay for this, Rune," Margret threatened.

"I already have," he said, then walked away, this time for good.

Xander had awakened from his sleep of death. He had no memory before the time of his dying. No flashes of light from the aurora borealis darted across the heavens in greeting. Bewildered by his whereabouts, he raised his head from his icy sleep but kept his body circled in the snow. Raw instinct was his only guide. He sniffed at the frozen air and snarled at the idea of food. Furious winds blew past but not through him; his thick fur layers protected him well enough. Parts of him winced at the bitter bite of the arctic winds — the parts newly healed. His senses instantly told him he lived in a harsh place, a cruel place, a place where survival depended on his know-how and his alone. He wasn't a part of any pack.

His ears pricked. Howling called across the wild. Xander sat up, then stood, able to do so without falter. He sniffed the icy air in all directions and tried to determine the source of the sound to best defend against it. His watch-blue eyes scanned the horizon for any predator, for any movement, for any sign of an attack coming. He had no trouble seeing. Everything was deadly clear. His fur ruffled in the strong winds. Hungry, he needed to hunt.

Howls cut through the air. Xander whimpered at the cries because he didn't know where they came from. He didn't try to howl in return, but instead folded back down into an icy circle. More calls from the wild made him stand again. His watch eyes instinctively scanned the twilight expanse. He kept his ears pricked. Silence blanketed the heavens and Native Earth.

Unsure of his next move, Xander stayed on alert and did not budge from his spot. Something held him there, but he didn't know what. To survive he needed to keep on the move; instinct gave him this impulse. Yet he stayed. He waited. Inherent in him, buried deep in a place beyond his present awareness, his gentle soul longed for the touch of his guardian's hand and for the company of his breed — one in particular. The tie of generations remained unbroken, yet hidden from his consciousness. He whimpered reflexively to trigger some connection to this moment, to why he stayed when he should go. He waited for more calls from the wild.

None came.

Only silence.

Only fierce winds and blowing snow swirled in the arctic air.

Xander stepped restlessly. He growled at his surroundings, at the unknown, at any predators that might be stalking him, and at the prey he needed to find. He couldn't afford to stand still and had to stay on the move. His stomach seized. He had to eat. He had to kill or be killed. In the next instant he took off to hunt in the wild, the same wild that had him so caught up only moments before.

Something stirred the seven dogs tethered in the Eskimo dog yard, Anya's dogs. Already agitated from their constant ties, sounds carried through the arctic air — cries from a place they could not detect. Their pack instincts collectively grouped, causing them to trace back and forth in the space their bonds allowed, restless and whimpering. All but little Thor sniffed the sharp winds to try and pick up any scent of what was to come. Curious, the pup watched them but didn't behave as they did.

Danger stalked in the open and here in the quiet. Flowers and Little Wolf in particular, sensed Xander's absence and yearned for his companionship. The rest yearned for the pack of old — the pack with their leader — Zellie — and with their strength — Xander. Reflex, impulse, and instinct brought all seven dogs to the same behavior and alert stance. Now Thor responded in kind and howled with his pack.

Anya heard all the noise. She came outside her hide tent but did not head in the direction of the set-up dog yard. She felt little kinship with the secured huskies. By this time she recognized they were her dogs, but she felt no tie to them, no sensation of camaraderie and belonging. Something was wrong inside her. She sensed that much, and more. Her gut told her danger stalked. Deep down she knew *something is coming; someone is there.* Instinctively she wanted to protect her dogs, yet every time she started for them, a pain deep inside would stop her. What part of her had been killed to cause this? How could she be so inhumane?

Anya wasn't proud of who she'd become. A coward, that's who. Controlled by fear, she was no good to anybody or anything, least of all to her dogs. They needed her, but she was afraid to approach them. Why? She didn't fear death — her own, that is. She did fear for others, and that was the grip that had caught her up. A part of her memory had returned — the memory lost at the point when Xander and Rune disappeared from her life. That day remained an awful day, and each one that followed only got worse. Loss and hurt consumed Anya, and she was left a cowardly shell of the spirited shaman she once was.

Vitya's company helped a little. They'd

been close since childhood. He'd been a good friend to her, maybe more. She let him come near and even talked to him again. Their conversations in her native Chukchi eased her troubled soul, yet made her homesick for her coastal village in Siberia. She didn't have full recall of every detail of the past year. Some of the danger she and Rune and the dogs were in, she could remember. She just couldn't remember feeling anything, as if she were dead inside. She could match names and places and faces, but she couldn't match any feelings with these recollections. Worse than that, she'd become a coward.

Here she knew her dogs cried out for her and for Zellie and Xander, yet she didn't go to them. No, she wasn't proud of who she'd become. No matter that she was shaman; she had no spirit.

Spirit?

Jolted to awareness, Anya remembered. Spirit was her husky counterpart in the Chukchi world of spirits beyond Native Earth! Her *Spirit was gone, just like Xander.* She had to be since Anya had no sense of Spirit, the same way she had no sense of Xander's life. It seemed obvious: they were both *dead.* Her beloved grandmother, Nana-tasha, was dead, too. If only her grandmother was with her. Nana-tasha might help her find her Direction again. In that, Anya might find the courage to save what dogs remained. In that, Anya might find the strength to forget she ever loved Rune Johansson.

Anya's *feelings* returned with a vengeance.

"Oh, Nana-tasha, you said you would always be with me. Where are you?" Anya pled. "I am spirit, yet I have none. I am shaman, yet I'm ashamed of my actions. I am a young woman, yet stay a helpless girl." Anya sat up and tried to hold back her tears, at the same time she reached in the pocket of her fur kerker for her knife — *a gift from the gods.* Carefully, deliberate in her actions, Anya took the crude little blade in both her hands and then sat erect, her spine taut.

In one swift motion she could drive the blade into her throat and rip it open. This would end her life the quickest, she thought. Her life's blood would be gone in a heartbeat. Wasn't this what she'd planned for Xander? Wasn't this the way she thought he could die the quickest and with the least pain? A swift strike would end her life, as she'd planned to end his. No one on Native Earth or in any spirit world that lay beyond had been dearer to her than Zellie and Xander. Their deaths took her arctic will to endure in this fierce wild. Their deaths took her Direction and left no trace behind to follow.

"Don't you see, Grandmother, what a coward I've become? Even in my death I show no bravery, but complain like a babe and blame Zellie and Xander for my failures. It is not their fault but mine that the rest are still in peril. I have not measured up to the task for which I was born. I was supposed to save the dogs, and instead I've let them die. Three are gone and seven are left. It's only a matter of time. Whatever is after us will get us in the end."

She had nothing left to give in this life but her death as sacrifice. If she gave up her life to the ancestors and to the Chukchi gods, she believed the rest of the dogs and Rune would be safer. Desperation had brought her to this. She had to do something, anything, to help save their lives, so she'd wrongly convinced herself she must be bringing unneeded danger to the dogs, since she was the one possessed, not them. Her hands began to tremble, but she made sure she held fast to her knife and closed her eyes for the last time.

A fine, cool mist settled over her. If she had opened her eyes, she might know its source, but she did not. The mist comforted

Anya in this difficult moment and helped her settle. Only when her trembles turned to tingles — when her fingers went numb — did she open her eyes and look straight at her hands. Skin and bone turned to mist then back to flesh, sparkling in vaporous shimmers. Her knife fell to her lap. She couldn't hold onto it. Her stomach churned.

Was this *Spirit* returning to her?

All the times before when this happened, her human shape was being pulled into the world of spirits to take the place of her husky counterpart. A surge of energy, *Spirit's,* pulsed through Anya and helped her stand up straight. For the first time in weeks, she felt uplifted. She hadn't lost her Spirit after all! Spirit had survived and so would she!

Cool mist still rained softly through the air inside Anya's Eskimo yaranga. Only the Chukchi called their homes yarangas, but Anya felt as if she were back home in her Anquallat village, with the return of her husky. Spirit's reappearance wasn't the answer to all that troubled her, but it meant everything to not feel so alone.

Anya shut her eyes and listened to the unearthly sounds coming across arctic winds. They were howls from far, far away — howls so distant only ghostly spirits might hear them. These soft cries rained down from the heavens, much as the cool mist that comforted still. With her eyes kept closed to better listen, Anya embraced the sounds; their touch soothed her the same as when she would put her hand to Zellie's soft, thick fur for companionship and comfort. Startled by this connection to her beloved, dead Chukchi dog, Anya opened her eyes.

For the faintest of flashes in time . . . *she saw Zellie.*

Held in the momentary magic of this fought-for belief, Anya watched her beautiful, black and white leader dog struggle to hold some kind of shape on Native Earth. Anya feared that the slightest move might chase Zellie from her.

Zellie fixed her watch eyes on Anya and gave a soft whimper. The moment she did, her image instantly misted away.

"No, come back!" Anya cried out and grabbed at the air as if this might have some effect. Her action was so fast, Anya didn't realize her hands had not returned to flesh and bone but still sparkled in mist and magic themselves. She didn't notice and she didn't care. Her heart ached, she loved Zellie so. The impact of the moment hit Anya all over again.

Zellie had brought Spirit back to her!

Zellie had traveled from the other side of life and risked losing her eternal resting place in heaven, to help Anya!

Once crossed to heaven, a dog cannot return, or so Anya had always been taught. As life is sacred, so is death. Anya feared for Zellie's soul. That she'd struggled to reach Anya no matter the cost to her unto eternity, would sustain Anya for the rest of her life on Native Earth. After such bravery from Zellie, Anya dared not show cowardice in the dark days ahead.

It is time.

It begins again.

Nana-tasha's words, Anya clearly recalled.

Her grandmother, like Zellie, risked much to come near, for this was what Anya sensed in the mist from the world of spirits, and from the part of her that was born into that very world. Danger loomed in the distance, coming ever closer. The Great Crag widened. Gloom seeped from the heavy air. To Anya it felt as if the winds had turned to glue and shut down all arctic whispers. No Direction called to her.

She had seven dogs left.

Some will live. Many will die.

No truer words remembered. Anya had to protect the dogs without Rune's help. His handsome image flashed in front of her, but she chased it away. She had to.

This was not a time to think of love, but a time to think of fooling death.

"Say, Zeke, how many saloons do you think there are in this gold-fever-town?" Homer Jessup put the question to his longtime friend and mining partner, Zeke Raney. They'd both made the long trek down from their mountain cabin, and then past the Pioneer Mining Company operations, among others, into the frontier city of Nome for a change of scenery and to catch up on any news. In truth, both men worried over Anya and Rune and their sled dogs. The young'uns could be long gone from the Alaska District, and neither Zeke nor Homer would blame them. Bad stuff followed the young'uns. Stuff from nightmares and dark places. Bad stuff and bad people, both veteran miners agreed.

Zeke and Homer had welcomed Anya and Rune and their dogs, and offered safe haven for them, no matter the risk to their own lives. Unexplained things had happened to them and almost killed them. Something came at them; they couldn't say what. Then their cabin burned, but didn't burn down? It didn't make any sense. It didn't seem real.

What made sense, what Zeke and Homer could reckon with in the real world, was the danger of wolves and other predators, and the danger of storms in the North even more ferocious than predators — *not* the unexplained.

They kept their rifles at the ready, but Anya and Rune told them never to raise their guns to a wolf. "Live and let live. Leave them be," Anya had scolded. Shoot, Zeke and Homer found themselves in a fix, not automatically pulling the trigger against the wolf packs that roamed the frozen hills. After a time, when no wolves and no unexplained predators came at them, they kept their rifles pointed only at game for the supper table. They let up their guard fully and even left their rifles in their cabin when they trekked down to the mines to work.

Both veteran frontiersmen knew how to live a simple life, an uncomplicated life. They chose to carve out such a life in the Alaska wild. Survival was tough enough; no need to go complicating it further and worry over things they couldn't explain. Better to leave the unexplained be.

But they did worry over the whereabouts of Anya and Rune and their Siberian huskies. Rune had gone down to Nome to meet up with somebody, but they didn't know who or what that was about. Then, when Zeke and Homer were away working, Anya left without a word as to why. She took her dogs with her. She must have had a good reason to leave in such a hurry without saying why. The men stewed over what might have happened to all of them. The young'uns were good kids who had accepted their help and were grateful for it. It didn't set right with Zeke and Homer, the way they had left and didn't come back or send any kind of word.

Something had to be wrong, bad wrong.

Their worries mounted, so much so that both men decided to leave their winter work in the mines and head into Nome. Jafet Lindeberg, their boss and the owner of the Pioneer Mining Company, told them they could take a few days off, but expected their shovels to hit gravel come the end of the week. Loyal employees, Zeke and Homer would do just that. In the meanwhile, they meant to do a little investigating and find the young'uns. They were not used to the hustle and bustle of the frontier city. Life didn't seem so simple in Nome, and this made them anxious to get back to the isolation of the tundra and the mountains beyond.

"I say nigh on to a hundred," Zeke finally

answered his friend.

"A hundred what?" Homer mumbled back; his full attention was on the fancy gal that just passed by their table in the Discovery Saloon.

"Saloons in Nome, you old sourdough! Git your mind off that gal and back on why we're here in the first place," Zeke grumbled.

Homer watched the woman cross to the other side of the saloon, his mouth agape.

"Dammit, Homer, I know it's been a long time since you've seen a female, but quit actin' like it. You look like a dag-nabbed fool." Zeke poured a shot of whiskey from the bottle he'd ordered and paid for in gold dust. He always kept a stash of his earnings in gold dust for just such an occasion. Important thing was: keep your gold hidden. If a man didn't, a man risked claim-jumping or worse. Zeke didn't have a claim staked, but his carefully stowed pouch of gold dust might just as well be. Too many crooks in Nome nowadays, he believed. A lot probably came from Dawson in the Yukon, to pick what pockets and steal what claims they could. When Dawson's gold dried up, here they all came-a-calling in Nome, looking for nothing but trouble.

"And it ain't honest trouble, that's for sure."

"What's that you say, Zeke?" Homer asked and helped himself to more whiskey.

Zeke scratched his beard, then pulled his worn, brimmed cap down low over his brow. He didn't want anybody noticing him. Crowded saloons made him uncomfortable. Nome made him uncomfortable. There had to be twenty thousand people living here if there was one! *Makes a body nervous,* he repeated mentally.

"Homer, do you even remember what you asked me?"

"Sure do."

The pair stared each other down.

"I'm waiting, Homer," Zeke challenged.

Homer squirmed a little. He had trouble with his memory. He'd never had much learning and thought that could be why. Zeke had a lot of learning and was smart. Zeke knew him good and well, his ways, good and bad. Still, Homer wished he could answer Zeke's question right.

"I-I wanted to kn-know if you see any spittoons around here," he said guardedly.

"There's one over yonder," Zeke said flatly and indicated the direction with a nod. "Handy when you need it, old friend."

Homer beamed. He'd answered Zeke's

question right.

"That supper was damn good," Zeke said, the corners of his mustached mouth crinkling to a smile. "Fancy cooking once in a while won't kill us, I reckon."

"Guess not," Homer chuckled.

"*Hallo* there, fellas."

Neither Zeke nor Homer had noticed the man approach.

"Well I'll be . . . how are you, Sepp?" Zeke leaned over the table to better shake the man's hand. "Join us, will you?"

"Homer," Sepp said, and gave him a quick nod before taking a seat.

"Good to meet up with you, Sepp. Good to have a drink in my hand and not a shovel, eh," Homer said and laughed.

"*Ja.*" Sepp agreed and smiled. A healthy outdoorsman, a capable smithy, a fisherman, a decent wrestler, and natural-born skier, Leonhard Seppala, "Sepp," was still relatively new to mining work. Small in physique, he stood five feet tall. His build was small, but he was fit as they came; a tough Norwegian who worked for his longtime friend, Jafet Lindeberg, at the Pioneer Mining Company, same as Zeke and Homer.

"Have a shot of whiskey with us," Zeke offered and grabbed up an empty glass off a nearby table.

"I don't take much to drink but I'll have a *snap* with my friends," Sepp said. He downed the whiskey in one gulp and set his glass hard on the scratched wood. "My wife Constance will give me a fit if I come home, *drukket,*" he joked.

Zeke and Homer didn't have wives, but they got Sepp's joke. Zeke wouldn't mind having a couple of young'uns. He wouldn't mind being a father. A wife he didn't want, but kids and dogs, he'd take on in a heartbeat. He realized he felt downright fatherly toward Rune and Anya. An old salty frontiersman, no woman would want him. No woman would want to live the way he did, so isolated from the rest of the world. But soon as he met Rune and Anya, they took to him and it made him feel damned good . . . and damned responsible for their welfare, their dogs included. Zeke took another shot of whiskey. He needed to buck up and find his kids, he mentally lectured without realizing he thought the word, *his.*

"I started same as you, Homer," Sepp said in answer to the question just put to him.

Zeke turned his attention back onto the conversation.

"Driving horses and a wagon? I never done that, Sepp," Homer admitted.

"*Ja,* well I drove a wagon with horses and sometimes now, a *slede* with dogs. I went with a gang to help stake claims for our boss and had to learn to handle the big dogs. They are something, they are. Weigh more than I do, some of them," Sepp joked.

"Like it, do you, dog driving?" Zeke asked.

"*Ja.*" Sepp sat back in his chair, and the satisfied look on his face said it all.

"Zeke and me, we had to learn to fill a slip scraper to clear sluice boxes. Did you know about that afore you came to Nome, Sepp?" Homer asked.

"*Nej,* I didn't know the first thing about the mines. I used to farm but I never did shovel work like we have to here, in the gravel. When the rains pour in the mines and I put shovel to gravel, I think sometimes I'm going to open up the whole Arctic Ocean underfoot," Sepp joked.

Zeke and Homer laughed. They knew exactly what he meant. It could get so wet everywhere when the rain storms don't let up, a body felt like they're working the Bering Sea instead of gravel.

"I'm a little man, fellas, but I tell you the rain and the shovel work haven't stopped me." Sepp's pleasant expression grew serious. "Just makes me work harder. More exercise to ski well on the slopes and dog

90

drive endless hours. I do what I do, that's it."

"Yeah, and from what I hear, you can mix it up pretty good in a fight," Homer praised.

Sepp smiled again. "*Ja,* I can."

Zeke knew Sepp was tough. Sepp got into scraps to help chase away shyster lawyers and claim-jumpers, all without the law seeing him. Zeke and Homer had mixed it up once or twice themselves to help immigrants keep their claims. It was tough in Alaska, where the law was sometimes nowhere to be found when it came to protecting your hard-earned gold dust. Zeke thought of the fight that Rune and Anya might be in — a fight for their lives.

"Sepp, Homer and me, we're in Nome looking for a couple of young'uns with some Siberian huskies. Have you come across a Chukchi girl named Anya and a young seaman by the name of Rune? Rune is a Norseman like you with the heart of a Viking like you," Zeke said. The description seemed to fit.

Sepp wore a puzzled look but it wasn't over any question about his ancestry.

He'd never heard of "Siberian huskies" before.

CHAPTER FOUR

Rune had had time, too much time, to realize he'd deserted Anya and her dogs when they still needed him — all because he was jealous of Vitya. That he'd let something so petty as his feelings get in the way of saving Anya and her dogs' lives ate away at him. His father would be back from his last trade stop in Vladivostok any day. The moment Rune saw the *Storm* dock in Seattle's harbor, he'd find his father and let him know he, Rune, planned to return to Nome before the winter was out.

In fact, Rune wanted to leave as soon as he could. The approach would be sketchy. A decent steamer could get past brush ice and sludge ice, but pack ice, no. This time of year the pack ice should be far enough to the north to not send problems south. Small fragments of brush ice and sludge ice with the consistency of honey wouldn't halt passage, but separate masses of pack ice would.

Rune believed he'd be able to reach the edges of the Yukon by steamer. He'd hop on any boat, large or small, fishing boat or ferry, going in the direction he needed. Then, if he were lucky, it would take two months to cross the Alaska Territory by dogsled and reach Nome on the Bering Sea coast.

Two months!

Cold fear shot through him. Fear like ice. He had to be made of ice to have left Anya in the first place. He hoped to God Anya and her dogs would still be there, alive and unharmed in two months' time. He hoped by all the gods of the Vikings, too. Odin was a ghost, a powerful one who reigned in the world of the living and the world of the dead. Rune believed this now; the past year had convinced him. It was Odin who'd summoned him to Anya's side. Rune had left her side. He felt only shame and didn't care what price he'd have to pay to the gods for deserting Anya. But Anya . . . he hated to think she might have to pay for his deeds, her and her dogs.

If his travel went without problems, Rune could make Nome by March, a month before the next running of the All Alaska Sweepstakes. He thought of the race because Fox and his three teams of Chukchi dogs meant to compete in the biggest race of the season. Like Anya's seven surviving original imports, Fox's dogs could also be in danger. Something wanted Siberian huskies dead; something from a dark place in a dark world, and not any part of this one, Rune knew.

All of Rune's memory had returned with ringing clarity the moment he heard his sister repeat what she'd done to Anya and the dogs: Inga, along with his own mother. He ought to have learned his lesson years ago, that love and family didn't mix, at least not in his. He ought to be done with love, period. Yet he knew he wasn't.

He loved Anya.

She was ice seal and she was mermaid — both rare and beyond his reach. She was pretty and soft and when she smiled, he went all funny inside. When she looked at him, he could feel his body ache for hers. These were grown-up feelings. That's how Anya made him feel, grown up and ready to love her. But what he wanted would never happen.

Anya didn't love him.

She loved Vitya.

She was beyond Rune's reach.

It hurt, but he had to accept the truth and get past his upset feelings so he could be of some use in the battle ahead. Love and war don't mix either, he realized. When he found Anya and the dogs again, he would fight with everything left in him to win her safety from the dark spirits after her and her dogs. He wouldn't try to win her love, not anymore.

Memories of Xander and Zellie and the rest of the sled team raced over tundra and ice in his mind's eye. To have been their dog driver for a time was a deep honor. He didn't have the words to describe his devotion to the brave Siberian huskies. They risked their lives to escape to the Alaska Territory. Some had died. Seven were left. The danger wasn't over. He'd lost his Viking sword in the last fight with the deadly Midgard serpent, but at least he'd *slain the serpent,* as Odin had commanded him. Still, Rune had come to trust in the security of the sword. He wasn't looking forward to entering any war of ghosts again without it.

There were more serpents to slay.

Still agitated, isolated, left alone, and not exercised for long periods, none of the tethered huskies had been able to settle down as they might, in the wake of the newest snowstorm. They'd been fed. Hunger wasn't the problem. They knew how to hunker down in a circle and put their bushy tails over their snouts for protection and warmth, yet all the seven either sat or stood in place. The winds blew past and over them, but arctic spirits didn't call to them. The pup, Thor, yelped for his mother, but Flowers didn't look his way. She put her watch eyes toward the figure that approached. So did Midnight, Midday, Magic, Frost, and Little Wolf.

The pack came alert.

Despite the fierce snowstorm, none moved. Even Thor stopped yelping, stood on all fours, and faced the same direction as the rest. Snow pelted them. Midnight's black coat frosted to gray. Magic's copper-red fur faded in the storm. Midday was barely recognizable except for the blue of her eyes. Frost and Little Wolf's watch eyes shone through the storm with equal brilliance. Thor lost his spots, and was fluffy white now.

All of the dogs experienced the uncomfortable sensation that they were tied down and could not fight as a pack or run away. What was coming at them had them trapped. Their leader, Zellie, was gone. Their strength, Xander, was gone. Mushroom was gone. Their canine instincts charged this cold reality through each dog, all but Thor, since the piebald pup had no memory of the time before, as they did. If given a chance, Thor might have recognized his father, Xander, because of his natural-born, keen senses. He did not face this test. Along with the rest of the pack, he faced the unknown, his droopy-blue watch eyes trained on the unrecognizable shape that approached.

Flowers screeched first. They were wails of joy, not upset. The rest of the pack caught on right away to why Flowers howled in such a way — *Anya.* Their guardian had returned to them! Impulsively, the dogs jumped hard against their tethers. Snow flew every which way. Midday and Magic screeched their passionate calls, singing low and almost mournfully, they were so happy. Each dog craved Anya's touch and her guiding hand. No matter the rough swirls of snow and wind that pounded them, they felt a halo of safety gently cloud over them.

Their guardian had returned. To their canine instincts, she led them out of darkness and into the light. Night turned to day in a heartbeat, in the time it takes to give life, or take it. The twilight of winter still reined in the skies, but the Chukchi dogs only saw light, their hearts lifted so by Anya's return. She was one of them. She was home.

Anya already had her blade pulled from her pocket before she reached the outlying dog yard. A brief flash of memory took her to the moment she'd first set Zellie and Xander and all the Chukchi dogs free in her coastal village. She'd used the same blade. It hadn't been snowing then, at least not hard like it was now. The winds howled as loudly as the dogs, even more shrilly.

She came upon Thor first and slit his leather bonds to free him. The pup tried to jump at her and lick her face but she had the others to think of, and quickly felt for the next dog and the next tie. The near blizzard was blinding. Midnight lunged at her, much as Thor had, in a show of the same affection. She longed to hug him, but instead turned to the next dog, Midday, and cut her from her post.

Anya almost giggled at how playful the dogs appeared, reminded of how Xander used to knock her over in play. Her heart filled with such a memory, but she couldn't let it get to her, so busy was she with the task at hand. She found Flowers next, then Magic, then Frost, and at last . . . Little Wolf. He'd dropped weight. Instantly upset by her neglect of him, she pocketed her knife, then knelt down and circled her arms around the gray and white runt.

"I am here, Little Wolf. I know you miss your big brother. I know you do. Be easy. I am here," she cooed.

As if in understanding, the Siberian runt pushed his muzzle against her neck and did not back away, but pressed into her and whimpered low. If an animal could cry, he was crying.

It broke Anya's heart to feel the pain Little Wolf suffered. The rest too, she realized. They all suffered. She'd neglected them. They missed Zellie, Xander, and Mushroom, the same as she did. By now all of the freed huskies surrounded Anya, pushing at her where they could, barking in short moans, and wagging their tails in pure excitement. All was a flurry of happiness.

It was Anya's turn to take energy and heart from their obvious show of affection for her. She loved them. Zellie and Xander could never be replaced, but she'd come to love these brave Chukchi dogs. They had waited for her to come back to them. She was humbled. She was one of them in the world beyond. She was *Spirit.* In this world on Native Earth, she determined to stand with them and fight for the survival of their line. She was born to this world to save them and she would, or die trying.

It was just as well Rune was not here. Much as she wanted to see him again — she did not want to see him die. In a bizarre way, she was also relieved Xander was gone. The whole episode of his passing was too painful to revisit in any way. She didn't want to think of the details of his passing unless forced, unless such memories could somehow help the rest survive.

Her experience with Zellie crossing back from the other side to help her rejuvenated her to the fight, but made Anya worry over Zellie's place unto eternity. It might be lost forever . . . *because of me.* No, she didn't want to put Xander's passing to the other side in any kind of jeopardy, as she had Zellie's. Better to forget all about him if she could and let him rest in peace.

The storm wasn't giving up. A part of Anya wanted to shoo the dogs away to find shelter agreeable to them, but she didn't want to let them stray too far. She didn't know what could be out there waiting for them. At that moment Midday and Midnight pounced on her and knocked her down, knocking sense back into her. These Chukchi dogs were used to storm after storm with no cover. They were used to traveling hours on end, on the icy hunt with no rest. They were used to little food along the way. She didn't need to worry about protecting them from the snow and wind.

This wasn't the ice storm she expected.

That was yet to come.

She couldn't predict where or how the next strike would come, but she knew it would. All she could do was keep her dogs close and her knife closer. Vitya would help. Chinook would help. Their help could only go so far, for they did not have the gift from the gods, as she and Rune apparently did.

She was a Chukchi shaman summoned by the Gatekeepers. Rune had been summoned by his ancient Viking gods, by Odin himself. She and Rune both communicated with their ancestors, with the dead. Of this, neither Vitya nor Chinook would have any understanding. Besides, the less they knew about the ice storm coming, the better. They would be safer, she believed. Whatever was after her and the dogs would find Vitya and Chinook innocent. She would pray to the Morning Dawn for this wish to become fact.

"Anya! Anya!" Vitya ran up to her and the dogs.

The dogs knew Vitya, for he was one of the humans who fed them. They felt little kinship with him, but his approach didn't upset them. He was not an enemy.

Anya faced Vitya. The wind whipped past.

"You are with the dogs!" Vitya yelled. "I couldn't find you! I was afraid for you!"

Anya reached up to Vitya's firm jaw and touched him there.

"I am good. Do not worry." She did not yell.

Vitya smiled down at her. He was tall, like Rune.

"Come back with me," he mouthed more than spoke.

Anya shook her head in a firm no.

Vitya's handsome dark countenance turned into a frown.

"I will not leave my dogs," she told him in a clear voice. "I will not."

"Then I will stay," Vitya said in Chukchi. "You still do not have on your mittens," he scolded.

Anya warmed inside to him. She remembered he'd used those very words with her so very long ago, and right before he'd kissed her. She remembered his kiss, too.

"Thank you," was all she said and smiled at him.

The untethered Chukchi dogs gathered round the two humans, the scene one of family and home. Thor jabbed at Anya and Vitya's legs at every opportunity.

For the first time in a very long time, this was not such an awful day, Anya thought.

■ ■ ■ ■

The golem was upset but not overly so. True, the guardians of the Chukchi dogs were back in their right minds, but they were not back together. He knew this from the Raven god of the Chukchi who did his bidding. The Raven god sent its minions to track and observe what they could in the far-off reaches of Alaska, and kept their beady eyes on Anya and Rune. When reports came back that the two were not working together anymore, the golem relaxed. He needed this news from the world of dark spirits because the world in which he lived in body — the world that had him still imprisoned — called on him now to do the work for which he was born.

The final communist revolution had begun, and in a few days he would be free. Heady with the power soon to be his, he did not want to waste time worrying over the guardians of the Chukchi dogs. He would stamp them out like a dead cigarette when necessary. Let them squirm and struggle a while longer. He would enjoy their upset. He looked forward to their deaths, theirs and their dogs.

No *kulaks* would live, not in his Russia!

One thing did nag at him, despite his approaching freedom from his cold and dank prison cell. He had no sense of the one Chukchi dog that had escaped. The Raven god had no word about the black and white wheel dog. Fiery *Hel* had no report, either. The dog was probably dead, yet the golem snarled as a wolf might, a wolf on the hunt.

Xander had no sense of the pack, dog or wolf. He had no sense of the time before. He had no sense of the time to come. Only the present lay in front of him — the cruel terrain of the arctic wild. Dispirited, isolated, alone, and indifferent to all but his basic needs for survival, he'd disappeared into the wild and was shielded from unnatural predators as if he wore camouflage. Because no spark of recognition ignited within him for any ties to his past, he'd rendered himself immune to spirits, good and bad. This shielded him — his loss of Chukchi spirit. This is why Anya could not find him. This is why the golem could not find him. But Zellie had.

She'd managed to awaken from her sleep of death to hear his silent cries. The Gatekeepers had stirred her to alert and to form into some kind of being that could travel worlds beyond time and space — worlds no living creature could trespass. It weakened her in death, to try to come to some kind of life to help Xander and Anya.

And now Zellie found herself lost in the vast, cold expanse of the gaping breach between worlds, a breach she had no part in causing. Yet the gap widened. Zellie's claws nearly gave way into the abyss. She'd broken with the ancestors. She would pay. The Great Crag had caught her up and held her in its unforgiving shadow. She'd been here before, at the edges of the deep, icy crevasse . . . and lost. Once her claws gave way this time, there would be no next time in any place, in any world. No one waited to help pull her sled out of the darkness. The ancestors had turned from her.

Zellie was alone.

Xander, too, was alone. He had no awareness of Zellie's deadly struggle for existence. Whimpers and soft howls reached his ears from depths beyond Native Earth that nudged at Xander's awareness, yet he didn't question their direction. He ignored them. Only predators caught his attention. The part of his Chukchi spirit that might have heard Zellie had all but faded into the severe arctic landscape. His ears pricked to the growls and snarls and caws that came at him, growing louder and forcing him to full

105

alert. He knew to survive, only that.

"But Rune, you must not leave Seattle. You must stay here to stay safe," Lars ordered his son the moment Rune shared his plans with his father, to set out for Nome as soon as possible.

"*Far,* I have to go. I made a promise to Anya, and I broke that promise. I mean to keep it now and find her," Rune tried to explain. He needed to be careful with his words and not give up the secret of the runes. If his father knew Rune spoke to ghosts, then he really wouldn't let Rune leave, believing he wasn't right in the head. On that, his father could be dead-on, yet no matter. All that mattered was getting to Nome and getting to Anya.

Lars sat back in his worn leather office chair. The hinges creaked.

Rune didn't take any seat, but stood by one of the large windows overlooking the Seattle harbor. The scene below looked ordinary enough, with ships docked and sailors busy loading and off-loading goods. All but one of the seven vessels in the Johansson shipping fleet were in view. The *Storm* needed repairs after its last voyage and was in dry dock. Just as well, Rune thought. He didn't need the vessel to get to the Yukon and then across the Alaska District. He needed a sturdy sled pulled by good dog teams and the guidance of his Viking gods. He needed the help of ghosts. No, his father wouldn't understand that!

"Rune, I forbid you to leave. You're too young and can't make the kind of journey you're talking about!" Lars criticized. He rubbed his clean-shaven cheeks hard in frustration and worry, then rested his elbows on his desktop. His son wasn't looking at him. This wasn't going well. When Lars regarded Rune, he saw a young boy, a boy who would maybe give him a second chance to be a good father. Lars wanted that chance. He also feared for Rune's safety. His nightmares still came at him in the dark hours when he tried to sleep. Something was still out there waiting to get at his son. He could feel it, even in his sleep. It was as if the dark elves of ancient times had come back to haunt him and taunt him with their warnings over Rune.

"You don't trust me, *Far.* You never have." There, Rune had finally spoken the truth. Even though his father had let him captain the *Nordic* across the Bering Sea to Anadyr, it wasn't enough to prove himself to his father. After all that had happened during the past year, after all that Rune chose to tell him about what he'd gone through with Anya and her dogs, it still wasn't enough. Disappointment was all Rune felt; that and regret over not having left Seattle before his father returned from the far North and then Vladivostok. Why had he waited for his father to return? For *this*?

"You're wrong, son," Lars mumbled to himself, trying to find the courage to tell his son what was in his heart and worried he wouldn't say things right.

"I'm wrong, am I?" Rune didn't care that he sounded cruel.

"*Ja.*" Lars spoke in a clear tone and rose from his chair to begin crossing the room to his son.

Rune watched him, caught off-guard by the upset he saw on his father's face. He'd never seen his father look anything but in cool command. He didn't look that way now. Rune braced for what was wrong, for what *else* he'd done to have his father so upset with him.

Both men were tall, at well over six feet, and Lars faced his son. Shoulder to shoulder they were a match. Strong and well-muscled in build, they could have just stepped off a Viking ship of old, having sailed the arctic waters and made a conquering return. Still blond with a full head of hair, Lars looked younger than his forty-two years. The gray was there but invisible to most. His wrinkles told a different tale. The outdoors had weathered him, but not necessarily aged him. Attractive like his son, age would never dampen his good looks.

Rune stared into his father's faded blue eyes, and set his jaw. He really didn't want to hear this. He was done with family, even his father, the way Rune felt at the moment.

Mistakenly, he'd thought his father believed he'd grown up and was a man. Mistakenly, he'd thought his father considered him a full deck hand now, a captain in fact. More than that, Rune had warmed to his father when Lars stepped in to do what he could to help Anya and her dogs while Rune was across the Bering Sea. Rune thought he could trust the changed feelings in his father, the changed feelings for him, his son. He could not. Lars was still giving him orders, telling him he was too young, and making it clear he didn't think Rune was capable of getting back to Nome by dogsled or any other route!

Rune just wanted his father's approval and his love — very simple, all of it. Rune hated to admit this to himself. He hated that he cared about his father. He hated that he cared about Anya. He hated that he loved them both. If the great Odin had such great powers, why couldn't he strip Rune of these awful *feelings*!

Deep down Rune knew he shouldn't test his Viking gods, especially since he needed help to help Anya once he returned to Nome. In the war of ghosts ahead, he needed Odin's help, and Odin's wolves. *The wolf and the dog battle as one.* Rune hadn't forgotten the prophecy and his promise to do his part. The ice storm was coming. The scar at the back of his neck — the sign of the gods — singed to the point of pain, and signaled as much. He'd been given this mark and this task at birth. If Rune believed anything now, he believed this. He believed something else.

This parting from his father might be their last. Rune didn't expect to return from the Alaska frontier, not this time. This could be a battle to the end. He wasn't scared, but ready to fight for Anya and her dogs. He owed her that much. Who was he kidding? He owed her everything! Meeting her was the one, best moment in his life. He wouldn't have another.

With his father, either. This was it.

Rune set his jaw hard, as he saw his father do, still facing him dead-on. Rune hurt inside. He wished he could tell his father

110

that, but wishes were for fools. His mother had fooled him and so had his sister. All his life he'd believed they had some kind of good feelings for him, some kind of love. They did not and they never had.

Rune had been a fool. With his father, too, he realized. He'd been a fool to think his father had learned to trust him and to care beyond spouting out orders and commands aboard ship or bidding Rune "do this" and "do that" on land. Life was all about trade stops and making money and building his shipping business, and nothing about father and son.

Rune forgot his father had just said he wanted Rune to "stay safe." He didn't hear all that his father said, so focused on what his father had not said. Rune still waited for Captain Lars Johansson to give him the wheel and mean it.

"Rune, I am a man of few words. You know that of me," Lars began, the tension in his voice obvious. "I have things I must say. You must stay and listen."

Humph. Rune turned his back on his father and stepped closer to the adjacent window. He peered outside and followed the flight of gulls over the shipyard. *Orders again.* You "must" stay and you "must" listen.

Lars left Rune alone when he wanted to embrace his son and pour out his heart. He couldn't, not now; not with Rune so unwilling to listen. He didn't blame Rune. He had not been a good father. Lars meant to change that, starting now.

"*Runa`* Johansson, if something ever happened to you, I could not take that. I could lose all I have, all my *dampskips,* every one of my *skepps,* and my business, but it would be nothing to me. If I lost you . . . that would be everything. I would await my own *dodsfall . . .* that's all that would be left for me." Lars choked back his emotions, unable to say more.

Frozen to the moment, to his father's longed-for words, Rune stayed silent and still. He couldn't turn back to his father. He couldn't let his father see his face and know how much those words meant. Rune was afraid he hadn't heard right. Maybe he'd just dreamed this up because he wanted to believe it.

"*Runa`*, I could have given you the wheel when you were *nio ar gammal,* you were that ready to captain any *skepp* in my fleet. There's no one I trust more than you in the wheelhouse to cross any arctic waters, ocean or sea," Lars made clear.

Since nine years old?

Why *nio*? Why that age and that number?

The number nine flashed before Rune. He momentarily forgot his father.

Nine dogs.

Nine serpents to slay.

Room number nine.

Nine hours at sea.

Nine miles to go.

The number cropped up in his life the moment he met Anya — when the hand of the guardian brushed the hand of the runes. Nine was significant to the Viking heritage he shared with his father.

Rune inhaled sharply, his attention back on his father. Scared to death to face him, he still feared he'd misheard him. Rune didn't know what to expect, what he should say or do. He hated being so afraid, but he couldn't help it.

"As your *far, Runa`,* I can't let you go," Lars said in a quiet rasp.

At that, Rune turned around and instinctively grasped his father in a tight hug.

Lars put his strong arms around his son.

Rune had saved up for this moment all his life. He didn't try to hold back tears, not caring now if his father saw him cry. His father believed in him, that he was a man, full grown and to be trusted! All he'd ever desired from his father his whole life

113

he got in the touch of his father's strong arms around him.

Nio times over, he loved his father.

Nio times over, his father loved him.

After long moments, Rune forced himself away from his father's comforting shoulder. His face was wet with tears.

So was Lars's.

Rune wiped his sleeve across his nose and straightened his spine.

"I have to leave, *Far.* I have no choice in this. You must understand and you must trust me."

Lars's faded blue eyes covered over in moisture. He used his hands to wipe them dry, then stared into the determined, clear blue vision of his son.

"So *I* must take orders now," Lars tried to joke.

The corners of Rune's mouth crinkled into a smile.

"I can go —"

"*Nej, Far,* you can't go with me," Rune interrupted.

Lars heaved a sigh. His son had his mind set. His son must have good reason to leave. *Like before.* Lars thought of the time when Rune had taken off for Siberia on the *Nordic.* For good reason, Lars repeated mentally. Rune knew the risks. So did Lars, at least

114

those that came to him from the dark elves in his fitful dreams. Those dreams had to do with Rune's birthmark at his neck. Lars regretted the naming of his son. It was too late for regrets. Time was up.

"Then you take my love with you, *Runa`*, to help keep you safe, *ja*?"

Rune swallowed hard. New tears threatened.

"*Takk, Far.* I will," he managed to say.

Having his father's love might not save his life in the ice storm coming, but it would help him endure to the end.

CHAPTER FIVE

"Chinook, let me go with you on the hunt," Anya offered enthusiastically. "My dogs need the exercise. They need to pull a sled and to work. They've been cooped up far too long. Please, Chinook, let us come with you."

The wise hunter, village leader, tradesman, and experienced dog driver eyed the Chukchi girl with skepticism. Her dogs had been in his village all of this winter season, idle and restless to run. He knew Anya had kept them there on purpose, for their protection. From what, he didn't know. *Something was out there. Something was coming.* His native instincts told him as much the moment he first met the Viking boy, Rune, and then Anya. Bad spirits followed their good spirits. The reason Chinook helped shelter Anya and her dogs all this time was because she had the good spirits with her. He did not believe the bad spirits that followed the youths were after him or his people or his dogs, but *hers.* So far, nothing had attacked.

It would be a risk to take Anya's Chukchi sled dogs on this hunt.

"You hunt the seal. You hunt the caribou. I can help hunt the seal. My dogs will find the seal holes no matter how far they must run across the ice. My dogs will give you fresh meat for your homes, for your children's stomachs. A hundred miles across the frozen waters won't slow them. You can trust in them, Chinook," Anya said resolutely.

He did not doubt her words. She spoke true. The reason he wanted to breed her dogs with his Alaskan huskies was for the speed and endurance the Chukchi dogs would add. But Anya forbade any outside breeding. Her mind was set, and Chinook couldn't convince her otherwise. This had something to do with the spirits of her people, he realized. She kept her dogs separate from others for good reason. He decided not to ask what that was. Better to not disturb the spirits and anger the gods in the heavens, on Native Earth, or in the Deep. Besides, Anya was a Chukchi shaman, he'd come to recognize by this time. She was special.

Three Eskimo sleds would leave his village to hunt the caribou.

Two would leave to hunt the seal: his sled and Anya's.

Chinook would not risk the lives of others, but he would risk his for this brave young Chukchi shaman. He felt fatherly toward her and would be proud to call her daughter. But for the young Viking and the young Chukchi, Anya was alone. Rune must have had a good reason to leave. No one was left to help Anya but Vitya and himself, Chinook reasoned. She had no one else, no other home.

"Sit, Anya. The fire will warm us." Chinook shrugged off the hood of his parka and crouched down by the central cookfire inside his winter tent.

Disappointed Chinook had not agreed to take her with him on the hunt, she stubbornly did as he'd asked and folded down into a cross-legged sit. Her hide leggings caught a couple of sparks from the fire and she quickly swatted them out.

Chinook took out his tobacco pouch and lit his pipe. He'd been looking forward to this hunt and the chance to break from his usual routine of working his trade store on the outskirts of Nome. Hesitant to take Anya with him, he was more hesitant to leave her in the village. He feared something might happen to her. If it did, he wanted to be there. He had some fight left in him. His warrior roots had not died inside him. He was Eskimo — Yupik and Inuit, he considered himself — strong and of the people.

Anya watched Chinook puff on his pipe. She realized he was thinking things over and that she must give him time. Hope seeded and grew that he might agree to take her and her seven sled dogs with him to hunt the seal. She relaxed a little and blew out the breath she'd held tightly until now. The idea of running free once again over the ice steadied her. Yet when this made her think of the times growing up in her home village, and made her remember Grisha and her people, she tensed again. She'd left them alone to face their fate, while she and her dogs journeyed to this new land to face theirs.

Anya had no choice.

She'd learned that much, having come this far.

Suddenly upset, Anya felt the burden of being a Chukchi shaman — a guardian and healer of her people. It caught in her chest, the sagging feeling she *wasn't* helping her people — those she'd left behind — being here on the Alaskan frontier. Should she try and return? Should she try and warn her village of the ice storm coming and the danger they faced? Prophecy had warned her of the danger; the arctic winds whispered that some would live and many would die. Anya intuitively knew the whispers spoke of the Chukchi dog and the Chukchi people. She intuitively knew the whispers warned on both sides of the great sea. It was her task to stay on *this* side and save *these* dogs.

She'd been born for this purpose.

The watch-blue eyes of the Gatekeepers bore through her spirit and soul and sent a shiver through her. She must keep to her purpose. But shouldn't she try to save her father, too? There, she'd gotten to one of the main reasons for her upset: *Grisha*. Agitated, Anya shook her head to clear it. Grisha was only her stepfather. Grisha had traded her away to the evil Mooglo. Grisha didn't love her.

But she had to face the truth: she did love him, after all.

She was forced to face another truth: there was no way she could help him.

Chinook studied Anya's troubled expression. He had to do something about that.

"Anya, you and your dogs come with me on the hunt," he declared loud and clear.

She beamed from ear to ear and scrambled to her feet.

Chinook got up himself and then settled his pipe back between his teeth. In the next second it was almost knocked away, Anya's hug was so unexpected.

"I put it there to honor Xander," Anya told Vitya, defending her action.

He'd finally noticed the necklace he'd given her over a year ago, the ivory carving of a husky, hung above the door flap outside the Eskimo tent he shared with her. Why he hadn't spotted it before puzzled him. It was in plain sight all the time!

"To honor Xander?" he repeated in Chukchi, buying time to think on this. So she hadn't tossed his gift away as he'd thought. Maybe she did care. Maybe she did love him. Lighthearted, he shot her a quick smile.

"Yes, Vitya," Anya responded. "When Xander went away, when he died, I had to mark this place to honor his passing." It hurt to talk about Xander, but she wanted to explain things to Vitya. His gift had meant a lot to her during their separation, and she needed him to know that. "I-I never took your necklace off until-until then, when Xander passed," she whispered, and

121

felt her voice going and her energy for this conversation with it. Instead of more words, she reverently arranged and rearranged the husky carving, just so, in its place of honor.

Vitya understood and could see her distress. He shouldn't have been so jealous of Rune Johansson and think the Viking seafarer was the reason she didn't wear his gift. Xander was. That Xander had died was a great loss to his Anya. Vitya stepped closer to her and put his hand over hers, the same hand she rested atop the husky carving.

Anya turned into Vitya's arms.

"Hold me, Vitya. Please," she begged in a hoarse whisper, fighting the tears that welled inside her — tears for Xander and Zellie and for Mushroom — perhaps not equally born, yet heartfelt and genuine all the same.

Vitya had waited for this moment and pulled her close. He tried to hold her gently, but his arms tightened at the feel of her. She needed him and he needed her. They were meant for each other. Anya was *his.* All he wanted to do now was get her safely back home to their village in Siberia where they would marry in Chukchi ritual and ceremony. She'd been shunned by many in the village. He couldn't wait to marry Anya in front of them all and prove to them how

122

wrong they'd been to turn from her. Vitya did not like the shamans in his village. He did not like Grisha, either. He couldn't wait to stand up to them and marry Anya right under their noses, for what they'd all done to her. Once married, he would protect Anya and regain respect for her among the people.

Impulsively, he pulled Anya closer against him and tightened his grasp around her. She was his to protect and to love.

"Vitya, you're suffocating me," Anya had to tell him, even though she took great comfort from him. He understood how upset she was over the loss of her dogs, but she couldn't breathe in his vise-like hold! She hated to complain, but she really couldn't get a breath.

He didn't seem to listen.

"Vitya!" she shouted at him now. "Let me go!"

This time he did.

She quickly took a few steps away, out of his reach. She halfway expected him to laugh at her actions. As children, sometimes this would happen after they'd roughhouse in play, then split apart, often sending them both into spasms of laughter. But they were not children anymore and Vitya didn't crack a smile. His look caught Anya off-guard.

His handsome expression drew her in. His dark intensity mesmerized.

Did he mean to kiss her?

Did she want him to?

She stared at his mouth, suspended in the hypnotic moment. Would she be more disappointed if he kissed her or if he didn't? The question hung in the silence between them.

When his lips twitched slightly at their corners and then turned into a broad smile, Anya had her answer. She was disappointed he didn't even try to kiss her.

Seemingly unaware of Anya's thoughts, Vitya shook his head at himself and backed away a few more steps from her. He said nothing and looked sheepish.

Anya had to smile. She forgot about the kiss she'd expected, and remembered all the years of friendship between them. Besides, he looked so stricken.

"Vitya, I'm going to hunt the seal with Chinook," she told him, changing the subject and the mood.

"No, you must not!" he roared.

"You cannot tell me what I must do or not do, Vitya!" She could be just as loud and warrior-like as he.

Until we're married, he thought to himself. A husband watches over his wife and tells her what she must do and must not do. It is the Chukchi way. Anya was stubborn. He loved that about her, yet he looked forward to the time when she would listen and obey. Shaman or not, she would first be his wife.

"I need to go on the hunt, Vitya. So do the dogs. We need to run free. It has been too long," Anya explained, forcing her tone to soften.

Vitya did understand. The reason Anya released Grisha's dogs in the first place was to let them run free and not be caught and traded away at Markova, separated for all time on Native Earth. In freedom the pack stayed together, to Anya's thinking.

"I will come, too," he said.

"No, Vitya. I want to go alone. I would ask you to watch over the pup, Thor. He will want to come with us, but he is too young. If he's free to run, he will follow and something can easily happen to him. All seven of my dogs are precious to me, Vitya. You know that. They each must be protected. They each must live. Please do this for me, Vitya," she asked. "Please watch over Thor."

Vitya wanted to refuse her but he couldn't.

"I will go back to the dog yard of Fox and help to train for the big race. The dog drivers will be disappointed not to see you, but

I will tell them you will return soon," Vitya said.

"But, *Thor*?"

"I will keep him tied and keep him with me. Do not worry," he assured her.

"I do worry, Vitya, for all of us. You know that. I am shaman and I worry for our dogs and our people. Something is trying to hurt us. You know that. I have told you," Anya admonished, despite knowing she hadn't told him everything. She never would. Knowledge would put him in too much danger.

"Thor will be all right," Vitya assured her a second time. "It is you I am worried about, out on the ice where the hunt is not always easy. There are dangers over the ice. *You* know that." It was his turn to scold.

Anya's face took on a faraway look.

Vitya knew he was right to remind her of the dangers that waited for her.

"There is danger for us everywhere," Anya muttered aloud, her look still trained on the snow-covered tundra that surrounded the Eskimo village. There were perilous cracks and crevasses on land and in the ice. The ice storm had gotten Zellie and Xander and Mushroom. Maybe even Rune. She couldn't let herself think of him, not now. Now she must think of the six Chukchi dogs with her on the seal hunt. They desperately needed to run and to hunt. She had to keep her focus on their safety, only that.

What could he do? Anya had made up her mind, and Vitya knew there was no changing it. He would take the pup and go to the dog yard of Fox and try to communicate with the dog drivers. They managed to understand each other through some sign and a few shared Eskimo words Vitya had learned. He'd even picked up a little English, but a very little.

On impulse, he took down the necklace Anya had placed over the door flap of their tent and placed the husky carving around her neck. He'd made it for her, to keep a part of him with her always.

She tried to take the necklace off, upset to have it moved so from a position of honor for Xander.

Vitya put his strong hands over hers and forced the necklace back around her neck.

"Anya, this is the only way I will let you go on the hunt without me. This will help keep you safe. If you do not keep this around your neck, I will go with you and so will Thor!"

Anya jerked her hands out of Vitya's. The necklace felt heavy around her neck, like an albatross. The sensation unnerved her. She wanted the carving to stay in its place of honor, but had little choice with Vitya so insistent she wear it. Maybe she was being too hard on Vitya. She hated to see him worry so. She relaxed her posture and her expression and even tried to smile. The necklace would have to stay with her. The spirits would not punish her for this, she hoped.

"Chinook is waiting for me to harness the dogs. He's given me a sled, a good one made of hide, bone, and wood. This will be a good hunt, Vitya. You will see."

It was Vitya's turn to hope that her hunt would be a good one with no one hurt. He'd have trouble keeping his mind on things until he saw her again.

Xander kept at his half-eaten arctic hare, devouring it as fast as he could. Instinct told him to eat and run before being found out by other predators. His hunt for food had been a hard one, and he wouldn't give up his meal without a fight. Just then he stopped eating and sniffed the frozen air. He smelled wolves coming at him from opposite directions. His canine instincts told him they were from different packs. They might be in a fight over territory or his food. He was caught in between. They would kill him over both. Scanning the horizon surrounding him, he saw no sign of wolves, but knew they came, scouting, stalking, ready to kill. They were hungry. They needed to survive, as did he.

His best chance was to run. Every instinct in him jarred him to this simple reality. He would have to leave the rest of his kill. Against so many of the enemy, he would die. Outrunning the enemy was his only chance. No song of the ancestors rose within him, only the chorus of survival in the wild — heard in calls across tundra, mountain, and ice from the raven, the ptarmigan, the snowy owl, the wolf, the wolverine, the caribou, the bear, the fox, and the unmistakable screeches of caught prey. To ignore such a chorus would mean a quick death.

Xander knew it, and so he ran.

Zellie's formless being picked up his flight in the wild but could do nothing to help guide him. The Great Crag had trapped her and would not let her go. The breach between worlds widened. The edges of the Great Crag shook. Sacrifices had to be made. Zellie struggled to gain some sort of shape, enough to defy the gods and free herself to help Xander and Anya. This was not conscious because she was dead, at least dead in any sense of awareness on Native Earth.

In the world of spirits, she was still very much alive. It was her place in eternity she risked, yet she fought the Great Crag and defied its powerful hold on her. These sensations through timelessness sparked electric and reflexively, invisible to any but the Chukchi gods. She'd ignited their wrath and was paying the price, caught in her own war of spirits.

The Gatekeepers kept their watch eyes on her and on Xander, forbidden by their ancestry to do otherwise. It was the Chukchi way and could not be disturbed, even for ones so in need of their help. The whimpers that cried out and filtered down now through mist and snow to the reaches of Native Earth were the gods themselves, shedding tears for their own.

Zeke and Homer finally found out where Anya and her dogs were, but only by chance.

Sepp had not seen or heard of her and her dogs, but one of the barkeeps in the Discovery Saloon remembered "the half-breed girl." It was his business to remember everybody. He'd seen the unusual girl on Front Street before the last sweepstakes, but not since. He said the girl had been with the dog driver of the very last team to leave Nome. The girl seemed out of place to the barkeep, which is why he remembered her. When asked, the barkeep said he suspected if the girl was still around, she'd have likely gone off to live with the Eskimo, her and her dogs, since he hadn't caught word of her still being in Nome. He would have heard about her if she was still in the frontier city. Most everybody came through the doors of the Discovery Saloon one time or another. Word spread fast.

This made sense to Zeke and even to Homer, that Anya might live with the Eskimo instead of the white man, and maybe felt more kinship with them, especially with Nome being so big and all. The closest village outside of Nome was Chinook's village. Everyone knew Chinook because of his trade store. Zeke and Homer collected their gear and hurried out the Discovery Saloon. Zeke knew some of the *Eskaleut* language, enough to get by, he hoped.

Both men wore trail shoes and had ice creepers in their packs, used to travel on foot across the frontier. Zeke also kept a glim and matches in his pack from the old mining days. He didn't need a candle to dig at the Pioneer mines, but a candle could come in right handy out alone in the arctic dim of winter. They had two days left before Mr. Lindeberg expected them to return to work.

It was important to keep their jobs, but it was more important to find Anya. Both men were rugged sourdoughs and frontiersmen. Jobs came and went. Little Anya, she was different. So was the boy. The young'uns couldn't be replaced. The young'uns had something unexplained after them. Zeke and Homer needed answers. They meant to search until they got them. No amount of gold dust compared.

"Out of my way!" The golem swatted his guard aside as he might a nuisance fly, and charged through the now-unlocked door to his cement cell. Hit hard, the guard slid to the floor, knocked out. The golem barely noticed. He'd been held unjustly in this gray prison. All of Siberia would pay. All of Russia would pay for his unfair imprisonment.

The great revolution had started.

The revolution would end the lives of his enemies.

Thirsty for their blood, the golem downed the shot of vodka given him by one of his friendly guards, put in his hand just before he stepped outside the prison walls. The golem had made a careful account of his friends and his enemies over the long months and years spent in prison. He knew whom to punish. He knew whom to make afraid. There were many. Many would be fearful for their lives. Fear breathed life into the golem — fear he could cause in others. Death by fear was the strongest drink, better than any Russian vodka. The blood of others gave him life in this world and the world beyond.

"They will all pay, *Mah-ma,*" he spewed into the bitter cold before he got into the military truck that waited for him. The vehicle looked new and shiny and ready to help him lead Russia into powerful agricultural and industrial times. First things first, he reminded himself as he eased back against the passenger seat and took out his cigarettes. He looked at the driver to scrutinize his face, but not for any conversation. Faces were important to remember. The golem had trusted few before his imprisonment and trusted fewer now, even his communist comrades. Any face can turn on you, any time.

Pain split through his head, this one worse than the last episode. He fumbled to strike a match and light his cigarette. His hands were shaky, one of the effects from his severe headache. The headaches also caused the voices in him, those in his head, and in his mind's eye. He'd suffered headaches most of his life and always listened to the voices brought on by them. The golem didn't think he was crazy. He knew he wasn't. He was special. His *mah-ma* had alerted him to his powers in this world and the world beyond. He alone would hold dominion over both.

Fear would pave the way for him — fear in both worlds.

The ice storm raged on in the world of spirits, and now he would unleash a storm in the world of man. As the ice storm killed in one world, so it would in the other! He brought the ice storm! He brought death to his enemies!

The golem blew out the smoke from his lungs. They burned like acid, like fire. The tobacco didn't satisfy. It usually helped calm his headaches and helped him think more clearly, having a cigarette. Voices came at him from too many directions. He strained to concentrate.

Which were his enemies?

Which were his friends?

All of the faces that flashed in his mind's eye were enemies. He didn't see any friends.

Cough. Cough.

There were many comrades who waited to serve him, *many.* He had no doubts here. When he spoke on the streets in Moscow, hundreds, then thousands, listened to him. More gathered around him all the time. Russia was changing from the old. The peasants wanted him to strike down any of the Czar's leftover rule and become their leader, to bring food and work and power to the people.

Cough. Cough.

He'd fooled the peasants. He'd fooled his Bolshevik comrades, too. With his leadership, none were safe. He held dominion over them, he and he alone. His power had no limits. This fact eased his chest and stopped his coughs. His head felt better, and he relaxed against the cold leather seatback.

"Better. Much better, Mah-ma," he rasped in a whisper.

The gray-uniformed driver kept his eyes forward and stayed silent. If he heard his passenger, the driver seemed to know better than to say anything. The snow picked up. It was a long road ahead to get to the appointed train stop, and he didn't want to make any mistakes or cause any accidents with his new commander. He didn't want a bullet in his back. That's how the Russian army stayed strong — afraid a bullet could come at their back any time, any place, if they didn't stay in line and in the fight. Whether you were a top commander or bottom-ranked soldier, it didn't make any difference when the trigger was pulled.

The driver kept his focus on the icy road. He shouldn't complain. He had food and he had work. He wanted to keep his life. No, he wouldn't complain. An eerie feeling hit as he drove his new commander to the train, the feeling that no one would dare pull the trigger on this commander because he would never let them. They'd be dead first.

The golem ignored his driver and threw his cigarette butt out the window, then rolled the frosted glass back up. Immediately he lit another smoke. His body craved the taste and certain comfort of a satisfied draw. First things first, he mentally repeated. He must stay organized. He must keep his thoughts straight and the worlds he ruled separate. He had time before they'd arrive at the train junction and he'd board for Moscow. First things being first, he must concentrate now on what was left to do in the war of ghosts he waged against the Chukchi and their dogs. Some were dead, but not enough.

The same way he'd fooled the peasants

and many of his comrades, he'd fooled some of the gods of the guardians who tried to protect the Chukchi and their dogs. Powerful in the dark world of spirits, this had not been hard for the golem. The Raven god, the fires of *Hel,* and the Midgard serpent did his bidding. The serpent was no use to him now, but the Viking sword could be. It rested in its deep hiding place beneath arctic waters and waited for his command. Other serpents could be stirred, other storms. The fight wasn't over. No *kulaks* can live!

With the guardians of the Chukchi kept apart, their powers against him were diminished. If they joined forces again, this could bring trouble. If they found a dog breeder across the Bering Sea from Siberia — *a despicable enemy kulak* — this could mean worse trouble. Three guardians together would be hard to best, even with his powers in the dark world of ghosts.

No, the golem couldn't take the chance that the — what he believed were weak and too small for his new Russia — Chukchi dog might be purebred across the sea. Purebred or not, the dogs were worthless to the golem. Not to the Chukchi. Their dogs brought them power. Their dogs brought them wealth. The golem couldn't understand why, not really. To him the Chukchi dogs were weak and small. Yet the dogs made the Chukchi *kulaks.*

The golem fumed. The Chukchi were his enemy. They meant to escape his mortal hand and fight against his communist rule. They meant to bring trouble. He, the golem, would visit trouble upon them first! He'd never let them escape. He would make sure they died and all of their worthless dogs with them! No one in Russia would know the Siberian husky ever lived. No one across the Bering Sea, either.

The golem still had much to do in the dark world of ghosts and in the real world of his communist Russia to rid both worlds of the stain of the Chukchi dog. The strong and heavy-muscled freight dog was needed in the new Russia to realize his vision.

"Apaches of the North," the golem scoffed out loud at how some described the far-northeastern Siberian people. "They will be the last to defy me, which is why they are the first to die in my new Russia," he said through clenched teeth.

The young soldier driving the truck swallowed hard. His nerves picked up, same as the snowfall. He didn't hear anything, he told himself. He counted the minutes until he could drop off his new commander at the train and knew he wouldn't feel easy until he did. Right now his best defense was to stay invisible.

CHAPTER SIX

". . . gloom still reigned underneath the
overhang of the Great Crag."
Yuri Rytkheu, *The Safekeeping of Names*

Grisha stared out over the frozen sea. He
didn't feel like hunting when he knew he
must. In spite of being able to provide well
for his family from the fair trades he made
for his Chukchi dogs in Markova each year,
he needed to hunt the seal, the whale, and
the walrus to ensure a good food store for
his family. The arctic air bit at his leathery
cheeks. He did not feel it. Gulls squawked
overhead. He did not hear them. His harnessed dog team tried to bolt and begin
their hunt without waiting for their master's
order. Some yelped and some barked in
earnest.

Grisha did not notice, too concentrated
was he on the stark horizon before him. The
dim skies gave off little light. He squinted

to better spot any sled that might be returning to the village. His Anya might return home. He must be ready to welcome her. This had become a ritual every day, in the same spot — where land met the sea ice — at the same time, waiting for his Anya to return.

But today he needed to hunt the seal. His son, Uri, was coming to join him in the hunt, not his Anya. Grisha remembered seasons gone by when little Anya begged to come with him and he had said no. Why had he said no to his daughter? Why had he denied she was his daughter all those years? To his own mother, Nana-tasha, he'd denied her. He'd said Anya was not a part of him. She was not of his blood. He'd been wrong to say such a thing, he realized. Anya was a part of him, as much a part of him as the arctic itself, as the tundra under his feet and the life-giving ice that held them all to Native Earth.

The ice held all life within its crystal hands, Grisha believed. In the summer seasons and in the winter seasons, the crystals give life and take life. It is the beginning and the end. It keeps secret its pathways of food and plenty for life in the seas. It keeps secret what will stay warm enough to live and what will turn to ice and die.

Grisha believed the ice could take his life anytime and he would deserve such a fate, for what he'd done to Anya. He'd traded her away! Maybe that's why he stared out over the icy expanse every day; he needed to believe the ice would be forgiving and would protect Anya and bring her home where she belonged.

He was her father. She belonged with him. That he would never be able to tell her killed him a little more each day.

His night terrors had faded and with them, his fears that something bad was going to happen to the people. His wife chided him over such nonsense, his sons, too. Haunted by bad dreams, Grisha was unsure what to do. Angry outbursts overtook him for a time, but no more. His wife, Gyrgyn, still whispered her sharp upset that he considered Anya his true daughter. "She is *not* of your blood! She is *gone* from you now!"

Grisha longed for the time when his first wife, Tynga, was alive. She was Anya's mother and the only wife he'd loved. He'd blamed Anya all these years for Tynga dying at her birth. He'd blamed Anya for not being of his blood. When bidden to do so, Tynga welcomed another man to their yaranga, as was custom. Anya's father was a nameless white man, a whaler with no face and no place in Anya's life. All this time he'd punished little Anya for things not of her doing.

He'd traded her away like one of his dogs.

The Gatekeepers would shut their doors to him at his death.

His punishment was deserved.

Thor had broken off his leash and disappeared.

Vitya realized too late that he'd not put an extra tie on the frisky pup. Vitya should have known better, especially with Thor wanting to take off after Anya and her dogs the moment Anya left the Eskimo village. Thor had given Vitya a fit. Almost six months old, the pup was still too young to train for the hunt. He wasn't big enough or strong enough yet to face the arctic ice. He'd escaped Vitya's watch.

If anything happened to Thor, Anya would be heartbroken. Vitya couldn't do that to her — cause her any more distress than she already suffered. Just when she'd started to feel a little better, being able to take her dogs and go on the hunt with Chinook, here he up and lost Thor!

Vitya didn't think there would be any harm in taking Thor with him when he went to the Ramsey mines to help Fox and the other dog drivers train their imported Chukchi dogs for the big race coming up. In fact, Vitya didn't want to lose sight of the pup, for Anya's sake. It was for Anya's sake, too, that he'd promised to help train the three sled teams to race. He couldn't win for losing, it seemed. Frustrated and angry at himself, Vitya walked back over to the post where he'd tied Thor in the crowded dog yard. The thick hide strap had been gnawed right in two! Thor had more gumption than Vitya realized, and sharper teeth.

It was late in the day; the twilight skies gave off little light. Vitya had an idea where Thor might have gone: after Anya. He'd find the spot where she took to the ice of the Bering Sea and start from there. All Vitya could do now was hope nothing happened to the pup along the way. Vitya quickly motioned his goodbyes to the dog drivers and indicated he needed to find "Thor."

When Fox heard about Thor, he worried more than the other drivers.

He knew how upset Anya would be over the missing pup.

Chinook's Alaskan sled dogs were fast, but Anya's dogs ran faster. This made Chinook smile. He admired the abilities of the

Chukchi dogs and still wanted to breed them with his. Anya had said no to this. Every time Chinook would ask her, she said no. But Chinook knew of the big group of dogs brought from Siberia by the miner, Fox Ramsey. News traveled fast across the frontier despite the vast distances separating mining camps and villages of the white man and the Eskimo. Chinook ran the trade store just outside Nome. He heard many things, often, and usually before others in the surrounding area.

When time came, Chinook would trade for some of the new Chukchi dogs. The men who trained the dogs for the next sweepstakes would say yes after their dogs ran a good race, a winning race. Fox Ramsey and the other dog drivers wanted to win races. They did not want to breed dogs. They did not worry over the pure bloodlines of the Chukchi dog as Anya did.

Anya was shaman and Chinook respected her and her wishes in this. The spirits guided her and her actions. He would not interfere. Anya and the boy, Rune, had sacrificed much to bring their dogs to this frontier. Some of the dogs had died. More might. Chinook could do little to help other than offer shelter and what protection he could. Good spirits guided Anya and Rune, but bad spirits stalked them. Chinook had no weapon against the bad spirits. Native Earth could quake and rip open and swallow up the people. The heavens could bolt open and bury the people in blinding ice and snow. All in a heartbeat, in the time it takes to give life or take it away.

Chinook shuddered against the possibility. His thick fur parka did nothing to keep out the cold reality that if dark spirits wanted to bring trouble, they would. Anya and Rune fought powerful dark spirits. Chinook had realized this from the first. He knew the risks he ran, helping the young people and their dogs. Yet he took it. To do otherwise would defy the gods of his people. The Eskimo and Chukchi were enemies in times past. No more. Native spirits guided them as one people now, Chinook believed. The shamans were holy to both.

"Hurry, Chinook!" Anya shouted over her shoulder.

His sled was too far behind to hear what she'd shouted but he knew she called out. Sound traveled with more speed than his sled obviously did, he chuckled to himself. At least Anya was all right. He took a moment to shake off his worries about bad spirits being after her, and then cracked his braided whip to the side of his Alaskan team, to hurry them on. Hungry for the hunt, he struck his whip against the ice a second time, careful to keep its lash far enough away to do no harm. His dogs got the message and raced toward the icy horizon, in the direction of the disappeared team.

"Whoa!" Anya called to her dogs when she didn't have to. They had already slowed, detecting the seal hole ahead. Her blood pumped, just like her dogs'. The hunt felt good and renewed all their spirits. The thick ice and snow cover of the winter season did not deter them from finding the ringed seal hole. Luckily the snow cover was fairly even and not curled up in wavelike forms that could stop a dog team in their tracks. High winds could cause this and make finding any path over the ice nearly impossible. The dogs had run well and traveled a long distance. The skies had stayed clear. No storms brewed overhead. Anya knew her dogs could keep going, no matter how far. But there was no need.

She had time to wait for Chinook to catch up. It might take hours for any seal to show itself and come up to the breathing hole for air. A good hunter is a patient hunter. A good sled team finds the seal hole and then waits patiently for their master to strike the killing blow with a harpoon or heavy wood club. The Eskimo call their club a *hakapik*, Anya had learned. It has a hammerhead and a metal hook on its end. The hook is used to drag the kill across the ice.

Anya knew Chinook used a harpoon, just as her people did. This killed quickly with no suffering to the animal. The strike was straight in the skull of the seal. The glassy look of death was unmistakable. There was no blink reflex when tested. This clean kill was a good kill. The animal's life had been sacrificed to feed, house, and clothe the people. The animal's life would not be wasted. The Eskimo called the seal *nayiq*. Here on this new frontier, the life of the *nayiq* would not be wasted. Its life would go toward harpoon lines, oil for lamps, booted moccasins, dog harnessing, clothes, windows, and food.

Anya's own *kerker* was sealskin. It offered protection from the cold and did not wear out, as warm now as when she'd first helped Nana-tasha make it for her. Her grandmother had far better sewing skills than Anya but never criticized Anya about this. "You were born to Native Earth for other things," Nana-tasha would say, then give Anya a pat on the head as if she were a pup.

Anya's chest caught at this endearing

thought.

In a way, she was a pup.

Finding it easy to slip into thoughts of the past, Anya had to focus on the present. As much as she missed her grandmother and the dogs she'd lost, she had to think about the living. If she lost her focus, she might lose another dog. This was her worst fear. Since she fought the dark spirits alone, with Rune gone, a bad feeling crept through her as if a part of her had been weakened. The wolf and the dog *do not* battle as one. When she was with Rune, she felt better about their ability to fight the unknown together. She'd come to lean on Rune's strength and depended on his help. He was gone. She'd best get used to it. He wasn't coming back.

Anya impulsively prostrated herself on the snowpack to pray to the Morning Dawn and all the Directions to help guide her in her renewed fight against the evil that came after them. She was shaman. It had been far too long since she'd prayed to her gods.

The dogs watched her but did not give up their positions. All were in harness and all stepped restlessly by the seal-carved hole in the ice. Aligned in pairs, Flowers and Frost took the lead spot, with Little Wolf and Midday next, then Magic and Midnight. This was a change in the lineup for them.

They trusted their guardian's hand. They would adjust. Aware of their guardian's actions, they were also aware of the hunt and the kill. They whimpered and barked in anticipation. They were all born to run, to hunt, to endure.

Instinctively imagining herself one of the pack, Anya worried they could be picked off, one by one, separated from the rest and sent on an ice floe into the Great Crag, forever vanished. Predators would do that, find the one that straggled behind or showed a moment of weakness, then strike quickly. She had the dogs in pairs, tethered in loose formation, and did not place Flowers as leader by herself. She'd thought to put Little Wolf in the basket of the sled if need be. In watching him run across the ice this day, he'd done well despite his dropped weight and downhearted behavior over missing Xander. The little runt had run hard, and she couldn't be more proud. He was true Chukchi, a pure spirit she must protect.

Wasn't this her task? Wasn't this exactly what the Gatekeepers expected of her — to protect the purity of the Chukchi dog? The pure lines of generations of Chukchi heritage must not be bred away. Their strength, endurance, and gentle nature must not be forgotten. Their arctic will must prevail.

Some will live. Many will die.

This prophecy pounded in Anya's head like the loudest of shaman drums. She didn't need to go into any trance to realize it was up to her to help ensure *some will live.* Coming to this new frontier was the only pathway open to try to keep alive the spirit of the Chukchi. She was the first of her kind, born of the spirits for this task.

The dark predator after them was also born of spirits, dark spirits. The longer this war of ghosts raged against her and her dogs, the more she'd become convinced that the enemy was not of Native Earth alone, but from another world, deep and deadly. She'd been summoned as guardian in this war. Rune had been summoned, too. Without him she was weaker, but she'd keep up the fight as long as she had breath in her.

She got up off the ice and brushed the crystals from her cheek and then replaced her fox-trimmed hood. The weather had taken a sudden turn and winds picked up. It snowed lightly at first, with flakes dancing and darting by like random flies. This changed to disruptive swirls that hampered Anya's vision. She listened carefully for the Directions to speak and help Chinook along his way. Her dogs had quieted.

The ice rumbled under her feet.

The seal, the walrus, and the whale swam these frozen waters.

Anya peered hard through the building storm looking for Chinook's sled and team. They must start the hunt. Their prey neared. To lose the vital animal would be costly.

Yes, the golem contemplated. It would be.

Fire broke out and raged aboard the modest steamer traveling the Inside Passage of the Alaska District. It happened so quickly, the crew in the engine room couldn't fight it and couldn't escape. All three of the young seamen perished. Those left alive jumped ship to attempt the swim to shore. The frigid water temperature could kill them, but better that than death by fire. Some might make it to land and survive hypothermia, but they took a big chance, jumping into the icy water.

One lone soul stayed with the boat: Rune Johansson.

Rune had signed on to the ferry steamer out of Seattle, needing to work his way up the Inside Passage to Skagway. The icy waters were not frozen here, as they were farther to the north. Glaciers loomed in the distance. The Mendenhall Glacier was home to Juneau. After Juneau, the last stop along the Inside Passage was Skagway. The frontier city boasted of ten thousand residents, all come for the gold. After Skagway, either by the Yukon route or passage along the edges of the Gulf of Alaska, Rune meant to get to Seward in the Alaska District to procure supplies and a sled dog team.

From Seward, by his calculations, he would have close to two thousand miles of snowy ground to cover to make it to Nome. He'd brought some money for this purpose, but preferred to work his way along the route to not cause any talk about his travels. He didn't want to be noticed, period. There were gold-hungry miners and claim-jumpers wherever he went. He didn't want to cause any stir with them or with anybody else. He sure wasn't going to make the mistake of shying up to any fancy girls in any saloons along the way. He'd made that mistake once and lost all his money to thieves at the Nugget Inn in Nome. Besides, he didn't want any fancy girl.

Rune wanted Anya. She was part ice seal, part mermaid, and, he wished, part his. He thought of her inviting smile, her lush lips, her luminous eyes, the softness of her cheek and how she must be as soft all over. He hadn't even kissed her yet! Imagining such a kiss stirred him all up. His body reflexively leaned to her image. He thought of her sweet fragrance whenever she neared, of the melody in every word she whispered, of how his skin came alive under her touch, and of how she made him feel with just one look . . . like a man . . . a man in love and ready to wed.

But she didn't want him.

She wanted Vitya.

Rune had told himself this before — before leaving Seattle in the first place to find Anya and her dogs. He'd been summoned by the gods of his ancestors to help protect her and her dogs. This was his purpose, his only mission. When he found Anya, he didn't expect her to fly into his arms. He'd buck up and deal with his disappointment. He'd had to all his life. Why should this time be any different? It wouldn't be. Love came at a high price, too high for Rune. There was a price to pay for feelings. They always came back at him.

It hurt to love when love wasn't returned. He wished he could change and be somebody Anya could love. Never religious before meeting her, he was now. He'd trade his soul to be somebody Anya could love. But even if he could change, there was no guarantee of Anya's feelings. No, it wouldn't be right to trade away his soul for love, not for the love of his family, his mates, and not even for the love of his life — *not even for Anya.* There wouldn't be much left of him, and he'd be no good to anybody.

His life took him to the oceans and seas. He never wanted to be landlocked. That's what feelings did to him, he realized; they kept him landlocked and made him doubt himself. Doubts didn't help anybody navigate their way. Feeling sorry for yourself didn't help, either. Self-pity wasn't wise and it wasn't for Rune. Doubts weakened a man. He couldn't afford to weaken. He needed to stay strong and stay in the fight.

That's exactly where he found himself at this point — along the Alaska District's Inside Passage in a life and death contest with the fires of *Hel*!

The instant Rune caught wind of the fire onboard the steamer, he'd no doubt who caused it. This wasn't any simple fire started in the steam room. It started in *Hel.* He realized right away: the battle had begun again. *The wolf and the dog battle as one.* His reflexes were quick. Every muscle in him trained on the fight.

He was now naked to the waist. What clothes he'd worn had been burned off him during his attempts to help save his fellow crewmen. The evil after him had no problem killing the small crew onboard. They sacrificed their lives for him . . . *and for Anya . . . and her dogs.* Rune fought to save those he could, but the angry fire burned the men alive who didn't escape to the water. Only death quieted their screams, only that. Rune heard his own screams somewhere in his consciousness, but the battle raged on and he meant to slay this serpent! He had no sword this time. He had nothing but his own fists and his Viking spirit.

The ship burned around him as if he'd been put to sea in a Viking burial. The evil onboard had no intention of sending Rune to Valhalla, but to a merciless, shameful, helpless death. He had no sword to hold in his hand. The traitorous enemy laughed. Rune could almost hear the fires of *Hel* taunt him, the way the flames licked at him. Rune had two choices: death by fire or death by ice. There was little bravery in either.

He had to hold something in his fists in this moment of death. He grabbed up the nearest thing that wasn't on fire — a *sjorya* — a sailor's blanket, and managed to wrap himself in the heavy Norse wool to help protect him to the ship's rail. Then he jumped into the icy waters that waited below and left the fires of *Hel* behind.

His last conscious thoughts were of Anya.

Xander woke from a restless sleep. In the wild, no sleep ever went peacefully, he'd come to learn. Predators didn't allow for it. His senses had him on particular alert, waking just now. He scanned the dim landscape and looked for whatever might be coming at him. His watch-blue eyes were keener than ever and his vision crystal clear. Nothing moved on the crisp horizon. The wind was as still as death. No enemy scent flared his muzzle. He whimpered into the soft mist, as if this might have some effect and bring the enemy in view.

When that didn't work, he gave a gruff bark, several in fact.

Nothing disturbed the landscape. No sign of trouble.

He hunkered back down to his sleeping spot but did not sleep. His stomach groaned from hunger, yet he did not set out for the hunt.

Someone was coming. Something was there.

Xander got back up and sniffed the frozen air. His ears pricked at the winds suddenly picking up. The arctic winds spoke to him.

Someone was coming. Something was there.

This warning did not come to Xander in any clear thought or English language, but out of instinct and impulse traveling to him by way of the ancients — the generations of Chukchi dogs that lived before him. The message charged through the barrier of the wild that had become Xander's world. It charged from the reaches of the ancient world beyond Native Earth — the world where ghosts reign. There was power for the Chukchi dogs in this world and they used it now to try and warn Xander what was coming.

Xander didn't see or hear any imminent danger, but he felt it. Every muscle in his body alerted to it. This high alert put him on edge, only because he didn't know what it was that had him so stirred up. He lived by simple rules in the wild: kill or be killed. Eat. Sleep. Hunt and defend. This canine reflex, this feeling that warned of danger, was new. The sensation of *feeling* was new to Xander. Like humans, dogs sense feelings of love, of loyalty, of obedience, of despair, of loneliness, of longing, of dejection, of pain and sorrow — feelings beyond the basic urges to eat, sleep, hunt, and defend.

Xander had possessed no sense of anything beyond his need to survive until now.

When no one and nothing attacked, he hunkered back down in the same sleeping spot and then did something unusual. He closed his watch eyes against the winds blowing at him. He relaxed his ears against any more disturbing calls from across tundra and ice. He wasn't afraid. He was confused. Memories blurred. Sounds crashed together. Healed scars pulsed in pain.

Facing the wild had become routine for him.

The sensation of feelings had not.

This high alert put him on edge.

"Little Wolf! Little Wolf!" Anya screeched.

Everything had been fine up to this moment.

Anya had watched while Chinook harpooned the first seal to show its head through the hole in the ice. The wait had been hours long, but worth it. The kill was quick and merciful. The huge animal filled Chinook's basket sled and Chinook left soon after to cross the Bering Sea ice to his home village. He'd wanted Anya and her dogs to leave right away with him but Anya gestured she would follow and for him to leave.

The storm had kept up. Snowstorms were not as dangerous as ice building fast and furious, but whiteout conditions could be deadly. Chinook did not want Anya to become lost and he worried, despite the fact she had such skillful and swift dogs, and despite that she'd told him to leave.

For her part, Anya knew the seal needed to be cut and preserved. No time could be lost. She'd urged Chinook to go on without her. She was accustomed to snowstorms; her dogs were, too. Chinook mustn't worry, she'd yelled out.

He did worry but he did leave. Anya was shaman. He would do as she said. His dogs had started out without his command, and they were anxious to get going. Chinook didn't think about how odd this was — for his dogs to go before his command. With so much ice left to cross, he was intent on getting back to his village.

When Anya cried out for Little Wolf, Chinook could not hear her. He'd kept on and believed all was well.

It was not.

Anya had cut Little Wolf from his harness after Chinook left and then tossed her knife in the basket bed to save time. She'd assemble new strapping for him later. Already, she fought the storm. She'd decided to put Little Wolf in the sled so he could ride over the ice on the return trip. He wouldn't like it, but she would force him to ride. The storm blew hard, too hard for the little guy to make it without expending all his energy. He still needed time to strengthen, no matter the good showing he'd made today.

The remaining five dogs would keep a steady pace. This wasn't a race but a run across snowpack ice. Anya hadn't spotted any treacherous breaks in the ice on the way out and didn't expect any on the way back. The snow and fog didn't deter her, and she knew it wouldn't put the dogs off course, either.

But when Anya turned around to collect Little Wolf, he'd disappeared.

"Little Wolf! Little Wolf!"

Despite the blowing snow, she could see the wide range of ice well enough to spot any movement. Accustomed to arctic conditions her whole life, she could see through storms as well as any hunter. She didn't see Little Wolf! He would not have run off.

"Little Wolf! Little Wolf!"

Where could he be? The instant her focus shifted to the seal hole . . . *she knew*.

The rest of the dogs hadn't reacted or

noticed one of their own was missing. Now they did. With Anya's cries for Little Wolf, they absolutely did. Flowers, Frost, Midday, Midnight, and Magic all howled to the heavens. They strained against their harnessing and barked at the seal hole.

Anya didn't hesitate. She threw off her kerker and slid down into the icy depths below. Little Wolf might still be close enough for her to save. She meant to get him back up through the breathing hole before they both died.

The Chukchi huskies barked frantically and pawed at the edges of the seal hole; their ties easily becoming tangled in all the upset. Bound together and left alone by their guardian they could do little else. Each one picked up the sharp scent of danger. Their muzzles flared. Their muscles tensed. Each one fixed their watch eyes on the empty seal hole and would stay to the end.

Zeke and Homer paced back and forth in front of the Eskimo tent where Anya lived. They'd been directed there by one of the villagers. "The Chukchi girl was on the hunt over the ice," the Yupik said. Zeke's skills with the *Eskaleut* language proved good enough here. Anya and her dogs had been gone since early morning, they'd been told.

162

Zeke answered back that he and Homer would stay until she returned if that was all right. The villager nodded yes, then left the two white men at Anya's door flap.

The snow had stopped and the twilight gusts calmed. The storm was over. No matter to Zeke and Homer. It wouldn't go easy with them until they got what they came for: reassurance that Anya and her dogs and Rune were all right. They determined to stay put until they knew for sure.

Sudden shouts at the edge of the village drew their attention. Someone was coming. Maybe Anya! Both men took off at the same time, to find out.

It wasn't Anya but one of the hunters, Chinook. Zeke picked up on the name right away. Chinook had brought back a huge seal and was giving instructions to the men around him to prepare and preserve the meat. The Eskimo seemed in a hurry.

Zeke and Homer pushed through the circle of men.

"Anya!" Zeke shouted at the returned hunter. "Where's the girl! Where's her dogs!"

At Zeke's roar, the villagers backed away a little.

Chinook stared at Zeke, taking his measure.

"Are you friend to the girl?" Chinook quizzed and motioned for the two men to step forward.

"You bet we are." Zeke sounded accusing. "Where is she?"

"I do not know. She should be back, but she is not. I am going to find her," Chinook answered soberly.

"Yeah and we're going with you," Zeke shot back.

Chinook nodded his agreement.

"Can you drive a sled?" Chinook asked of the two.

"Sure," Zeke answered.

Homer sent Zeke a puzzled look, but Zeke ignored him.

Zeke had seen plenty of sleds driven. He was a fast learner. He'd have to be, for Anya's sake.

CHAPTER SEVEN

Thor found his way to the edges of the frozen sea, to the very spot where Anya and his pack started out over the ice. He'd had to take cover along the way. Human hands tried to grab him, but he ran past. Big dogs barked at him. Some growled. Some tried to take a piece out of him, but he ran past before they could. Instinct and sheer will kept him on the trail. He'd been left behind and he didn't like it. He belonged with his mother and with his pack. Gumption to catch up brought him to the spot where they'd left the land for the ice. Generations of Chukchi know-how brought him here.

Hit hard by something, Thor spun around in pain. Hit a second time, he cried out. Confused, he spun back around to run out over the ice to escape. Unsure what to do, which way to go now, he ran back to the snow-covered beach. It was mud and slush and ice and snow. It pulled at him and tried to break him down. Humans crowded everywhere and hid the sky. Hands poked and prodded and hit. Something big grabbed him up and threw him back out over the ice.

Thor landed hard and slid against jagged shards jutting from the ice pack. He yelped in pain. He didn't understand what tried to kill him. He wanted to find Anya and his pack where he would be safe. The pup managed to get back on his feet and reflexively shake his head to clear away the mud and slush and ice balls that clung. He'd been here before, to this dark place — where nothing wanted to let him live. His instincts remembered the time. His will to survive imprinted the experience deep within his makeup, no matter his youthful age. Because he was still young and rebellious, Thor turned to the ones he saw trying to hurt him and wanted to hurt them back. He barked at them in self-defense, daring another challenge. He had spirit — true Chukchi warrior spirit.

"Jeg ville ikke gjore det hvis jeg var deg," Leonhard Seppala warned the boy about to throw a mean, hard snowball at the pup caught out on the ice. Sepp repeated his warning in English this time. "I wouldn't do that if I were you."

166

The boy, the oldest in the group of young juveniles crowded at the edge of the Bering Sea, didn't lower his arm and started to throw his icy bullet at the helpless pup.

Sepp grabbed the boy's arm and wrested the snowball free, then crushed it under his mukluk. The boy matched Sepp in height, and he seemed surprised the short man who intruded on his fun was so strong.

"Hey, mister, you leave me be or I'll tell my father. He's bigger than you and will hurt you good," the boy said, loud enough so his friends could hear.

The others boys backed away but didn't leave the scene. They all had sheepish looks on their faces as if they knew what they'd done — what they didn't do. They should have stopped things before they went this far. They were used to doing what Walter told them to do. All of the boys were a little afraid of him.

Thor stopped barking. He didn't leave the scene, either. He faced off against them all. He hurt and reflexively needed to find Anya and his pack for comfort and companionship, but he stayed put, curiously watching the bad human who tried to kill him and the good human who tried to help him. One was a threat. One was not.

Bullies, Sepp thought as he scanned the

mean-spirited group of kids. From childhood in his homeland, he'd had to deal with such bullies. He always did and there was always a fight. He always won. His words at this moment were meant for the boy who threw the pup out over the ice like so much rubbish.

"You *stoppe na'. Det er feil.*" He was so upset for the poor little pup, Sepp reverted to his native Norwegian language. "You stop now. It is wrong what you do," he said in English this time. "You could have killed the pup. Are you stupid or just *mener,* just mean?" Sepp asked. "Both, I'd say," he answered his own question.

The boy didn't answer Sepp and he didn't run off. He seemed to be trying to figure a way to save face in front of his friends.

Sepp read the signs. He knew what went through the bully's mind.

"What is your name?" Sepp asked.

The boy didn't answer.

"Your name," Sepp said again, this time more forcefully.

Still, the boy kept silent. His jawline visibly tensed.

"Walter Moody!" an anonymous boy shouted.

Sepp didn't look in the direction of the shout-out but at the bully boy.

168

"I know of your father. He likes dog fights. He likes to see dogs hurt." Sepp shook his head in disapproval. "It is sad you want to be like such a father. Your father is stupid and your father is mean. Every dog here on the frontier is important, every one of them. They help us stay here and stay alive. It is stupid to hurt even one. It is mean. Do not be a *darlige gutt,* Walter. Do not be a bad boy," Sepp warned.

Walter stared at the ground and pushed his mukluk deeper into the snow.

Sepp felt sorry for the boy. His father hit him. Sepp could tell. His father made the boy afraid, and his father made his son into a bully.

"Clear out of here, all of you," Sepp told the boys.

They all did, right away. Only Walter hesitated a moment, seeming to hunt for the courage to look Sepp in the eye.

When he finally did, Sepp knew he was right about the father and felt sorry all over again for the son.

Then Walter took off in the same direction as the other boys.

Thor watched him leave, then trained his watch eyes on the human who did not try to kill him. His instincts told him to take off across the ice, but something held him to the spot. He didn't want to leave this human yet. The pup felt an odd kinship with the stranger and stayed curious about him.

Sepp watched the pup. He'd never seen the breed before. He'd never seen such gumption in any pup. Sepp was used to the larger breeds in the Alaska District, mixes of Eskimo dogs and just about everything else. Drawn to the young dog, he wondered about its injuries. The bullies had hurt the pup, and Sepp wanted to make sure he was all right.

Others passed by along the stretch of beach, but no one paid any mind to Leonhard Seppala and the piebald, spotted pup on the icy edges of the Bering Sea. Puppies ran around all the time. Owners were always chasing one of their strays, and needing to get them back home. Kids were always causing some sort of ruckus. Nothing was happening to catch any onlooker's eye.

But Thor caught Sepp's eye, and not just because he was being mistreated. The pup didn't look like any Sepp had seen around Nome or back home in Norway. Smaller than most, Sepp felt a kinship with the striking blue-eyed dog. Sepp wasn't big, either. The pup was tough and had a lot of heart, the same as Sepp. To survive on the Alaska frontier, you had to be tough, and you had to put your whole heart in the struggles and challenges faced every day. You had to be fast, strong, and enduring. This pup had all of these qualities. Sepp could see it in the determined set of the head, in the clear focus of the watch eyes, and in the fearless stance of the multi-speckled pup.

Its coat was spotted with shades of gray and black and copper-red, all woven together in a pattern of thick fur and pure husky. The pup's distinctive expression was the most striking to Sepp, with its intelligent, sky-blue eyes set against coal-black fur. White fur coated the chin and muzzle area and ran down all four legs and the undercarriage of the bushy tail. Quite a picture, this little husky, Sepp thought again.

Thor had been studying Sepp in his canine way. He waited for the man's next move. Thor had an urge to go to the man, but he had a stronger urge to go to Anya and his mother and his pack. The lines between his pack and this man blurred, as if they were part of the same pack, the same family. Thor whimpered slightly at this queer sensation. Confused as to what he should do, he whimpered louder and stepped restlessly on the ice. He turned in a semicircle, then back around to face the man. Then he put his muzzle to the heavens and began to howl instinctively for some kind of help, some sign what to do.

Sepp took a knee and gave out a kissing sound to Thor, as he would do to speed up his sled team. He wanted the pup to come to him. The pup was upset. Anyone with half a brain could see that.

Thor stopped howling when he heard the kissing sound and took off . . . toward Sepp.

"There's a good boy," Sepp said the moment Thor reached him. Sepp didn't see any blood. The pup's thick fur likely hid the bruising injuries. Sepp let the dog sniff and explore his hands and face before making any move. When Thor affectionately licked Sepp's hands, and then his face — all of it — Sepp dared a hand to the pup. The pup's curled tail wagged. The pup accepted him. Sepp felt relieved. The two were getting to know each other. The idea struck Sepp then and there to take the pup home to his wife. Constance would love him.

Sepp already did.

"Hey! Hey!" A young man yelled behind Sepp.

Sepp stood up and turned around to the youth coming toward him. He held Thor in his arms.

Vitya breathed a sigh of relief when he spotted Thor with the small man at the sea's edge. Vitya had guessed right. Thor meant to head out over the ice and find Anya and join the hunt. Thor was alive! His Anya would not have to grieve over losing another dog. Yes, Vitya breathed a huge sigh of relief.

The instant Vitya reached Thor he put a hide loop around the pup's neck and held on to the rest of the leash. He let the man keep holding Thor, grateful the man had found Anya's pup. He smiled broadly at Thor and the man holding him.

Disappointed, Sepp realized he couldn't take the pup home to his wife. It must belong to this Eskimo. Or was he Eskimo? Like the pup, the youth didn't look familiar to the area. Sepp unconsciously hugged Thor closer. He didn't want to give this pup up to the stranger, not yet.

"Is this dog yours?" Sepp questioned.

Vitya didn't understand the exact words but he guessed what they were about. He nodded his head in a yes.

"Th-thank y-you," Vitya managed in English and then reached for Thor.

Sepp's arms felt cold without the pup close. He could see the pup didn't protest, so he wouldn't.

"What's his name?" Sepp asked.

"Eh?" Vitya had trouble with this question.

Sepp reached out and gave the receptive pup a scratch behind one of its furry ears before pointing directly at the dog and saying again, "Name?"

Vitya nodded enthusiastically now. "Thor. Thor," he repeated.

Sepp ran his hand over Thor's head and scratched again behind an ear. *Thor* was one of the Viking gods, a part of Sepp's Norse heritage. Thor was a fitting name for such a fit pup.

"*Farvel,* Thor. You are a *bra gronlandshund.* You are a good husky, you are," Sepp pronounced, then took his hand from Thor and walked away.

Thor whimpered after him.

Sepp heard but could do nothing. The little husky already had a home. It would not be with him.

The worlds of the Chukchi spun round. The gods talked in whirls of spirits and whispers. Their time on Native Earth was in great peril. Their time unto eternity was in great peril. They had done what they could for the human guardians of the Chukchi — Anya and Rune — and could do little more. The threshold between spirit and mortal flesh had been crossed. The guardians faced great trials, both of them. Their time on Native Earth teetered between life and death.

The dark spirit after the Chukchi was powerful but weakening due to distraction, not any lack of resolve. The demonic golem meant to wipe out the Chukchi dog and destroy the people. The golem would succeed. The gods knew the prophecy. *Some will live. Many will die.* This prophecy was not argued among the gods. The idea the gods could do nothing else to hold it back was.

The notion that only the human spirit could prevail on Native Earth sounded thin and unacceptable to some ghostly minds. Surely the ancient spirits from two such powerful worlds as the Chukchi and the Vikings could provide help. The Creator god and Odin transcended time and space, life and death, here and the hereafter, in a swirl of worlds passing by and brushing together in an instant of communion and communication. This is how all life and spirit went on. This is how worlds helped each other in the beyond — in the layers of time after time.

Some will live. Many will die.

This far-reaching prophecy spoke to life not just on Native Earth, but in other times and places in the history of all existence. Recorded history teaches the hard lesson that while some will live, many will die. Pompeii lay in ruins. The Mayans, the Anasazi, and the Minoans had disappeared. Ancient Greece fell. Sparta and Athens had vanished. So had the Roman Empire vanished. Whether by sword, by act of nature, or something else . . . these civilizations vanished.

But did they?

The spirits did not argue about this. *Some will live,* the prophecy foretold. Civilizations did not disappear. They did not vanish. The spirits traveled among these same ghosts from fallen ancient worlds. These ghosts lived in the swirls and brushed by the same worlds, waiting to be summoned to the fight when needed. This was how the ancestral ghosts of the Chukchi and the ghosts of the Vikings brushed past — *the hand of the guardian brushed the hand of the runes* — summoned at the same time to the fight against the demonic golem.

There was no argument among the spirits over this. The battle was engaged, hard fought, and not over. The argument came with worry over their guardians falling. Then, no human spirit would be left alive to prevail against the golem. Some of the gods were sure there was a way to span the breach and help, especially the Morning

Dawn. The other Directions agreed. Their arctic whispers had a far reach. In this, the ravens of the Vikings related.

The Creator god did not agree, nor the Earth god. Odin did not agree. The risk was too great. The unnatural breach caused in Native Earth widened. Its edges cut a dangerous path that threatened all of them. The lines between worlds — the lines separating one world from another — one time from another — were too unstable for the gods to keep crossing. If broken, worlds would tumble and crash into each other and all would perish.

It was up to the young guardians on Native Earth now. They were on their own.

The dissenting spirits quieted.

The Gatekeepers kept their whimpers to themselves and kept their watch eyes on Anya and Rune.

Still caught in a web of her own making, Zellie's flagging spirit wriggled beneath the Great Crag. She fought to hold on to awareness. She fought to hold her amorphous, husky shape and keep her voice. She'd already crossed back over the carefully constructed lines between worlds to the side of Native Earth, and defied the gods in doing so. Any moment her shape would turn to soulless dust. She had to break free before it did.

Lars tore off his spectacles and got up from his office chair so fast the worn leather swiveled and creaked in protest. He kicked the chair full away, he was so upset over Rune. Every window in his spacious office was edged in snow and ice on their outsides. Lars cursed the ice, cursed the winter, cursed the biting temperature, and cursed the day he let his son leave for Nome. He charged over to one of the windows and stared down at the Seattle harbor in view, to try and glimpse Rune. His son might return, believing his journey was a fool's errand this time of the year. A father could hope.

Lars put his fingers against the cold glass and splayed them as if he could somehow make contact with Rune in doing so. It was the sea and the ships below that gave Lars the impulse. Many a time Lars had stood at this very window and watched his young son help load and off-load cargo and chase around after crewmen, wanting to learn the ropes from them. If Rune wasn't climbing on board one of the Johansson ships in the harbor, he'd already found his way onto another. It did little good for Lars to lecture his son on the dangers of his actions. Rune didn't listen. If he did, he didn't say anything back. Lars remembered how his determined son would stand in front of him and look right at him. In fact Lars couldn't remember a time when his son didn't look him in the eye. Rune never looked away when he was in trouble, but always faced it, the same as his Viking ancestors. Lars imagined they never looked away from trouble, either.

Was that what his son was doing, facing trouble?

If Rune were in trouble, there wasn't a damned thing Lars could do about it! Frustration and fear crept over him and forced his hands from the glass. He backed away from the window, scared for his son. His nightmares had returned. Old worries haunted him. In the light of day, Lars tried to push his worries away but it didn't always work. Like now.

It wasn't just Rune's safety Lars worried about.

It was Rune's inheritance.

Margret made threats to take Johansson and Son Shipping from Lars and from Rune. Margret wanted Lars and Rune to pay for what they were doing to her and to Inga. The divorce was getting ugly, when Lars thought it would be a simple thing to end their marriage. He'd thought wrong. Margret meant to do anything she could to strike out at him and Rune, even though Lars had promised to provide for her and for Inga for the rest of their lives. It wasn't enough to Margret. Because all she cared about was money, she believed that was the worst thing she could do to Lars — take all his money. She'd hired top lawyers in Seattle to accomplish just that.

Lars didn't need this headache, but he had no choice. He had to fight this legal battle at home while his son fought a far more dangerous one to the north. Both fights were important, Lars realized, important to win. When Rune returned safe, Lars wanted Johansson and Son Shipping to be waiting for him. In a sense, Margret had already killed their son with her lack of kindness and refusal to love him. Now she wanted to kill his inheritance by taking it from him. It disgusted Lars, but the truth of Margret's unconscionable actions couldn't be ignored. Greed will do that, he supposed. Greed and bitterness can make you forget you were ever a mother or a wife.

Lars didn't trust Margret to keep her complaints against him open and above-board. She would do whatever she could to get Johansson and Son Shipping from him and from Rune. Not every lawyer could be trusted to represent the truth. The truth can be changed. The right amount of money can twist the truth. This concerned Lars. This could bring down his world and his son's along with it.

As much as Lars wanted to take out after his son, he had to stay in this fight at home and win it for Rune. If he didn't keep a careful eye on Margret in the months to come, the price could be high, and Rune would have to pay it. But as soon as the ice broke off Nome's shores, Lars would have the *Storm* there for Rune to board. He refused to think Rune would not be there. His son had skills beyond the average seventeen-year-old. Rune would be eighteen before Lars saw him again.

Lars swallowed hard.

When he reaches eighteen, not *if*.

The night sky dimmed to twilight. Light snow picked up. The wolves pawed at the snow. Nervous about their next meal and agitated over the threat of a challenge to their territory, they dug at the ice in antici- pation of the fight ahead. All of their senses sharpened in the process. Hunger usually drove their actions. Not this time. Survival did. Nine wolves followed their leader, a huge black wolf. The magnificent animal ruled in the wild and faced down every challenge. His pack followed him willingly. Behind him they were safe. Behind him their stomachs stayed full. Behind him, they had pups. Behind him, they stayed alive.

The frozen tundra, mountain terrain, and icy landscape had been home to the ancestors of the wolf since the coming of the Ice. Generations lived and died in the cold regions of the Alaskan frontier. Their cries rang across the open, echoing their claim to this vast territory for all to hear. Their howls signaled the beginning of life and its end. The best chance to live was with the pack. The easiest way to die was being left alone. No wolf ever strayed far without good reason. The weak could lag behind. The strong could be sent to scout food. An attack from a rival pack could splinter the group. The wild was dangerous, but then, so was the wolf.

The great black wolf sniffed at the obvious danger coming his way. A storm brewed. Heavy snow blanketed the air around him and closed in. Every hair on him bristled; every muscle tensed. His chest pounded. His ears pricked to the silent landscape and his eyes trained on every part he could see.

Any movement would alert him to the fight ahead.

There would be a fight.

His relied-upon instincts alerted him to it.

Whatever came at him from the unknown wild, he would kill. It was what he knew, what he always had to do to stay alive and to protect his pack. His claws sharpened reflexively. His jaw tensed; his fangs salivated, ready for the fight.

His pack backed away, sensing the danger faced. Wolves didn't fear much, but they feared whatever was coming now. They whimpered and moaned, pacing restlessly.

Something was coming. Someone was there.

The great black wolf stood deadly still, disturbed by the queer sensation that this kill would be different. His feral senses confused him. Winds brushed across his thick fur, ruffling him. He peered through the twilight storm at the icy expanse and saw nothing. He kept his ears pricked. Still nothing; no sounds traveled across the wild to alert him to this different danger. He instinctively circled full around, trying to better pick up the unknown scent.

It was everywhere.

Then it was upon him.

■ ■ ■ ■

Fox couldn't get Anya's lost pup off his mind. He looked out over his dog yard at his own Chukchi dogs in hopes of seeing the little guy scrambling among them. Maybe the piebald pup had wandered back from wherever he'd disappeared. The dog yard was crowded but organized and well set. The huskies were each tethered to their own posts with enough room around their crude shelter and straw bedding to move, eat, and sleep reasonably well. They had protection from the weather and attention to their needs. Fox felt good about their care, but grew more uncomfortable every day about their competition in the upcoming sweepstakes.

Word had gotten around that he meant to race three teams of Siberian huskies, and that he had his dog drivers set. John Johnson would be one of them. The only reason all of the locals didn't label the Siberian huskies as "rats" was because of Johnson's well-known ability to drive a sled team with speed and skill. Locals had begun to take notice of his dogs, too much notice, Fox thought. He should have expected it. Good mushers had good reputations. Johnson was one of them. Fox was a dog driver, too, but still new in the area, having come to the Alaska District the year before to join the family mining business. Now, sled dog racing was Fox's business.

He was in love with the sport and was wealthy enough to follow through and secure his own teams from Siberia. Last year's showing proved to Fox that the Siberian huskies made a big imprint in the snow on the Alaskan frontier. Their path carved deep. Their path would last. He would make sure of it, running three teams in the next sweepstakes. No one would call the unique sled dogs from Siberia rats anymore. These amazing animals stirred Fox's blood and whetted his competitive appetite. He wanted to win the next All Alaska Sweepstakes and he would, with these dogs. They had something special and he planned to show just *how* special, in the sweepstakes. If he didn't cross the finish line first, John Johnson might, or his third dog driver, Charles Johnson. With three teams in the running, they would all do well, Fox predicted.

With word already spread of his intentions, Fox found himself looking over his shoulder to see who watched him train his dogs. Charles Johnson and John Johnson trained with him, but more often than not, John would take his team off and be gone for days, exercising his team on his own. John liked the open territory better than areas around Nome. The quiet and solitude suited him. Fox had no problem with this. He relied on John to train as best he thought. Fox wasn't worried about any of his teams entered in the sweepstakes. They were all Chukchi dogs and all great racers. He and Charles and John were just going along for the ride. Fox chuckled to himself at this thought, but it had a ring of truth to it.

So did the fact that locals were not the only ones to watch out for, who might be looking over his shoulder. Fox couldn't put his finger on exactly what troubled him, but something or someone seemed to spook his dogs. When they started to bark or howl at odd times, Fox would rush to the dog yard but see nothing, no one. This happened too often for it to be nothing. Fox wasn't imagining it. He'd always have his gun ready but never spotted wolves, wolverines, bears, or any other predators. The very idea of an unknown predator out there spooked Fox.

He had enough to worry about with the upcoming race. Worry over anything else distracted him from his purpose. He'd gone all the way across the Bering Sea to Siberia to get his race teams, not to mention his investment of time and money in them. The idea that something or someone waited in dark shadows to pounce on his dreams for the Chukchi dogs just wouldn't go away.

There it was.

He couldn't do anything about it. As hard as he worked, as soundly as he slept, as exhausted as he was at the end of every day . . . *there it was.*

Did the pup's disappearance have anything to do with dark shadows all around?

"Keep the *heid*!" Fox lectured himself. Here he was putting worries together as if any of it made sense. He needed to get on with his business and not act like he was *mad wi it* drunk. The lad, Vitya, would find Anya's pup. Fox's dog teams would stay safe and be trained up proper. One of his teams would win the next sweepstakes. The lad, Rune, and the lassie, Anya, would be all right in the end. Fox would bring pride to the name of the *Siberian husky* in the Alaska District.

"There, all said and done *noo*," Fox affirmed his predictions, then gave a nod in the direction of the dog yard. The dogs were watching him. None slept, and all appeared stirred. Fox scanned the landscape for a sign of any trouble. He didn't see or hear anything out of the ordinary. The dogs should settle soon and he should relax and not worry so much.

He headed back toward the Ramsey Mining office, knowing full well that wouldn't happen. No sleep for him tonight. He'd stay on guard and watch over the dogs.

CHAPTER EIGHT

"He's awake, Pa. Come see."

Doc Adams put his precious store of chloroform safely away in his medicine cabinet and joined his daughter. Lucy had sat vigil with the boy ever since he'd been brought to them for care three days ago. With the boy's extensive burns and almost drowning in the half-frozen waters of the Passage, the doc really didn't think his patient would survive. Maybe the boy shouldn't come awake, the doc thought. Burns meant pain. Burns usually meant a slow death from infection. Doc Adams shook his head. He'd never seen such a case where a body suffered the effects of burning and freezing at the same time.

A doctor for the army, Adams completed his duty at his northern post in the District of Alaska and was in route home to Colorado when he decided to stop in Skagway and try his luck with a shovel instead of a scalpel. He didn't have any. Even so, he sent word to his wife and daughter to join him. "There is adventure aplenty here and enough patients to keep a roof over our heads and food on the table," he wrote. As it turns out, he was lucky. His wife and daughter did join him, and he did not succumb to gold fever like so many others.

Skagway marked the end of the Inside Passage water route or the beginning, whichever way a traveler might be headed. It was a jumping-off place for the gold fields of the Yukon. It also meant an overland journey in the opposite direction toward the Gulf of Alaska if the intent was to reach Alaska's northern territory. Either way, the journey never proved an easy one. Winter meant ice and snow. Summer meant a flood of melt and mud.

In Skagway, Doc Adams cared for white and Eskimo alike. He cared for gold seekers, fishermen, fur trappers, storekeepers, saloonkeepers, ladies working the line, and immigrants from the Outside — some good and some bad. It didn't make any difference to the doc if he were removing a bullet, a nasty fishhook, glass from a broken whiskey bottle, or the end of a pickax from somebody's back; he put out his shingle for all in Skagway, law-abiding citizens or not.

He had to laugh at this. There wasn't much law in the boomtown of ten thousand.

The numbers had started to drop when the gold became harder to find. Life in Skagway wasn't easy, and the doc wasn't going to make it any worse for folks by refusing to help those in need. The notorious Soapy Smith had been one of his regulars. The outlaw couldn't seem to stay out of trouble. He had company in that. Times were tough and so was the territory. A body had to be tougher than it to survive; to some that meant being on the wrong side of the law.

"Pa, will he make it?" Lucy asked her father as she kept her eyes on their patient. The boy had the bluest eyes she'd ever seen. Her heart skipped a little. Almost disappointed he'd awakened, she couldn't sit such easy vigil with him. She couldn't put a cool cloth to his brow or apply new salve and change his dressings without her fingers trembling. He'd see and know she was nervous. He was a stranger and she shouldn't feel so drawn to him.

Doc Adams didn't answer his daughter's question.

The front room of the Adams's cabin served as the doctor's office, with two hospital bunks, an instrument table, a medicine and supply cabinet, a small library of medical books, a desk, two wood chairs, well-placed kerosene lamps, and one electric light, only recently made available. The army had taught Doc Adams well. To be fit and ready for duty, a soldier had to be outfitted properly. Army-trained docs were often the best on the frontier. Hard to get the supplies and medicines he needed, being so isolated from the main core of medicine to the south, the doc did what he could with fees earned, to keep his medical bag and office up-to-date and ready. His hospital bunks rarely sat empty. Now was the exception, with the boy his only patient.

Rune came awake slowly, as if out of dreams and not any nightmare. It was Anya he saw in front of him. *Anya.* He had to touch her and make sure this was real but when he tried to move, he couldn't. Pain had him pinned down.

Anya, I love you.

He tried again to reach for her, not embarrassed by his thoughts. She needed to know the truth. Relief burned through him and freed his arm. Anya was *alive.* Tears stung at him everywhere it seemed. It took effort but he managed to brush the side of her face with his fingertips . . . down her comely cheek . . . over her soft lips . . . under the curve of her shapely chin.

This wasn't Anya!

Rune forced his swollen eyes wide open. His injured arm fell away from the unfamiliar girl. He tried to turn his head to see where he was, but he couldn't move. Pain kept him immobile. His vision blurred and he blinked hard to clear his focus. Despite everything holding him to the spot, he raised his head enough to see in front of him — enough to see all the bandages over his arm . . . over both arms . . . across his chest . . . down his legs!

Memory flooded in. Hit hard with remembering the fire aboard the steamer, Rune's head fell back to the bed. He cursed the fires of *Hel*!

All the crew had died, everyone set on fire or forced to a frozen death. He'd chosen ice over fire. So why wasn't he dead? He should be, especially since all the crew had unknowingly given their lives for him. Guilt shot through him, same as the pain. He couldn't save them, not even one. Dark spirits from *Hel* killed the crewmen to get at him.

Rune forced his thoughts to the present. He tried to speak to the girl with him, but words wouldn't come. His mouth felt like somebody had shoved straw down his throat. His tongue tasted like charred cotton.

"Wa-water," he managed to rasp. The sides of his cracked lips struck something agitating. When he forced himself to reach past the pain and touch his face, he realized what it was: more bandages. Jarred to the reality of his condition, he knew he'd been burned pretty badly. He thought more about how odd it was he'd lived through the fire and the icy plunge into arctic waters than he did about how serious his condition really was. In the back of his mind, he knew he might die.

He wasn't afraid to die.

He was afraid he wouldn't find the answers he needed.

"Here, take some of this," Lucy said gently, at the same time putting her arm beneath Rune's pillow to lift his head. She held the cup of water in her other hand and put its edges to Rune's mouth. She knew it hurt for him to move, but he needed water. The burns drained water from his body. He needed to drink as much as he could. "Take small sips," she coaxed.

He did, but he didn't like it. The water went down well enough. It wasn't that. It wasn't the pain, either. It wasn't even the bandages all over him. He didn't like being helpless. He didn't like anybody having to take care of him. Used to being on his own, none of this felt good to Rune. Unless he was dead, he didn't want to be flat on his back covered with a bunch of bandages and having some stranger doing for him!

The girl seemed nice enough. Then Anya's image flashed in front of him and he imagined *her* taking care of him. That he might not mind. *Anya,* thinking of her and how much he cared for her, and how much he needed to find her, forced him into a fit.

"Pa! Pa!" Lucy screamed.

Doc Adams rushed over.

"Lay him flat," he instructed.

Lucy deftly removed the pillow under Rune's head. His blue eyes rolled upward and his body went rigid with the shakes. Saliva foamed out one side of his mouth. His teeth clenched. No object could be inserted to prevent him from swallowing his tongue. The bed shook. Rune's body creaked and groaned like a ship about to wreck at sea.

Lucy had never witnessed anybody having this strong a fit. She stayed at her side of Rune's bed and met her father's eyes. Doc Adams stood opposite. They shared the same understanding. The longer the fit went on, the more convinced they both were that their patient wouldn't come out of it alive. No one could withstand the severe injuries he had before going into such a state, much less endure the battering a fit caused on top of them. The boy had burns. The boy had suffered the effects of freezing. His heart and his lungs could not take much more. The boy would not come out of this.

Tears gathered at the corners of Lucy's eyes. She already grieved the boy's passing. The three days she'd spent at his side made her feel close to him, as if she knew him. They would have become good friends. She felt drawn to him even in this moment of loss. Life was cruel. Life was not fair. Lucy didn't believe in miracles. Few came her way on the rugged Alaska frontier. She didn't expect one now. Even so, she sent a prayer heavenwards to save her patient. "If anybody deserves it, he does," she softly whispered.

Doc Adams saw the agitation on his daughter's face. His distress almost mirrored hers. Out there somewhere, a mother and father would have to grieve over the loss of their son. He had no idea of the boy's identity and no idea who to contact. His family might never know about their son until they met their Maker. The doc believed in the hereafter, but he was more concerned about the moments left in this boy's life.

Rune's fit suddenly quieted. He lay flat and board-like. His breaths were shallow to negligible. His lids twitched ever so slightly.

"Son," Doc Adams said, and leaned down closer to his patient. "You're a brave boy and a good one, I know. My daughter and I are here with you and we will not leave you. My name is Matthew and my daughter's name is Lucy. We —"

"Rrr-Rune."

It took effort but Rune managed to speak. He needed to thank Matthew and Lucy for helping him. He couldn't believe he was still alive and wasn't at all sure he wanted to be.

The silence of the depths below the ice roared in Anya's ears.

Desperate to find Little Wolf, she had no time for silence. She needed to hear where he was, to see where he was, to take hold of him and take him back above the ice. The shaman in her could save the helpless husky! Desperate to believe this, Anya strained to move her body through the freezing waters. She strained to see ahead of her and at the same time, to keep the seal hole — Little Wolf's way to safety — in her sights. There was some light, enough to see shadows pass and faint rays shimmer through the layers

197

of ice above.

In no way did she expect to survive this, but she expected to save Little Wolf's life before she died. Her lungs were strong and she'd always been able to hold her breath a long time. She depended on that now. She had a minute or two of air in reserve. That was it. The cold temperatures already dug into her, clawing for her life's blood. She could feel her insides turning to ice.

Then she heard it. A tiny howling waved thickly past.

Little Wolf!

She cried out in answer, desperate for the captured husky to hear her. "I'm coming. I won't leave you," she screamed against the flow of ice and water trying to stifle her call. What part of her wasn't frozen cried for Zellie and Xander and Mushroom, too, in this life and death moment. Her mind still worked, but only barely. She needed at least to make the same promise to Little Wolf that her grandmother made to her when they had their final parting.

I will always be with you. When you rise up and when you lie down, I will be with you.

Little Wolf can't die alone. If I can't save him, I have to be with him!

The power of love, the power within every living being, drew Anya and Little Wolf toward each other as they struggled to get close. Whatever had grabbed the husky had finally let go. When Anya spotted him, his watch eyes fixed open and his body faltered on each sway of the Bering Sea depths, taking him ever downward. The husky had a hint of life left in him. Anya could sense it and swam as hard as she could toward him. When at last she held onto him, her eyes meeting the blue in his, he attempted a whimper and then his lids closed. In the next instant, his body flickered and shimmered and then disappeared, much like a candle burning out.

Little Wolf was with the Gatekeepers.

Anya could die.

The Chukchi dogs stayed gathered around the seal hole where their guardian had disappeared. They watched and they waited, but when she didn't return, this left them vulnerable and agitated. Besides their human guardian, one of their own had not come back. The pack would not leave this place, this patch of ice in the great open. They were tied to it as much as if tethered to the strongest post. They had no leader, but they did have Chukchi spirit, each one. This husky spirit held them together and held them to the spot. Loyal to their own, they would not leave.

After a time, the dogs started to settle, but then did not. They could not, with their ties entangled so. One barked at the other in frustration over their predicament. Their restless movements, backing to and fro and pacing in circles, miraculously freed the partially caught harnessing. The dogs seemed to sense what to do, how to get out of trouble. They knew their positions in the line and intuitively worked to regain them. The gangline was still attached to the sled. The dogs settled down in their formation in front of the sled, ready to run when told.

Whimpers ran down the sled dog line. The whimpers turned to unsure howls. This was not any call to the wild but a call for the return of their guardian and their pack — all of them — Zellie, Xander, Mushroom, and Little Wolf. The names did not run through the dogs' senses but images did. The empty positions along their harnessed line did. Midnight was the first to stop howling. The alert black husky picked up a familiar scent from across the ice. The rest quieted, all at once, and sniffed the same icy air.

Ravens suddenly squawked overhead. The pair echoed their call and then flew off.

Spirit at last found the left-alone Chukchi dogs.

Zeke and Homer elected to run alongside Chinook's team rather than guide their own. They were hardy enough for the trek over the Bering Sea ice but not skilled enough to guide a sled team with any kind of speed. Speed was important. Time was important in the hunt to find Anya and her dogs. They had ice creepers in their gear and put them on instead of snowshoes. Both made pretty good time this way and kept up with Chinook and his sled team; at least they kept Chinook in distant view ahead. Out of breath but not out of determination to help find the girl and her dogs, Zeke and Homer pressed on. Hell, they'd been ice fishing before. This trek was nothing, they kept telling themselves.

Loud barking and then shouts called out to them from up ahead.

It was Chinook.

He must have found Anya!

The veteran miners did their best to hurry to the scene. They thanked their lucky stars it wasn't storming. They could make out black dots on the horizon but little else. The closer they got to Chinook, the Eskimo and his dogs came into clearer view. When they realized Anya's dogs were there but not Anya, both men's spirits plummeted. Something had to have happened to her. She would never leave her dogs.

"Where's Anya?" Zeke yelled out to Chinook on his approach.

But Chinook didn't look at Zeke and he didn't answer him; he was too busy staring at the unfamiliar husky in the mix with Anya's dogs. The unique white-masked husky favored an ice seal, all dusky-brown and silky in fur color and trim, with luxuriant brown eyes that sparkled almost like blue ice. The contradiction didn't match. Chinook looked again and thought he saw the dog's eyes shade from blue to brown, as if it were a changeling. This wasn't possible. This didn't happen in any husky he'd ever seen.

But then maybe this wasn't just any husky.

Because Chinook believed in the spirits and the shamans of his people, he could believe this of the beautiful husky in front of him, staring back at him just as hard. The spirit was female. What's more, she wore no collar around her neck but instead had an ivory carving of a husky tied there. Chinook had seen that carving before. He couldn't remember where, but he knew he'd seen it.

"Chinook, where's Anya!" Zeke demanded again, as if Chinook could make her appear. Zeke wasn't looking at any of the dogs now, but at the Eskimo.

In that instant, Spirit disappeared across the ice; vanished in a heartbeat — in the time it takes to give life or take it away.

Chinook watched the Chukchi spirit disappear from view. She was fast. She was strong. He had hopes she would endure. He turned to Zeke but couldn't tell the upset miner the truth, at least what he thought was the truth — that Anya just took off over the ice. The moment he remembered the carving, he recognized her.

Anya was shaman. Her husky spirit gave her away.

"Chinook, where's the girl?" Zeke asked quietly, more to himself than to the Eskimo.

Chinook stayed silent.

Zeke hadn't noticed the dog that had just run off, too concentrated on his worries for Anya. Now he looked at her dogs. She clearly wasn't with them. He squinted out over the ice in all directions. He could see for miles with the storm let up; there was no sign of her. Whatever had happened and wherever that was, her dogs were on their way back without her. He eyed the dogs more carefully. One was missing. No, three:

the big black and white, a copper-red and white, and the small gray and white runt. Zeke counted only five now.

"What do you think, Zeke?" Homer edged closer to his friend and Anya's dog team. "This ain't good."

"Nope, it ain't," Zeke agreed.

"Are you thinking what I'm a' thinking, that something what can't be explained done this?"

"Maybe," Zeke answered Homer. He didn't want to admit it, but the truth hit him hard. Whatever had tried to get at Rune, yonder in the hills at their place, might have gotten to Anya. Zeke had been a mountain man, a miner, and in the territory long enough to see just about everything, or so he'd thought. There was bad stuff and bad people for sure, but you could put a gun on whatever came at you. Not with the varmints after the young people and their dogs. You can't shoot what you can't see.

Chinook let the two white men talk. He could tell they knew more about Anya than he'd thought. They knew about the dark spirits after her. They knew about, "something what can't be explained."

Flowers barked and stepped restlessly in place; Midnight and Midday alerted in the same way. Frost nosed the air and then looked at the sled's basket. Magic was already putting her muzzle beneath the caribou sleeping blanket.

All three men had their eyes on the copper-red husky. The blanket moved.

Anya had been listening to the exchange between Zeke and Homer. She wanted to let them know she was all right and show herself, but hesitated. She wasn't full back into her mortal body yet.

Spirit had saved her.

Anya hadn't asked for any help, but her Spirit must have pulled her back to life in the beyond, to save her life on Native Earth. Anya's stomach still churned from the change between worlds. She hadn't expected this. She'd expected to die under the gloom of the Great Crag, a sacrifice she was willing to make for Little Wolf. Sobs welled and screamed inside her for the brave young husky. He'd loved Xander, especially. They were together now; at least she believed that. Reassured Little Wolf had been taken to the Gatekeepers, she'd watched him shimmer to crystal sparkles in the icy depths at the moment he passed on.

Grateful she'd reached him in that precious moment of his passing, Little Wolf knew she was with him. When she touched him, he knew. His lids stayed open for her, and he didn't close his watch eyes to life until she came. His strength and loyalty shone to the end. He wasn't alone, set adrift on an ice floe and separated from his pack. Anya believed this with all her heart. Little Wolf was in heaven sleeping next to Zellie and Xander and Mushroom, waiting to help pull all their sleds through to eternal rest with the ancestors.

All four dogs had sacrificed their lives to save the one — *the one who will save them.*

Anya understood it wasn't her.

Certain events can bring great clarity. The brink of death can do that. It did for Anya. Her last earthly heartbeats shined a light on the vision she'd had in dreams of a faceless guardian come to help the Chukchi dogs and the people. There were three guardians of the Chukchi and their dogs. She was one. Rune was two, the moment *the hand of the guardian brushed the hand of the runes.* The man without a face became guardian number three, the moment Spirit saved Anya. This notion was as clear to Anya as if she'd just traveled through a hole around the Pole Star to hear the words in person from ghosts in worlds beyond.

Maybe she had, but she couldn't be sure.

Of one thing she was sure.

It was more than a notion that her Spirit

held a connection to the man without a face — the man she'd imagined in dreams, driving a Chukchi sled team, and then without warning, falling into a dark abyss to his death, the dogs with him. All this because of the breach caused in Native Earth by the demonic predator after them.

Spirit had just brought her back from mortal death. Could Spirit do the same for the guardian from her dreams? Anya had no clear reason to believe this, but she did believe Spirit held the connection between her and *the one who will save them.* Anya and Rune were both needed to help save *the one.*

But Rune was gone. Anya had to forget about his help. She had to forget him. Her feelings for Rune couldn't have picked a worse time to plague her.

Right now, with so much at stake, Rune's handsome image loomed in front of her. She had to chase him away. Many lives were held in the balance, not just hers and Rune's. Anyway, she didn't return from near-death for him.

He'd left her and he wasn't coming back. He didn't love her. How many times did she have to go over the painful truth to believe it? How long would it take to forget him, in this world or in any other?

Anya forced her thoughts to the present and away from Rune.

The human spirit must prevail. Her human spirit must prevail. This was the message from the gods, from her beloved grandmother, and from her dear huskies lost — the message she heard on arctic whispers and in the deep silence of the ice. Dead, Anya would be no help. Dead, her people would lose her unique connection to the spirit world. She was a part of both worlds. She was born to Native Earth for the purpose of saving the Chukchi dog, and born to the world of the ancients to save their husky spirit.

She didn't need the gods to whisper this to her or tell her that the ice storm still advanced and brought death to the Chukchi. Their troubles were not over. They'd begun anew, Anya realized in this moment of clarity. Her dream of the faceless guardian was proof enough that *someone is coming . . . something is there.*

Chinook had a good guess who and what made the caribou blanket move. He'd give her more time to show herself. She deserved the time after what she'd been through. Her dogs recognized her scent and her presence. They didn't wait as patiently as he did. The copper-red and white husky, Magic, was about to give Anya away.

Anya felt Magic's cold nose and reflexively rubbed the dog's muzzle. Despite wanting more time to gain her composure, she wanted to hold onto the curious copper-red and white husky more. Her dogs needed her. She needed them just as much. With four of their pack gone, and young Thor left behind, the dogs looked for her guidance and companionship. They could withstand many things, but loneliness hurt the most.

"Say —" Zeke didn't finish his thought before pulling the caribou blanket up for a look-see, himself. "Yippee!" he yelled like a schoolboy at recess.

Startled, Anya tried to smile at Zeke, at Homer and Chinook, too, the second her eyes met theirs. She knew she looked a fright but that part didn't bother her. Explaining the reason why did. To buy time, she stayed quiet and stayed put.

"Girl, what are you doing, scaring us so bad?" Zeke accused in a fatherly, concerned way. "You look half-froze, for mercy's sake. Let's get you up and into something warm. That parka of yours is all ice. Why, you look about as blue as some of this here ice we're standing on." Zeke took hold of one of Anya's arms and Homer stepped over to take the other. Together they gingerly helped her up from the basket of her sled and were quick to toss away her parka and wrap her in one of Chinook's native parkas he'd brought along. Zeke held onto her like a baby, then carefully set her down in the bed of the watchful Eskimo's waiting sled.

"What are you doing scaring *me* so bad?" Anya tried to joke. "You should be up in the mountains where it's safe and not out here over the ice," *where it's not,* she couldn't help but think.

"I'll tell you, young lady, where me and old Homer should be is right where we can help take care of you and your dogs, that's where." Zeke's chest caught a little at his own words and he tried to hide this from anyone catching on.

Cough. Cough.

Anya tried to cover her own upset. She really had to cough, though. Her chest pained her from the cold. Her weakened lungs pained her from the cold. Her whole body hurt from it! Numb in some places and stinging to needles in others, her body was still in shock from her deadly plunge. How long she'd been under, she'd no idea, except that it was long enough to see Little Wolf die, caught up by an evil that was none of his doing.

Cough. Cough.

My knife!

"Say, young lady, you stay put," Zeke cautioned her when she tried to get up and out of Chinook's sled.

Her dogs whimpered at the exchange, distressed themselves over their guardian's upset.

Chinook's native huskies stayed quiet, all sixteen of them sitting or lying down to rest on the ice. Chinook stood at their head; his guide whip was directed to the ice and not to start any run. Gulls sounded in the distance, the bark of the seal, too. Groans of the walrus and moans of the great whales ricocheted along the icy layers of the Bering Sea. The dogs would pick up on these sounds and prick their ears, alert to the hunt. So engaged, they paid little attention to anything or anybody else.

Anya tried again to get out of Chinook's sled but this time Zeke and Homer held her back.

"You need your rest, girl," Zeke tried to calm her. "You near froze to death and you need to stay warm. What's got you so bothered?"

"My knife," she answered simply, too weak and exhausted to say anything but the truth.

"You need your knife? Is that what this is about? Shoot, I'll fetch it for you," Zeke assured her and nodded to Homer to keep a hold on her. Zeke figured the cold had gotten to Anya's head and she thought funny. He'd play along so she wouldn't get any more upset than she already was. Lucky to be alive, the girl was. He couldn't care more about his own daughter, if he had one.

Chinook didn't interfere. Anya was shaman. She knew what she was doing.

Zeke covered the ice needed to reach Anya's sled and checked all around the basket bed for a knife. The winter twilight allowed just enough light for him to see. The day was done, but days and nights didn't come and go on the Alaska frontier like they did on the Outside. Summer light and winter dark were the times to mark and none other mattered. Right now Zeke could see well enough in the winter dark.

"Found it," Zeke announced and held Anya's knife high for her to see. He replaced her wet parka in the basket. The knife must have fallen out of its pocket or some such, since he'd found it beneath the tossed parka. Otherwise, her sled had been empty except for a supply of fish for her dogs. He didn't see any supplies she might have brought for herself, just her dogs. His heart went out to her all over again.

"Please, give it to me," Anya whispered

hard. It hurt to talk. The cold air burned like fire when she breathed in and out and opened her mouth to speak. Anya realized how close she'd come to death before her Spirit saved her. Another few seconds underwater would have killed her. No world would be open to her after that.

"Here you go," Zeke said and placed the knife in Anya's waiting hand.

She closed her stiff fingers around the crude blade. Without Rune here to help, she didn't think she could make it without her "gift from the gods."

It is time. It begins again.

Someone is coming. Something is there.

CHAPTER NINE

The demonic, steely-gray wolf snarled to its pack to follow him across the icy crevasse.

One mistake in their footing and any or all of the nine wolves could drop to their death. The pack hesitated and stepped restlessly in place when their feral instincts told them to run away from the powerful predator. Those same instincts told them to stay. The beast threatened. His takeover had been swift. All nine had witnessed what the beast had done to the great black wolf that had fathered their pups, provided for them, and protected them since the beginning of their time in the wild. The fight was over before it started. The out-of-nowhere gray wolf didn't fight fair. No challenge was issued. Death just came — striking in a heartbeat — in the time it takes to give life or end it.

The pack suffered from the loss of their leader. They were still stunned from his killing and were left vulnerable because of it. None challenged the menace that had taken over, but none would accept him as their leader. Feral intuition told them he was not one of them. He came from a place they feared the most: death, the end. There was life and there was death. Their great black leader meant life. The intruder meant death. This cold awareness hung over each one in the pack. It wasn't a matter of *if* they would die, but *when*. If any had a chance to run, they would take it.

The demon snarled again. Its fangs dripped in anger at the pack's rebellion. The dark spirit within the *wolf-born-of-ashes* would kill each one of them if they didn't obey him. He always enjoyed the kill. This time was no different.

In a hurry to find the Chukchi dog that escaped him, the golem dug deep in the darkness to find a way to get at the misplaced dog. He knew where to find the guardians and their six dogs still alive, but couldn't find the escaped black and white husky. It was vital to find him. Time ran short. The two worlds in which the golem existed called on him at the same time, and left him torn between duties in each of those worlds.

Released from prison in his physical

world, the revolution in Russia was beginning. Freed, he would see that it kept up.

In his world of dark spirits, he needed to end the rebellion waged against him there, to free his time and attention for the great revolution.

The war against him was the same in both worlds. The Chukchi threatened his power in both. The dogs of the Chukchi gave the far-north Siberian people their power. The solution was obvious and the same, no matter the world: destroy the dogs of the Chukchi.

The golem had simple rules to achieve this, whether by execution from bullets or a slicing strike from dark spirits. Follow the dogs and follow their guardians. Keep the pack separated from each other and from their guardians. Kill each one the moment you can. Give no warning. Take no prisoners. Use their own against them when you can.

In this the golem had been successful. He'd turned the Raven god of the Chukchi against their own and he'd spirited the fires of Viking *Hel* to his side. Only one failed him. The Midgard serpent had been sliced in two by the boy. But the boy's sword belonged to the golem now, and he meant to find a time and place to put it to good use. The boy lived because of the Viking sword, but now he would die because of it; the golem would make sure.

Changing his shape and being used up too much of the golem's power. He must not dwell too long in the reaches of spiritual darkness at any one time. Just like the arctic seal, he had to surface for air and refuel. The trick was not to leave any trace of a breathing hole and become easy prey. On the hunt for the escaped Chukchi husky, he'd no intention of becoming the hunted.

No predator could get to him on Native Earth.

The cry of the wolf was his.

Rune lived, but barely.

He'd lapsed into unconsciousness on the fourth day of his recovery, and Doc Adams doubted he'd come out of it this time. Just as well. His pain was too great and his injuries too many for the youth to fight off. He suffered from hypothermia and the loss of his skin integrity. Where his skin wasn't red, it mottled to an ashen color or patches of white. The burn of the ice, Doc Adams thought. The combination of freezing and burning at the same time was just too much.

With no way to get liquids into his patient, the doc worried over fluid loss. The burns robbed the boy of any chance to heal, taking all the water in his body to the burn site and leaving none in the core of his body to help him survive. The doc had treated burn patients before. He knew how they suffered. He'd treated frostbite before, especially living in the North, in the District of Alaska. It was common to lose fingers or toes from the effects of frostbite. Death sometimes resulted in severe cases.

When the boy, "Rune," awakened on the third day, Doc Adams thought he might have a chance at life. He'd even taken a few sips of water. But when the boy passed back into unconsciousness, his chances went from zero to none. *What a shame. What a shame.* A tough army doc, Doc Adams didn't believe in miracles. He hadn't seen any in his lifetime of service. Right now, he wished for one to save the boy's life. If the doc couldn't help him, maybe the Almighty would.

Where before, the doc didn't think the boy would or should live, right now he wasn't so sure. He'd seen a look in the boy's eyes of sheer determination and arctic will — that's what the doc called it here in the frozen, unforgiving, arctic territory. Sometimes gold miners had that look. Sometimes soldiers in the fight. Sometimes even a lady who worked the line. Each one looked death in the eye, and spit at it. But the doc had never seen that look on a patient practically laid out in death on one of his hospital bunks.

Rune had that look.

The boy meant to live and just might have enough arctic will in him to do it!

"Pa, I have new bandages ready," Lucy said quietly, coming up to the side of Rune's bunk, opposite her father. "I'll take care of his dressing changes and apply new salve, Pa," she told him. "I know what to do."

Doc Adams was proud of his daughter. At fifteen, she already made a good nurse, and he'd see to it she made a fine doctor. When he could, he meant to send her south to medical school where she could train in a one- or two-year program. Women made fine doctors. For the present, he did what he could to share all of his army schooling with her. As a doctor, he didn't like what he saw in his daughter's eyes when she cared for Rune. He could tell she cared for him beyond nursing the boy back to health. He worried for Lucy almost as much as he worried about Rune's recovery.

"All right then, Lucy. I'll leave you to it," he said in a professional tone. "I have to get to the postal station and pick up the supplies I hope have arrived. Are you going to be all right, alone here with our patient?" He could have kicked himself for sounding like her father just then.

Lucy didn't look at him, but at Rune, when she answered, "Yes."

Doc Adams grabbed up his fur parka and pulled the flaps of his cap close over his ears. Weather had moved in, stormy weather. He almost laughed at the notice of snow and picked-up winds. When was it not stormy in Skagway, summer or winter? Mud or ice — take your pick. He looked over his shoulder at Lucy and Rune one more time before he opened the door and headed outside into the cold.

Lucy pulled the lamplight closer. She meant to do a full dressing change and application of salve to all the wounds. If she hesitated and thought about anything but her task, she couldn't go through with this. The idea of causing Rune any pain troubled her, even though he was out. So did the idea of seeing any fresh bleeding. She must not think about anything but completing her medical tasks with as much skill as she could.

Fear caught in her throat. She slowly removed the thick cotton layers over Rune's middle. She'd do her best to keep his

220

privates covered but she had to redress the wounds over his lower stomach. In one quick move, she exposed the area in question.

"Eeek!" Lucy screamed.

Rune had his fingers clamped around her wrist. He hadn't opened his eyes yet, but he didn't have to, to know what the girl was about to do. Coming slowly out of his punishing sleep, he'd heard the doc and Lucy talk. He understood the doc was Lucy's pa. He also understood the girl would see him *everywhere,* and he didn't want that. Sick as he was and needing her help, he was still shocked at the idea she'd look at him all over. Given the shape he was in, he shouldn't care, but he did.

"You should let go," Lucy said, her voice strained. "I can't help you unless you let go." She did her best to keep calm. No matter how sick he was, Rune was strong. He might not be right in the head, injured so, and she needed to be careful with him. Her pa was gone for the moment, and she didn't have any way out of this if Rune got crazy. She would have trouble restraining him. Too much trauma and he could die on the spot, she knew.

Rune forced his eyes open.

"The light. Get rid of it," he ordered and

didn't mean to snap at the girl. She meant him no harm.

"All right," Lucy said. "You have to let go of my arm first."

Rune's loosely bandaged fingers fell away from her.

Lucy turned down the wick of her lamp.

"Better," Rune said. "Thanks."

"You're welcome," she answered shyly. The rich timbre of his voice surprised her. Mesmerizing, like his eyes. She felt a flush creep up her neck.

"It's Lucy, right?"

"Yes."

"I'm Rune."

"I know," she said and smiled.

"When did I te—"

"Yesterday when you woke up, you said your name, Rune," she carefully explained. She knew how important it had to be for him to know details. The questions would come, about his accident and how he'd been brought here. She tried to mentally prepare. His injuries were extensive. She knew he knew that. This wasn't going to go easy.

"I'm hurt bad," he said in a flat tone.

"Yes," she said. She wouldn't lie.

"Can you and the doc fix me so I can get out of here?"

"We can try," Lucy answered as honestly

as she could.

Rune stared hard at the pretty girl with long ginger hair before he spoke again. She looked at him straight-on and didn't seem repelled by his appearance. He had to look like some kind of monster, all frozen and burned at the same time. His head flooded with flashes of Anya and her dogs, and what he needed to do to help them.

Both of his stiff hands went to the bandages at his head. Everything hurt. It didn't matter. He wasn't going to look good to Anya when he found her, but he couldn't let that stop him. He'd already decided to help her even though she didn't love him. She loved Vitya. That wasn't important. Anya's safety was. The dogs' safety was. After that, nothing much mattered.

"All right then," he told Lucy. "Go ahead."

"This might hurt," she cautioned.

"Go ahead," he repeated and lowered his arms, then shut his eyes and braced for his treatments. Whatever it took to get up and out of here, he'd do. The pain, he'd endure. And a little embarrassment was nothing. The alternative was death, and that was something he couldn't afford to let happen. Not yet.

Zellie's ghostly existence held together

under the Great Crag, enough for her to keep alive, her awareness of Xander's movements on Native Earth. She drew energy from the crashing seas below the ice and the life-giving arctic air above, fueled by these ancient layers in time. Her ties to any kind of existence at this moment came from her ties to the ancients. She was Chukchi, in life and in death. Instilled with these instincts unto eternity, she still had them within her soul when she crossed back from the other side.

The gods could not strip her of these inborn instincts as punishment for her actions. Instead they held her beneath the sacrificial crag and meant to prevent her from returning to the Gatekeepers. A Chukchi husky, pure in heart and ghostly spirit, she was overtaken by the urge to break free and help Xander. Her arctic will for such a daring feat was bred into her — a part of her no one and nothing could strip from her . . . even caught . . . even in death. Alerted at the moment to Xander's fight for life, her instincts sharpened.

Worlds ever brush past. Their boundaries are sacred. To test them is a risk. Good and Evil spirits — in all the layers in time — buzz in agitation at any test to their spheres of existence. It's the Unknown that all fear, ghost or mortal, spirit or flesh, god or golem. To upset their balance in time is to risk the future of all, for all of time.

Born with intelligence, speed, and endurance at her core, Zellie acted on instinctive Chukchi impulse. This led her into the Unknown. She didn't smell fear, only the scent of the hunt. She would leave her gentle nature behind. Every instinct in her alerted her to the fight ahead that Xander faced. Her energy would be used up fast; her keen senses told her as much. Whispers from the ancients pricked her ears. Some came with her to the fight. She sensed the Directions near and followed their guide.

The gray golem stalked Xander.

The golem's pack had vanished; all nine were dead by his kill or nature's cruel hand. He didn't care, and didn't have much time left to stay in this shape of a wolf. It drained his power. He'd already stayed too long in the world of dark spirits and needed to return to his physical being. Danger gnawed at him. Anger and agitation drove him on to hunt for the escaped husky. He needed this kill. He craved it. His fangs dripped with anticipation. He'd enjoy this death more than most. No one dared challenge him. Not the Chukchi. Not their dogs. He'd kill them all.

The golem's yellow eyes scanned the snowy landscape, then stopped short at the black mark on the frozen horizon — *the escaped husky! Finally!*

The golem's claws came out. The scent of death soothed him.

The husky lay in the open, exposed, helpless. The husky didn't sense its trouble. The kill would be easy. The gray wolf slowly stalked the unsuspecting dog, so not to alert him.

Run! Run! Run!

A piercing howl rang in Xander's ears. He jarred to alertness. His world spun. His senses brushed the crisp air. Every layer of his fur ruffled at the familiar contact. He recognized the howl. The message came through loud and clear. To ignore it meant sudden death, and so he ran, taking off in the direction of Zellie's call.

The wolf gave chase.

Xander ran as only a Chukchi dog can, across the open, up and down the rugged hills beyond, and then across more open land to the valley of blizzards with its steep slopes and hidden crevasses. A wrong step would mean death, yet Xander didn't hesitate to follow the call in the wild.

Zellie led Xander to the point where she'd dropped into the deadly crevasse, killed by dark spirits. Her ghostly presence knew just where to guide Xander — where to lure the predator after him. Her howls pierced through blowing snow and blurring wind to bring Xander to her. The instant he reached her, she jumped through him and with him across the abyss, so Xander might reach the other side.

He did.

Xander didn't fall. He didn't falter. Zellie held him within her soul, to keep him safe.

The wolf leapt at them. Its hot breath steamed close before it slipped into the darkness below, gone in a heartbeat. The beast's feral cry muted into the cavernous depths, then fell silent.

At that moment the twilight suddenly cleared. No snow blew. No winds blurred. The valley of blizzards had uncharacteristically calmed.

Xander whimpered softly in the stillness. Zellie was gone. Her presence vanished with the wolf. Lonely for her, Xander hurt all over again — his watch eyes on what might have been.

"*A'write,* lassie," Fox greeted the moment he entered Anya's home in Chinook's village.

Anya had begun to think of the Eskimo

winter tent as her home. She didn't think *yaranga* every time she entered. She didn't expect to see walrus hide instead of caribou hide anymore. A lifetime ago she'd lived in such a tent. No more. The great sea stood between her and her Anquallat village. When memories of home haunted her, she tried to push them away. These memories returned in dreams that haunted at night and nagged her in the light of day. Her fitful dreams were not limited to memories of home and had grown worse since she'd lost Little Wolf and almost frozen to death herself.

That was two months ago in the white man's time.

Though part-white, Anya walked every step on Native Earth in the footsteps of her Chukchi heritage. Even so, she lived in the white man's territory at present, or at least in close proximity. White and Eskimo alike shared the land here. The land belonged to no man, Anya maintained. No spirit either . . . no *one* spirit, that is. Trying to hold back spirit would be like trying to hold back time. Anya was glad for this. Otherwise she would not be alive.

Her Spirit had saved her life two months ago.

Anya had worried her counterpart in the

spirit world had died because a part of her had died, with so many Chukchi dogs lost. Zellie, Xander, Mushroom, and Little Wolf were all gone. Their suffering killed a part of Anya every day. The arctic air did not always soothe and Anya could feel her shaman instincts dull from grief. She worried over this with six dogs to protect. She had to keep the dogs safe and deliver them into the guardian hands of the faceless dog driver from her dreams. The dog driver was *the one*.

The passing of time had not let her forget about this dream-turned-nightmare. The way to salvation for them all depended on her remembering details. Every shaman instinct left in her foretold of a new guardian of her dogs and her people. She tried hard to remember the details of her dream, doing her utmost to invoke the trance of shamans for help. If she could have found the red, magic mushrooms used for such a drugged trance by the shamans of her people, she would have swallowed one in a heartbeat. So many lives depended on her.

She remembered the dog driver raced a Chukchi sled team. Under attack from dark spirits waiting in shadow, they all plunged over the cliffs of the great sea to their deaths. Their screams and blood coated her

in sweat every time she woke from such fitful slumber. When she awoke in such a state
and tried to shake off her distress, it never
worked.

"Lassie, ah dinnaeken why you look so
doon?" Fox said as gently as he could. He'd
come here on a happy errand and didn't
like seeing Anya upset. He took a seat across
from her on the floor, each of them on opposite sides of the cookfire.

Anya reached over and stirred her pot of
stew meat. She never liked bear meat or
cooked meat, really, but bear tasted a little
better if done. Cooked-away blood of the
bear didn't nourish her. Raw fish did, that
and raw seal or whale or caribou. The iron
taste of fresh blood held off sickness and
fever and fueled the soul, all of them. Each
Chukchi had more than one soul, just how
many, she didn't know.

Fox sniffed the stew.

"You could use a few *tatties* in this," he
suggested.

"Tatties?" she said, a smile crinkling the
corners of her mouth. The word sounded
funny. She knew a lot of English words and
some Scottish, thanks to Fox Maule Ramsey. But *tatties,* she hadn't heard of.

" 'Potatoes,' the folks around here call
them," Fox said, glad the lassie looked a

wee bit brighter.

"Yes, I know potatoes." Her smile broke into a full grin. "You're right. They might help tame this nasty bear."

Vitya suddenly appeared through the door flap and sat down with Anya and Fox. No snow blew in. The day was clear.

"Me eat," he said in his best English. He picked up one of the wood bowls and dipped it into the stew, letting it slop on the sides. "Hungry," he said between slurps and bites. He didn't use a wood spoon and scooped up the stew in his cupped hand. The warm stew didn't deter him.

Anya and Fox both broke out laughing.

Fox wasn't going to correct the Chukchi youth. A lot of miners slurped up their vittles just the same. Table manners didn't rank too high on the Alaska frontier. Having something to eat in the first place did.

Anya mentally shook her head at Vitya, but found his sudden appearance welcome at their cookfire. She and Vitya shared this tent, and kept their sleeping blankets well separated. Fox's arrival was welcome, too. It was nice to have the companionship of friends who helped her forget her fitful dreams. Her shaman spirit felt sharper in their company.

"The dogs," Anya said to Vitya. "Are they good?"

"Yes," he answered in Chukchi in between bites.

Anya nodded her accord and sat back, able to relax more. All of her dogs were tethered in the same dog yard as before, only now they had frequent visits from her and Vitya, and had exercise time in front of a sled. Sheltered so, they were as safe as Anya could keep them, given the situation. Chinook appointed some of the young people in the village to keep watch, too. If any of them saw something wrong, they were to sound the alarm. Pounding a drum would signal the trouble. Anya had selected the one that could make the most noise, and this was set nearby her dogs.

When Anya saw to her dogs, she always brought her knife.

When Vitya had charge, he took a loaded rifle with him.

This routine went on day in and day out, and had for the past two months, with no sign of new trouble. Anya cautioned everyone to keep up their guard. The young people obeyed. She was shaman. The boys respected her and the girls were in awe of her. The drum, they believed, held the power of the spirits. They watched over the drum same as they did the Siberian huskies. The shamans in Chinook's village left her alone. In their holy minds, she was not possessed. In trouble, yes, but not possessed of evil spirits. The shamans embraced Anya and her dogs and agreed to give them shelter.

Anya relaxed by the cookfire with Vitya and Fox, knowing the children in the village kept up their vigil. She had faith in the Eskimo children to signal any danger. She tilted her head back, then rotated her neck from side to side to get rid of any telltale stiffness there. Her neck felt good. So did the rest of her. It surprised her to feel normal. Accustomed to anything but, she hugged her arms together to make sure of them. An old habit, she acknowledged to herself. She was a medium between worlds and never knew exactly when she might pass from one to the next. To reassure herself that she was intact on Native Earth, she rubbed her hands along the sleeves of her native dress. The soft hide soothed and eased her worries.

Dress! She had on Rune's gift. She'd meant to get rid of it, but instead, she had it on!

In rapid motion she slipped her hands away from her arms and made believe she tended the cookfire. If Vitya saw — if he knew she wore Rune's gift — he would be bothered at her obvious dismay.

Anya knew Vitya liked her in that special way. She knew Vitya suspected she liked Rune. She more than liked Rune, but she couldn't let Vitya know the truth. Not after their long-ago kiss, her first and only kiss from any boy. Vitya had come all the way from across the great sea to take her back with him to their Anquallat village. She understood that. He didn't have to tell her; she just knew.

How could she break Vitya's heart and tell him of her already-broken one over Rune? In time she would tell Vitya, when things were easier for him. Now he battled like a Chukchi warrior for her and her dogs. He'd been wonderful, and she refused to hurt him. She'd wait for the right time. This was not it.

Vitya's safety mattered to her. She wished she could find a way to get him home to Siberia, to a village safer than this one. She wished the same for Grisha and all in their coastal village. The Morning Dawn might help her. So might the Directions. It wouldn't hurt to ask. A way might open to her through prayers to the gods. The watchful Gatekeepers never deserted her, she believed. If she put her whole heart in it, she might find a way to help Vitya and her people hide from the darkness that hid in shadow and waited to strike.

Her *whole heart,* she thought heavily. When Rune left, he took most of her heart with him. What she had left she gave to her brave huskies. She'd best find something left over for her dear and just-as-brave friend, Vitya. The last thing she wanted was to see him hurt. He'd sacrificed so much for her; then so had Rune.

"Lassie, what do you say?" Fox asked her a second time.

"About what?" she answered, her concentration on Vitya and then Rune finally broken.

"What do you say about the sweepstakes . . . tomorrow?" Fox underscored.

"The race is tomorrow?" Anya shot up and threw her arms wide. "But that can't be! It's too soon, much too soon!"

"I *dae nee kin,*" Fox said, in true Scottish form.

"You what?" she said, dumbfounded.

Fox walked over to her and spoke quietly and in clearer English this time.

"I do not understand your surprise, lassie." Fox spoke deliberately. "We have been working and training and getting ready

235

for race day together. My teams are ready. My dog drivers are ready, same as me. You and Vitya need to be at the start to cheer us on, lassie. I stopped by to make sure you will be," he explained, unable to hide his excitement over the sweepstakes.

Race day is tomorrow. Of course it is. Anya knew that. What she didn't know was if she was ready. Were the three Chukchi teams ready? Were their dog drivers ready? Were any of them ready for the dangers that surely would be hidden in the shadows, waiting to strike?

It's too soon, much too soon to race!

Anya realized she wasn't ready to face tomorrow — not without Rune.

CHAPTER TEN

Rune turned the wool sailcloth over in his hands. The *sjorya* had saved his life. He'd grabbed it up before jumping over the side of the blazing steamship. The moment was burned in Rune's memory.

He ran his fingers over the warp yarn of the sailor's blanket, made from the wool of Norse sheep. This same wool was used by his Viking ancestors to make square sails sewn together with hemp rope; sails strong enough to withstand rough seas and fierce winds. Tallow was used to grease the sail-cloth and help waterproof it. The wool absorbed water without becoming wet. It insulated against heat and cold, all at the same time. This was why he was still alive. Rune marveled at the gift of his ancestors in his hand. It brought him back from the shadows of death.

Lucy Adams had explained everything that happened the day he was scooped out of the icy waters of the Inside Passage, frozen and burned at the same time. Two months ago. The Eskimo fishermen who found Rune saw the boat burning in the open waters of the Passage. The night sky was on fire, they'd said. The three men carefully traced their steps to the edges of the ice to look for survivors, even though they didn't expect to find any. Ordinarily the fishermen would never tread so close to the icy edges of the dark waters. The layers of ice could not be trusted to support their weight.

But something alerted them to keep going; something in the winds around them guided them — a howling, they thought. Wolf or dog, they could not tell. The spirits spoke to them, the Eskimos explained. They would not question the spirits.

Rune certainly agreed with that.

Lucy went on to tell him what happened next.

The fishermen spotted an ice floe drifting closer to them. It surprised them, since ice floes never came this far in. Ice floes stayed with icebergs in the waters of the north and did not drift along the Inside Passage, even in the seasons of winter. Layers of ice would break off with the melt of spring, but not like this. This ice floe drifted *to* the Eskimos and not away. They waited for the ice to drift closer. The night sky was still on fire and helped light the scene.

First the fishermen saw the jagged ice along the sides of the floe. Then they saw a cloth or maybe a blanket, caught on one of the shards jutting from the floe's toothed edges. Then they saw a body caught up in the blanket. That's when the ice floe came close enough for the Eskimos to reach for the dead man.

"The moment they lifted you onto safer ice," Lucy told Rune, "they believed you were dead. They dared not remove the blanket from your parched and frozen body and brought you here for proper burial. This was the wish of spirits, the Eskimos said. The spirits led them to you and the spirits brought you to us."

Rune didn't doubt any of it. He owed his life to the spirits of the dead, Viking and Chukchi both. They relied on him to get to Anya and her dogs and refused to let him die until he did. Rune couldn't come up with any other explanation for why he'd survived. He wouldn't try. All his efforts now needed to focus on getting out of Skagway and getting to Nome.

Two long months had passed.

Anya *had* to be waiting for him. After all

of this, she had to be. Rune was beyond anxious to find her, but knew it could take another two months to get to her. Winter persisted and conditions would still be rough for travel by dogsled, if not impossible by ship. The summer melt would take its time arriving. Rune couldn't wait for that. Besides, he'd relied on the kindness and generosity of the Adamses far too long. There was no comparing them to his own family, so he didn't try. He could never repay the doc and his wife. They accepted him into their home and cared for him as if he were a son. The doc had even given him a measure of gold dust to help pay for his needs ahead.

With Lucy it was different. He felt brotherly toward her, but he could tell she felt more than that for him. She didn't feel sorry for him, as he'd expect any girl to, seeing his injuries.

His convalescence had been slow-going. His wounds started to heal, but he stayed bedridden. Every time he'd try to walk, he'd fall down. His arms, too, had weakened to near uselessness. It was all hard to figure, the doc had told him. Doc Adams could find no reason for his paralysis. Then the doc had to admit he'd never seen someone burned and frozen at the same time, and the wounds heal the way Rune's did. There would be scars, but most would fade over time.

The doc had come up with his theory for why: the instant freezing Rune experienced after suffering burns actually treated the burn areas. Somehow the ice had put out the fire on him and had a miraculous countereffect. The doc had never seen the like, and likely never would again. Unfortunately, the healing effect of the freezing weakened Rune's muscles and bones and prevented full use of his arms and his legs. Further, the doc said, Rune's temporary paralysis could be from the severe cold Rune experienced when he plunged overboard. At least this was the doc's best theory.

Rune had a much different theory but if he said anything, the doc would think he was crazy. Rune kept quiet and kept the *sjorya* in his hands. The Norse wool blanket had protected him the same as if he'd held a Viking sword in his fist when he jumped overboard. Maybe he'd *slayed another serpent* after all, in escaping death this time. He prayed to Odin he had.

He hoped Odin listened, but had no guarantee. During these long weeks of healing, Rune had no sense of the Viking god or of Odin's wolves or his watchful ravens.

241

Rune would clutch the *sjorya* to him and pray the ancient spirits stayed just as close. The truth, he didn't know. He still put his life in Odin's hands and believed his Viking ancestors were responsible for his miraculous recovery.

Why else would the *sjorya* have saved his life?

Then there was his birthmark, his "mark of the gods," according to his father.

Despite his traumatic injuries, the mark at the back of his neck was unfazed. Rune could reach up now and feel it; its raised edges were clear. The mark was a connection to his ancestors, and it wasn't burned away. The scar he'd had since birth protected him; Rune was sure of it. The slightest touch to his neck, and a cool sensation soothed and eased his pain. Where before the mark had given him headaches, now it healed and comforted him. At least this was Rune's best theory.

Rune almost looked as he did before. He never cared about his looks and didn't at this time . . . except for what Anya might think of him. The skin over his body, over his arms and his legs, was scarred, but most of the healed areas were flat and indistinguishable. These, Rune didn't care about. His muscles had regained their strength and his mind regained clarity. No one would guess what he'd been through. But his face might give something away.

A deep scar ran across one cheek, as if he'd been sliced with a sword. The same kind of clear-cut scar ran across his chest. The scars left the appearance of his having been in a knife fight instead of a fire, the doc had said. The doc couldn't figure why, and he couldn't figure why these scars didn't heal like the rest. Rune had a good guess. He wouldn't mention this to the doc. Doc Adams wouldn't believe anything about demonic ghosts trying to slice Rune up with his own Viking sword! The doc likely wouldn't believe something from another world could break through to his and hunt him down and try to kill him.

That was precisely what Rune believed happened. *Nine serpents you must slay*, Odin had said. Rune had lost count of how many he'd killed so far. Clearly there were more, and clearly they were not just after him.

The thought of any blade slicing Anya or her dogs scared Rune into quicker action.

"I will pay you back," he assured the doc.

"Don't worry about it, son," Doc Adams said.

"I will pay you back," Rune repeated.

The doc smiled and gave a nod.

Lucy leaned against the wall behind her for support. She knew Rune was leaving today and the knowledge hurt something awful. Maybe he'd come back one day. She had to cling to this hope. It was all she would have left of him.

Rune made sure of the pouch of gold dust in his pocket. The assay office wasn't far from the doc's house. Rune would get the money he needed for clothing and gear and then strike out for Seward. In Seward he would get a sled team outfitted and then begin the long journey across the Alaska frontier to Nome. He had a lot of time to make up, and he didn't plan on taking another two months to do it!

Rune shook Doc Adams's hand in good-bye. Mrs. Adams stood close. Rune gave her an affectionate nod. He wanted to hug her but didn't know if he should. When he turned to say his goodbyes to Lucy, she ran into his arms. He hugged her back. He owed her so much and could never repay her, not with money or with the same affection she had for him. His heart belonged to Anya.

"Lucy," he began softly, breaking their hug to look down into her amber, tear-filled eyes. "I will never forget you. You are a healer. You have a good spirit within you.

244

Never doubt how special —"

Lucy didn't let him finish. She ran into the next room and shut the door behind her.

Mrs. Adams approached Rune.

"It's just puppy love, son. She'll get over it."

Rune felt awkward and gave Mrs. Adams a stiff nod. There wasn't much else he could do except make sure he repaid the doc and his family the hard-earned money they'd just given him. Their life in Skagway wasn't easy. Johansson and Son Shipping could help change that. Lucy would be able to go to medical school in the south. Rune wished only the best for her. She *was* special. He meant every word he'd said to her. He would never forget the girl with ginger hair.

Gulping past his surprise feelings over leaving the Adamses and their home, he made a beeline for the front door, opened it, and abruptly left. Feelings always got him in trouble. He had to shake his feelings for the doc and his family and get his focus back on track — the track to Nome. The sunstone of the Vikings worked for him at sea. He prayed he'd have the same guide in his hand on the overland trek ahead.

Fox Ramsey knew the risks out on the trail

ahead. They'd be worth it if one of his teams won. But not if any of his dogs or drivers died. Nothing was worth that.

He looked over his shoulder for anything unknown that might give chase.

All he could do was keep a good lookout. He'd cautioned his other dog drivers to do the same throughout the race. This had been a general caution, not about any specific threat. Fox couldn't explain what exactly troubled him. He just knew something might be out there, watching and waiting for them. That warning would strike the rugged dog drivers as plain crazy. Fox hoped it was.

Fox, Charles Johnson, and John Johnson reviewed the sweepstakes stops out of Nome, together: Hastings, nine point one miles. Cape Nome, thirteen miles. Safety, twenty-two miles. Solomon, thirty-three miles. Topkok, forty-seven point two miles. Timber, fifty-nine point seven miles. Council, seventy-five miles. Boston, ninety-five point six miles. Telephone, one hundred ten miles. Haven, one hundred twenty-four miles. First Chance, one hundred sixty-five miles. And Candle, two hundred four miles, the halfway point. The miles covered by the end of the race would total four hundred and eight.

Fox's sled teams were harnessed and ready, lined up one in front of the other along Front Street waiting for the start gun. Fox and his dog drivers had taken up their positions. The three teams of "Siberian Wolves," as they were again listed on the chalkboard at the Board of Trade Saloon had been put smack dab in the middle of the lineup. Unlike before, where they'd been dead last. At ten sharp the start gun would send the first of the twenty teams in the 1910 All Alaska Sweepstakes on their way.

Fifteen minutes would separate each team to allow a margin of safety for the dog drivers and their mix of dogs: malamutes, native huskies, and foreign imports alike. This time the Nome Kennel Club allowed whips to be used as guide only. The same rules as last year in all other things applied. The safety of the animals and their drivers held the top spot. The race would be dangerous, run across rugged terrain in oftentimes whiteout conditions, same as the year before.

The crowd of race watchers gathered, breathing a collective sigh of relief at the difference between the start this year and the one last year: no sudden blizzard hit Nome to threaten the day. In worry that one might, a few had their Bibles tucked inside their parkas. Chatter among folks that lined up three and four deep along Front Street focused mainly on who bet on which sled to win, and not on any fears over the End coming. Still, some had their Bibles just in case.

Albert Fink, the Nome Kennel Club president, worried about something else. Trouble when results started to come in. That could be as early as the Solomon or Topkok checkpoints, respectively, at thirty and fifty miles out on the course. Teams that withstood the challenging terrain and all range of weather conditions would not finish until after day three at best; still, information about how everybody was doing along the way would be messaged back to Nome by telegraph. Every call in would be chalked on the board. That's what worried Albert. He checked his Smith & Wesson pistol to make sure it was loaded and ready in case he needed to fire a warning shot to settle down the crowd — anxious bettors all.

How bets had been placed at the Miners and Merchants Bank of Alaska or the Bank of Nome, Albert couldn't gauge. In the buildup to this year's sweepstakes, talk had ranged from no mention of the smaller Siberian huskies to nothing but. Competition cut through the air in Nome and its surrounds, and stirred up talk over whether the three teams of Siberian dogs entered would run as well as upstart Rune Johansson's had the year before. Some thought yes, yet many thought no. It was those in the middle Albert worried about. How had they bet? If the Siberian dogs did poorly, there could be anger. If they performed well, there could be anger. Either way, Albert didn't want those emotions to turn into any kind of fight.

The Nome Kennel Club president wondered why the boy, Rune Johansson, had not entered the sweepstakes this year. He'd halfway expected to see him lined up with the rest this morning: his dogs, too, in hopes of capturing the ten thousand dollar purse. Fox Ramsey had a whole passel of the Siberian imports running today. Maybe the boy's dogs were in the mix. Still, Albert wondered about the boy and where he was, if not here on this important race day.

Albert looked at his pocket watch. Ten o'clock on the nose. He took up his place next to the start judge and pushed his worries to the back of his mind. The day was sunny enough. No clouds. No storm coming. The sled teams stood harnessed and ready. Their drivers were in position. The checkpoints and telegraph lines were set. The Nome Kennel Club had good people at each stop to offer assistance to the dogs and drivers when needed. Communication the whole way should be good. Reporters from the Outside had their pads and pencils ready. All bets had been placed.

The start gun fired.

The first sled took off.

Albert hoped for the best, yet prepared for the worst. To do otherwise would be foolhardy.

Anya went with Vitya to Nome, to Front Street for the race start. After Fox's teams took off, she planned to return to the Eskimo village, to her own dogs. There she would sit vigil and invoke a shaman trance to keep her watch eyes on the Chukchi dogs running in the sweepstakes, in case she or her Spirit might be needed. Yet all she could invoke at the moment was fear that Rune didn't stand alongside her, in case he might be needed, too.

Together, they were a force to be reckoned with. Apart, they were vulnerable.

Like it or not, she and Rune had been appointed guardians of the Chukchi; both set on this path by their own gods. Born to separate traditions, she and Rune had been brought together for the same purpose: to save the Chukchi dog and help the people. She was no ordinary girl and Rune was no ordinary boy. They both talked to the dead. They both communicated with spirits long dead. These differing spirits singled them out for a purpose on Native Earth greater than themselves.

Anya might only be fifteen years old and a child to many, but she had wisdom beyond her young years. Her beloved grandmother had forewarned Anya of the great burden placed upon her by the Gatekeepers and the gods of their people. Nana-tasha always told Anya she was special. Anya fully understood why, at this moment, where she stood at the edges of the race start — at the edges of the Great Crag — and where the Chukchi dog had to race yet again, for survival.

It is time. It begins. Someone is coming. Something is there. The wolf and the dog battle as one. The hand of the guardian has brushed the hand of the runes. The ice storm is coming. Some will live. Many will die.

It is time. It begins. Someone is coming. Something is there. The wolf and the dog battle as one. The hand of the guardian has brushed the hand of the runes. The ice storm is coming. Some will live. Many will die.

These arctic whispers repeatedly

251

drummed in Anya's head and sounded on every heartbeat until she got their message: the ice storm is here!

Anya understood what she had to do, but she didn't know how to do it without Rune. The hand of the guardians must brush the hand of *the one.* She and Rune both had to find the third guardian. All together they would be a force of three and could better fight the ice storm. There was strength in numbers. She was alone now and the risks were great. The fear of failure loomed large.

Vitya stood by her side, but he was not a guardian. He was her friend and a brave Chukchi warrior, but he was not appointed by the gods to fight the ice storm. However welcome his help might be, Anya knew Vitya could not help in the war of ghosts. The last thing she wanted was for him to be the first to die of the two of them. He deserved long life on Native Earth. He didn't ask for any of the trouble that surrounded him just by being so close to her.

It hit her again, how important it was for Vitya to return home to the people and go into hiding until the ice storm passed.

It hit her again, how important it was to warn Grisha and all in their Anquallat village, to hide from the darkness coming, too!

In the end there was no safe haven from

the ice storm. Anya knew that, but she had to try so that more might live. She had to fight the prophecy of death. Finding a means to do this wouldn't be easy. Rune wasn't here. Zellie, Xander, Mushroom, and Little Wolf were not with her. Death had reduced their pack to six Chukchi dogs.

Many Chukchi dogs were set behind the start line now, to race in the sweepstakes that would take them across the Alaskan frontier. Their numbers were great. Forty-eight were going to race today, all Fox's Chukchi dogs. This time, one of the Siberian teams *did* need to win and not just finish well. The memory of Zellie's death flashed painfully in front of Anya.

Zellie sacrificed her life to help the Chukchi get to this race start. Anya's chest caught. Her tears for Zellie would never dry. But maybe, just maybe, Zellie's keen watch eyes were on them at this important moment, awakened from her sleep of death, not to help pull their sleds through to heaven, but to make sure they didn't fall into the same dark abyss that she had.

Anya's fingers twitched inside her fur mittens. Her hands begged to pet Zellie and Xander and draw them close. Anya balled her hands into fists. She would have to wait until she passed out of this world and into the next to touch her beloved friends and companions again. She couldn't save their brave husky spirits on Native Earth, but she sensed they would forgive her in the next world, once they were reunited. She prayed to the Morning Dawn that they would.

Though Anya worried for the dogs about to race, she worried more for her own.

There was more on the line for her dogs. The Chukchi dogs today had to run for notice, but her dogs still ran for their lives.

Her instincts, husky and human, told her as much. The fact that she was female told her as much. She'd felt the injury to Flowers, Magic, and Midday — the injury to their female core — as if she'd been cut herself by demonic spirits meant to end the pure bloodlines of the Chukchi dog. The traitorous Raven had attacked the three females. The claws of the Raven tried to tear out the lines of inheritance by destroying the dogs' ability to conceive. Anya remembered their squeals of pain and their grief afterwards.

But Flowers beat the Raven. Flowers conceived Thor.

Maybe Magic and Midday could conceive in time. Anya thought so. Why else would the Raven and the fires of *Hel* and the darkest of spirits still be after them? Her dogs held the key to the future of the Chukchi dog and its untainted bloodlines. Whatever was after the people was after their dogs for this reason. Maybe the third guardian had something to do with this. Anya hadn't puzzled this out. It was up to her human spirit to do it — her spirit and Rune's. The gods of the Chukchi and the Vikings stayed in the distance. The Directions stayed close but only to whisper on the winds, not to intervene in her troubles.

Anya understood. She'd accept this hard reality a little better if Rune were here instead of Vitya. She wished Vitya was safe at home and Rune was safe at her side. She'd no way of knowing if either wish would come true.

The start gun fired.

The race was on!

Anya had no more time for wishes. She had to focus on the Chukchi dogs about to take to the race trail, and do her best to help them if trouble came. She was a Chukchi shaman. She was born to Native Earth for this. The moment she could, she would return to her Eskimo tent and wait — the same as Spirit would do from her world beyond.

"Aren't you gonna watch the race start,

Sepp?" Homer put his question to Leonhard Seppala, who was packing his gear for a trip to help stake another gold claim for his friend and boss, Jafet Lindeberg.

"*Nej.* Sorry to miss it. You tell me all about it when I get back," Sepp good-naturedly threw over his shoulder, and kept to his task.

"I figured you'd for sure want to see the Siberian huskies race," Homer tossed back.

Sepp turned around at Homer's words.

"The *gronlandshunds* from *Sibir,* you say?" Sepp remembered their talk before about Siberian huskies. He'd never heard of them until his friends mentioned the particular breed.

"You want to say that in English for me?" Homer joked.

"*Ja,* sure, sure," Sepp offered right away. "You mean the huskies from Siberia that you told me about a while back."

"The very ones," Homer answered enthusiastically. "They're fast as lightning and are gonna beat the pants off the rest. You can take that to the bank."

Sepp's brow furrowed. He needed to leave, but he wanted to know more about the huskies from *Sibir.* Sepp liked working with the freight dogs he'd been assigned to drive, and had become pretty skilled in their care and running. Some weighed as much as he did, but that didn't stop him from learning to dog drive and getting the job done. Employed by his friend at the Pioneer Mining Company, Sepp had to learn to do a lot of jobs he'd never intended when he left Norway nine years ago for Nome. Such jobs came with the territory in Alaska.

Just then Zeke entered the mine quarters.

"Hey, Sepp, c'mon with us to the race start. They're getting going soon. Boss says we can take off the morning to watch. It's like a Christmas holiday around here. This is the biggest race of the season." Zeke's enthusiasm matched Homer's.

Sepp shook his head at both of the tough old miners. They sounded like boys let out for recess. The huskies from *Sibir* must be the reason. They must be something special. He thought of the pup he'd rescued from the bully boys. That pup was special, Sepp remembered thinking. He would have brought the little guy home to Constance. His wife would have loved the piebald husky with blue eyes. He would have, too.

Sepp didn't have any holiday time to go stand along Front Street and watch other sleds take off. He had to get his freight sled loaded and his team harnessed up. The other miners going on the same job were waiting for him. Jafet Lindeberg was Sepp's boss, too. More than that, the two had been friends from Norway. Jafet had talked Sepp into coming to Nome after the gold and had given Sepp a job at his mining company. That's where friendship stopped. Sepp wouldn't take advantage of Jafet by not doing any and every job required of him as an employee of the Pioneer Mining Company. He made sure he earned every penny of his ten-dollar-a-day pay. He wouldn't take the morning off and go watch any race, not even this big one.

The competitive spirit in Sepp sparked at talk about the huskies from *Sibir.* If the dogs were fast as lightning; that would be something to see. Sepp didn't learn to dog drive to race dogs, but to work them. He enjoyed his time out on trips like the one he was about to take; he enjoyed working behind a sled and guiding the muscle of the malamutes pulling it. When first asked to drive a team of freight dogs, he'd been reluctant. No more. It beat shoveling and earned him more pay. That he enjoyed dog driving was extra payback to him.

"*Takk,* thank you for the invite, boys," Sepp said, his eyes still on his packing and not on the two miners. He needed to make sure of his supplies. To head out on any frontier trail without the right gear could be

258

costly. He'd lived in Alaska long enough to know that much. No matter how well you think you know the land and the trail, there are always surprises, especially in winter. A storm could come up on you any time, same with winds and blinding snow.

Then there was always the *isen*. The ice always waited for you, Sepp realized. One wrong move meant trouble. A wrong guide of the sled or an unseen crevasse meant trouble for the dogs and for him. Sepp took care and took his time where he could, to avoid trouble. A successful journey into the wild out over *isen* took guts, smarts, and a lot of luck, to Sepp's thinking. So far he'd been lucky on his ventures, but he'd heard about others who had not been.

Sepp marveled at the mail carriers who drove their freight sleds through the un-known wild, isolated mile after isolated mile, week after week, year in and year out. No man on the frontier was tougher than the ones who carried the mail, Sepp told himself. Every one of them had his respect. Their dogs had his respect, too. They pulled loads that ordinary dogs could not. So did Sepp's freight mixes of malamutes. A man on the Alaska frontier had to be tough, but his dogs had to be tougher. This had proved true too many times not to be fact.

"So, what will it be, Sepp?" Zeke asked, waiting more patiently than he felt like doing for an answer. Time ran short. They needed to get to Front Street on the double.

Sepp had finished checking his gear and cinched the pack tight before he turned around to the two men. Darned if they didn't look like boys at Christmas, on their way now to watch the Siberian huskies race. He almost wished he could go with them. If he didn't have a job to do, he would.

"Next time, maybe," he said. The corners of his mouth hinted a smile.

"That's a year away, Sepp," Zeke joked.

Sepp didn't have an answer for his disappointment at hearing this. He'd felt the same disappointment when he had to return the husky pup, Thor, to its rightful owner.

He didn't have an answer for that letdown, either.

CHAPTER ELEVEN

"With the aurora borealis flaming coldly overhead, or the stars leaping in the frost dance, and the land numb and frozen under its pall of snow, this song of the huskies might have been the defiance of life, only it was pitched in minor key, with long-drawn wailings and half-sobs, and was more the pleading of life, the articulate travail of existence . . ."
Jack London, *The Call of the Wild*

Xander missed his pack. He missed his guardians. He missed his old life and was weary of this new one.

His senses turned in a different direction and away from the wild in the exact moment he survived his leap of faith across the sudden, icy crevasse. Instinct told him to veer from its deadly edges, but Zellie's spirit took him over it safely to the other side. In canine terms, he'd had a sudden change of heart over his loyalties.

His survival took him by surprise. He'd expected to find death on the other side of his forced jump, not life. This rattled him and shook him to new senses and awareness.

Where before he'd lived solely by his instincts to kill or be killed — with all his senses to that one simple rule of survival in the wild — now his senses turned him in another direction. This one confused him. This one led him out of isolation in the wild to a place long forgotten. This one led him home.

To Xander the instinct for home made him remember his human guardians and his husky pack. He saw their faces, heard their voices, remembered their scent, and felt their touch. With them he'd known companionship, safety, loyalty, and love. Without them now, he suffered the pangs of loneliness.

This made him vulnerable. This would make him hesitate in living by the rule of kill or be killed in the wild, and increase his chances for dying. When he remembered the loving touch of his guardian's hand or the comfort of having his pack close, his watch eyes would be focused on home and not the hunt. One wrong move, and he'd become easy prey. These impulsive flashes shot through his senses like familiar whispers on the arctic winds — just as loud and just as clear as before *the time of his dying,* when his memory faded from awareness.

Xander's present confusion left him exposed. His defenses were down. He reflexively pointed his muzzle to the heavens and wailed in half-sobs to the Gatekeepers, to Zellie, and to the ancients of his breed. His mournful call to spirits spoke of the struggle ahead to find his way back home. He didn't call for help, but for arctic winds to carry his whispers to the worlds beyond, to those who came before him. His cries to imagined spirits gave him company in his loneliness.

Lars should have heard from Rune by this time. Too much time had gone by without word. Rune would have sent a telegram. Lars didn't want to think of the reason why he had not. He refused to think something bad might have happened. His heart refused to accept the possibility, but his head told him otherwise. No matter how worried he was about Rune, Lars wasn't a quitter, and he wouldn't quit on his son! He wouldn't give up on Rune and lose hope. Rune must have a good reason for his silence.

Exhausted from lack of sleep, Lars kicked

back from his desk and got up from his leather swivel chair. He'd slept in his office all night; at least he'd tried. He called JOHANSSON AND SON SHIPPING — so the signage outside read — home now. His name was on it, and Rune's. The doublestoried, brick office building provided a comfortable enough place to live. Besides, he preferred living near the sea to being landlocked. Seattle's harbor was welcoming. Its stately residences on the *best* streets were not.

Margret and Inga lived there.

He'd given them the house and had no regrets. It wasn't his home anymore, and he didn't try to fight for it in any court proceedings Margret started against him — against him and Rune. The case had just ended. Margret had lost her suit to try and take his life's work from him. Her high-paid lawyers were good, but his were better. The case was never open and shut, and Lars knew that. He knew that because truth didn't always win out in a court of law. A well-argued case did. Where one court might have ruled in his favor, another might have given his now ex-wife Johansson and Son Shipping. Nothing was obvious and evident when it came to the cold business of law.

The only reason any of this mattered was because of his son. Lars wanted Rune to inherit the family shipping business. More than that, he wanted Rune to work alongside him, captaining one of the *skepps* in their fleet that traded to the north. Maybe Lars would get into the passenger ship business as well. The future could hold any dream you wanted in America, if you were willing to work hard enough for that dream to become reality. Lars never doubted his son's work ethic. He always reported for duty — sick or well, rain or snow, liking his assigned job or not.

That was what had Lars so worried at the moment. Rune always reported in. He hadn't yet. There had been no word from Nome. Lars couldn't focus on why, but he could focus on when he planned to sail the *Storm* to Nome and rendezvous with his son — when the *isen* began to break. The time to head into arctic waters was when the ice let you. Lars's best calculation for arrival outside Nome was mid-June.

If he were any kind of explorer or scientific voyager, he might have icebreakers at his disposal. If so, travel might be possible in spring. Lars knew that icebreaker steamers coming from far distances to the Arctic often had to stop mid-journey and set up camp for the winter wherever they could find safe haven. Lars hesitated.

Was there ever safe haven in the Arctic?

For his own peace of mind in worry over his son, Lars would leave this question open. Lars would find out soon enough, as soon as he got to Nome himself. To be safe, he wanted a backup plan. He'd have a trusted crew navigate the *Nordic* behind the *Storm.* If all was well with Rune, Lars would send the *Nordic* to appointed trade stops north and return to Seattle with his son on the *Storm.* Once they returned, he and Rune would make a new home together as father and son — Johansson and Son Shipping in sign and in fact.

Rune had left for Nome three months ago for good reason. Lars didn't have any details. He had to respect Rune's decision, but he didn't have to like it. He didn't like the dark elves invading his fitful dreams, either. Some nights were better than others. Some nights he slept a couple of hours, and some nights he kept the electric on and tried to work. Lars pushed his work aside. This wasn't about him anymore, but about his son.

Lars wouldn't worry about finding any peace of mind until he found Rune.

■ ■ ■ ■

The Chukchi dog had escaped him again.

Rune Johansson hadn't burned to death.

The golem paced back and forth in his recently set-up quarters in Moscow. A big part of the advancing communist operation to reshape Russia into a mighty industrial and agricultural power, he cursed his recent failures in the world of dark spirits. He couldn't blame the Midgard serpent or the Raven god this time for the dog escaping him. The fires of *Hel,* either. The golem had only himself to blame. He'd reshaped from his human form into the killing spirit of the wolf. It didn't work. The dog got away.

So did the golem.

At the moment of death for the wolf, the golem spirited to life in his human form on earth . . . just in time. He'd used up a lot of his otherworldly powers already and only had so much left in him when the Chukchi dog tricked him into falling into the unseen crevasse. His powers were enough to get him out of trouble and escape the same fall and the same fate as the wolf. It all happened in a heartbeat, in the split second that means life or death.

The golem's attention had been on the

dog when he should have put more on the guardian. The golem couldn't blame the fires of *Hel.* Once started, the fire should have killed the boy; the fire or the frozen waters, either one or both together should have done the trick. Here again, the golem had been fooled by the *kulaks*!

The Chukchi would never win in the end.

They would die, and their dogs would die out.

Not one for panic, since he held dominion in the world of humans and spirits, the golem nevertheless did worry about the one weapon the Chukchi still held over him: their guardian strength. As long as he kept the guardians of the Chukchi separated, their power to slow the inevitable ice storm stayed weak, almost quiet. Joined together, their power would strengthen. The two guardians had caused enough trouble for the golem, but he'd taken care of them and separated them to prevent more. If ever they rejoined and added the one more guardian to their watch, this spelled trouble for the ice storm.

The golem scratched his days-old whiskers and then poured himself a shot of vodka. He had one drink, then two, before he took a seat at the large table provided in his office for meetings with his subordinates. In ten minutes, his comrades would start to file in. He had little time left to put his attention to his troubles in the spirit world. He'd have to make time and make sure Chukchi strength continued to weaken and die out. This called for an accounting.

The guardian with her six dogs was one problem to watch.

The guardian trying to get to her was two.

The one yet to be seen was three.

The guardians could not be allowed to come together with their Chukchi dogs and fight against him. Human or spirit, wolf or serpent, Raven or *Hel,* by sword or by bullet or by ice storm — he would never let them!

The moment Fox's three sled teams safely crossed the start out of Nome, Anya raced back to Chinook's village and to her own Chukchi dogs. No storm brewed that she could tell. No sudden change in the weather foretold of more danger. Anya wasn't fooled by this. The dark spirits hid in shadow and waited to strike at first chance. She couldn't let down her guard. To best do this, she would keep watch with her dogs instead of going to the Board of Trade Saloon and keeping watch there, as she'd done before.

Rune had raced then.

All nine of her dogs had raced then.

This time was different. She had to trust in Spirit, and Spirit had to trust in her. This time Anya had to rely on her Spirit to keep watch over all three dog drivers and all three teams of Chukchi dogs. Spirit would lead from her position in the beyond, and Anya would follow, both harnessed together in guardian spirit. Anya would let Spirit take over if trouble hit. At the same time, Anya had to stand firm on Native Earth and position herself with her own dogs and keep watch over them and keep her knife — a gift from the gods — ready to make her own strike.

The fragile lines between worlds had to be crossed if necessary. It was the only way to try and stay safe. It was a risk both Anya and Spirit were born to take. The tiny holes around the Pole Star opened for them to make such a crossing. In so doing, the fragile lines between worlds stayed safe. The layers of lives in the worlds of the Chukchi, both human and spirit, remained protected. The ancestors and the unborn depended on it.

Anya was shaman. Her Spirit was shaman. Their holy paths to each other crossed in a heartbeat — in the time it takes to give life or end it.

"Anya, what are you doing?" Vitya finally

caught up with her. She'd taken off out of Nome so fast, it took him awhile to even realize she'd left. When he did, he had a good idea where she'd gone. He'd been right, with the exception of one thing. He didn't imagine finding her sitting square in the middle of her six dogs, holding onto all their ties at the same time. Even odder to him, the dogs seemed fine with it. Their watch eyes followed him as he came up on the scene.

It took Anya a moment, however, for her watch eyes to focus on Vitya. She'd already gone into a trancelike state of mind, listening for arctic whispers to guide her.

"Are you all right?" Vitya had to ask. Her look was so far away.

"Yes." She didn't feel like saying anything else. She didn't feel like explaining things to Vitya. He knew she was shaman. Why was he even asking? Annoyed, she tried not to show it. She didn't appreciate her concentration being broken, even by Vitya.

Anya looked away from him.

Vitya was hurt. He wanted to help her. He wanted her to *want* him to help her. Ready, willing, and able to help her in all things, it hurt Vitya that she shut him out. When she became his wife, things would be different. A Chukchi wife listened to her

271

husband's roar and answered right away in a soft, obedient whisper. Anya was stubborn and liked to do things on her own, but that would all change when they returned together to their Anquallat village and married. He respected that she was shaman, but she would be more respectful of him when he became her husband.

Vitya didn't try to talk to her again. He could see that wasn't a good idea. The dogs lost interest in him, too, it appeared to him. They didn't watch him anymore. One by one they burrowed and curled down into a circle in the snow, all forming a circle around Anya, even Thor. Vitya expected the young husky to want to play and romp, but Thor behaved the same as the rest. The scene took on a ceremonial appearance to Vitya. He could swear this was some kind of ritual that shamans performed to communicate with spirits. Then Vitya realized that's exactly what it was.

Anya was a Chukchi shaman.

He was a Chukchi warrior.

He would keep silent, and he would keep close.

Rune had made it to Seward without trouble. Familiar with the Gulf of Alaska, he'd headed in a direction out of Skagway that followed its edges. In Seward he'd secured supplies, a rough map of his intended overland route, a sled, and a husky-mixed team of twelve sled dogs, all thanks to the generosity of Doc Adams and his family. Rune felt well enough. No aches and pains slowed him down. No weakening of his muscles plagued him and threatened paralysis. The clear weather cooperated.

He felt fit and ready to begin his long journey across the Alaska frontier, except for one thing. While the scars from his burns had all but disappeared, the scar from his birth felt on fire.

This sign from the gods meant danger. Rune didn't know what kind. He'd have to fight the fear all the way from Seward to Nome . . . without his Viking sword. The only weapons he held in his hands now were the imagined sunstone of the Vikings in one and the map marking his route in the other. They'd have to be enough. He didn't have his relied-upon sword anymore. Someone else did and used it against him. It struck out of arctic shadows. Rune would have to avoid the shadows and stay in the light of the coming spring.

He couldn't help but think how much easier the journey ahead would be if he had Zellie as his leader dog — Zellie and Xander and all the rest of the brave nine who ran in the last Nome sweepstakes. He remembered the feel of their guide and their muscle and trusted in their every move. A rookie dog driver himself, the Chukchi dogs were not rookies to any trail they had to run. Fast, enduring, and infused with arctic will, his team of nine would brave anything. They did, at the risk of their own peril. Every mile of the race marked a new risk. Not one dog ever turned away from that risk.

Zellie had paid for it with her life. Xander and the rest of the team had survived, but only to face more risks . . . more death. Mushroom might have died at the hands of a cruel mine boss, and Xander's death might have occurred when he was outnumbered in a vicious dog fight ring, but Rune had no doubt what had really killed them. It was the same evil that still chased after Anya and the rest of her dogs. All of them, Rune included, had been outnumbered from the very beginning in this war of ghosts. More evil forces had joined the dark side in battle against them. The sudden strikes from too many shadows told Rune as much. Only one force had been added to their own side by Rune's count: the pup, Thor.

Rune hadn't forgotten what Anya told him

on that last day, about Xander and Flowers's pup. At this moment Rune regretted not going to see the little guy. He should have. The idea of the pup struck a fiercely protective nerve. It was the same nerve that was hit when he thought of Anya and the dogs left alive. Rune needed to make sure evil left them alone. He couldn't do that until he'd reached them in Nome. Until he saw them with his own eyes, he wouldn't rest easy. Humph. Any idea of resting at all along the trip ahead struck him as funny, not the kind of funny to bring any laugh. He had two months of fear for Anya and her dogs to go before he'd rest, period.

Rune forced his thoughts to the trail ahead and took out the crude map drawn for him. It showed the fur trade stops out of Seward, the same stops used for hundreds of years, he'd been told, to carry supplies and provisions back and forth from coastal to interior destinations. Rune supposed the route had been used for thousands of years, not just hundreds. Land and sea trade was as old as everything else around here; they came with the territory.

Some sections of the route were likely older and more often used than others, making them easier to follow. For those sections less used and not clearly mapped,

Rune would rely on the sunstone of the Vikings for direction. The Arctic Ocean was never far. He felt its vibrations. He could almost feel its icy waters surge and whip beneath his feet, no matter that he was on land. The sensation brought comfort in the knowledge that his Viking ancestors, and his connection to them, were never far. Good. He needed all the help he could find for the fight ahead.

The first stops on the map would take him over Moose Pass, then to Portage, then on to Eagle River. Maybe he'd be lucky enough to find a roadhouse and shelter for his dog team at the designated stops. The journey ahead wasn't the all-important Nome sweepstakes, but it felt like it to Rune. This race would end in Nome and was most certainly a race for the lives of Anya and her Chukchi dogs. But that's where any common ground ended. Unlike in the sweepstakes, where Rune's sled and team crossed the finish in just over eighty-three hours, this one would take longer, by two months.

"Mush!" he called out to his new team of malamute mixes. They wouldn't be as fast or as enduring as Siberian huskies but he could rely on their strength and skill over familiar ground to get him there all the same.

■ ■ ■ ■

In seventy-four hours, fourteen minutes, and thirty-seven seconds after he'd crossed the start of the 1910 All Alaska Sweepstakes out of Nome, District of Alaska, John Johnson crossed the grueling finish first. Fox Ramsey's team crossed second, with a time of seventy-six hours, nineteen minutes, and twenty-two seconds. Scotty Allan came in fifteen minutes behind Fox, with Charles Johnson close behind Scotty, crossing in fourth place.

Saloons all over Nome buzzed with the news. The Board of Trade Saloon, race headquarters, was no exception.

Not only did locals call John Johnson "Iron Man" Johnson after the race, but they called his sled dog team of Siberian wolves, *Siberian huskies,* now. No one would call them *little rats* again, either. How could they? Three out of four of the top teams finishing their prized sweepstakes were all underrated foreign imports bought in Siberia, brought to Nome, and raced under the ownership of Fox Maule Ramsey. The winning dogs had no malamute mix, native Alaska blood in them. They were not any kind of freight dogs or heavily muscled dogs meant to pull loads. The smaller Siberian dogs were meant to pull light loads over long distances, and do it *fast*.

To locals, they were meant for something else from that moment on: dog racing.

A mix of their own dogs with the unique Siberian imports spelled future winnings. Crossing bloodlines made sense. When Siberian speed was bred with Alaskan strength, no one could catch the husky mix in any race. Bred to live and work in the north, the two groups of huskies proved themselves before any cross-breeding. But imagine the breed . . . *after*! The same idea occurred to more than one race watcher, and more than one plan was already underway to combine the breeds.

The noisy, crowded Board of Trade Saloon boomed with excitement about the race results posted. Spirited conversation went in all directions from, "I told you so," and, "I always knew the little huskies were fast," to, "I never would have figured on them running so good." Bets had been heavy on Scotty Allan to win again, but other bettors had spread out their wagers on other teams in the field. A few bettors admitted now they'd put their money on the imports to win. And boy, had they been right as rain to do it! The bettors who didn't fare as well didn't get mad and pull out their guns. The crowd was still in awe over the showing of the Siberian huskies.

Not only did the dogs race well, but they had some of the best dog drivers in the District of Alaska to run them. John Johnson and Charles Johnson wouldn't have bothered with the Siberian imports if they didn't think they were worth it. Fox Ramsey wouldn't have invested so much time and money in them either, if he didn't think they were worth it. Besides that, Fox just finished second, ahead of Scotty!

It was a thing of wonder, the 1910 All Alaska Sweepstakes.

Albert Fink kept his gun hand ready and kept at his same appointed table where he took up his position every year at race time. As president of the Nome Kennel Club, he sat near the black chalkboard that marked down every race team's progress, or lack thereof, at each stop along the way to Candle, then back to Nome. If a team had to drop out, a moan would pass through the crowd. If a team didn't check into the next stop on time, worries would go out around the smoke-filled saloon. All eyes would go to the telegraph for word of what went wrong. The race pretty much followed the remote telegraph lines, and communication from each checkpoint was highly anticipated.

When the stops at Haven and First Chance — the two stops before the two-hundred-four mile, halfway point at Candle — were posted, it was evident the Siberian teams were doing a good job in the race. That's when Albert lowered his gun hand and rested his fingers over his Smith & Wesson pistol, expecting trouble.

But none came.

The atmosphere in the Board of Trade Saloon reflected the exact opposite. In fact, a rousing cheer for the underdog sled teams would go out every now and then. More whiskey would be poured, and more reporters from the Outside would head to their newspaper wires and telephone lines to spread word of events as they came in and were posted on the chalkboard. Murmurings of Iron Man Johnson's progress could be heard over talk of others. He was an expert dog driver, and the crowd expected him to do well, but without an Alaskan dog team in front of his sled, they didn't realize how well until they saw the latest postings.

The crowd cheered for Scotty Allan and their own, too, but a grudging respect for the Siberian imports had taken hold and didn't let go. Those still gathered in saloons or along Front Street after the last sled team crossed the sweepstakes finish were still caught up in the grip of excitement over the Siberian huskies. The four-day race meant a four-day holiday and everyone, white and Eskimo alike, celebrated the race finish in true holiday spirit.

Everyone, that was, except Anya.

Her Spirit, either.

Tense and on guard for three days and as many nights, Anya and her counterpart in the spirit world were instinctively happy at the race outcome, but their watch eyes still trained on the darkness surely after them, the darkness that hid in shadow and *did not strike.* Why? Why miss such an opportunity to bring down the Chukchi and their dogs? If the Chukchi teams had been forced to quit or even perform poorly in the race, such an outcome would be just as disastrous as death caused to the people.

Yet, no dogs had been struck down.

No dog drivers had been harmed.

If the evil after them did not strike here, at this opportune time, then where was it?

After Rune?

After Grisha?

After more innocents?

The evil that hid in shadow would never give up an easy victory so willingly. Zellie had been struck down at just such a time. Anya and her Spirit together couldn't save the beloved husky. This time Anya was forewarned and ready. Her Spirit was ready. Still, they were worried. They had no reason to believe more Chukchi dogs wouldn't meet the same doom, despite their combined, close watch.

Agitated, Anya got up and paced around the circle of six dogs that watched her and were alerted to her confusion. A few whimpered. The rest sniffed at the danger in the air.

Spirit raced along the edges of the Great Crag, running dangerously close to the expanding breach caused in Native Earth. Edges everywhere ran thin.

Anya didn't know what to make of any of this. She'd had dreams, fitful dreams about what to expect. In dreams she'd seen the Chukchi dogs lose their footing on the race trail and never regain it. All at once and all together, the dogs were sucked down a jagged, icy embankment, then thrown over cliffs to the frozen sea below. Their claws were pulled out and their paw pads bled, in desperate attempts to save themselves. No decent foothold waited below to catch their bloody fall — only death, for the dogs and their dog driver. It all happened in a heartbeat, in the time it takes to give life or end it.

This deadly foreboding had put Anya on full alert for the running of the 1910 All Alaska Sweepstakes. She expected to be called on by mist and magic to help save one team, or all of them. This time she meant to be in time to prevent such catastrophe. When no signal came, when no whispers on arctic winds struck her awareness, Anya couldn't get rid of the bad feeling deep down inside her that the trouble wasn't over. She had an even worse feeling that it had just started all over again.

"Anya!" Vitya called out as he ran up.

Anya stopped her pacing and waited for his report from the race finish. She'd already heard from Chinook which team won and which teams came in right behind the winner. Her fears that a Chukchi sled team might not come in first had disappeared, only to be replaced by new ones. She needed reassurances from Vitya. He'd agreed to watch the Chukchi teams cross the finish line and not return to Chinook's village and to her until they did.

For her part, she could not desert her post with her dogs and see the race's end herself. To do so invited trouble. Her full attention had to stay with Spirit. The best protection

Anya could offer any of the Chukchi teams depended on her decision.

Anya trusted Vitya to find out if any of the dogs or dog drivers had been hurt. Did each dog that started finish? Did any of the dog drivers encounter problems? Was Fox all right? Were John Johnson and Charles Johnson all right? Did anything strange and unusual happen to any of them? Did any whips come out of nowhere and strike? Vitya's English was poor. Anya knew that. Still, Vitya was the right one to eye each dog and each dog driver and check for problems. Vitya would know right away if he spotted injury or something unusual with the dogs.

He'd worked with Chukchi dogs all his life. He would know.

Fox and Vitya communicated well enough by this time. At least well enough for Fox to let on if things had gone bad on the race trail. Fox would want Anya to know right away, so he'd make sure to get the news across to Vitya. When Fox finished tending his dogs, he would come himself to talk to her. He should have time to celebrate the win and the great showing of all three of his Chukchi teams in the sweepstakes. She should allow him the time, no matter how anxious she was to hear every detail of the big race just run, and no matter how she longed to thank each dog driver in person, especially John Johnson.

His win meant more than he realized. She could try to explain this to the tough, frontier dog driver, but then how could she? She couldn't, not in any way he'd understand. If he were *the one,* she might try, but John Johnson was not the third guardian. He was not the man without a face in her dreams. Even though John Iron Man Johnson just won the Nome sweepstakes and was a champion of the Chukchi dog, he was not a guardian. His spirit did not speak to her.

Anya swallowed hard. She sensed that time was running out for her to find the third guardian. Her fears rekindled that she might not.

Her mood brightened a little, seeing the happiness on Vitya's face — seeing his pride in such a big win for the Chukchi dog. She felt the same pride. She mentally thanked the Morning Dawn and the Directions for their guidance. She thanked the Gatekeepers for their watch. In quick prayerful whispers, she even thanked the rest of the Chukchi gods and Rune's Viking gods for any help they might have given. Anya sent her whispers to the heavens and to the wild.

The gods had been silent far too long.

Some had stayed with her to help guide her and keep watch. Others had not. The truth of this kept Anya on full alert. It was up to her, to Rune, and to a third guardian, so that some might live. But she didn't have Rune to fight at her side, or the third guardian. This reality set her nerves on edge and her intuition agitating. The danger she faced wasn't over. In fact it got worse the moment Iron Man Johnson's sled came across the finish in first place.

Anya had never been so alone, in body or in spirit.

CHAPTER TWELVE

"Victory awaits him who has everything in order — luck, people call it. Defeat is certain for him who has neglected to take the necessary precautions in time; this is called bad luck."
Arctic and Antarctic explorer, *Roald Amundsen*

Jafet Lindeberg reread his friend's telegraph message, sent from Eagle, District of Alaska, to him in Nome, eight months earlier.

Jafet had kept the message safely stored in his desk drawer. Roald Amundsen was a good friend and a fellow Norwegian. The pair kept in touch as regularly as they could. If things had gone according to plan, Roald's vessel would arrive in Nome waters any day. Roald would have switched from his smaller, forty-five-ton fishing vessel, to a larger icebreaker steamship for venturing out into arctic waters. He used the smaller vessel to maintain his way along the arctic coastline from Canadian territory into Alaskan territory. The waters along the coast were too shallow for any kind of large vessel.

Whether exploring in the South or in the North, Jafet never knew what expedition his friend planned next. Roald meant to get to both poles first. That much Jafet did know. Roald put together expedition teams as hardy as himself. He'd also taken advantage of the local native cultures along the way and taken careful note of their survival skills — skills such as replacing wool parkas with warmer and more waterproof animal skins and hunting meat for his crew's table. Fresh meat contained fresh blood. At sea with no fruit or means to prevent scurvy, meat provided a fruit source. Animals produce their own vitamin C.

These native lessons served Amundsen and his men well when isolated in the freeze of winter, land or sea. However, there were no lessons about predators that loomed, other than to avoid them. Amundsen had earned more than one broken bone to show for this hard reality. He'd been attacked by polar bears numerous times. Dangers in the Arctic were never far away.

Jafet agreed. If a body on the Alaska

frontier didn't understand the dangers it faced, respect those dangers, and even embrace them, a body wouldn't live very long. Anyone coming to live in arctic territory or its surrounds needed to learn that lesson fast. To Jafet's thinking, most folks came to Nome for the gold. He had, too, at least after he broke his contract to help bring reindeer from Siberia to the Alaska District. He'd decided it would be better economically to get into the business of finding gold. That proved an understatement.

He'd not only found gold but was wealthy, very wealthy. To give back some of his good fortune, he wanted to bring electric light and power and water works to Nome. With so much profit from his Pioneer Mining Company, he believed he owed it to the people who lived in the frontier city he helped establish.

Right now he wanted to think of a way to help his friend Roald, and contribute to his chances for success in any expedition Roald undertook. Money, Amundsen could always use, Jafet thought, but whenever he'd offered funds to support his explorations into the Arctic or Antarctic, Roald said no. So maybe he'd been wrong to want to give money. But Jafet had an idea now about what to do for his wilderness-exploring friend.

The moment Jafet heard the news of how well the Siberian huskies had performed in the All Alaska Sweepstakes, he thought of Roald Amundsen. Roald used sled dogs on his expeditions. When a ship was marooned in ice, dogs on board could be put to good use. A dog sled could pull men across ice to safety, where a trapped ship could not. Dogs could also pull men out of trouble on land. Their sleds carried supplies for survival and exploration into unknown wilderness.

If the dogs ever had to be dog food, Jafet didn't want to know. It was a hard thought to reckon with. He'd heard stories of expeditions and what had to be done to survive. Leave that for the ship's log to set down and not bring such last-resort news home. Roald had never shared such news with him. Leave it at that.

Soon Roald was going to attempt a voyage and trek to become the first explorer to reach the poles. How soon and to which pole, Jafet wasn't certain. Of one thing he was certain. Sled dogs would be needed — fast and enduring sled dogs able to pull small loads over long distances in harsh weather, with little rest and even less food. What better dogs for this important, expeditionary purpose than the proven, newly crowned Siberian huskies! Jafet felt good about his idea. Roald would not turn down the offer of well-trained Siberian sled dogs to take on his expedition team.

Jafet intended to put this offer out there when Roald arrived in Nome. He'd make him the promise of delivery of the Siberian huskies at the time needed. All Roald would have to do was say when. It occurred to Jafet that he needed to talk to Leonhard Seppala, first. A good friend to him as well, Jafet needed to enlist Sepp to do the training once the Siberian huskies were acquired. He'd leave it up to Sepp just how to get the right dogs together for an expeditionary team. With so many huskies from Siberia already here, it shouldn't be hard to get enough to meet Sepp's sled dog standards.

Jafet had to laugh at this thought. Before Sepp came to Nome, he'd never been around a dogsled team, much less driven one. Mining meant not just having good men to shovel gravel and run the sluice or start up the dredge, but good men to dog drive teams that were needed to pull heavy loads of supplies, day in and day out, from one mine to the next. Sepp had to learn how to dog drive for the Pioneer Mining Company, and, to his credit, he did. And he was damned good at it, Jafet had to admit.

He was surprised at how well Sepp took to driving a freight sledge pulled by a team of malamute mixes. Most men Sepp's size would have been intimidated by the large freight dogs, not Sepp. He never had a problem getting the dogs to listen or getting them to work. It had all been a surprise to Jafet, but a good one. Sepp was reliable. Jafet would count on that trait in his good friend, in securing and training up a reliable team of Siberian huskies for Roald Amundsen's expedition to the pole.

All he would have to do was say when to Sepp, and the job would get done. He'd sent Sepp with a sled dog team and two men on horseback to stake a new claim for the Pioneer Mining Company in the hills well beyond Nome. As soon as Sepp returned, he'd get Sepp's word on it.

"Lassie, *ah dinnaeken* what you want from me?" Fox answered Anya, puzzled by her question.

He didn't understand why she thought he could just come up with a steamer to take Vitya across the Bering Sea, back to their coastal village. *Aye,* he had traveled by steamer before, with Rune on one of Johansson and Son's steamers, when Fox made passage to Anadyr, Siberia, and traded for his seventy huskies. That was almost a year ago and he hadn't seen the lad, Rune, for a long time. Too long, Fox thought. He and the lad had made an agreement, and Rune had stuck to his part and got Fox safely to Siberia and back again, all of the huskies, too. The journey was not without its rough patches, but they'd made it, and that's what counted.

Besides the fact that Rune wasn't around to steer any steamer across the Bering Sea, it was too early in the season. The ice hadn't melted enough to allow safe passage. If that wasn't enough, Vitya obviously didn't want to leave without the lassie. Fox could tell that right away. He'd known for some time how the Chukchi lad felt about Anya and could understand the lad's objections to going anywhere without her.

"Fox, you have to help us," Anya pleaded. She hated to sound so desperate, but she didn't see any other way out of this problem without Fox's cooperation. He was important in the white man's world. He was important in mining. He had money and means. He had many Chukchi dogs. Best of all, he had a good heart and she considered him a trusted friend.

"No!" Vitya stepped in between Anya and Fox.

Anya fumed at Vitya's interference.

Fox stood back from the two.

"Anya." Vitya turned down his roar at her. He spoke in pure Chukchi now. "I am not going home without you. You are coming with me. We are going to marry. We will have many children; children to help us raise many Chukchi dogs. It will be a good life, a happy life. I am not going home without you," he made clear.

Anya knew this was coming, but she didn't expect Vitya to say such things in front of Fox, even if Vitya spoke in their native tongue. She loved Vitya in so many ways, but not like he wanted — not like a wife should love a husband. She owed Vitya so much. He'd been her forever friend and had always been there for her, back home and here in this new land of Alaska. He'd sacrificed so much to make sure she was safe. She needed to make sure he stayed safe, but that couldn't be at her side. To stay near her meant danger for Vitya. She had to get him home.

Something else struck Anya at that moment. Her troubled thoughts turned to her stepfather, Grisha. She had to make sure he stayed safe, too. Maybe she should go back home with Vitya to make sure they, and all in her Anquallat village, escaped the evil that was after the Chukchi dogs and the people.

There *must* be a safe place to hide from such shadows of death.

She was shaman, a holy woman to the people. She must find a safe haven for them. If she went home with Vitya, maybe she could find it. This idea had struck before, but she hadn't thought it out. It had been the cause of more than one fitful dream. She had so many. It was hard to keep an accounting anymore.

If she went with Vitya, who would watch over her dogs!

Anya's nerves fractured and tore her up inside. She couldn't take her dogs with her, back to the very place they'd escaped! She couldn't defy prophecy and challenge the Chukchi gods and all the ancestors! To do so would bring great risk. Her dogs risked so much already, so *some* might live. Zellie, Xander, Mushroom, and Little Wolf had been lost in the war of ghosts. If Anya took the surviving dogs with her, *none* would live. The Chukchi dog would vanish from Native Earth in a heartbeat.

How could she leave them and go with Vitya? She was their guardian, entrusted to watch over them. Rune was their guardian, entrusted with the same watch. She went over this again in her head as she had countless times.

She and Rune both communicated with the dead, with spirits. They could better see what hid in shadow and waited to strike than others who did not have their connection to the spirit world. The hand of the guardian brushed the hand of the runes. She and Rune had been appointed guardians, both summoned by the gods of their separate traditions, to meet the same challenge: to save the Chukchi dog.

If only Rune were here now and could watch over Magic, Flowers, Midday, Midnight, Frost, and little Thor.

Her stomach churned as if all the spirits in worlds good and bad spun inside her, whirling and swirling their plans. She couldn't fight off her fears for her dogs if she left them with anybody but Rune. She couldn't leave them, but if she didn't go with Vitya, he and Grisha and everyone in her home village might pay for it with their lives.

If forewarned, they could leave.

They must leave.

The people must leave.

"All this *blether* is for nothing, lassie," Fox

said, trying to break into Anya's obvious concentration on something else. She had a faraway look that got to him. The poor lassie suffered. She worried so over her dogs and Rune, too, he guessed. She likely missed the Viking lad. *Aye,* Vitya was here with the lassie, but she missed Rune. Fox wasn't any kind of matchmaker, but he felt like one at the moment, worrying over who might win the lassie's heart when all was said and done.

Vitya hadn't moved out of the way and he wasn't going to.

"What do you mean?" Anya asked, going around Vitya to Fox.

Fox smiled at her maneuver.

"I mean that all this talk goes for nothing. I *cannae* come up with a steamship for you this early in the season. Even if I could find a captain willing to take Vitya to Siberia, only icebreakers and explorers can get across the still-iced-in waters. Lassie, it is *nee* possible *noo.*"

Anya needed a miracle. She needed two. She needed to find a captain to take her and Vitya across the great sea, and she needed to find the third guardian — the faceless dog driver — to watch over her dogs while she was gone. If spirits wanted to poke and pry and squawk inside her now, let them speak up and tell her just who the guardian was!

Fox watched Anya hug her arms close as if in pain. He hated to see her so upset.

"Lassie, tell you what. I'll ask around for news of any steamships coming this way. Could be I'll find you a captain after all. *D'nee* look so *doon*."

Vitya stood behind Anya and put his hands on her frail shoulders. She never ate enough. When he got her back home, he'd not only marry her, but make sure she listened to him and let him take care of her. It was about time someone did.

Anya reflexively stepped out of Vitya's reach. The hint of a smile caught at the corners of her mouth at Fox's last words. Maybe she'd have her miracle after all. Maybe the impossible was possible.

She and Vitya said their goodbyes to Fox and left his mining office. His dog yard was close by. Anya realized Fox was a good guardian over his dogs. She didn't worry for their safety. They'd run hard and run fast and fulfilled their destiny. His Chukchi dogs earned their well-deserved rest. The evil that had pursued his three teams had turned away the instant the race was won. Not so for her and her dogs.

For them, the ice storm didn't give up . . .

but picked up.

Rune arrived at the Big River Roadhouse after a full day's travel. He'd save crossing the Kuskokwim River for tomorrow. He kept to the same schedule every day and every night, running his team eighteen hours and resting six. The dogs did all right with this routine, as long as he built in needed breaks. Where the trail proved too exhausting, he made sure to water and rest the animals. If any dog showed any sign of injury to its feet, he'd stop and check them all out. Bad weather didn't slow him or his dogs down the rest of the time. The animals kept their muscled shoulders to the stormy trail and so did Rune.

He was relieved he still had skills enough to dog drive. It had been awhile since he'd been called on to learn to race huskies.

On this night he'd sleep outside the roadhouse shelter, with his dogs. He wanted their companionship, being on edge more so than usual. His mind had started to play tricks on him again. All day he saw Zellie harnessed in the lead position of his dog team, and Xander harnessed in the wheel position, right in front of his sled. He'd blink away such an impossibility only to see the Chukchi pair reappear in the mix with his malamute team. Copper-red and white Mushroom would show up in his swing position if Rune blinked wrong. Maybe he needed to rest more.

Snow didn't blind him, but something did. He just didn't know what. Something caused him to see Anya's lost dogs — all three dead — all three lost to her, and to him.

He'd been traveling with these same dogs for a month. Today was the first time he'd seen Zellie, Xander, and Mushroom helping pull his sled. Why now? What could this mean, besides him being so tired he was seeing things that weren't there? His birthmark singed at his confusion. He slapped a hand to the back of his neck, trying to chase away pained thoughts. When his fingers brushed his scar, its raised edges scorched his spirit . . . and got his attention.

The hand of the guardian brushed the hand of the runes.

All three dead and gone Chukchi huskies — Zellie, Xander, and Mushroom — were trying to help him get to Anya and her dogs. He was needed there, *now*!

Rune convinced himself this was the message intended.

He couldn't get there by mist and magic. He had no sword from the gods. He had only the sunstone of the Vikings in one hand and a map of the trail ahead in the other. What he also had was weeks more travel before he'd cross the Yukon River at Kaltag, then make it to the juncture of Unalakleet and the Norton Sound. There he'd follow the Norton Sound around to Golovin, then Solomon, and finally to Nome.

It would take him another month to get to Anya and her dogs.

He prayed to the Almighty, to Odin, and to the Gatekeepers, he wouldn't be too late.

"Roald Amundsen you say?" Fox greeted the man introduced to him when he entered the Pioneer Mining Company office of Jafet Lindeberg. He thought he'd heard the name before but couldn't place it.

After making rounds in Nome and asking about any ships soon to anchor in the area, Fox got an earful. The ice melt had begun in earnest, and that meant shipping lanes would start to open up to trade, whaling, and exploration on both sides of the Bering Strait, Russian and American. Trade and whaling had been conducted for centuries along both coasts of the two nations. Both coasts were a part of Russia until 1867, when the United States had bought the 586, 412 square miles of Russian America for

7.2 million dollars from the Russian Empire. Not everyone in Nome was in the know about these details, but Fox ran into enough that did in order to find out what he needed. Active shipping through the Bering Strait was about to commence.

In fact, Russia had recently let foreign companies establish businesses in their northeastern regions for trade and ore, like the U.S. Northeast Siberia Company and the Hudson's Bay Company. The Yukon gold rush might have been the reason for this, Fox thought. He wondered if relations with Russia had always been so friendly-like. Born and raised in Scotland, he'd never paid attention to talk of nations so distant and different from his own. He knew there was a line drawn in the Bering Sea between Russia and America, borders between nations being important. A man's life could depend on knowing whether or not those lines could be crossed.

It sounded to Fox as if Russia and America didn't much mind who crossed when. That could change. He hoped not for a long time — long enough to help get Anya and Vitya over the Russian borderline and back to their home village on the Siberian coast.

"*Ja,* that's my name," Roald Amundsen said and put his hand out to shake the

302

young Scot's.

"*Awrite! Noo* I can place you. *Noo* I *ken* who you are. *Ah didnee* expect to ever meet the likes of you. A real pleasure, Roald Amundsen," Fox repeated and shook his hand again. Fox didn't know much about shipping lanes and trading and such, but he had heard of the famous explorer. He didn't think any man could have more gumption.

"*Ja* and he's a fellow Norwegian," Jafet Lindeberg threw in with a smile.

"I'm a Scot." Fox stated the obvious.

All three men laughed.

Jafet sat down behind his desk and Roald in a seat nearby.

Fox took a chair opposite both men. He needed to get down to the business of why he came here in the first place. Problem was, he didn't know how to start the conversation without sounding like a fool in front of such an important man — important because Roald Amundsen knew about so much of the world that Fox did not. But Fox was here for the lassie. He'd best get to it.

"Jafet, *d'ye ken* of any way two passengers could get over to Siberia this time of year? It's important or I wouldn't be here asking."

"What passengers would need to cross the

303

Bering Sea?" Jafet questioned. "It's not a trip made often from Nome. You went on one of the few last year. It took big money, I'm sure. You've got my curiosity going with this, Fox."

Fox pulled his tartan cap off and turned it over in his hands.

"I would be willing to pay out more money if you know of any captain going that way," he said to Jafet. He didn't look at Roald Amundsen during any of this. He forgot all about the famed explorer, so worried was he over the lassie and helping her in any way he could.

"Don't you have enough on your hands with mining and dog racing?" Jafet said lightheartedly. "Your big win with your Siberian huskies isn't enough to keep you occupied, I suppose."

Fox had to smile at that. The owner of the Pioneer Mining Company was right. Fox had plenty on his hands, plenty to keep him in his own mining office and tending to his racing dogs.

"I've been telling Roald about your dogs. I don't suppose you want to sell them to me," Jafet suggested. He wasn't joking anymore.

"No," Fox answered right away. He didn't think he should say anything more. He wanted to keep good relations with Jafet and the other mine owners. He didn't want any problems with any of them, but he didn't want to let go of or sell any of his dogs, not yet. Even though he'd allowed Iron Man and Charles Johnson to keep training and caring for the Siberian teams they'd raced, he'd instructed them not to take any offers on their sale. Soon enough the breed would mix with Alaskan huskies. He knew that, but he wanted to put it off. His competitive sense ruled here.

"Too bad, Fox. I'd make you a good offer for a sled team," Jafet said.

Uncomfortable with the subject, Fox turned back to his problem at hand.

"About my passengers —"

"What passengers?" Jafet interrupted with his same question.

"The lassie who brought the Chukchi *dugs* here before I did," Fox answered honestly. "She's one, and a lad from her same village in Siberia is another. His name is Vitya. He came with me on my passage to help with all of my *dugs*. If not for the lassie, no one in Nome would even know about the Siberian husky. They would never have made it across the Bering Sea. She's a special lassie and I want to help her. She needs to go home. She needs to take her friend with

305

her. This is why I ask you, Jafet Lindeberg. Do you know of any captains going west anytime soon?"

"*Ja,* he does," Roald Amundsen answered for his friend. "I might be going west, far enough to meet up with a Russian trade vessel to take your passengers on to Siberia. If not, I will take them myself to Provideniya at the tip of Chukotka. My icebreaker will get your passengers home, Fox Ramsey," the veteran explorer said.

What Amundsen didn't say was that he knew of the suffering caused to the Chukchi because of the Russian Empire. Many in the seafaring world did. The far northeast Siberian tribe had been subjected to multiple attacks over hundreds of years. Whalers brought back the stories. Roald believed them. Chukotka held riches the Russians wanted. Roald was glad to help in any way he could. If he could get two of their put-upon tribesmen home, so much the better.

"The lassie still has her *dugs,*" Fox heard himself say. He hadn't meant to say anything about Anya's dogs. Surprised and grateful to have Roald Amundsen's offer of help, he blurted it out. "How much can I pay you?" Fox quickly asked, hoping to cover up his revelation to the two men. "I will go to the

Bank of Nome and withdraw what you need."

"No," Roald said. "No need for any money. I'm going in that direction anyway." He stretched the truth.

"Will the girl take her dogs with her?" Jafet broke in with his question.

"I don't know," Fox answered honestly. He was sorry he'd mentioned Anya's dogs, but it was too late to take back his words. Fox could almost hear Jafet's thoughts spinning about her Siberian huskies. Maybe Jafet wanted to race his own team in the next sweepstakes. Fox's shoulders slumped. What was the use? Happy that Anya could get home to Siberia, he was unhappy he'd said anything about her dogs.

They belonged to the lassie and not to him.

They were not his to talk about.

"When you find out, let me know, Fox." Jafet kept on the subject of Anya's dogs. "I might just know someone who could look out for them."

Fox frowned at Jafet Lindeberg. That was a queer thing to say, he thought. What did he mean, look out for them? He was that close to asking Jafet what he meant but stopped short of saying anything further. Instead, he turned to Roald Amundsen.

"I *cannae* thank you enough. When would you leave?"

"The sooner the better," Roald told him. "Tell your passengers . . . what are their names again?"

"Anya and Vitya."

"Tell Anya and Vitya to get their things ready and be prepared to leave in three days," Roald said. "If need be, we'll figure out something for the girl's dogs. Find out if she's taking them or not."

"I will," Fox agreed.

"If anything comes up in the meanwhile, I'm staying at the Nugget Inn. Get word to me there."

"*Aye,* Captain Amundsen." Fox gave him and Jafet Lindeberg a polite nod and turned to leave.

"Fox," Jafet called behind him. "Don't forget to tell Anya that I know someone who could look out for her dogs."

Fox blew out a heavy breath and opened the door to leave. This wasn't going to be an easy conversation with the lassie, no indeed.

CHAPTER THIRTEEN

Xander crept along the edges of the sudden drop-off into darkness. The darkness meant death. His canine senses alerted him to this reality on every step across the wild, every step back home to his guardians and his pack. But the crisp air carried no scent of home. The arctic winds gave no sign of which direction he should go. Old scars haunted him. While he wouldn't collapse in a full fit, weakness would strike his muscles and bones and slow his step. Forced to, he would have to sit for a long period until he recovered. During these times, his watch eyes blurred. This confused him but did not stop him.

Bad memories flashed in front of any trail he tried to take. Whips struck at him. Gunshots cracked the skies. Fangs caught at his body. Blood spattered in his path. The bear attacked. The wolf did not, but the gray beast that came out of nowhere did. Kill or be killed. Xander survived. The beast did not. Zellie did not.

Xander missed Zellie. He missed Anya and Rune and all the others in his pack. When their faces flashed in front of him, his keen senses alerted to the trail ahead and he got up and moved with purpose. At times the scent of home struck his muzzle, and he picked up his step. Instinctively he knew he was still far away from his loved ones. When he lost their scent and the trail ahead confused him, he'd tilt his head to the heavens and howl for their companionship.

Alone in the wilderness, he ached to be home.

Zeke and Homer had put in a full month's work at the Pioneer mines and were in their quarters packing up to head home to their remote cabin in the hills well outside Nome. Both men preferred the isolation of the mountains to the crowds in town or at the mines. They'd stayed at their mine quarters rather than trudging home each week, wanting to check on Anya and her dogs routinely. Grateful she'd survived her ordeal over the ice in the Bering Sea, they still worried over her and Rune. The boy had been gone a long time. No telling if he was ever coming back.

"*Hallo,* fellas," Leonhard Seppala greeted them as he came inside their shared quarters. He saw the miners packing and intended to do the same thing. Constance expected him home. He had more on his mind tonight than usual to talk over with her. Jafet had given him a new job. It would mean more time working with sled dogs and less time at the mines or at home. Sepp loved to work with dogs. Constance knew this. She loved dogs, too; so much so that he'd wanted to bring the bullied husky pup home to her. Thor was the piebald pup's name, he remembered. Sepp had wanted to keep the young dog but that hadn't worked out. He didn't bring a new dog home.

Now, that might change.

"Zeke, Homer," Sepp said. "I've got a question."

"Sure, Sepp," Zeke muttered, then stopped what he was doing.

So did Homer.

"Did you fellas ever find the Chukchi girl and the Viking boy and their Siberian huskies?"

Zeke wore a quizzical expression, surprised Sepp remembered the details of their conversation at the Discovery Saloon. It had been awhile.

"Sure did, Sepp," Zeke told him. "At least

the girl; Anya is her name. The boy, Rune, left Nome. We don't know where he is or if he's all right. Sure hope so."

Sepp listened with more attention than he usually gave to the miners. He hoped the boy was all right. Most of Sepp's attention went to his work and his long workday. Little else got his notice. Right now, the idea of *Sibirsk hunder* most certainly did.

"So Anya is here?"

"Yep," Zeke assured him.

"She is here with her dogs?"

"Yep, she's here with her dogs, if that's what you're asking," Zeke said, puzzled over this.

Sepp looked Zeke and Homer straight in the eye.

"Would you fellas take me to her? I would like to meet her and her dogs."

"Why, Sepp?" Zeke questioned.

Fair enough, Sepp thought. He'd like to keep his business personal, but in this case he couldn't. He needed Zeke and Homer's help.

"Jafet Lindeberg has it in mind for me to work with Siberian huskies instead of mala-mute freight dogs. He wants me to put together a Siberian husky sled team and train them up for a polar expedition some-time down the road. I don't know when that

312

might be, or if it will ever be. I also don't know who else to ask but you fellas. Would you help me and let me meet Anya?"

"I can tell you right now, Sepp, the girl will flat-out tell you no if you ask her to give you any of her dogs," Zeke said, his tone a bit angry.

"That's the truth of it, Sepp," Homer agreed.

Sepp picked up the protectiveness in the voice of both miners for the girl, Anya, and for her dogs.

"It can't hurt to ask? Right, fellas?"

"Suppose not, Sepp." Zeke softened his tone. "If you've a mind to meet Anya, let's get going. She's in the Eskimo village just outside of town. It's late, and we all have to get home sometime this spring."

"*Ja,* sure," Sepp said and left his gear on his bunk to pack later. "I'm right behind you fellas."

Anya ran shaky fingers over the necklace Vitya had given her a lifetime ago. She took the husky carving from around her neck and reverently placed it back atop the door flap of her Eskimo tent. This was where she'd left it to honor Xander, and this was why she returned it to its rightful place. Vitya had foisted it on her before she went seal hunting with Chinook, but she'd brought it back safely . . . for Xander. Spirit had brought it back safely, she corrected. In a way, the necklace came back from the dead. If only Xander could.

No matter how hard she tried to use her shaman powers to sense the time and the place of his death, she came up empty-handed. The last time she saw him, he was too injured to live much longer. Even if he had somehow survived, he'd been gone too long to still be alive. He would have come back to her. He had to be dead. That she didn't have to use her own knife to kill him gave her little comfort. She should have been with him in the end. He hated being alone.

Anya wiped her tear-streaked face, then wiped her wet fingers on her dress.

Rune's gift. She'd meant to get rid of it, but it was all she had left of him, except for memories. The soft hide dress brought Rune close when she knew he was far away, where he'd probably stay — far away from her. Just as the last time she saw Xander, the last time she laid eyes on Rune haunted her.

Vitya had come out of nowhere and held her in a tight embrace outside her tent. Her emotions wore thin. She'd just left Xander alone inside. He was dying. The next thing she knew, *Rune* came out of nowhere! Right away she broke out of Vitya's hold and ran up to him.

She'd hugged Rune close, but he didn't hug back.

That hurt refused to heal. It never would. The wool of his sea jacket still brushed her cheek. She'd feel cold until the day she died without his arms around her. She remembered the tension she felt coming from him, with his taut-muscled body against hers. He'd been upset with her. She had trouble remembering exactly why. It had to do with Vitya, she thought. She wasn't sure.

What hurt almost as much as Rune's rejection of her was his rejection of the dogs. He knew how important it was to stay and watch over them. They depended on him, same as her. He was sent from the gods to help the dogs, same as her. It didn't make sense that he'd left so sudden-like.

As she'd done many times before, she went over the scene in her mind's eye and tried to remember details. Upset herself then, it was hard to recall what happened and what words were exchanged. Rune had said things, but for the life of her she couldn't remember what! He'd asked about Xander. They'd talked about Thor. Then she yelled after Rune to come back, when she saw him leave. There had to be more in between. If only she could remember.

A sudden intuition hit. Anya called on the arctic winds to jostle her memory.

They worked in a heartbeat of mist and magic.

She remembered the hurt look on Rune's face when he saw her in Vitya's arms. That look unlocked the rest of her memory. She could even hear Rune threaten Vitya.

"Keep her safe. If you don't, I'll find you."

Then Rune left.

Anya put her cold hands to her flushed cheeks. Her world spun, but in a good way. She understood what had made him leave. It was the same reason she'd wanted him to stay. Slowly, Anya lowered herself to her knees and then prostrated flat on the floor of her tent, to pray to the Morning Dawn and the Gatekeepers, to keep Rune safe and one day bring him back to her.

He loved her after all.

"Lassie!" Fox abruptly called from outside Anya's tent. "We need to have a *wee blether.*"

The unwelcome interruption forced her from daydreams of Rune. Her tilting emotions quickly leveled. She stood up straight.

"Come in," she called back to Fox. Vitya was still with her dogs, keeping watch.

Fox pulled back the door flap and charged inside. His face was all smiles.

"I've got *braw* news for you, lassie. You and Vitya have a way to get home," he said in a hurry. "In three days you can both be on your way!" He didn't say anything about her dogs. The subject would be a tough one. Captain Amundsen would take them if Anya wanted. Fox didn't know what pot this might stir. There was more than met the eye as to what stirred around Anya and Rune and their Chukchi dogs. No, Fox didn't know about all their troubles.

"You mean it?" Anya stood frozen.

"*Aye,* lassie," he confirmed.

Spirits swirled everywhere, not inside Anya to upset her, but in the misty atmosphere of her hide-covered tent. Drums of shamans sounded in her ears. Their calls to the ancients echoed against the hide-covered walls in chorus.

What did Fox's news bring, besides spirits?

Anya strained for awareness.

Why now, and why so many spirits?

Their calls deafened her. The instant she put her hands over her ears to defend against the onslaught of noise, everything silenced in a heartbeat. Anya slowly lowered her hands to her sides. She understood the calls. They were calls to battle: *It begins again. The ice storm is coming.*

The Chukchi girl in her turned warrior in that moment. Viking spirits turned her to shield-maiden. She must fight now. With her crude blade in one hand and her human spirit in the other, she must fight the evil after the Chukchi dog. Fox's news signaled the start of the final battle. There was no going back.

She must follow her gut instincts and her heart of a husky to vanquish the enemy. She must get Vitya to safety and try to convince her people to seek shelter from the ice storm. She must warn Grisha. Fox had just found a way for her to do that, but he couldn't help with her greatest challenge: to find the third guardian of the Chukchi dog.

She could trust only the third guardian to keep watch over her dogs while she was away. Her dogs couldn't go back with her. She would never do that to them. Anya had to find the faceless dog driver from her broken dreams.

She only had three days left to do it.

Rune had been making good time, he thought. At this rate he might make Nome sooner than expected. The weather had cooperated. He'd been able to pull his sled

318

out of Iditarod without any slowdown and, according to his map, Dishkakat was up ahead and Kaltag after that. Once he made Kaltag, he'd cross the Yukon River. The trail to Nulato wasn't far from the river crossing, but Rune wasn't going that way. He would head for the edges of the Norton Sound instead. Depending on the ice, he'd either cross it or follow the rest of the trail overland to Nome.

The possibility of serpents lurking beneath the Sound wouldn't affect his choice.

The condition of the ice would.

Rune had to go on his gut instincts from now on and not listen to any dark elves whisper dangers in his ears. His instincts told him to choose wisely. He intended to do just that.

He must keep alert and keep going if he wanted to get to Anya and her dogs before it was too late. This last thought agitated worse than any nightmare dark elves could cause. In restless dreams or in the light of day, the road ahead was clear to him.

Keep alert.

Keep going.

This refrain rang in his thoughts as he paced his sled along the carved-out trail. The sled ran so smoothly that he reflexively checked his dogs again to make sure Zellie and Xander didn't run in harness with them. He felt their presence. It was the oddest thing. He couldn't shake the feeling and actually didn't try to this time. How wonderful it would be to have the Chukchi dogs he'd come to love run with him one more time.

But that could never be. They were dead. As much as he believed in the gods of the ancients, he didn't believe in life after death — in the mist and magic of the hereafter, maybe, but not come back to Native Earth. Too bad, he thought. It would be a marvel to run a sled with Zellie's intelligent guidance and Xander's shrewd strength. The experience of the All Alaska Sweepstakes would never be his again. Rune swallowed a lump of pride. He'd had the thrill once. He did have that.

The Chukchi dogs were the marvel. Zellie and Xander and Mushroom ran the race. Their amazing performance had nothing to do with him and everything to do with generations of careful breeding. Gentle-born, they left this trait home when on the race trail and put their all into speed and endurance. Pride welled up again inside Rune. From the start, the Siberian huskies had taken to him, of all people. No one could ever take that away.

Rune was getting off focus, letting his feelings drive his sled now.

Keep alert.

Keep going.

Better, Rune thought. Don't think about what can never be, but what will be if he didn't keep a sharp eye on the trail ahead. Anything could slow him down. Anything could be waiting in shadow to strike, land or sea. He'd learned that lesson well enough by this time. Rune urged his sled team on, giving out a kissing sound to speed up the dogs. They immediately responded to his command. He didn't need to crack a whip over them. It wasn't that the dogs had slowed down, but he had, with his thoughts of what could never be.

Rune blinked against the site up ahead. His eyes were playing tricks on him again.

"Whoa! Whoa!" He stopped his team of twelve so suddenly, they slid in their tracks before they could come to a complete halt. None collided, but they came close. Half of the dogs barked in protest. The other half stared ahead in the same direction as Rune.

Something was coming.

The black and white husky ran up on them all so fast, it took Rune by surprise. Rune stood frozen. Disbelief coursed through him. His malamute team didn't seem fazed by the newcomer; the dog was no threat to them. Some whimpered a greeting. Some danced restlessly in their harnessed position. Some sat silently and trained their eyes on their surroundings, ignoring the new dog.

Not until the lushly furred, hard-bodied, black and white husky nearly knocked Rune down, jumping all over him, did Rune realize it was Xander! No ghost. No made-up vision. But Xander in the flesh!

"Good boy, good boy," Rune praised through his tears. "You stayed alive. You stayed alive. Good boy." Rune knelt down and hugged Xander tight. He welcomed every kiss on his face, lick on his hands, and push against his body Xander gave him. The two ended up in a pile in the snow, so happy to see each other again. The shock of their meeting would take awhile to wear off.

The scent of home overwhelmed Xander. He was close, having found one of his guardians. He was close. Instinctively, Xander sensed this. Whimpers built up inside him at his intuition. Flashes of memory of Anya and his pack spurred him to bark.

Rune sat up.

"It's all right, boy. I think I understand," he said in a quiet voice, then reached to give

Xander scratches behind his ears. Rune met Xander's watch-blue eyes and saw the pain of a lifetime in them. The animal had been through a lot. To have survived his ordeals so far, then to have found Rune in the isolation of the vast Alaska frontier, was nothing short of a miracle. How Xander had managed to find the arctic will to live, Rune could never know. All that mattered was he had.

Anya believed Xander had died!

Rune couldn't wait for her to find out he had not.

"Hey, boy, let's get you checked and make sure you're all right," Rune said in his still-quiet voice, and ran his hands over Xander's back, his legs and paw pads.

Xander stood still and didn't protest.

Rune could feel scars. *Like mine,* he thought.

"We've both beat the devil," he said, more lightheartedly than he felt. They'd beat the devil so far. They had a ways to go yet in this fight. Rune didn't let the dark reality discourage him. This was a happy day. He couldn't wait to see Anya's expression when she saw her beloved Chukchi dog again. For that matter, he couldn't wait to see how excited Xander would be, either.

"Fella, you want to pull a sled again?"

Rune asked, at the same time rifling through the gear in his sled basket for more harnessing. Rune didn't think he could add Xander to his team without causing some disturbance to his malamutes. It was worth it to take a little time now and get everything sorted out so Xander could run with them the rest of the way to Nome.

Xander's friskiness picked up when he saw Rune's actions. He gave out short barks in excitement.

Rune didn't want to put Xander on a leash or put him in the basket of the sled. Xander wouldn't like either one. What he thought Xander would like was to work in his familiar position in front of the sled. Huskies were working dogs. Xander was no exception. Even after all the animal had been through, he'd rather work than ride.

At the next rest stop in Kaltag, Rune would water and feed Xander. Xander had fended for himself in the wild for a long time. That's what Rune intended to give him, time. Rune thought of the sled dog command and would go easy on Xander. The husky wouldn't have to mush until he was ready.

After two days of searching for the third guardian, Anya came up empty.

She didn't have any more names on her list to check out. Fox had written down all the names of all the dog drivers in and around the Nome area, for her, with a careful explanation of each one so Anya could commit his list to memory. She was better at ciphering than reading words. Counting the two she already knew, the ones who drove for Fox in the sweepstakes — Iron Man Johnson and Charles Johnson — she'd found the eighteen others Fox had listed, twenty in all. There *had* to be more. She tried not to panic, but tomorrow she and Vitya were supposed to go with Captain Amundsen and begin their journey back home across the great sea!

She'd looked into the faces of all the dog drivers on Fox's list, and none of them spoke to her spirit. None of them matched her instincts. Her human, gut instincts would lead her to the third guardian, she was sure; so far, nothing. In truth, she had no idea who or what she was looking for. Unnerved, she couldn't sit still. If she had to go looking all night for the faceless dog driver, so be it.

Her best bet, she'd thought, in trying to find the third guardian, was to search out all the dog drivers within range that she could, thinking one of them was likely *the one.* This would be the quickest way, and she only had three days. Anya had planned on this working, but it had not. Her instincts came up empty. She had no sense of ease from any of the men she'd met.

She couldn't leave her dogs alone without a safe guardian, and she couldn't take them back to the very place they'd had to flee!

This was an awful day.

There was no end to it.

"Anya, it's me, Zeke! Me and Homer have come to see you," Zeke suddenly called from outside her shuttered tent.

Usually happy to see the two trusted miners, she wasn't happy this time. Their visit needed to be quick. She had a lot of work to do between now and tomorrow morning. To hurry Zeke and Homer along, she went outside to greet them. Despite how she felt, she wore a smile.

"Howdy, young lady," Zeke said. "You're looking fit as a fiddle."

What was this about? Zeke usually didn't greet her like that. She looked at Homer. He appeared uneasy. This made *her* uneasy. They had to be bringing her bad news. She straightened to her full height of five-feet-two inches and waited to hear what it was.

"Uh . . ." Zeke hesitated to tell her the real reason they were there. The young'un wasn't going to like anybody wanting her dogs, much less even talking about them. "Uh, we've brought somebody here for you to meet," Zeke finally spat out.

Anya almost laughed, but stopped herself. No one was with them for her to meet.

"This here is —" Zeke stopped when he didn't see Leonhard Seppala. He turned an accusing eye to Homer. "Where in the Sam Hill is Sepp? He was right with us?"

Homer kept quiet and pointed in the direction he'd seen Sepp take off.

Anya followed Homer's direction and took off herself, running toward the stranger who headed toward her dog yard! This awful day had no end.

Zeke and Homer took off after Anya. This wasn't going well.

The man's back was to her when Anya arrived at the dog yard. At first sight, she didn't worry about the man so much as her dogs. They were loose! She'd get at Vitya for letting any of them off their ties. It wasn't safe. He knew it.

The dogs hadn't gone anywhere, but had gathered around the stranger. In fact they all seemed playful, the way they wagged their tails and whimpered in excitement around him. Anya's anger at Vitya faded, seeing that her dogs were all right — better than all right, it seemed.

They'd only acted like this once before . . . around Rune.

Anya's heart pumped. Her thoughts raced ahead. The stranger's back was still to her. He could be any dog driver, really. She shouldn't get her hopes up that he was the one. Swallowing hard, she took careful notice of his short stature, his thick head of tawny hair, his fur parka and native mukluks, and his mesmerizing effect on her dogs. They were listening to him, responding to his tone, and stayed gathered close.

As much as she wanted the stranger to turn so she could see his face, she wanted to turn and run back to her tent, afraid to face him and find out the truth of the moment. She didn't run away, but stayed frozen to the spot.

When Sepp noticed the Siberian huskies stop their play and shift their attention to someone or something behind him, he turned around to see who or what it was.

"Hallo," he greeted the moment he saw the pretty girl there. She looked half-native, half-white. This had to be Anya, the girl who brought the huskies to Nome. These were her dogs, lucky girl. The pup, Thor, was one of them.

From Anya's fixed expression, Sepp didn't

think she was happy to see him. Any hope that he'd leave the Eskimo village with these dogs vanished. He felt a little uncomfortable that he'd come on ahead to see her dogs, before seeing her.

"I am Leonhard Seppala. Sepp, to most," he said, trying to break the tension he felt between them. The corners of his mouth hinted a smile.

Anya's spirit soared, the instant she beheld Sepp's watch-blue eyes. The faceless dog driver in her fitful dreams finally had a face and a name.

The third guardian was Leonhard Seppala!

CHAPTER FOURTEEN

Out of time and out of patience, the golem slammed his office door on his subordinates, comrades all. He couldn't trust certain soldiers among his men. They were good soldiers, but not always for *him.* Suspicious, the golem believed the traitors wanted to take his place and take over leadership of the great cause to turn Mother Russia into an industrial and collectivized superpower.

Let them try.

The threat of harm to their families worked to keep men in line if they faltered in the cause. Threats didn't always work. Three among his top aides plotted against him. He had proof. He'd take care of the traitors tomorrow. Their executions would instill fear in the rest of his men. Fear was the golem's best weapon in this world and in the world beyond.

He was out of time and patience there, too.

Traitors were everywhere.

The guardians of the Chukchi dog had joined forces. This gave them power, power the golem didn't want any *kulak* to have. Two guardians had just turned into three. If he could, he'd execute the Chukchi girl, the Viking boy, and *Leonhard Seppala* tomorrow with the rest of the collaborators who plotted against him. The guardians could not be allowed to gather in full force. At least the Chukchi girl had done the golem one favor: she'd identified the third guardian for him.

The golem had enough on his human hands. Forced to, he put striking down the newly found-out and most dangerous kulak in the hands of dark spirits. Just as dark spirits readily brought news of the kulak to him, they would readily carry out his commands.

The golem eased down in the chair closest to him and lit a cigarette. The room had emptied out. The next time his so-called comrades gathered again at this meeting table, three of the chairs would be empty. That would satisfy. But it wasn't enough to satisfy his thirst for the blood of his enemies. He imagined the three guardians of the Chukchi dog sitting at this same table, then slowly raising his gun hand and taking careful aim at each one before he pulled the trigger.

In the end the golem would win in both worlds.

It was only a matter of time.

"Well, I never." Zeke pulled off his cap and scratched the top of his scruffy head.

"Me neither," Homer piped up.

Both miners were awestruck at Anya's taking to Sepp, and wanting to give him her dogs for safekeeping. It wasn't that they should have the dogs for safekeeping instead of Sepp, but that Anya would leave them with anybody, especially now. Bad things followed the young'un and her dogs. Zeke and Homer wanted to help, but they couldn't do much more than hide her dogs away up in the hills. That hadn't worked out so good before. Nope, Zeke and Homer were fresh out of ideas about what to do.

They reckoned that Anya wasn't, since she was giving her dogs over to Sepp.

She must have good reason and trust in Sepp, but she'd only just met him. If they were hearing right, she was departing Nome tomorrow and leaving her dogs here with Sepp. Both veteran frontiersmen stepped closer to better listen to the conversation going on.

"Promise you will protect them and protect their bloodlines. They cannot mix with other breeds. Promise me," Anya asked of Sepp.

Leonhard Seppala frowned at this. He didn't understand why the *jente* would trust him so quickly with such a task, since it was so important to the girl that the breed stay intact. She didn't know him, yet she trusted him enough to say what she did? Thor ran up to his side then and licked Sepp's hand.

Sepp melted at the pup's affectionate gesture. If he agreed to Anya's conditions he could take the piebald pup home to Constance — Thor and the five other Siberian huskies — right now. Sepp wanted to, all right. He realized he'd never wanted anything more. He felt an instant connection to them all. It caught him by surprise.

If he took the dogs, he needed to be upfront with Anya.

"My friend, Jafet Lindeberg, has asked me to find Siberian huskies to raise and train for expeditions. This is why I wanted to come here, for your dogs," Sepp admitted.

Anya stared into Sepp's watch eyes for long moments.

"When I return, I will help you," she promised him.

Completely puzzled by her response, yet

completely willing to take, and take care of, her *Sibirsk hunder,* Sepp nodded his agreement.

"*Ja,* then good," he said.

"You are Viking!" Anya exclaimed. Her expression brightened to a big smile.

Sepp burst out laughing. He'd been called a lot of things since coming to the Alaska frontier, but never a Viking.

"*Ja,* the Vikings were my people in the old days. I come from Norway." His smile matched Anya's.

They each felt a connection in that smile.

Their guardian spirits brushed hands.

Zeke and Homer stood quietly and listened to the two of them. Neither of them smiled, since their mouths gaped open. They'd never seen or heard the like. Their thoughts mirrored each other's. No matter how old you get and how much you think you know . . . you don't know Jack!

Anya's expression turned deadly serious.

"Thank you, Leonhard Seppala. I will return at the end of summer, with the First Light of Frost," she promised. "If I am not back, do not think of me again. You must watch out for my dogs and only them. You must fulfill the prophecy," she said without realizing her words.

"What prophecy?"

Gasp! Anya recognized her mistake in saying too much.

She couldn't take back her words and had to think of something, fast. The third guardian was never meant to know of his great purpose. He would never talk to ghosts as she and Rune did. If Leonhard Seppala learned the whole truth, he might run from it! His unwavering human spirit was the reason he'd been summoned by the gods. He could never know the danger he faced.

His ignorance of this truth might save his life.

Anya knew Leonhard Seppala was a marked man, or would be as soon as the dark spirits after them all found him and a way to get to him. She believed that the less he knew, the better off he'd be in throwing demonic predators off his trail. He didn't talk to the dead. He didn't invite spirits to his door as readily as she and Rune did. Dark spirits had to play by Sepp's human rules. It would make their hunt more difficult; not impossible, but at least more difficult and maybe even slow them down.

Anya played for time now. She hoped she had enough time to get back to Nome with the First Light of Frost. She prayed nothing bad would happen before then.

Sepp stared at the *jente* hard. The girl appeared young enough to make up stories, but old enough to know better. No one talked about things like *profeti* in Nome! Gold was all folks talked about, gold and dog racing. Anya was part native, and maybe it fit fine with her beliefs to talk about such things. That had to be the reason for it. She was helping him out, giving her *Sibirsk hunder* over to him. He liked her. She had gumption.

"I just meant —"

"*Nej,* you don't have to say anything." Sepp stopped her from finishing. He wanted to save her any embarrassment. "I can take your dogs?" He changed the subject.

"Yes," she answered with her head and not her heart. The last thing she wanted was to part with Flowers, Magic, Midday, Midnight, Frost, and Thor, but it was the first move she had to make in the fight ahead, so that *some might live.* All the dogs watched her, alerted to her actions as always. She'd been their only guide, with Zellie dead and Rune gone. They would have to let their new guardian guide them over the next seasons, until she returned home to them.

Flowers started to whimper. So did Midday and Magic. Anya tried to turn a deaf ear. She knew they sensed something was up. When she collected all their harnessing and gave it to Sepp, the rest of the dogs started to bark, even Thor. How could she look into any of their watch eyes, knowing she had to leave them? Tears started to fall. She let them.

"Thank you, Leonhard Seppala," she whispered to Sepp, then got out of there as fast as she could. She dared not look back for fear of changing her mind.

"*Nej, takk,* Anya. Thank you," Sepp whispered on the wind as he watched her disappear.

The ice conditions were not good. The uneven melt would be too risky. Rune decided against taking the shorter trail over the Norton Sound, favoring the safer overland route along its edges. He thought of the time before over the Sound, when his Chukchi team pulled his sled out of harm's way — when the serpent found them. Zellie was alive then.

Rune watched Xander run in harness. Xander must remember what had happened here. He must remember Zellie's guide. He had to miss her; still, he didn't miss a step on the trail. *Good boy,* Rune thought. The whole way from Kaltag, Xander hadn't faltered. Good boy. Xander lived up to the reputation of the tough yet gentle Chukchi dog. He was fast, strong, and enduring.

Rune couldn't wait to reach Nome, and he couldn't wait for Anya to see Xander.

Unable to cross the Norton Sound, his arrival would be delayed. For Anya's sake, he wanted to get there fast, but for his sake . . . maybe not. He could only imagine how happy she'd be to see Xander, but he didn't know how she'd react when she saw him. The last time Rune and Anya saw each other, she'd hugged him. He still felt that hug and smelled her sweet fragrance.

Her not wanting him to leave was what kept him going all these months. It took him time to remember what she'd said, but he finally did.

But what if she wanted him to leave when they saw each other again?

Rune tried to shake off his doubts. They didn't matter by this time.

What really mattered were Anya and her dogs. He needed to find them alive and well before he let any other feelings in. There was that word again, *feelings.* Feelings always got him into trouble. But they could also get him out . . . if Anya had the same feelings for him. He thought she did, but he had no way to be sure.

There was the gash across his face. Would she be repelled? Maybe she wouldn't want to hug him anymore. The cut across his chest he could cover up, but not the other.

Then he remembered Vitya. This memory struck a jealous nerve.

Vitya had feelings for Anya; that was no secret to Rune, after seeing Anya in his arms. How could he have forgotten? The problem was, he hadn't. Nor had he forgotten his worries that Anya seemed to care for her Chukchi friend. Boyfriend more like it, Rune hated to admit.

Suddenly these last miles to Nome, going through Golovin, Solomon, and Chiukak to get there, would be the hardest to travel. Rune couldn't let himself fill up with fear that Anya might reject him. He needed to keep alert and keep going. The journey from Seattle had already taken longer than he'd planned. If he feared anything, it should be that.

He gave a kissing sound to his team to speed the dogs up.

Xander already had.

It was fifty degrees above zero, if one. The summer weather in Nome allowed for easy travel by land and sea. The frontier city buzzed with traders, whalers, miners, tourists, and local businessmen and women — some with families, and some on their own.

339

The population in Nome still thrived, but the numbers had dropped from the Gold Rush heyday of twenty thousand people. A prospector had to go farther and work harder to get the gold since much of the gold in and around Nome — on its beaches or in the nearby hills — was either mined already, played out, or claimed by larger companies.

Still, Nome bustled as a frontier city because of its prime location on the Bering Sea and its resources of gold and fur in the wild. White and Eskimo alike shared the territory. The steadfast Eskimos inhabited the area as they had for centuries. The Russians had combed through their lands. Now more newcomers glutted their coasts and pushed across their wild. They endured this influx of the white man, not only living alongside them but sometimes helping to save their lives. The Eskimos knew how to survive in the Arctic and would share their knowledge if asked.

By example alone, they gave the white man vital survival lessons.

Chinook was no exception. By his deeds and by his word, he had stood by the newcomers — the Chukchi girl and the Viking boy and their dogs — no matter the threat to him in doing so. Anya was shaman. Rune walked with spirits. The spirits guided their dogs. Chinook knew it and believed it because he believed in the spirits of his people. The gods lived in the heavens, on Native Earth, and in the Deep. Their presence gave him peace. But bad spirits sometimes broke into that peace.

Bad spirits chased after Anya, Rune, and their dogs.

It would take more than offering shelter to help them escape the bad spirits. Ever since Anya left with the Chukchi boy, and then left her dogs with the white dog driver, Chinook had asked the shaman in his village to pray for their safety. The rituals and traditions of his people would help watch over them all, Chinook had to believe.

Summer weather meant good summer trading to Chinook. He went back to work at his trade store, with Anya gone from his village, and her dogs, too. There he could keep a better ear out for news of any trouble. His trade business was always brisk. Locals talked as much as they traded. If anything had happened to Anya, to Rune, or to their dogs, Chinook thought he'd hear about it.

The door to his store burst open. Chinook looked up, then got up from his seat behind the counter. Ghosts came in — two of them.

Rune charged in with Xander!

Chinook stood stock-still in disbelief.

Rune had come back to Nome, and Xander had come back from the dead.

"Where is Anya, Chinook?" Rune demanded. "Where are the dogs? I went to your village. They are not there! Where are they? Where is Anya? Are they all dead? Are they, Chinook? You tell me, and you tell me *now*!"

Xander whimpered at Rune's side. He reflexively put his head under Rune's hand, needing a scratch behind his ears and reassurance things were all right. His canine senses told him they were not.

Chinook read the fear on Rune's face and heard the same fear in Xander's cries.

"They are not dead. They are all alive." Chinook made sure to be clear with such important words.

Rune relaxed enough for his hand to feel Xander beneath it. He reflexively scratched behind Xander's ears and felt some of his own tension let go then. *They are not dead. They are all alive.* He repeated the words over and over in his head so that his heart could believe it.

But then he tensed up again and let go of Xander.

"Chinook, where are they?"

"The dogs are here and Anya has gone

back to her home village."

Chinook's brutal honesty hit Rune hard. Her dogs were close, but Anya was not. His heart sank at this news.

"Did Vitya go with her?" Rune asked before he could stop himself. He didn't want to know anything about Vitya!

"Yes."

Chinook's simple answer complicated Rune's life more than anything else ever had. The girl he loved had chosen the boy she loved. It wasn't Rune. In a way, he was glad he'd missed Anya's leaving — leaving him.

"When did they go?"

Chinook frowned at Rune's continued distress. Why wasn't news of Anya's safety calming him? As soon as he'd asked himself the question, Chinook knew the answer. Rune had feelings for Anya. He was jealous. Chinook understood, but he wasn't sure what to say to bring ease to Rune.

"At the end of the winter season, weeks ago."

Rune didn't think to ask how or who took them. He tried not to think at all.

Xander whimpered low at Rune's side but didn't try for any more scratches behind his ears.

Chinook wanted to ask questions about

how Xander could be alive and how he ended up with Rune, but his questions could wait. The boy was too upset for such conversation.

"Where are Anya's dogs?" Rune asked in a flat tone.

"With a dog driver at the Pioneer Mining Company," Chinook said and tried to keep the same lack of emotion to his voice as Rune's.

"What's his name?"

Chinook answered, "Leonhard Seppala."

"C'mon, Xander," Rune ordered, worried all over again about Anya's dogs. Her dogs were working the mines! They could die from their labors alone, if not from the whip of a cruel dog driver or a bullet from a just-as-cruel mine owner!

The door to the trade store stood open. Rune charged outside with Xander behind him, without a word of goodbye to Chinook.

The steadfast Eskimo understood. He sent prayers to the gods to go with Rune and the black and white Siberian husky. Xander's watch eyes had turned bright again. The blue of the sky shone in them. A miracle Chinook would not question. He must get word of their safe return to Zeke and Homer in the distant hills. The miners must learn of this miracle.

■ ■ ■ ■

Anya and Vitya would be home soon. Their coastal village lay just ahead.

Vitya was excited.

Anya was anything but.

The two traveled together, but that's where any similarity ended in terms of their responses to coming home. Their Anquallat village was home to Vitya, but to Anya home lay across the great sea with Flowers, Magic, Midday, Midnight, Frost, and Xander's feisty pup, Thor. Her dogs were the only home she longed for now. Not this one.

She needed to return to Siberia to warn Grisha and her people of the ice storm. They must listen to her warning and escape the iron hand of evil that would come down on them all. There was a chance some might live if they heeded her words. Anya already knew many would die, no matter what she said. But she had to return, and she had to try.

Anya didn't expect her stepfather, Grisha, to listen to her or even talk to her. He'd traded her away. He didn't respect that she was shaman. He didn't care if she lived or died, but he might care about others in the village. He might also listen to her warning about the Chukchi dogs. They were all in great peril. She must make Grisha understand that much.

He was a dog breeder.

The ice storm was coming for him — *especially him.*

"Anya, hurry," Vitya chided. "You walk too slow."

She kept walking slowly, and would go slower if Vitya didn't keep trying to hurry her up. Vitya was anxious to see his family. She was not anxious to see hers.

Grisha was her only relation in the village and that wasn't by blood. Her stepfather had reminded her of that enough times. He blamed her for her mother's dying when she was born. Anya never blamed Grisha for that, but she did blame him for trading her away. Mostly, she blamed him for never loving her as she did him. Somewhere deep inside her, she always had. His rejection of her would be fresh when she saw him again. Some hurts never die.

As upset as she was about Grisha, she thought of Rune. His handsome image warmed her cold hands and eased her nerves for the day ahead. She couldn't wait to return home, to him. Wherever he was, was home — same as with her dogs, but not the same. She loved her dogs, but she was in love with Rune Johansson. Thinking of him now made her shiver. She wasn't cold, quite the opposite. Any ice between them had melted.

When she could get back across the great sea, she'd look for him, and keep looking until she found him. Their destinies were harnessed together, and no dark spirits would keep them apart. Let them try, Anya challenged.

In this world or the next . . . *let them try.*

"Anya, look there! Grisha is coming!" Vitya roared.

Anya stopped walking and stood deathly still. She straightened her spine and stared hard at the black speck across the snow-covered tundra that grew larger as Grisha came into view.

Rune didn't care about the late hour. He and Xander were headed away from the Pioneer Mining Company office and set out for the hills beyond, where Leonhard Seppala, Sepp, supposedly lived. Rune's nerves grated. Glad Anya's dogs didn't work at the mines, he still didn't know what kind of condition they'd be in once he found them. Sepp could just as easily be a cruel dog driver as not.

Xander kept pace with Rune. The loyal

black and white husky's company helped keep Rune on his path. A part of Rune wanted to find a place to stop and sleep all of this unpleasantness off, or at least try. He couldn't do that to Xander. His pack was close. Xander needed to know they were all right as much as Rune did.

Rune saw a log house in the distance. Its chimney smoke greeted him. The house sat against a backdrop of open tundra. Tall evergreens crowded around the front. The midnight sun lit the friendly landscape in welcome. Rune relaxed a little, but stayed on his guard. So did Xander. The husky's watch eyes were focused on the scene ahead, same as Rune's.

Dogs started to bark, then to howl.

Rune and Xander heard them at the same time.

Xander took off in a heartbeat.

Rune let him. His pack called out to him.

Rune hurried, but he didn't run. He fixed his eyes on the closed door of the house and expected the dog driver inside to open it any time. There was too much commotion outside for him to stay inside. Sepp would want to know what was causing such a ruckus. Rune even expected Sepp to come out with a gun in his hand. So no, Rune didn't run, but approached the house carefully. Besides, he needed a little more time to get past his uneasiness in meeting Leonhard Seppala.

As predicted, the front door opened and a man came outside. He wasn't wearing a gun but a friendly smile on his tanned, outdoor face. In rolled-up shirtsleeves and corded pants, he could be any frontiersman. He looked tough enough, too. Shorter than Rune imagined the dog driver to be, there was no mistaking his Viking spirit. Rune had the same spirit. Fiery blue eyes didn't lie. He and Sepp had the same fight in them, the same heart of a Viking. This took Rune by surprise. He hadn't expected to feel such kinship with any stranger, much less this one.

"*Hallo,*" Sepp said and put his hand out for a shake as if nothing at all was going on in back of his house. The excited barking hadn't stopped. Howls ricocheted in all directions.

Rune almost laughed but stopped himself. He caught the accent in the stranger's voice. He was Norwegian. Rune shook the hand offered.

"Are you Leonhard Seppala?"

"*Ja.* Call me Sepp."

"Did Anya give you her dogs?" Rune accused more than asked.

Sepp put his hands up as if he had nothing to hide. He didn't.

"*Ja.* I am keeping watch on them," he said, and took his hands down. "Are you Rune Johansson?"

Sepp's question caught Rune off-guard.

"How do you know my name?" he quizzed, suspicious of Sepp all over again.

"The *jente,* Anya, said you might come along. And you have," Sepp said, his smile back.

Rune stared down at his feet and dug one foot into the slushy ground.

"What else did she say about me?" He could have kicked himself for how stupid he sounded!

"To let you help keep watch over the dogs," Sepp answered right away.

Rune looked at Sepp again. He tried to puzzle this out, what Anya had said. As if Sepp might have answers for him, he scrutinized the likable Norwegian from head to toe. Rune towered over Sepp.

Sepp didn't seem fazed by Rune's study of him. He'd spent years ignoring what others might think of him. He was good at it.

"The black and white Siberian husky that ran around back of my house, is he yours?"

"He's Anya's," Rune didn't hesitate to say.

It was Sepp's turn to wear a look of surprise.

"His name is Xander, and Anya thinks he's dead," Rune explained, with little reason not to. Anya had evidently entrusted Sepp with her dogs. If Anya trusted Sepp, then Rune decided he would, too.

"My wife Constance is around back at our kennels with Xander" — Sepp carefully pronounced the name — "and the rest. Come with me and let's have a look at the happy reunion," Sepp invited enthusiastically.

Rune didn't have to be asked twice. He took off in a run, much as Xander had minutes before.

Sepp grinned and shook his head. Young people usually made him smile. They were always running off and getting into some kind of mischief. Rune probably wasn't any different. Then Sepp hurried up, too. It would be a sight to see the Siberian huskies reunited. He could hear how excited they were. Xander had to be one of the first to cross the Bering Sea to Nome. Sepp was honored to have him.

Rune found Xander running back and forth, going kennel to kennel, rubbing muzzles with all of his pack in turn. This was why there was so much barking, this and recognizing Rune. Rune could see the husky pack separated by wood planks and wire-strung fencing, each in his own kennel. The Chukchi dogs had been accustomed to posts and tethers or running free, not to being housed in a kennel.

"Sepp, release the dogs. It will be fine. They won't go anywhere." Rune tried to be polite in all his excitement.

Leonhard Seppala did just that. This boy knew dogs, these in particular. They were certainly excited to see the boy. Sepp trusted Rune Johansson.

Flowers was let go first.

Tears stung Rune's eyes when he saw her put her head against the side of Xander's, then jump away, only to lick his muzzle again and again. Her whimpers matched Xander's, both huskies reveling in the moment. Flowers suddenly ran over to Rune and jumped up in excitement, then ran back to Xander.

Sepp went down the latches to each kennel and opened them.

Magic was next, then Midnight. The two joined in the mix with Xander and Flowers before quickly running over to Rune and then back. Once released, Frost and Midday piled on, leaving only Thor. When the pup was released, he didn't rush up to

Xander like the others, but kept his distance. He sensed the big moment. This was his father returned. He remembered Xander's scent and the watch eyes of his father. From that one time when he had time with his father . . . *he remembered still.*

The rest of the pack tussled and played in happy reunion, barking among them at Xander, and at Rune.

Xander pulled out of the group and looked at Thor. He sent out short barks for the pup to approach. Thor padded slowly over to him and then lay flat and rested his head on his paws in a submissive posture. This was his father. He instinctively lay down at his feet. He would wait for what to do next. His instincts did not guide him any farther than this.

Xander sniffed at the air and picked up Thor's familiar scent. He remembered the pup. Thor was his. As close to death and as shut down as he was when he first picked up the scent of his pup . . . *he remembered still.*

Xander bent his head and licked Thor's husky mask in that recognition.

Thor whimpered and got up right away, licking his father wherever he could find a spot.

Sepp's wife, Constance, turned into her

husband's shoulder.

Rune heard her muffled sobs. She was probably caught up in the same emotion he was. He realized he liked Sepp's wife. She had a good heart for huskies. That mattered a lot, especially if she were going to help keep watch over them.

Sepp caught Rune's eye and nodded toward Xander and his pup.

"That's something, isn't it," Sepp said quietly.

Rune smiled and wiped away a few more of his tears. He didn't care that anyone saw.

A few minutes passed before all the dogs began to settle.

"I am going to put the dogs back in their kennels," Sepp said and began doing just that.

"Hold on, Sepp," Rune interrupted and tried to stop him. "Why? They won't run."

"I believe you, but I have to for their protection. Other animals might come close. I have to keep these *Sibirsk hunder* separated and safe," Sepp tried to explain.

"No," Rune disagreed. "It's cruel to keep them away from each other. They should stay together but be free to run."

"*Nej*, Rune Johansson," Sepp said. "It is not cruel. The huskies will be fine. It is what Anya asked me to do. 'Promise you will protect them and their bloodlines,' she said. 'They cannot mix with other breeds,' she said. When I make a promise, Rune Johansson, I keep it," Sepp finished, his fiery blue eyes still on Rune.

Rune believed Sepp. Anya would say these things to him. She would.

"What else did she say before she left?" Rune had to ask.

"That when she returned, she would help me," Sepp said, then continued with what he was doing.

When she returned?

Rune tried not to get ahead of himself and celebrate this news, but Anya meant to come back! His heart raced at the possibility.

"One more thing she told me, Rune Johansson," Sepp added. He'd finished putting all of the huskies in their respective kennels without protest and turned his focus on Xander. Sepp had a pat on the head for him but no kennel.

Rune held on to hear Sepp tell him one more thing.

Sepp looked at Rune.

"Anya said she would return by the end of summer. She said that if she did not, I should not think of her again. 'You must watch out for my dogs, only them,' " Sepp

355

finished, his tone dead serious.

Rune put a hand to Xander and scratched him behind his ears. He needed the comfort of having the loyal husky close. Wheels began to turn in Rune's head. Anya's words were all caught up in them. He needed time to sort them out.

Time he didn't think he had.

CHAPTER FIFTEEN

Dark spirits whispered frantically among themselves. No enemy spirits must overhear. The Raven brought news that had them stirred.

Two guardians of the Chukchi had joined forces against them! They walked together now on Native Earth.

The dark spirits hadn't expected this so soon. They needed more time to round up their own forces and gather strength for the final battle. The Raven god of the Chukchi and the fires of Viking *Hel* still did their bidding, but the dark spirits didn't trust how long their betrayal to their own would last. Paranoid and suspicious by nature, evil spirits trusted no one and nothing. They trusted their powerful leader, the golem, but only him. Their trust of him was born out of fear.

Fear was the best weapon in any battle —

to hold troops together or to bring them down.

Thus, the golem ruled in their dark domain.

Two guardians had joined forces against them! This put the dark spirits in a dangerous place: up against a more powerful battlement than theirs. Enemy spirits had to be laughing at them. This, the dark spirits could live with. If the golem laughed, they could not.

He had ways of killing even after death. The golem must not find out about Rune Johansson and Leonhard Seppala joining forces on Native Earth. The Raven god must not betray the dark spirits, as they did their own, and take the news to the golem.

This worry set the dark spirits off-guard. Instead of going after Rune and Sepp, they plotted against the Raven, to find a way to destroy the Chukchi god first. This was the wisest choice, they all agreed. It should not take long if they plotted together. Once that was done, they would bring the golem's ice storm to the guardians and their dogs — *no kulaks can live.*

On her guard, watching Grisha approach, Anya looked for the harpoon he might be holding in his hand for her. He'd tried to trade her away and she'd come back. He would be angry at seeing her and still angry over the fact she'd released his dogs almost two years ago. Grisha would not have forgotten, and he would never forgive her. His right to kill her in their homeland still stood.

So did her right to defend herself, she thought. She'd lived in the land across the great sea under different customs and laws of life and death. The Alaska frontier had taught her much. Even though she was back under Grisha's laws, she didn't have to accept his will. She had her own arctic will. She had the right to defend herself.

Her knife rested deep in the pocket of her fur kerker. She still wore her sealskin parka in spite of the warm day. This day reminded her of the time she'd left her grandmother and her village so long ago. That day had been warm. Her parka had irritated her skin, but she'd kept it on all the way to Markova. Beneath her parka, Anya wore Rune's soft hide dress. It was adorned so beautifully with beads and embroidery, she thought of her grandmother. Nana-tasha wore such dresses. This thought helped give Anya courage to face Grisha and the threat of death he brought.

Grisha did not guide a sled and dog team

toward her. He did not have a harpoon in his hands. This surprised Anya, but she still held her ground against him. He had on the same kerker as she and the same hide leggings. His hood was off. His wiry hair brushed up in the stiff breezes. It wasn't coal black anymore, but shades of snowy gray. He'd aged. Anya shouldn't be surprised by this change, but she was. She never thought anything could affect her cold stepfather. Least of all her, she couldn't help thinking. She'd never had any effect on him.

He *never* loved her.

"Hello, Grisha!" Vitya called out in a Chukchi roar.

"Hello!" Grisha called back to Vitya, but his eyes were on Anya.

Frozen to the spot, defiant, Anya didn't look away. She made sure of her knife, ready to use it. Grisha had traded her away without as much as a goodbye for her. She had no hello for him. Her heart pounded. The Chukchi warrior in her alerted to the moment. She must prevail.

Grisha stood in front of her by this time . . . but that was all? He didn't say anything or do anything but look at her? His eyes had changed. Once clear and determined, they'd blurred to slushy gray. Tears caught in their corners. Grisha never cried. Anya refused to believe he cried now. He would never cry over her. She kept her hand over her knife.

Anya studied Grisha's face; the change in him shocked her. He looked worn down and worn out. The same wrinkles and crags in his weathered complexion were there, but his expression had changed. No one looking at him today would believe he was ever the strongest warrior, the best dog breeder, and the most able leader of the Chukchi in their homeland!

Unaware she did so, Anya pulled her hand out of the pocket that held her knife. Still unaware of her actions, she put that same hand to Grisha's face, moved by its broken expression, to give him some kind of comfort.

"My daughter," Grisha whispered and pulled her into a tight hug. He put all his heart into the arms he held around his child — the child he'd abandoned and traded away.

This moment had taken father and daughter a lifetime to reach.

Anya cried against Grisha's shoulder and hugged him back with all the love she'd saved up for fifteen years to give her father.

Vitya stood back to give them room for this meeting. He could only guess how Anya must be feeling. Hard as it was, Vitya decided to wait to marry her until she settled back into life in their village. By the end of this summer season and before the first frost, she would be his wife and they would live in their own yaranga. He wasn't worried, just impatient.

Anya was *his.*

He'd gone all the way across the great sea to fetch her back.

She was *his.*

"*Awrite,* laddie!" Fox said the instant he spotted Rune coming his way. Fox had just come inside his mining office but hadn't shut the door behind him. "It's about time you came to visit," he joked. He'd seen Rune since he'd returned to Nome, but the lad hadn't come to his mine digs and his dog yard yet. "Sit yourself *doon* and we'll have a *blether.*"

"*Hallo,* Fox." Rune readily followed his friend inside.

Xander followed them both.

"There's a good *dug,* Xander," Fox praised the handsome husky, all the while giving his head a friendly pat. What a relief that the dog still lived.

Both men settled into wood chairs on opposite sides of Fox's desk.

Xander settled beneath it.

"I'm *that* glad you're here, lad," Fox said, starting the conversation. "I'm curious about you and Sepp working together. He's a good man and a good miner and dog driver for Jafet Lindeberg. Sepp hasn't been working at the Pioneer mines. News travels fast around here. I thought maybe you could tell me the reason, since you *bide* with him *noo*," Fox said in a friendly way.

Rune had to smile. He guessed how curious Fox must be. He trusted Fox. His motives were always good. Rune didn't mind that the Scot wanted to know about his working relationship with Leonhard Seppala. The love of the Siberian husky linked them together, Sepp included.

"We're keeping watch over Anya's dogs until she returns," Rune told Fox.

"Are you *noo*? It is *braw* news the lassie is coming back."

Rune sent a silent prayer to the heavens that she would. He'd come up with a plan to make sure. That's where Fox came in and why Rune had come to see him.

"Tell me, lad, does keeping watch mean you're going into the *dug* breeding business?" Fox asked good-naturedly. "If it does, I'll take more."

Rune chuckled at this.

363

"It does. If Anya and Sepp give the go-ahead, you'll have more Siberian huskies," Rune offered. "That's a ways off, Fox. Sepp needs more time and more dogs to successfully breed the Chukchi dog here."

Rune didn't want to place Fox in the middle of danger again. The less Fox had to do with him and with Sepp, the better for his Scottish friend. Rune wasn't fooled by any letup in the trouble that followed him — and now Sepp. Demonic spirits still followed. Rune didn't want the dark spirits that hid in shadow to keep after Fox.

"*Aye,* I thought so!" Fox enthused. This was good news to Fox, that Sepp wanted to breed Siberian huskies. Fox meant to keep on mining and keep on dog racing, but not become a breeder himself. News of the tremendous showing of the Siberian husky still ricocheted throughout the Seward Peninsula, with many requests already to breed his winning sled dogs with their Alaskan husky mixes. Since he wasn't a dog breeder, he was *that* glad Sepp wanted to be.

"Fox," Rune said, needing to get to it. "I've wired my father and asked him to meet me here in Nome as soon as he can. He's on his way and will arrive within the week if the weather holds. I'm taking the

Storm he's bringing, across the Bering Sea to Anadyr. I want to trade for more Chukchi dogs for Sepp's breeding kennels. Do you want to come with me for more dogs? I wanted to make sure before I left Nome. I owe you."

What Rune really wanted to tell Fox was that Fox had helped save the Siberian husky breed by rescuing so many of them from Russia, and by their doing so well in the last sweepstakes. The huskies were no longer called rats in the Alaska District. They had a strong footing on the American frontier and would never lose it. Rune came to this conclusion on his own. No spirit had to spell it out for him. But Rune was not about to say anything to Fox and get any worries stirred — maybe one day they would have that conversation, but not now.

"*Haud* on, lad. You *d'nee* owe me anything. I have all the *dugs* I can handle but *noo* that I think on it, Iron Man Johnson might want to tag along with you. He's been talking of trading for his own team of Siberian huskies. I'll talk to him and see if he wants to go. If he does, will you take him?"

"*Ja,* I will." Rune was happy to help Fox in any way he could. "Tell him to be ready within the week."

"*Aye,* laddie," Fox said and put his hand

out to shake on it.

Rune waited at the dock in Nome for any sign of the lighter boat that would be ferrying his father from the *Storm*. The venerable steamer was the pride of the Johansson and Son fleet, to Rune's thinking. He couldn't wait for his father to get here and he couldn't wait to get going across the Bering Sea to Anadyr. A lot depended on the trip — everything, in fact. He meant to find Anya and bring her back safely to Nome, to her dogs . . . and to him.

Xander would come with him. He needed the beloved husky to help find her. Once in Markova, Rune meant to strike out in search of Anya across the tundra in the direction of her coastal village. He needed Xander to pick up her scent and had no doubt he would. There was another reason to have Xander be the one to find her: so Anya would believe he was alive. Rune didn't think she'd believe anything but her own eyes.

She'd lost Zellie, but not Xander. Rune couldn't wait for Anya to know it.

Besides Xander, Rune needed his father to come with him. After they reached Anadyr and off-loaded their goods for trade, then made it to Markova by boat or overland trek, and when Iron Man Johnson had traded for his dogs, the *Storm*'s crew would be ready to return to the ship. Rune might not be back with Anya yet. His father would need to keep the crew settled for the wait.

Anyone but Lars Johansson himself might not be able to.

Reports were coming out of Russia that troubled Rune and others in the seafaring trade. Rumors of trade being cut off rumbled up and down arctic sea corridors. Russian troops might use their sabers and guns against intruders in their trade markets. It had happened before, and history could repeat itself. The carefully guarded balance of trade between Russia and the markets to the West could easily be upset.

Rune wanted to get Anya and clear the Gulf of Anadyr, along with his father, crew and all, as soon as possible. He didn't want any of them caught up in Russia's economic and territorial battles. He and Anya and Sepp had their own battle to fight. They didn't need any part of this one.

Rune thought of his last trip to the Markova Fair, last year with Fox Maule Ramsey. Both men had witnessed what Russian troops could do if ordered: kill in a heartbeat. Rune still couldn't shake the memory of seeing the native Even gunned down alongside his sled dog team of twenty huskies. The troops didn't worry about shooting the man, so intent were they on killing his dogs — all executed with a bullet to their heads.

It could happen again in the same heartbeat. Rune couldn't save every dog, but he had to get to Anya, and get her out of Siberia, to try and save her dogs waiting in Alaska. The gods of her people and his had destined them for this task. He didn't think about failing.

He didn't think about Vitya, either. *Ja,* Anya had gone back to her home village with Vitya; and *ja,* Vitya wanted her like a husband wants a wife, but Rune couldn't let this matter with so much else at stake. All of their lives depended on prophecy of the ancients right now. The past had caught up with the present and foretold the terrible future. This notion came to Rune in dreams, or maybe in his nightmares. He couldn't remember which. His dreams were all fitful. They'd stay that way until everything was over.

Rune spotted his father on the lighter boat that approached Nome's dock. Lars Johansson was taller than most and hard to miss in any crowd. The ferry had boarded crew and travelers from three different ships anchored out in Nome waters.

"*Hallo*, son!" Lars called out, and waved.

Rune had never been so glad to see his father. He pushed old memories of thinking his father didn't love him or believe in him from his mind. Rune was happy to be proved so wrong. He had family again.

"*Far! Hallo!*" Rune called back.

The two embraced. Lars gave his son a hefty slap on the back.

"I didn't have to do all that worrying over you after all," he joked, but then gave his son a second look. "Rune, what happened? How did you get that?" Lars touched Rune's cheek where he wore the deep cut.

Rune pulled away.

"It's nothing." Rune tried to shrug off his father's concern for him.

"*Nej*, it is something, Rune Johansson," Lars said. "Maybe you will tell me on our way back across the sea. I am patient." He tried to joke, but his worried expression gave him away.

Rune could almost read his father's thoughts. There had to be other injuries Rune hid from him. The slash across his face wasn't just any cut made by any blade. It looked too deep and too calculated.

Rune looked his father in the eye. They were the same height and a match in many

369

ways. Both could be Viking warriors of old.

"I am good, *Far*," Rune reassured him. "I would tell you if I was not."

"*Ja?*" Lars asked again.

Rune gave his father an emphatic nod yes.

"*Sa bra*," Lars said, then good.

Rune needed to get his father's fix off of him and onto the trip ahead. Lars's faded blue eyes still held a sparkle of fight in them. Good, Rune thought. His father could be counted on to help. Rune needed every hand on deck, even the captain's. Rune would ask his father to take the wheelhouse of the *Storm*. That might fool any dark spirits after them.

"*Far*, we're giving a dog driver a lift to Markova. His name is Iron Man Johnson."

"Iron man?" Lars smiled his surprise at such a title.

"I'll explain later," Rune said. "I want to help the dog driver trade for a team of Chukchi dogs. I made a promise that I would."

Lars smiled at his son. He knew that once Rune made a promise, he kept it. He liked that in Rune. His son could be counted on. Lars had family again, and it felt good. He and Rune could count on each other, no matter what. It sounded to Lars like one of those no-matter-what times might be coming up with a rough passage back over the Bering Sea. It was summertime, but the Arctic couldn't guarantee smooth waters. Humph, Lars gritted to himself. The Arctic never guaranteed anything.

"Come with me to Leonhard Seppala's house for tonight," Rune said, and scooped up Lars's duffle. "I want you to meet him and his wife. They're good people, *Far*. Tomorrow we'll get loaded and ready to strike out for Anadyr, all right?"

"*Ja,* all right, son," Lars agreed. "Maybe we take one more day to prepare the *Storm,* Rune. Is that all right with you?" Lars's eyes held a twinkle.

Rune smiled at his father, then nodded it would be.

The two hurried alongside, as any father and son might, on their way home at day's end. To onlookers nothing appeared out of the ordinary. To Lars and Rune, this walk home together was anything but normal.

Anya didn't expect any greeting from Grisha's wife, Gyrgyn. She'd been right to have low expectations. Of her stepbrothers, Rahtyn and Uri, either. None welcomed her. They barely spoke to her but for a nod. Anya sensed why, and she didn't care. She sensed they were jealous of her dead mother, Tynga. Grisha had truly loved Tynga. He loved her still, Anya believed. She rightly believed he'd never loved Gyrgyn and had married her only to have sons. Anya wondered how he felt about Rahtyn and Uri. The older boys seemed to worship Grisha but Grisha gave them little attention.

Anya was shaman. She wasn't here to worry over Grisha's family. The first-born of her kind to Native Earth — part spirit and part human — she was born to help all the Chukchi. She would treat Gyrgyn and her sons like all the rest. She would worry about all of them the same. Picking up on Gyrgyn's greedy nature the instant she entered the spacious yaranga where she grew up, Anya easily recognized Gyrgyn's gold fever.

Living on the Alaska frontier for so long, Anya understood how the desire for riches could destroy a person's life. It was eating away at Gyrgyn. Her fear of losing the riches she had, being married to an elite dog breeder like Grisha, was written all over her sour face, and in every cold movement. Where before Anya never realized the extent of Gyrgyn's greed, she did now.

Greed had no place in Chukchi culture and tradition. It was a hated trait.

Anya wondered if the shamans in the village who'd accused her of being possessed by bad spirits all her life would pay her a visit in her father's house. The last she saw of them, they wanted Grisha to run her through with a harpoon and kill her. They were jealous of her, as her grandmother had warned. Anya was a medium between worlds and didn't need to invoke a trance to talk to spirits. Spirits came looking for her.

Anya looked around the familiar yaranga and ached to see her grandmother fussing over the cookfire. Nana-tasha was the only light in her world as she grew up in this Anquallat village, Nana-tasha and Vitya. Anya sighed. She wasn't sure how things would go with her childhood, forever friend. Vitya loved her as a husband did. She loved him like a brother. Relieved he was home safe, she wondered how long he would remain safe.

How long before the ice storm would come?

"Anya, child," Grisha said as he entered through the door flap of their yaranga. They were alone. Gyrgyn and her sons had left.

"Father, I am glad you are home. We must talk," Anya said.

"Yes, talk. This is good," he agreed, and sat down opposite her at the cookfire. Grisha sat attentive. His daughter was shaman.

She spoke to spirits. He would listen to her.

"I have something very important to ask of you," she began.

"Is this from spirits?"

"Yes," Anya said, thinking it best. It would be easier for him to believe if the spirits spoke directly about this. In truth, they had.

"What then, my child?" Grisha waited quietly for her to talk.

Her nerves were on edge. She wanted to say this right. Nothing between her and Grisha had ever been so important.

"An evil storm is coming for our people and our dogs. It is not the Czar. It is not the Cossacks this time. It is not any warring tribe. There is an evil that will soon rule in our land. That evil sends a killing storm to us. You and all in our village must leave this place. You must take our dogs. You must protect them from the coming ice storm."

Grisha looked to Anya as if he'd expected this news. He listened carefully to her and did not get upset. She tried to reason why, and couldn't. He stared hard at her before he began to speak.

"Our people face into storms every day, child. We are born in storms, and we die in storms. The ice gives life. The ice takes life. Our ancestors lived through ice storms and so will we. It is our way. We will endure, child. That is why we are hated. We can take care of ourselves in this harsh place because of our dogs. They provide a good life for us. Without our dogs, we cannot endure. The evil after us knows it."

Anya listened to Grisha, transfixed. She could hear Nana-tasha talking through him, he sounded so prophetic. She'd expected to hold his hand through the conversation but instead, he held hers to give *her* comfort.

"The spirits are wise to speak to you. You have always kept a good watch on our dogs," Grisha kept on. "They have chosen a wise guardian."

Anya sat bolt upright. Grisha had said *guardian*! She peered from walrus-hide wall to walrus-hide wall in their yaranga, expecting to see her grandmother whispering in his ear. How else could he know she was a guardian of the Chukchi dog, unless Nana-tasha told him? Anya shot a look back at her father.

He had a gentle smile for her, and said nothing more.

Anya tried to settle by the fire again. More needed to be said. She saw no point in holding back.

"I am in a fight to save us and our dogs," she poured out. "I have seen the other side of the great sea, and it is our only hope.

Chukchi bloodlines can be re-born there. I tried to protect the nine dogs I first took there, and now there are only six left — six to save us, father, only six. The evil after our dogs followed me across the great sea, and follows me still. It wants to destroy us and wipe our dogs from Native Earth, so that it would be as if they never lived. This same evil follows you because you are a breeder of Chukchi dogs."

Grisha sat back on his heels and placed his hands over the cookfire to warm them. Long moments passed before he spoke again.

"I can help you in this fight, daughter," he said, his eyes still on the cookfire.

Anya's instincts sharpened to her step-father.

"I will give you ten of my best young dogs. You take these Chukchi pups across the great sea, and you save our bloodlines and our people," he told her. "I am proud to call you daughter. One day we will meet in the great beyond of our ancestors, and I will sit with you again, just like this, around our family cookfire, and we will speak of these times and how we met them as Chukchi warriors. I have no weapon to give you in the fight but our dogs. You will choose wisely, I know." Grisha's tight expression softened. He held Anya's gaze with his. "Take my love with you tomorrow and keep it for all time."

Tears streaked down Anya's face. She didn't care that Grisha saw her cry. Her tears were for him. Choking back upset, she struggled to get her words out.

"I will take . . . your love with me . . . only if you keep mine," she whispered to Grisha, and put out her hands for him to take.

Grisha took up her hands and briefly kissed each one.

"It is done," he said and let go of her. "You select the dogs you want and leave in the morning."

"But Father, where will you and the others go to escape the ice storm coming?" Anya asked anxiously. This whole conversation was going way too fast.

"Child, we will not run from the ice storm," he told her. "We will face into it as our people have always done. We will endure. We will endure because of you, my child," he said in a whisper. Then he straightened his spine and picked up his voice. "You must cull your last pups from your last litters and leave your home for the last time."

"Father, no!" Anya panicked. "You can

find a safe place! You must try!" she pled.

"You are shaman, but I am your father. I will do what I must for our village. I will keep watch. This is our home. We will not leave. It might be a long time before the ice storm comes. It might be a short time. You cannot know. I cannot know," he whispered, so softly now it was hard for Anya to hear him.

Anya fought her distress and tried to find her voice.

"Then I will go and select the pups and leave in the morning, as you tell me, Father." Her head spoke, but her heart broke.

Grisha nodded in Anya's direction, but he did not rise and stand. He could face the ice storm coming, but he couldn't face his daughter's leaving.

She'd only just come home.

CHAPTER SIXTEEN

". . . In the evenings, when darkness
descended over the water, and the ice
was lost from view, the sailors' hearts
filled with hope that they had outrun the
white death on their heels. But by
morning, as soon as pale dawn rose over
them, the ice shone more brightly than
morning light, and the sailors, standing
around in despairing silence, could hear
the grind and crackle of the ice floes."
Yuri Rytkheu, *The Chukchi Bible*

Rune could feel the water tumble and hear
it roar beneath the *Storm*'s hull. The Bering
Sea would not stay quiet on this crossing.
Natural disturbances, he could fight. Super-
natural ones caused by dark spirits could
turn this summer passage to winter ice in a
heartbeat, and trap the *Storm* and everyone
on board. Rune meant to keep alert and
keep his watch over these arctic waters. On

land or over water, whether he drove a dog team or steered a *dampskip,* the dangers that hid in shadow and waited to strike were the same. He had to keep watch over both.

On impulse, he ran his fingers over the deep cut on his face. Nothing human had done that. The inhuman bastards would try again. Rune cursed the gutless dark spirits that hid in shadow. The wolf and the dog battle as one. This was not just Rune's fight.

A sudden, sharp chill — like a blade — sliced across his cheek, then down to his chest, marking the wounds he'd suffered in both places. Rune reflexively touched his face. He knew what the chill was: the cold cut of death. It was coming back to strike again, and not just him. He couldn't let anything happen to Anya and the dogs because of him, because he'd lost his sword to the Evil after them.

He had to think about what to do.

Rune immediately traced his thoughts back to the time he slashed the Midgard serpent in two. His sword was swallowed by the deep then, he thought. Was it still? Was it buried somewhere in the sea . . . or was it stolen and back in enemy hands? Rune could visualize the enemy, at least one of the phantom predators after them.

He thought of Mooglo and remembered

what the yellow-eyed, inhuman evil had said to him in Nome after Mooglo had stolen his sword, then offered it back to Rune. Mooglo told Rune to "take the sword," because Mooglo could "steal it again, when and where he wanted."

Was that what happened? Did the snaking serpent, Mooglo, have the secret of the runes now? Had he stolen the sword from the deep? Rune already knew the answer to that. The cuts across his face and across his chest — the same cuts from when he was struck by his own sword in the dark waters of the Inside Passage — burned like fire. Fire and ice didn't kill him then. But the Evil after him and Anya and the dogs would try again.

Dammit! Why hadn't he put all this together before? Time had been lost because of his poor thinking, time Rune didn't have.

Xander was on the main deck of the *Storm* and stood next to Rune. He sensed Rune's upset and put his head beneath his guardian's hand. Canine instinct alerted him to the moment. Xander needed to be comforted. He waited for Rune's companionable reassurance.

"Good boy," Rune said, when he noticed Xander, and stroked Xander behind the ears. "We'll find her. We'll find Anya. Don't you worry, boy." Somehow saying the words helped Rune believe they would find her. He had to hold onto that hope, that and the hope he'd find his sword.

Hope wasn't good enough.

Only actions counted.

The scar at the back of his neck, the one symbolizing the secret of the runes, jolted him like electricity. Rune stiffened his spine. The fight was on. He curled his fingers in tight fists around the ship's rail and stared out at the open sea.

Xander jumped enough to get his front paws to the rail and faced out over the watery horizon alongside his guardian. Like Rune, Xander kept his watch-blue eyes open for any signs of Anya and Zellie. Old habits die hard, and some never die at all.

Vitya sat alone in his yaranga. His family had left the walrus-hide dwelling setup for him. His father had given up coastal life for a life on the tundra, following the reindeer. Vitya was not surprised. He'd known of his father's plans. Stirring the pot over his cook-fire, Vitya let the bits of bone and meat warm before he ate. When Anya was his wife, she could cook for him and for their children. He would craft a polog, just for her. Their sleeping box would be made of the softest of arctic furs. Vitya meant to use seal and reindeer and polar bear to line their marriage bed. To hunt the polar bear, he would go north along the coast, to the ice.

Anya would have the best yaranga and the best sleeping box in the whole village. The shamans would not dare shun her. No one in the village would dare shun her again. Vitya was a good hunter. For Anya, he would become a great hunter. They would have the best sled in their village, too, and the best team of Chukchi dogs to pull their sled across the ice. He would help Anya raise pups, and together they'd become dog breeders, same as her father, Grisha.

Vitya couldn't be happier for Anya, that Grisha had accepted her as his daughter. Vitya would never have let Grisha harm her with the threat of a harpoon or trading her away again. It had occurred to him before to harm Grisha for his mistreatment of Anya, and for not telling Vitya what he'd done with her the time Grisha took Anya away from their village. Everything seemed well now. There was no need for any reckoning with Grisha.

Vitya's food simmered over the cookfire. He should have removed it so nothing would cook through. His mind wasn't on his food, but on Anya's soft lips. They'd shared one kiss, only one. His Anya had been a girl of thirteen then. Now she was a woman of fifteen. He looked forward to sharing many more kisses with her — *with my wife* — in their lifetime together.

"Vitya," Anya called through the door flap from outside.

He jumped up and nearly bumped into her, he rushed so fast to greet her when she came in. He didn't say anything and tried to cover up his embarrassment.

Anya smiled at him. The smile faded fast. She had things to say. She sat by the cookfire and waited for Vitya to sit across from her.

"Vitya," she said in a whisper. "Please come and sit. I must talk to you."

He stayed by the entry.

"Please," she whispered again.

This time he did as she bade him.

Anya looked at him with all the tenderness her heart held for her forever friend. His dark midnight eyes mirrored his dark hair. His handsome features and strong build would win any girl in the village. How she wished he didn't want to win *her.* Their lifelong friendship had turned to love for him, but not for her. She loved another.

It would be wrong to stay in the village with Vitya. He deserved better, much better than her. What's more, her life carried her back across the great sea to protect her dogs. Summoned to the Alaska frontier by the ancestors and the gods of their people, she could not disobey. The cost of disobedience would be deadly.

The Gatekeepers would keep watch over Vitya, she had to believe. She would pray to the Morning Dawn every day for the rest of her life they would.

"I am leaving the village, Vitya. In a short while I am taking ten of our pups and —"

"To trade at the Markova Fair?" he interrupted, suddenly energized. "I will go with you," he said and started to get up.

"*No,* Vitya," Anya whispered hard, and grabbed his arm for his attention. "Please sit back down. I must go alone."

"I'm listening," he gritted out. He didn't roar. He didn't whisper. His voice went flat.

"You know I am shaman. Because I am, I must fulfill my duty to our people. That duty takes me away, back across the great sea. I cannot tell you more than that. I cannot put you in more danger than I already have. You risked much to come and find me, Vitya. I will never forget you for that, and I will never be able to make it up to you," Anya poured out.

She knew she spoke too fast, but she had

to keep going or she would never finish, her throat was so tight.

"Vitya . . . Vitya, I know," she carefully began, "I know you wish for us to marry and live out our lives together, but you must know that is not possible. Our destinies are not the same, my dear friend. This is where we must part forever. It is for your good and the good of our people. Danger still follows me. I must leave here. But do not fear for me. The spirits of our ancestors protect me and our dogs. Those same spirits keep watch over us all. Do not fear. Promise me, Vitya," she pled softly, her voice strained.

"Promise *me* something, Anya," Vitya responded. "If your path takes you to Rune Johansson, never send word to me of it. I will have to learn to live without you, but I cannot live with the fact you chose the Viking over me!" His voice built to a roar.

Anya's insides roiled — spirits, good and bad, whirled and swirled and poked and jabbed. So many things had her caught up. Vitya's upset was only one of them.

"I promise," she finally answered.

"Now go, Anya. Please *just go.*" It was Vitya's turn to plead, then he fell silent.

The same as before, when she'd had to part from her father, her head spoke, but her heart broke. She got up quickly and left Vitya alone by his cookfire. His tears fell. She didn't have to see. She'd broken his heart and would never forgive herself for not loving him the same as he loved her.

"I wish you Godspeed, son," Lars said and hugged Rune.

The *Storm* had been able to reach the Siberian coastline, since the Gulf of Anadyr was not iced in as it had been on Lars's last voyage. The waters in Russia cooperated, not only melting in the gulf, but the rivers, too. Rune would be able to take the supply boat and head down the Anadyr River to Markova. Two crewmen would go with Rune and the dog driver, Iron Man Johnson. On their return to the *Storm,* the crewmen would sail the boat, and Rune and the dog driver would guide the huskies overland. Lars's chest caught.

Rune might not come back with the dog driver. He might not come back at all . . . unless he found Anya.

Lars wanted to go with Rune, but he agreed that he needed to stay with their *skepp.* The men on board would be anxious over the rumors of Russian *dampskips* trolling arctic waters, wanting to run off any intruders to their land. If need be, Lars might have to weigh anchor and move out of harm's way. He wouldn't go far. He meant to leave Siberia, all right, but not without his son and the girl, Anya.

Old worries haunted anew. Lars's fitful dreams made sure of that. The dark elves had been busy telling him Rune was in a lot of danger and so was Anya. Serpents were everywhere, hiding in shadow, waiting to strike. Lars had his own serpent — the *Storm.* He'd get Rune and Anya safely back across the Bering Sea or die in the fight for all their lives. Rune was family. Anya might become family too, if Lars was right in believing his son loved her.

Yesterday they were just kids to him, but today that changed.

Rune and Anya lived in a very grown-up world with grown-up troubles. This realization hit hard, especially now, as Lars watched his son leave with Xander. The intrepid black and white husky meant a great deal to Rune, to Lars, too.

"Godspeed to you both," Lars whispered under his breath.

Anya finally had the ten frisky pups she'd selected in harness for their journey to the Markova Fair. The watch-blue-eyed group represented a mix of color, with some black

388

and white, some copper-red and white, and two in shades of gray. Relieved she'd gotten this far, it was her best plan to save the young Chukchi huskies — to get them crudely trained to the harness and then get them to the Markova Fair. Every year, breeders brought their dogs and goods for trade to the important gathering. People came from all over Siberia to find new dogs and make a better bargain for them.

Anya pinned her hopes on the strong possibility that others from outside Siberia would come to the fair this year as they'd done before — when the *Storm* came.

There had to be a ship from the outside in Anadyr. There must be. It was the only way she could get her young Chukchi huskies safely across the great sea to Nome. She needed to find a friendly ship. She didn't think Captain Amundsen would be sailing by their shores again anytime soon with the offer of a ride. She didn't think any Russian ship would help her. A Russian ship would be no friend, but would probably try to take her prisoner and then kill her dogs. Let them try, she mentally challenged.

If anything happened to her, all could be lost. The drums of the ancestors would fall silent. The Gatekeepers would close their eyes for the last time. Anya had her eyes wide open to this truth. No, she didn't trust any Russian ship to help her. She would trust a ship from the outside. Her dogs' lives depended on it.

The pups she'd culled took to their harnessing well. Anya knew why: because past generations of Chukchi dogs ran with them, gentling them, yet strengthening them at the same time. The pups ran with the arctic winds at their back and in their heart. Their speed at such a young age surprised her. Their desire to run and not stop did not. These traits would carry forward for the generations to come. Anya couldn't fail.

She had to get these pups back to Leonhard Seppala.

They, together with the six already in Sepp's hands, would determine the future bloodlines of the unique Chukchi dog. Thousands of years of careful breeding for careful purpose rested on the shoulders of the sixteen chosen. Fiercely protective of the young dogs that currently ran in front of her sled, Anya ached to see Flowers, Magic, Midday, Midnight, Frost, and little Thor. She smiled to herself. Thor might not be so little by the time she saw him again.

She would see him again, wouldn't she?

Her mood dampened at the idea she might not. Then, when she thought of

Zellie, Xander, and Mushroom, she felt worse. She wouldn't see them again, either. They'd left Native Earth. So must she, to be with them again in true spirit. But she couldn't leave Native Earth, not yet. She had a battle ahead of her. They all did. This was no time for her to lose focus, to forget her purpose.

Anya blew out a breath and set her jaw. She had weapons to use in the battle coming, four of them. She had her knife to fight off the dark spirits after them. She was still shaman and would use her Spirit to fight every shadow in every crevasse that jumped out at them. She had skills and the know-how to survive in any arctic wild, in this world or in the world of spirits. She had found the third guardian — *the one* dog breeder who mattered the most.

Anya couldn't let herself think too long about who or what she didn't have, or she might lose her resolve. But she didn't have Zellie or Xander at her side and never would again, no matter how hard she prayed for her beloved huskies, including Mushroom, to come back to her. She didn't have Rune at her side, either. Would she ever see him again? It would take a miracle.

Then, she believed in miracles. Anything can happen if you do.

Anya pushed her sled forward to the Markova Fair. Her stomach suddenly acted up, the same as it had when she was a young girl — when spirits tried to get her attention with their confusing haunts and whispers. She didn't understand what they wanted then, and despite being older, she didn't always know what they wanted with her now.

Anya had important business in Anadyr and needed a clear head to keep her pups safe. She'd no doubt that bad spirits lurked around dark corners, hiding in shadow, plotting their evil. Unless she kept her instincts sharp, something could easily happen. She couldn't afford to have nerves. In that moment she realized it wasn't spirits stirring her up inside. It was fear, fear for Rune and her dogs. Her fears for them were not going away. She had to control her feelings and keep her focus, and become the Chukchi warrior she needed to be.

Quickly, she gave out a kissing sound to her young dogs, telling them to speed up. This moment called for fight and not fright. This moment called for her to be on her best guard. If not, this moment could be the last on Native Earth, not just for her and her people, but for the Chukchi dog.

It would be as if they'd never lived.

■ ■ ■ ■

As soon as Rune knew that Iron Man Johnson had met up with a translator so Johnson could trade for the Siberian team he wanted, Rune took off through the already crowded maze of men and carts and dogs with Xander. He'd instructed his crew that had accompanied them to Markova, to help get Johnson and his dogs back to the *Storm* if Rune didn't return in two days' time.

Rune knew he wouldn't be back in two days, but he didn't want the crewmen getting into any trouble or getting upset with him not there. Russian soldiers, or at least their spies, were in the mix of people, Rune suspicioned. His men would be jumpy and would want to get back to the ship. He understood this. He also understood that his father would keep the ship in the Gulf of Anadyr's harbor and wait for him for however long it took to find Anya.

Within reason, Rune realized.

If trouble came the *Storm*'s way, his father would have to steer clear of it. Rune wouldn't hold out false hope of the *Storm* waiting indefinitely for him, just as he wouldn't hold out false hope of finding

Anya. The reality was he might not. He hated to admit he might fail. He wouldn't leave Siberia without her.

Neither would Xander.

They had a pact of sorts, a silent understanding, Rune believed. Out of instinct and fierce protectiveness, they'd made their pact when they shared watch out over the sea — watch for Anya. They would keep on going until they found her and not turn back.

Rune abruptly did a double-take.

Xander growled.

Rune could have sworn he saw the face of the ugly evil with the yellow grin that had confronted him at the Board of Trade Saloon in Nome — the same evil who'd stolen his Viking sword and then plunked in down in front of Rune to taunt him.

Mooglo.

The phantom image vanished as fast as it had appeared. Rune signaled to Xander to keep going, when he knew Xander sensed the same dark presence he did, and wanted to rip out the demon's throat, as Rune did.

"C'mon, boy, 'On By,' " Rune said, giving the sled command to pass and not be distracted by anyone or anything. The fight was coming, "When I want and where I want." Rune remembered Mooglo's prediction and knew the demon meant every word. Whether in human form or inhuman, the evil after them *meant every word.*

Xander alerted to the fight coming. His keen senses sharpened. He reflexively buried his gentle nature. The call of the wild sounded through him: kill or be killed.

Like Xander, Rune itched to head into the fight, but first Rune needed to find Anya, and he needed Xander to help him. The Markova Fair was a maze, more crowded than when Rune was here before. He had an uneasy feeling about it, but kept on through the mass of men and dogs. He and Xander had to clear Markova, get out onto open tundra, and make their way up the coast. Anya's village lay ahead, somewhere out there.

The same uneasy feeling hit Rune again. When he scanned the crowd, he thought he might not be the only one who felt uneasy. Nerves ran high among the dog traders. Enemies waited in the shadows. The year before, a dog trader — one of their own, a man from the Even tribe — had been gunned down along with the man's whole dog team. It could happen again and at this fair. The crowd had good reason for nerves.

So did Rune.

The mark of the gods at the back of Rune's neck suddenly came to life. The scar pulsed hard but didn't hurt. Rune couldn't think on what this meant, probably nothing. But then, when he realized he was almost to the very spot where he'd first encountered Anya, he understood the message telegraphed. His senses instantaneously picked up on hers, at this spot. Their worlds had collided here when they'd brushed past each other.

If he could do it all over again and relive the same moment, Rune would have gone back and apologized to the girl he'd accidently bumped. He'd meant to go back at the time, but he was distracted by the sea of Chukchi huskies that all of a sudden had surrounded him; so distracted he forgot to catch up with the girl. He forgot all about the girl after that.

The girl turned out to be Anya. He didn't forget about her now. Plagued by worry, Rune involuntarily reached for Xander and needed to make sure of him.

Xander wasn't there. *He wasn't anywhere!*

Rune cursed himself for not putting Xander on a leash to better protect him. Somebody could have snatched him and claimed him as their trade, or worse — *Mooglo might have him.* The crowd that bumped past Rune didn't faze him. He stood deadly still, and strained to pick up any sign of Xander.

It was not the time to panic. Rune tried to keep calm, but his insides gave him a fit. Anya would never forgive him over this. He would never forgive himself. He shut his eyes and rubbed his face hard, desperate for some idea of what to do, where to look for Xander . . . and for Anya.

When he opened his eyes to the scene up ahead, he refused to believe what he saw. This must be a trick. His insides stayed coiled. He closed his mind against such deception, and determined he would *not* fall for such a trap. It wasn't Anya he saw. *This was Mooglo's work.* Mooglo must have conjured Anya's image to get to him. This must be a test of strength to see if Rune had any fight in him without his Viking sword. The demon spirit played with him and taunted him with Anya's image.

Rune balled his hands into tight fists. He was ready to slay this serpent any way he could, but . . . he wasn't ready to disturb the spellbinding image conjured, afraid Anya might disappear.

Every possibility of what this could be went through Rune's mind but the right one — that this was, in fact, Anya, and that she was all right. He was too scared to believe it; too scared that this Anya wasn't real. Mooglo's presence loomed. Anything could be going on. Rune stayed still, unsure of his move. He couldn't trust anything he saw, as much as he wanted to believe he'd found Anya.

But he had.

For her part, Anya hadn't seen Rune yet, so caught up was she with Xander.

Xander had come out of nowhere and easily overwhelmed her, the way he jumped all over her and showered her with affectionate licks and kisses. Literally thrown off her feet and sent tumbling into a world of ghosts, Anya struggled for some clarity of what was happening. What demon spirit had hold of her? This couldn't be real. This wasn't Xander come back to life. *This was a cruel trick.* Demons stalked her and wanted her dead.

That had to be it. She was dead. She'd suddenly died and gone to the Gatekeepers. How else could this be happening? Where else could she be but in heaven with Xander?

Then again, Anya didn't feel dead — she felt Xander.

His husky spirit matched hers in that moment of utter clarity. They were not dead with the Gatekeepers, but very much alive on Native Earth.

Xander was real — flesh and blood real!

Anya wanted to kiss the ground and thank the Morning Dawn for answered prayers, but she held onto her beloved husky instead.

"Good boy," she whispered tearfully against his fur. "My good boy." In that remarkable instant Anya felt Zellie's presence mist near. At least she wanted to believe it. Zellie cried the same tears as Anya, together in spirit. "Good girl," Anya whispered, needing to believe Zellie was close.

Her young Chukchi dogs were still in harness and didn't go anywhere, but watched the big black and white husky that came up on them, curious but not afraid. Fear wasn't something they had learned yet.

Anya's shaman spirit raced through her thoughts and forced her attention. She realized the gods had not deserted her after all. They'd brought Xander back to her. Instinctively Anya knew Zellie was the reason. Even in death, Zellie had worked some kind of mist and magic to save Xander. There could be no other reason. Xander had been too close to death — to the edges of the Great Crag — to come back to life on his own. Anya and Spirit hadn't helped him.

It had to be Zellie.

Who else's husky spirit would have defied

the gods but Zellie's! Once passed, Zellie didn't obey tradition, but broke bounds and passed back over to this side on Native Earth. Anya knew it, since Zellie had sent Spirit to save her when Anya tried to save Little Wolf, and all but died herself.

Good girl, Zellie. There's my good girl, Anya silently praised.

The shaman in Anya had her convinced of the truth. Drums of the ancestors didn't need to sound this out. Arctic winds didn't need to whisper in her ear. Some things you just know. Some ties can never be broken. But would the gods of the Chukchi allow Zellie back to her peaceful sleep of death on the other side? Anya had no way of knowing. She wanted to believe the gods had rewarded Zellie for her bravery and allowed her back with them. She would pray to the Morning Dawn for a sign that they had.

It was a miracle Xander was alive; one Anya hadn't prayed for, since she thought he was long dead. Even though she held on to him and could feel he was flesh and blood, she shut her eyes tight, then quickly opened them to make sure of what she saw. When she opened her eyes she saw a miracle all right — the miracle she'd prayed for but never expected.

Rune!

Anya slowly dropped her arms from around Xander and stood on weak legs.

Xander immediately turned to the pups in harness.

The young Chukchi dogs yapped in excitement, their brush tails wagging.

Anya managed to stay standing despite her body's reaction to seeing Rune again. She felt on fire, icy fire, it hurt so much to not touch him. Her insides heated to a burn. She melted in the light of his bluest of blue eyes. Nothing else in life held any meaning now but the promise of Rune's arms around her. She'd never been jarred to such womanly feelings, never for Vitya or for any other man.

Anya was scared.

Rune didn't make any move toward her. He might not feel the same way she did. Held to the spot and the moment, powerless to do anything else, Anya couldn't hold back her feelings. They frightened her. She couldn't control them, and she knew she'd just die if he didn't love her, too!

Then Rune had Anya in his arms.

Fiercely protective, he held her with all the love inside that he'd saved for her. He could finally let it go. This moment completed him. Anya was all he'd dreamed of and all he ever wanted. Her body fit against him and stirred him to desire her, only her. The scent of wildflowers filled his senses. He'd never wish for winter again.

The pair clung to each other despite the many passersby and barking dogs.

Anya and Rune were oblivious to everything around them.

Rune took Anya's arms from him and looked down into her impossibly beautiful seal-brown eyes. He held her hands and kissed each one before he put her arms back around him. Then he put his hands to her cheeks and touched her softly there before he directed her mouth up to meet his. Slowly he lowered to her and then crushed her lips with his kiss. The commanding pressure of his mouth opened hers to him. He held nothing back.

Neither did Anya.

How could she? She loved him. He was her match. They'd been destined to be together from the instant they first brushed past each other. Nothing had ever felt so right than to have Rune hold her like this. The feel of his lips on hers was mist and magic and wonderful beyond her wildest dreams. Urges she never imagined awakened within her. She never wanted Rune's kiss to end. This was the most perfect moment in all of her life. Flushed from head to toe, Anya wanted to stay on fire. She'd never wanted anything more.

Passions ran high. It was up to Rune to cool them down. He couldn't take this as far as his desire demanded, not yet. They must wait. They must wait to be together. When they made it back to Nome, he wanted to marry her at the first opportunity. They were young, but they were in love.

"Anya," he said in a strained whisper when he broke their kiss. He kept his eyes locked on hers to make sure she listened.

"We have to leave here. It's too dangerous. The *Storm* is coming to take us home across the sea."

"To Nome?" Anya exclaimed. Rune's words were like cold water on the fevered moment.

"*Ja,* my brave and beautiful Anya," he said and lightly touched under her chin. But then it struck him she might not want to go, the way he looked with the nasty cut across his cheek. Rune let his hand fall away. He didn't want to force her to look at him every day if his scarred face turned her stomach.

"Rune, what's the matter?" Anya saw the change come over him.

"My scar, does it disgust you?" he blurt out.

"What scar, Rune Johansson? I love you," she whispered against the wool of his jacket; the scent of the sea on him was bliss.

Rune gently pushed her from him to look into her eyes. They never lied. The love and devotion he saw in Anya's eyes reassured him she meant what she'd said.

"I love you, Anya *Johansson,*" he whispered hard, then gave her a wink to make sure she understood his meaning.

Anya's grin matched Rune's. She understood, all right. She couldn't help it and hugged him one more time.

"Anya, we must hurry," Rune told her.

She pulled out of his arms.

"I know," she said, and quickly sorted her thoughts.

"I have ten Chukchi pups with me, all young dogs we need to get to Leonhard Seppala in Nome."

"Sepp?" Rune sounded surprised although he knew he shouldn't be. He knew Anya had left her six dogs with Leonhard Seppala for him to keep watch over and protect.

"Yes, Sepp. He is a guardian of the Chukchi, like us, but not like us. He does not talk to spirits, but even so, he is the third guardian of our people and our dogs. He is the one summoned by the gods to be a dog breeder, the only one across the great sea chosen for the important task. He has been entrusted with the safety of our dogs, of protecting their bloodlines. If he fails, all will be lost. Nothing will be left but dust and memory. The Chukchi dog will disappear from Native Earth."

Things fell into place for Rune. He understood Sepp's importance. The human spirit must prevail on Native Earth. Sepp was that human spirit, and by his deeds the Chukchi dog would prevail.

Anya wasn't finished.

"You and I must protect Leonhard Seppala. We cannot let the dark spirits get to him. They will try. I have seen them in my dreams."

"I know. The fight isn't over." Rune stated the obvious.

"This final battle will be the most costly to our people and our dogs if we lose it." Anya barely spoke above a whisper.

Rune pulled Anya resolutely to him and encircled her in his arms.

"Then we will not lose it," he promised her.

Xander suddenly barked, stirred by new dangers coming.

So too, were the heavens stirred. The past

had caught up with the present on Native Earth and foretold the terrible future. Arctic winds picked up and whispered in frantic whirls and swirls around Anya and Rune. The ancestors echoed their whispers and lit the skies in waves of the aurora borealis. Ancient drumbeats marked the hour, their message clear:

It is time.
It begins again . . .
   It begins again . . . and then it will be
               done.

Chapter Seventeen

The golem took stock of his situation in both of his domains, in the physical world and in the world of ghosts. He'd achieved much within each, and he didn't intend to lose any more ground in this fight to the finish with the enemy Chukchi, or with any other traitors to his communist cause. They needed to be killed off — all the traitors in both worlds. He'd already taken care of those in his ranks who had tried to undermine his power. They were dead. Fear controlled the rest and kept them in line. If any stepped out of line to come at him, they'd be dead, too. It wasn't a secret to anybody, the golem's constant vigil on them.

The Chukchi and their dogs might suspect that he kept the same watch on them. At least their gods knew he did by now. He'd been able to draw the powerful Raven god away, and had forced the Raven to fly against the Chukchi. The same as he'd done with *Hel.* The fiery Viking god had burned out. The golem eased at this thought, reveling in his dominion over these deities. They had failed him. They had failed to finish off the girl and the boy and their dogs when they'd had the chance.

The Midgard serpent had split in two, but the golem had recovered the sword that did the deed, and would keep the secret of the runes out of the Viking boy's hands. Without it, the boy was helpless. The girl still had her gift from the gods, but the golem would get that, too. It was only a matter of time until she was as powerless as the boy, without her Chukchi knife. The time for play was over.

The golem tired of the cat and mouse game. He was done with halfway threats and too many survivors left on the killing field. The Chukchi girl and too many of her dogs still lived. The boy wasn't dead. The third guardian, either. The little man shouldn't cause the golem big trouble and would be easy to strike down. If the three guardians were together, they had more power to fight him, the golem knew. Then again, without their weapons from the gods, they were weak. They were mere mortals. They could be crushed as easily as a finished cigarette under his boot. He wouldn't give the mortals a chance to call on any of their spirits for help.

The golem laughed to himself — he'd call on *his* first.

Russia was doing his bidding and following his commands. He demanded loyalty from his troops and loyalty from every peasant, every farmer, every shopkeeper, and from every worker in every city and every village. Anyone who dared stand in his way would be crushed under his boot. A bullet would do that. So would a sword. Starvation could cause great suffering. Exposure to the frozen reaches of Siberia could cause even more.

Yes, there were many ways to conquer his enemies in the physical world.

The golem reached inside his pocket for his cigarettes. He needed to savor every plan he'd made and put into place to achieve absolute power in the kingdom of mortals. It would be easy, he thought. Few suspected him of anything but wanting to help them have a better life, working behind a plow or in a factory, for the new agricultural and industrial Russia. The peasants would go willingly to collective farms and into the machine age. The communist manifesto would reign supreme, and all would become comrades for the motherland. No one would have means over another, at least no one but him.

The golem stomped out his lit cigarette. The taste of the tobacco soured. He thought of the one enemy who still had the means to stand in the way of his complete dominion in Russia — the Chukchi *kulaks* and their bastard dogs!

The ice storm was coming for them.

The golem would see that it did.

Zellie's amorphous shape twitched.

Too weak to come to any awareness of the deathly realm she inhabited, she struggled reflexively in the ghostly web that had her caught. Her canine senses sharpened to her dilemma. This was not a good place. This was not any kind of heavenly place where the ancestors and the Gatekeepers kept their watch. She thought she'd made it back to them. They'd opened their gates for her to cross in peace.

But where was this place?

This was not a place for good spirits. Instinct told her as much. The same instinct urged her to break free and get out of there. She twisted in confusion, and struggled at the impulse to run. Splitting pain shot through her reflexes and silenced any cry for help.

A new death was coming for her.

A death that knew she could still hurt, if the right weapon caused it.

Zellie hadn't experienced any kind of killing sensation like this before. The pain was agonizing. She would endure until she could no more, then she would die all over again and be done with this arena of death. Her canine senses reeled out of focus. Her memory faded, and with it, the ancestors and the Gatekeepers. On some conscious level, she knew they would never call to her again. They would forget her place in time. She fought to bring their memory back, desperate to hold onto the generations of Chukchi dogs and home — *home with Anya and Xander.*

Sensations of loyalty and love and companionship and trust singed in the burnt air around Zellie, teasing and taunting her with the cruel reality she'd never know any home with Anya and Xander in any kind of heaven. Zellie sniffed at the ashes in the dead air, desperate to pick up any familiar scent. Her ears pricked against each pain that cut at her, and prevented her from detecting any sign, any howling, any guide from the ancestors that might lead her out of this final darkness.

411

But the trap was set, and Zellie was caught.

The horror of her first death would not be the last she suffered.

Lars Johansson scanned the coastline for any sign of his son's return to the *Storm.* It could be days, dangerous days, before Rune made it back on board. As for his son finding Anya, Lars didn't think that possible at this point. She could be anywhere. Even with Xander's guidance, the girl likely had disappeared. It was too bad, all of it. Rune and Anya were all caught up with dark spirits from dark worlds giving them chase. Lars couldn't fathom how any of this would end. Nothing was certain. Each day could mean life or death. Each fitful night's sleep could bring the same end. Lars had little control over events, but he could control his own actions. He would not leave Siberia without his son.

The crew knew better than to complain, but Lars understood their nerves. They were anxious to get underway. When the men returned shipboard with Iron Man Johnson and the dogs traded, they'd picked up on the nerves running through the entire Markova Fair. Dog traders were afraid of soldiers coming to strike them down along with their dogs. It had happened before and many feared it would happen again. Times were bad and getting worse, the Siberians had said, through translators and broken English. No one was safe. Something was coming. Someone was there. Spies were among them. The Siberians didn't want to stay at the fair any longer than they had to, the crew told Lars.

"Something is coming. Someone is here."

These exact utterances caught Lars's attention in particular. They were odd things for grown men to say, and sounded like something a child might fear. Then he thought again. Sure, when the ice came at them in winter at sea, fears ran high even among his own veteran crew. Grown men were afraid of something coming. That something was the ice, relentless, unforgiving, crushing, and killing. Lars better understood the comments from the Siberians now, and could picture the ice storm coming at them in waves of soldiers with their sabers held high and giving no quarter. Last year the ice storm targeted one dog driver and one sled dog team. This year could down another . . . and then another.

He didn't want his son or Anya or any of her dogs caught up in the waves of ice sure to hit. The ice storm could kill on land and at sea, Lars realized. His chest hurt at the realization — the pressure hard to bear. The ice storm wasn't just after the native Siberians, but after his son and Anya! Dark spirits fueled the storm, the same dark spirits that stalked him in night terrors and foretold the terrible future for Rune and Anya and the Chukchi dogs! The situation was worse than Lars had ever imagined. *Many will die before this is over. Dear God, do not let Rune and Anya be among them.*

Lars wasn't a praying man, but he prayed now . . . to Odin. This wasn't a task for the Almighty, but for the gods of his Viking ancestors. The worlds that clashed now had nothing to do with heaven and everything to do with the fires of *Hel.* Valhalla was at risk. The very world from which his ancestors were born, and where they now dwelled, was at risk of perishing. Lars had no way of knowing if his insights here had any basis, but it was how he felt. He couldn't shake the idea that so much was at stake; that the fight his son and Anya were caught up in was a fight to the death for more than one people, and more than one world. If he stopped to think about it, *it was crazy* . . . but it was how he felt.

Lars blew out a tight breath and scanned the Siberian coastline again. He was the captain of the *Storm,* and he needed to protect his crew and all on board. The sensible thing to do would be to pull up anchor and leave Russian waters. Then again, he was a father and needed to protect his son and Anya and her dogs at all costs. He believed in his heart that his crew would be with him in his endeavor if he gave them the chance to decide their fate. That moment might come, but it wasn't here yet. He strained to see any sign of Rune, any proof of life.

The wait might kill him and everyone on board. He was captain. He was responsible. It was the code he lived by. It was the code whereby choices had to be made.

Lars felt he had no choice but to wait.

Their Fate was in Odin's hands now.

"What's wrong, dear?" Constance Seppala asked her husband. She was worried about him. He never skipped an evening meal and never sat in front of their fireplace, stone-faced and silent. Tonight he'd done both. "Leonhard, you must tell me what bothers you so," she said softly, and knelt down by his easy chair.

Sepp didn't have an answer for his wife. On edge all day, he didn't know what nagged at him. Nothing was out of order at their home place. The weather was mild. No storm brewed. No predators stalked. There had been no sign of bear or wolverine or wolves. The dogs seemed fine. He'd exercised them as usual, and let them run in sled formation in front of the summer cart he'd made. Sure, they'd wanted to run like the wind over snow-covered tundra, but the snows had not come to stay in Nome. Soon enough, Sepp thought, about the time the *jente* would return for them.

He gently brushed his wife's hand from his knee and stood up. The fire was dying. He reached for two pieces of wood and rekindled the flame. The crackling sound frayed his nerves when they usually comforted. He thought of the *jente,* Anya, again. Maybe that's what had him so worried. The girl might not come back for her dogs. He wanted her to, right?

Ja, it was true he'd wanted her *Sibirsk hunder* to train as part of an expedition team for Jafet Lindeburg's friend, Roald Amundsen. Sepp was happy for the opportunity, it turned out. He preferred sled dog racing to mining and discovered he was pretty good at dog driving, especially with Anya's dogs. Her *Sibirsk hunder* were special. They made him look good, Sepp decided. Accustomed to the big malamute mixes, the smaller *Sibirsk* dogs required a different set of skills to drive them, skills Sepp didn't realize he had. He must come by it naturally. Why else would the *jente*'s dogs take to him so, and why else did he seem to fit right in behind their sled? The dogs listened to his commands and were quick to obey them. Half the time, he didn't even need to say anything before they turned where they should, or began to slow for good reason. Puzzled by this, Sepp flopped back down in his easy chair.

Constance picked up her knitting and sat in her rocker. She would wait for her husband to explain things and wouldn't press him further. In good time he would talk to her. He wasn't ready to now.

Sepp stared into the fire he'd just rekindled. This was all about the *Sibirsk hunder* and Anya and Rune Johansson, he believed. His nerves were on edge because of them. He hadn't figured he'd be so worried over the young people, over whether they'd come back to Nome safe and sound, but he was. Despite keeping watch on Anya's dogs, and despite knowing they were safe with him, he still felt on edge, as if something or someone was after them. Sepp never thought like this, and it bothered him. He dealt head-on with whatever problems came his way, always

417

had, and always would. Then what nagged at him?

Deep down, Sepp never wanted to give Anya's dogs over to any expedition. He wanted to keep them home with him and with Constance. The dogs belonged with him, he was sure. It just felt right. Why did it feel so right? The Alaska territory was a rough place, and if dogs were needed for an expedition, then so be it. This was sled dog country and the animals should be fine, but Sepp knew they might not be, on any trip, to any pole. Sepp had his answer then. He didn't have to ask himself why anymore. The *Sibirsk hunder* felt like family, almost blood-related, and he needed to protect them, at all costs. The moment he'd first spotted the pup, Thor, he'd known it. The attachment was strong from the start.

It struck Sepp hard that he needed to do exactly as Anya and Rune had instructed. The young people meant to protect the dogs. The dogs would not survive without them. If it were not for the young people, the *Sibirsk hunder* wouldn't even be in the District of Alaska. The knowledge came to Sepp, and he wouldn't question the wisdom of it.

What had Anya said before she left? "I will return at the end of summer, with the First

Light of Frost. If I am not back, do not think of me again. You must watch out for my dogs and only them. You must fulfill the prophecy. Promise you will protect them and their bloodlines. They cannot mix with other breeds."

He'd promised her and Rune he would watch over the dogs. The *profeti* must be what nagged at Sepp and kept him on edge still. No one in Nome talked about prophecy, only about gold and dog racing. But there it was, right in the forefront of Sepp's thinking: the *profeti* of which Anya spoke tied him to her, to Rune, and to the *Sibirsk hunder*. Like it or not, there was the truth of it. Like it or not, Sepp was caught up in the same dangers. He wouldn't turn away from the young people or the dogs, even if he had a choice.

He didn't, and he knew it.

Chinook never saw it coming. He'd just cleared his village and stepped onto the path toward Nome and his trade store, when Mooglo came out of nowhere and slashed Chinook's throat with Rune's sword. The golem made quick work of the Eskimo's life, ending it. The Viking sword gave the golem the added power he needed in the world of dark spirits, since his own had been diminished by the Chukchi spirits that tried to chase him away. They'd succeeded in chasing him away when he appeared as the great gray wolf. They wouldn't win again. The golem meant to get them all first.

As Mooglo, the golem could hold together long enough to finish the killings. He ruled in the world of the living and in the world of the dead, transformed into the Yukaghir. It was the best way to destroy the Chukchi dogs and their guardians who had escaped to the Alaska frontier. The enemies in Russia, he could easily strike down. He'd already started and made simple work of it, as he just had. The golem kicked Chinook's lifeless body and spat on the fallen Eskimo.

"Any friend to the Chukchi is an enemy of mine," the golem pronounced over the dead man. Putrid saliva oozed down the sides of his misshapen mouth. He raised the sword in taunting triumph to the heavens of the Chukchi. "You will not win this battle. I have dominion over you all. Your Raven god is dead. The fires of *Hel* can no longer come to your rescue. You will not survive away from Russia. You will not survive in Russia. You will not survive!" the changeling screeched and then slipped into the arctic shadows and disappeared.

The gods of all the ancestors, Chukchi

and Viking, heard this new call to battle. The breach between worlds gaped open and there was little more the gods could do to seal the deep wound in their generations of existence, caused by the demonic golem. The girl and the boy, both guardians — Anya a Chukchi shaman, and Rune a Viking warrior — were their only hope to save the Chukchi dogs. The third guardian was in the fight along with them. Their combined human spirits must prevail. The gods could do nothing more on Native Earth. Worlds ever brush past, both human and spirit, both living and dead. The guardians must win in both. It wasn't fair, but what is, when it comes to life and death?

It begins again and then it will be done.

"Rune, we have to hurry!" Anya blurted all of a sudden. "We have to get to Nome! We have to hurry!"

Xander whimpered at her side as if he understood the urgency.

"Anya, don't worry," Rune tried to reassure. "We'll be there soon."

"It's started . . . Rune," she said, suddenly breathless. "The evil after us . . . is already in Nome . . . and on the Alaska frontier. It's started its killing . . . and waits for us! The evil presence . . . I can't make out its shape . . . is angry and on the move, slipping in and out of arctic shadows, determined to kill. I'm scared, Rune . . . scared for our dogs and our friends." Her voice faded to a whisper. Then in the next second, she prostrated herself, facedown, on the deck of the *Storm,* to pray to the Morning Dawn and all the Directions for their help.

Xander howled his prayers to the heavens.

Rune could make out its shape, or so he thought. He pictured the ugly Yukaghir, Mooglo, and imagined the worst. The evil bastard had his sword. Rune watched Anya pray and listened to Xander's call of the wild. They had to win the war, for all their sakes, they had to win. But how, without his sword? He thought of Odin's words and remembered that he held wisdom in one hand and war in the other. To Rune, the sword symbolized war. But what did he have to symbolize wisdom? Rune held up an empty hand, almost expecting some kind of answer written there.

He wasn't disappointed.

The symbol for the secret of the runes etched across his hand in light scratch marks: one straight line with two smaller ones branching off. It was the symbol of the gods, the same symbol scarred at the back of his neck. This was the wisdom Rune sought. The ancient rune alphabet of the gods spelled it out for him in whispered thoughts: *words can cut like a sword.*

Rune had to outsmart Mooglo.

He had to be better at the killing game. Find the enemy, and Rune would find the way. His hands balled into tight fists. War and wisdom singed in both. He imagined himself in times of old — Viking times, where warriors took to their ships or to their ground and prepared for battle. He would shield Anya and her dogs with his life. This was *his* secret of the runes, his destiny met.

"Children," Lars called out from the window of the wheelhouse. He hadn't meant to say children and wondered about this slip. They were more grown up than ever to him at this moment, the way Anya and Rune appeared so tense with worry over their arrival back in Nome. Neither looked his way.

"Hallo there, you two!" he yelled over the crush of waves lapping at the *Storm*'s hull. A sudden squall had come up on them and surprised Lars. There had been no sign of any tempest brewing until this moment. No ice gave chase, the time of year being too early for such danger. Then where did this weather come from and what could it mean? Lars studied Anya and Rune and watched

423

them exchange hugs, and then include Xander in their circle.

It had to mean something Lars realized — the storm coming up all of a sudden and Anya, Rune, and Xander seeming to defend against it.

An eerie premonition hung in the air of the wheelhouse and gave Lars new cause to be afraid for the children. He couldn't imagine what dangers waited for them in Nome, but he knew the Alaska frontier wasn't going to be friendly. Dark elves danced in his mind's eye, clouding the wheelhouse window of anything but their taunts and jabs. Old fears surfaced, and Lars instinctively wanted to turn the *Storm* for Seattle. Even if he tried to turn the wheel away and change course now, it was too late. The wheel wouldn't respond to any human touch. The course was set.

The seal-brown and white husky raced wildly along the edges of the Great Crag. The worlds of the Chukchi swirled in upset. Instinctively, Spirit wanted to exchange places with Anya and try to help on Native Earth. She had to do something, and fast. Mooglo stalked Native Earth. What good was Spirit in the world of phantoms and fairies, when Spirit knew she could rip out

Mooglo's throat if given the chance in the world of humans? Spirit sensed Anya's fears and heard her prayers echo across the generations and layers in time of the Chukchi. She heard Anya's call of the wild: kill or be killed.

Spirit didn't want Anya to die. That was what was going to happen if Spirit didn't do something first. That was what she feared. From her high perch in the world above Native Earth, Spirit could foresee the danger ahead. She kept her watch-blue eyes on the scene below. Anya was a part of her, the human part. One of them would be sacrificed at the Altar of the Great Crag — but which one? Both could not survive the battle, no matter their arctic will. Canine instinct and a lifetime of reflexive behavior, ingrained in Spirit from centuries in time of the Chukchi, brought the message. The fight ahead would be to the death. Spirit didn't want the death to be Anya's. Yet at this point, even though Spirit could foresee danger, she had no way of knowing how things would end. She just knew one of their lives would.

The Great Crag widened.

The gaping hole in Native Earth opened its misshapen jowls, impatient for its next victim.

■ ■ ■ ■

Flowers woke up the moment her kennel clicked open. Then, down the line, the rest of Anya's dogs stirred as each of their kennel doors stood ajar. None of the Chukchi dogs barked. None made a sound or a move, not even young Thor. Out of impulse, all of the dogs sensed something was wrong. Magic sniffed at the telling air — rank with the putrid odor of death. She pointed her muzzle in the air, yet resisted the urge to howl to the heavens in distress. Midday and Midnight scanned the area around them and saw no sign of predators, but they had the overwhelming sense that *something was there.* Only Frost ventured outside his kennel but then returned and flopped down in a circle on his straw bed. This familiar action brought little comfort, and he stood back up.

The skittish huskies had no leader. Zellie was gone. They had lost their strongest with Xander not here. Their guardians had left them in this place. Their guardians would return for them. All of the dogs innately knew this. Anya and Rune meant to come back to them. But no one was here now to protect them from the newest danger.

Instinctively all of the Chukchi dogs wanted to escape the danger and run. It was how they always endured — outrunning their enemies. But something held each dog to their spot. Something kept them from running no matter how strong the urge.

Thor was the first to bark. Thor was born to the Alaska frontier, and it made the difference now between life and death for Anya's dogs. When the pup howled over the tundra, the wolf answered him. The cry of the wolf echoed in thunderous chorus and lit the skies in flashes of light, sparking electricity. Thor kept up his howling. Responsively, Flowers, Midday, Midnight, Magic, and Frost joined in. *The wolf and the dog battle as one.* This instinct of banding together in the fight ahead kept the dogs howling, and kept them from running away. They must hold their ground.

The cacophony brought Leonhard Seppala outside.

The rank odor of death instantaneously fell away.

The golem cursed the little man for his presence! The bastard Chukchi dogs would have run off, and the golem had plans to run them off the highest cliff into the deepest part of the Bering Sea! As it was, the golem wasn't yet prepared to kill the third guardian. He would be, and soon. He would take care of them all at once.

Mooglo wiped the sticky saliva away with his mottled sleeve. These next kills would bring such satisfaction. Cigarettes, where the hell were his cigarettes! He hid now in the shadows outside Nome, and forced himself to remain calm. His appetite for death overwhelmed him, but he had to control it for the time being. The Board of Trade Saloon was just across Front Street. Mooglo came out of the shadows and straightened his clothing. He wanted to appear normal, despite the fact that no one human could see him.

Enemy spirits were everywhere, and he had to fool them. Same as he'd done the year before when he went inside the saloon to return the Viking sword to Rune, Mooglo went through the doors of the Board of Trade Saloon and sat down at an empty corner table. The knotted whip coiled over his shoulder irritated him, but he didn't remove it. Instead, he found his cigarettes and struck a match to one, then took a deep inhale. The savory tobacco soothed his ache to kill, but only a little. He'd kill for a shot of good Russian vodka! Mooglo eyed the barkeep and wished the bastard dead for not having his favorite drink on hand. No sooner had he finished one cigarette than Mooglo crushed it beneath his dirt-encrusted boot and lit another.

Tired of the killing game, he'd make sure to bring things to a quick end.

Everyone would be here soon. Everyone would die.

The golem let the barkeep off the hook, not needing the vodka anymore. The kills ahead would satisfy him. His dominion in the world of the living and the dead would be complete. He blew rings of smoke into the thick saloon air and let them hang perilously before he took a clawed finger and sliced them in two.

Da, the kills ahead would satisfy.

CHAPTER EIGHTEEN

The new storm blown into the frontier boomtown set Nome residents on edge. Accustomed to rainstorms of late summer and snowstorms of early winter, and used to any abrupt change in Alaska weather, they didn't know what to make of the eerie day just turned to night. Something similar had happened right before the sweepstakes in '09 — right before a blizzard hit and knocked out eleven sled dog teams in the big race. Only then, night turned to day. The race was run in winter and not in spring, when natural light would have helped guide the racers. Night turned to day then, but the opposite had just happened.

The early night sky had Nome residents jumpy.

The Alaska frontier was always a worry, and everyone accepted it. Life was hard. Survival was hard. The icy waters and frozen tundra held few surprises by this time. In fact, nothing much surprised those who'd chosen to settle in the arctic north. Nothing came easy unless you'd been one of the lucky ones to hit big on the gold. Some who did stayed, but most left for a more agreeable life in a more agreeable place. Fighting the cold for food and shelter and the means to exist didn't appeal if you had gold in your pocket. An agreeable climate did.

Nome residents weren't the only ones jumpy at this time. News of Chinook's murder spread fast. The surrounding Eskimo villages kept their fires burning bright and kept their families close. No one ventured outside their huts unless to do so was absolutely necessary. Then, someone had to accompany them and stay on guard. Those who had guns loaded them. Those who had knives sharpened them. Chinook's murder and the sudden loss of daylight had everyone spooked. The village shamans could do little to ease anybody's nervousness. They were just as troubled over events.

Ceremonial gatherings didn't bring answers. The drums of the ancients kept silent. Good spirits were busy elsewhere, the shamans believed. This was a dangerous time. "We must wait for the danger to pass," the holy men advised. "Stay in your homes. If something comes at you, kill it. If something comes at your dogs, kill it. Villages must keep in close contact and help if called upon."

Everyone must be ready for anything.

The Board of Trade Saloon filled with townsfolk coming in to escape the odd turn of the day to night. While some were already at home with their families, others needed the peace of mind they always found when they met up with friends in the popular gathering place. Maybe somebody would know what the heck had brought on this dark turn in the skies. Answers could always be found inside the Board of Trade Saloon.

Who won the sled dog race? Who struck gold? What ship anchored off Nome? How many passengers are coming in? What supplies are on board? What accident happened at which mine? When is the mail due in?

It was natural for men to crowd inside the safe haven of the Board of Trade Saloon to find answers to their questions, especially to this latest stir-up.

"Jafet Lindeberg!" Albert Fink called out to the wealthy mine owner, and waved him over to sit at his table. As the Nome Kennel Club president, Albert always sat at the same table.

"Albert," Jafet bade him hello, then scraped out a chair and sat down. "I'll take a shot of that whiskey, Albert. I'll take two." Jafet didn't smile. He didn't feel like it.

Albert poured a drink for the mine owner, and another one for himself. Neither man cared much for drink, but both men wanted a drink now.

Jafet swallowed the liquor in one gulp, then motioned for another pour.

Albert complied and gave himself a second shot, too.

The two men were good acquaintances, if not friends. They shared associations in Nome, whether about legal advice or mining business interests. Dog racing had also been the subject of more than one conversation between them. It was hard to avoid the subject of dog racing in Nome. The All Alaska Sweepstakes held since 1908, with native mixed malamutes racing, set everything in motion. Then the imported Siberian huskies doing so well in the races of 1909 and 1910 guaranteed to keep the subject on the minds of most in Nome.

Dog racing was not on Jafet Lindeberg's mind at the moment, neither was the dark day.

"Albert, have you seen anybody new in

here? Someone you might be suspicious of? Someone you think might be on the wrong side of the law?"

The Nome Kennel Club president couldn't help but chuckle to himself. Most everyone coming to Nome looked like they might be on the wrong side of the law, and it turned out most of them were. He would have said that out loud to Jafet, but the mine owner wasn't in a laughing mood.

"No," Albert thought it best to say.

Jafet pushed his chair out and scanned the crowd in the saloon and ignored Albert. Gaslight burned the setting to a dim glow. The electricity had gone off.

"Exactly who are you looking for, Jafet?"

"A murderer is who I'm looking for. A cold-blooded killer is around here somewhere, and I mean to find him." Jafet leveled his words at the crowd in the saloon more than to Albert.

When Albert thought about it, there were a lot of men capable of murder in Nome. There were a lot of men willing to kill for the gold. Things had become more lawful nowadays, but danger always walked the streets and dug in mine tunnels.

"Who got killed?"

Jafet looked Albert square in the eye.

"Zeke Raney and Homer Jessup, two of

my best men. Both of 'em were old sourdoughs and tough enough to survive pretty
much anything on the frontier. They were
found this morning with their throats cut,
both in the same place, and likely both at
the same time. Maybe it's more than one
killer I'm looking for. I've never seen anything like it, Albert," Jafet confided. "Men
don't get their throats slashed around here;
they're shot or knifed in the back. No, this
is the work of a cold-blooded murdering
son-of-a-bitch from some place I've never
seen." Jafet reared back in his chair and
blew out a breath.

Albert had never heard such talk in Nome
— talk of a killer coming from some place
he'd never seen. Funny, but Albert suddenly
recalled the words of the crazy Bible
thumper of years ago. Joshua of Jericho, the
man called himself. The man had warned
of danger coming to Nome with the arrival
of the Siberian huskies. Albert thought him
a nut and didn't pay attention to his warning. He did now, because the man's talk
sounded as crazy to him as Jafet's words
about a killer coming from some place he'd
never seen. There couldn't be any connection — or could there be? Albert didn't have
any answer for Jafet Lindeberg or for his
own unease. It wasn't just the dark day that

stuck in his craw, but the notion that maybe the Siberian huskies *did* bring an unseen evil from across the Bering Sea.

Albert turned his empty shot glass upside down. He didn't feel like another drink. His hand automatically went to the holster of his Smith & Wesson pistol to draw comfort from the cold steel. Whatever was coming, he wanted to be ready.

Mooglo watched and listened to the exchange between Albert Fink and Jafet Lindeberg. His ghostly presence went undetected by the mere mortals. Stupid men! Mooglo burst out laughing. The sound of his own thunder gratified him. He, the golem, had killed the traitorous miners and the traitorous Eskimo! He, the golem, had slashed all their throats!

It was his turn to kill, and he would keep killing until the war was finished. It would be over soon. Anya and Rune and their dogs were visible now on the killing field.

No one could hide anymore.

Not any of the traitorous guardians or their traitorous dogs.

Anya's young Chukchi dogs stepped restlessly onto the beach in Nome. All ten were on leash, since Anya didn't want any of them to run off in the excitement of so many new sights and sounds. Each pair was on a double leash, then tied together on one line. Anya had named each one on the journey across the Bering Sea, in a mix of Russian and English. The exercise helped ease her nerves, besides being a necessity. It was important the Chukchi pups had names, not just to better follow their individual commands, but because they were family. The males she named Togo, Harry, Smoky, Kreevanka, and Tserko. The females she named Kolyma, Nome, Pearl, Dushka, and Sonia. The furry swirl of color they created — mixes of copper-red, black, gray, and white — couldn't be appreciated in the dim light of Nome.

"It's gone!" Anya whispered into the darkness closed in around her. Sharp winds cut at her from every which way. She ignored the winds and checked the pocket of her kerker again, the same inside pocket where she always kept her knife tucked — her gift from the gods. She knew she hadn't left it anywhere or lost it. She felt alone on the dark, unwelcoming beach, but for her Chukchi pups. Rune and Xander were up ahead, joined with Iron Man Johnson and the team of dogs he'd traded for at Markova. Captain Lars was still on the *Storm,* and hadn't taken the same lighter boat as they all just had.

Everyone on board the *Storm* had witnessed the dark turn of the weather and the day in the direction of Nome. "We need to brace for this and make sure the *skepp* is secure," Rune's father had said. "I will come on the next lighter boat. You both wait for me," he'd also told them. "Promise me," he'd added. Rune and Anya both promised they would, even though they both knew they would not. They'd already talked between themselves, and decided they didn't want to put Lars in any more danger than he already was. For his sake, they couldn't keep their promise.

Despite stiff arctic winds and despite the young dogs' restlessness, Anya stood as still as she could and strained to pick up any whispers on the wind. She strained to find the exact place she needed to be in her head and heart . . . to talk with the ancients. Any message from them might solve her problem, and she might know what just happened and who'd stolen her knife.

Then, in a heartbeat, she knew.

She didn't have to wait for ghosts of the ancestors to tell her who was the culprit. It could be no one but the evil demon after them from the start. The demon was here, in Nome. She didn't have to wait for the ancestors to tell her that she and Rune had no advantage over the demon, as she'd hoped they would. Anya might be shaman, but she didn't have her gift from the gods. Rune might be a Viking warrior, but he didn't have his secret of the runes. The two were left defenseless, she realized.

"What is it, Anya?" Rune suddenly came up on her. Xander was alongside.

The young dogs with Anya quieted and paid particular attention to Xander.

Xander had sensed trouble and pricked his ears to listen for any howls, for any guidance from Zellie. No matter that she was gone from him, instinct told him she was always near. Their spirits were connected even unto other worlds. He strained reflexively for any sign from her, and whimpered when he didn't pick up anything on the arctic winds.

"It's all right, boy." Anya held fast to her dogs' lead line, yet knelt to Xander and scratched behind his ears. She sensed his uneasiness. Hers matched his. Neither one of them knew Zellie's fate. She wasn't with the Gatekeepers at this time, or else Zellie would be alerted to the danger they faced and communicate through spirit. The emptiness she and Xander felt at the absence of

Zellie's spirit caused great anxiety to them both.

Thinking of Zellie's lost spirit stirred Anya's. That was it! *Rune and I are not defenseless. We have Spirit!*

"Anya, talk to me," Rune said. "We don't have much time."

She looked up at Rune and determined to keep herself just as calm as he appeared. She agreed. Their time had run out. The out-of-season, twilight-to-dark sky was proof enough.

"My knife has been stolen, same as your sword. We both know who must have done it. We both know who is here in Nome to kill us and the dogs. It's Mooglo. He might appear in some other misshapen disguise, but it's the evil after us all the same."

Rune knew she was right. They had to outsmart the devil. War and wisdom, he thought, and then, as if he held the sunstone of the Vikings in his hand for a compass, Rune scanned the beach for any sign of Mooglo. The ugly Yukaghir could be anywhere and do anything *any time*. Any shape could come at them any time. This war of ghosts was like no other, Rune believed. Nothing like it had been fought before in the layers of worlds known to the Chukchi, and the Chukchi had never been in greater peril. Rune's Viking gods knew this and had summoned him to fight at Anya's side.

How he loved Anya.

Rune would live with her or die with her. They were tied together for all of time. Worlds ever brush past, both human and spirit. He was meant to be with Anya. Nothing on Native Earth could force him to take back the moment he first brushed past her in Anadyr even if he could. That fated magic touch had set his course with hers in this world and in any other.

"Anya, hand me the lead line." Rune held out his hand to her, the same hand that held the sunstone of the Vikings, he believed. "Let's head to Sepp's. We can all be together there."

"You read my thoughts." Anya handed him the line and tried to smile. On the way she would tell Rune about her *Spirit,* and her plans.

Xander had already started out, accepting that he was the lead dog on this last, perilous trek into the ice storm.

"What do you mean, he's not here!" Anya hurled her question at the woman who answered the door.

Sepp's wife had opened her cabin door

the instant she heard someone pounding. Snow blew inside when she did. Jumpy ever since her husband left with the six Siberian huskies, Constance didn't like being alone in the eerie darkness of the Alaska frontier with her worries. "Couldn't I go with you?" she'd asked Leonhard. "I can ride in the cart or run alongside," she'd told him.

Her husband had given her an easy smile and then put more wood on their fire.

"I need you to stay here and be safe," Sepp had quietly reassured her. "This sudden storm is no place for you but the perfect place for me and the dogs to train. We will be fine." In fact he was going to hitch the six *hunder* in front of a sled and not a cart, since enough snow had fallen to allow it. This would make the training run go fast and their return early.

What Sepp hadn't told his wife was that something drew him into the storm.

The overwhelming pull made him uneasy, but he had to follow it. He'd never experienced such a queer sensation and thought he had to investigate. He couldn't do it in this weather without the dogs. Sepp didn't fear much in the Alaska territory, but he was afraid *not* to follow his instincts. He'd take his rifle and thought of predators that might be out there. He had to keep his wife safe and find whatever might be waiting to strike at his home first. No, Constance couldn't accompany him, even though he knew she wished she could.

Before he could change his mind, he'd given his wife a quick kiss on the cheek, taken up his rifle, and was out the door.

That was hours ago, and Constance was beside herself with worry. Conditions outside had worsened. If it were the middle of winter, she wouldn't question the storm. But this wasn't right. None of this was right. The deep snow, arctic winds, and ice build-up had her scared; scared for Leonhard and all of their family — all of the Siberian huskies in their care.

"Come inside," Constance urged the young people at her door. She recognized Rune and guessed the girl might be Anya. Constance pulled the iced-over door wide and held onto it for support. The winds howled outside and in. Her cozy fire died out. The inside and outside temperatures matched, both ice cold.

"Can the pups come inside, too?" Rune asked.

Constance looked past Anya and Rune and saw all the young dogs for the first time. She felt better right away at seeing the Siberian huskies.

"Yes, please, all of you."

Anya and Rune ushered the ten pups inside, snow and all. The room quickly filled. When Rune had the door secure, he and Anya scanned the dim cabin for any sign of trouble. Nothing appeared out of the ordinary, except for the dead fire.

"Let me rekindle your fire," Anya said, feeling every bit the Chukchi shaman turned warrior. She refused to let the evil Mooglo put the fire out again, hurried over to the fireplace, and had it started in a heartbeat. The room brightened instantly. "Keep piling on logs," she told Constance. "The fire won't go out again if you do." She'd started a Chukchi flame, and Mooglo couldn't touch it, Anya determined. The aurora borealis fought for the Chukchi and not the demon!

"All right," Constance agreed. She didn't know what was going on, but she knew that the young people who had just entered her home were here to help. There was no time for anything but to follow their lead and try to help, too. She was frightened she might never see Leonhard again.

Xander left Anya's side and padded over to Constance, then put his head under her hand, asking for a pat. Reflexively, he wanted to protect the third guardian's wife.

They were all part of the same pack.

Constance knelt down and hugged the blue-eyed husky.

"Thank you, Xander," she whispered into his furry neck, as if he understood her upset.

In his way, he did.

With the big black and white husky close, and with the new dogs just come inside, Constance's nerves eased a little. She didn't feel so alone.

Anya joined Rune by the closed cabin door. In that moment she felt the eyes of the Gatekeepers on her, and realized Rune's gods must be watching him in the same way.

"I told you about Spirit. She's our best chance to stop the evil after us." Anya spoke low and fast, so Sepp's wife wouldn't overhear.

"You mean our best chance to slay the demon, don't you?" Rune whispered back, unsure it would work. His heart thudded. He was scared Anya would never come back to him if she switched places with her Spirit.

"Rune, I have to do this. Mooglo has Sepp and our dogs. I know it. He's got them, and he's going to kill them. He has your sword and my knife. I know he'll use them. I know he *has* used them." Anya's tone turned desperate. Tears fell and she let them. "Rune, he's hurt our friends here," she said when she could speak again. "He's *killed* them. Chinook is dead and so are Zeke and Homer. The winds don't lie."

Rune took Anya in his arms for her comfort and his. He felt numb. *Killed?* The truth of Anya's words went beyond grief over their friends' deaths, to full-blown alarm for Anya and her *purebred Chukchi dogs* all over again. They could all die, and Rune might not be able to do anything about it!

But he had to.

"Rune," Anya tried to keep her voice from quavering. "Spirit is our only weapon. She can lead me to Mooglo. We don't have time for more talk, Rune."

"I know, but we're going to talk anyway," he told her, and took hold of her arm in an attempt to keep her firmly on Native Earth with him.

Mooglo wanted to finish Zellie off, but he'd wait. He wanted to drag out her torture more before she breathed her last. She was a problem for him. Her connection to all the worlds where he held dominion had to be cut. Whatever had kept her alive, even after her death, kept her alive . . . still. He had to kill it. The golem tired of trying to figure out what that was. The Chukchi ghost dog was in his grips now, and he had her trapped. She couldn't escape her suffering or her end. He'd finish all the others first, then her. He looked forward to his final kill in the world of the dead, before he returned to the world of the living in Russia — where he would kill again. The blood of his enemies gave him life, no matter the domain.

Mooglo blew out more smoke rings and jabbed each one through, before he crushed his cigarette beneath his unearthly boot and left the Board of Trade Saloon for good.

He brought the ice storm.

Da, this satisfied, indeed.

"Spirit can lead *us* to Mooglo, Anya." Rune underscored *us.* "I'm coming with you." He gripped her arm tighter to make sure she understood.

Anya tried to shake off his hold, but couldn't.

"Rune, you *can't* come with me," she rasped low. Constance mustn't overhear them. "Rune, you are not shaman, and you are not born to two worlds as I am. You can't come with me into the spirit world!"

"I carry the secret of the runes with me," he said and tightened his grip even more. "That's my pass into your world of spirits."

"But you don't have your Viking sword. How can you say you carry the secret of the runes? It is too dangerous for you to say such things." She tried again to shake off his hold. It hurt. "I have to go. Let me go, Rune!"

This time he did, only to grasp her hand and put it to the back of his neck, so she could feel the mark there.

Anya let her fingers travel over the scar's distinct outline. The mark was imprinted there. Rune didn't lie.

"Did you forget? I've had this mark of the gods since birth and *am* a part of two worlds," Rune exclaimed. "The blood of Odin's wolves flows through my veins. The wolf and the dog must battle as one, remember? You are husky and I am wolf. We must battle as one, Anya. Nothing we do in this world can kill the demon after us. We have to kill him in his world."

"But the human spirit must prevail. We must kill the demon on Native Earth, Rune." Anya fought her confusion and renewed fears.

"I know. You're right," he said and placed a kiss on her forehead. Then he took her in his arms and squeezed her to him, to his heart and to his soul, before he let her go. He needed to reassure her and explain. "The blood in my veins — the blood of my ancestors — can spill the demon's blood. I can help you in the battle, Anya." Rune had to swallow back the lump in his throat. "You and me, Anya. We might not survive, but others will. I have to believe that. I have to believe this is our purpose in meeting and the purpose for which we were born."

Anya stared up into his watch-blue eyes and knew he spoke true.

"The wolf and the dog battle as one," she repeated softly, and tried to crinkle the edges of her mouth into a smile, "so the human spirit can survive." This might be the last time she would see Rune in this world or any other. She felt queasy. Her stomach upset. Waves of nausea almost sent her to her knees, and would have, had Rune not been holding on to her.

Anya knew right away what was happening. She felt the drums of the ancients pounding inside her. Spirits closed in. Good and Bad. She could feel herself being drawn away from Native Earth and clutched Rune tighter, afraid to leave him yet. How could she face any kind of forever without him!

Rune cupped Anya's chin and brushed his lips to hers before closing his mouth over hers in a passionate kiss — a parting kiss.

Xander scurried over at just that moment.

Anya and Rune pulled out of each other's arms.

The black and white husky obediently stood at attention, the same as a soldier might do who waited for orders. Xander might as well have been hitched in front of a sled, listening for his next command. Generations of Chukchi dogs waited with him.

Anya and Rune's thoughts were a mirror image.

There was no guarantee Mooglo wouldn't come here, but it was unlikely he would before Anya and Rune engaged the demon in battle. The ice storm would stay outside of Sepp's cabin for the present, they believed. Constance needed to keep the Chukchi fire burning. The young Chukchi dogs would protect Sepp's wife and keep her safe and warm. They would instinctively know to do it. Young Togo took the lead, with Nome and Kolyma right behind him. The rest watched closely and then circled in, their pack mentality set.

Xander whimpered out of impatience. His reflexes held taut. His watch eyes were on his guardians and not the young dogs.

Anya had little time left to hold any human shape. While she still could, she reached out to Xander. So did Rune at the same time. Their connection was steadfast and their resolve clear, in this world and in

the next.
The wolf and the dog battle as one.

CHAPTER NINETEEN

Something pulled him deeper into the wild, the dogs, too. No matter how hard Sepp tried to command the dogs to "Come Gee!" or "Come Haw!" and turn them either way back toward his cabin, it didn't work, especially in the ice storm brewing. High winds and dropped temperatures made any headway, in any direction, nearly impossible. Sepp wanted to head back if he could, since he reasoned they were close to the Bering Sea at this point. Too close for any kind of comfort. The cliffs in this region were steep and the drop-off deadly. At the very least, the dogs would suffer terrible wounds on such uncertain icy ground. Any slip, and the sea could take them.

None of this made any sense to Sepp — imagining something trying to get at him and the dogs. A wild predator, he could understand, but not this unknown. A force beyond him or the dogs had overtaken them. It wasn't just the nasty turn in the weather. Sepp had been out in storms before, but never an ice storm quite like this. This storm was a monster, and one Sepp had never encountered before. Fingers of ice spread everywhere, it seemed, no doubt because of the dangerous winds. Sea fog closed in and blocked visibility. Snow fell over the ice in sheets, like the white death faced by sailors at sea.

Convinced he and the dogs had to be at the edges of the unforgiving Bering Sea, he knew the next move could be their last. Sepp reached inside the bed of his sled and checked his rifle to make sure of it — to make sure it hadn't frozen up, and to make sure it was loaded. Tucked under a caribou fur, his rifle was ready for whatever might try to come at him and the dogs. Sepp thought of Constance. She had to be frightened that he hadn't returned home. Too late to change things. He wished he hadn't left her alone. Then again, wishes never meant much on the rugged Alaska frontier, only grit and determination did. Sepp had both, and so did the *Sibirsk hunder* in his charge. Together they would live or die by such an unspoken code.

"Mush!" Sepp called out to the dogs, to

get them started and out of the fix they were in.

"Dammit!" Rune cursed the weather and cursed the fact he'd let go of Anya's hand to grab fur mittens for her. In that split second, she'd disappeared. "Dammit," he cursed again. He'd meant to travel with her into the spirit world, and thought he might even be changed into the wolf he claimed to be. He'd meant to rip out the throat of Mooglo. With the blood of Odin's wolves in his veins, he'd be nine times stronger and nine times more able to slay the serpent! What could he do now as a mere human against such a deadly enemy? *Dammit!*

Anya would have to fight Mooglo alone in the spirit world, without any help from him. Would Spirit be easy prey? Rune had no way to know. What powers did Anya's husky spirit have? He tried to remember what Anya had said about Spirit: *She's our best chance to stop the evil after us. She's our only weapon. Mooglo has Sepp and our dogs, and he's going to kill them. He has your sword and my knife. I know he'll use them. I know he has used them. He's killed our friends. Chinook is dead, and so are Zeke and Homer. The winds don't lie.*

The scar at the back of Rune's neck

throbbed. Icy winds assaulted. He barely noticed, so concerned was he over what to do, how to help save Anya and Spirit. If something happened to one, it could kill them both. He and Anya had never talked about the possibility but there it was, staring Rune in the face. Rune threw the fur mitts in his hands, the ones meant for Anya, into the maelstrom. The bitter winds swept them away.

Xander barked in protest and then howled to the heavens — to the aurora borealis that charged and flashed overhead, as if sounding the call to battle.

Rune hadn't noticed the skies before, due to the blurring storm, but he did now. Xander pointed this out with his howls. The skies were on fire! It had to be a sign but of what? Xander must know, the way he barked and forced Rune's attention from Native Earth to the world beyond. Rune studied the red skies and was reminded of spilled blood, as if the blood of the ancients was on fire overhead. It was an odd thought but it stuck in his mind. *Blood . . . his blood and the blood of the ancients . . .* Rune had the blood of Odin's wolves running through his veins. Xander had the blood of the warrior Chukchi running through his. *This was the sign.* The wolf and the dog battle as one.

"Xander!"

The intent black and white husky stopped barking and looked at Rune.

The ice storm blew around them and gathered in strength.

Rune's face and hands were covered over in ice and snow crystals.

Xander's fur was coated white.

Both the wolf and the dog held their ground in the dangerous weather moving in on them. The winds blew loud and fierce.

"Find your pack!" Rune yelled as loud as he could. "Find Flowers, and Thor! Find —"

Xander disappeared at once, into the ice storm.

Rune's sharp, feral instincts allowed him to follow.

Anya's disappearance from Native Earth set Spirit free. The full power of generations of Chukchi instinct, reflex, and keenness filled her seal-brown, husky limbs and gave her the strength to cross the boundaries between worlds. Their passing, hers and Anya's, was instantaneous. Only one could make it back.

Anya's vanished being in the spirit world quickly joined in whirls and swirls of snow lacing in frantic patterns through the ghostly air, as if the same storm brewed here, identical to Native Earth. The ancients over the many generations of Chukchi existence joined now at the edges of the Great Crag. The Pole Star dimmed to dark. The Gatekeepers saw. The gods stayed silent. The Directions stayed still, impervious to the polar vortex that had suddenly formed. Temperatures in the heavens dropped below freezing.

The unnatural pathway between worlds gaped open in a spiral of charged flashes and odorous vapors. The way had been forced open, and that was never meant to be. It would not hold long. The gods, Chukchi and Viking alike, knew it. The brink of extinction held them fast.

Anya was lost to them.

Their watch was on Spirit. She was at the breach, the point of no return.

The instant Spirit crossed the breach, the golem experienced a satisfaction unlike any before. He rubbed his gnarly hands together gleefully. He'd managed to lure the Spirit of the traitorous Chukchi to cross to his dark world where he could easily kill it. The knowledge that he'd created the breach between worlds in the first place fueled his appetite for blood, Chukchi blood. All *kulaks* must die! He would make sure.

The golem would kill as Mooglo in the world of spirits, and in the world of humans, he would kill as head of communist Russia. He had dominion over all and had few worries by this time, other than who to kill first. The ashes and embers of his parents glowed in the dark hollows of his demonic thoughts. They were proud of their son, or else they wouldn't show themselves.

His traps had been set. One Chukchi dog had to wait for her final death, caught in his inescapable web, but not the rest. The third guardian and the team he drove would die next. The golem would have time to destroy them before the traitorous Spirit of the Chukchi tried to interfere with his plans. She'd be next, and with her death, would come the girl, Anya's. The boy, Rune, and the last pure-blood dog, Xander, would finish it.

Da, the golem knew about the arrival of the ten Chukchi pups, but he wasn't worried. Without their *kulak* breeder, Leonhard Seppala, their bloodlines wouldn't stay pure. They would mix with all the other Alaskan huskies, just like Fox Ramsey's teams, and the Chukchi dog would be dead and gone from this frontier, and their fool guardians with them! The golem's work in this dark world of spirits would be done.

He could turn his attention to Russia, where he'd keep up his killing.

There was no stopping him anywhere in any world.

Worlds ever brush past, both human and spirit. Good and Evil are born into each. Some become master; some do not. Some suffer greatly; some do not.

Sepp didn't get very far with his team before they slid right off the edges of Native Earth. It happened in a heartbeat — in the time it takes to give life or end it. The trail dropped out from under them like a break in sea ice might do. Down they tumbled, over icy shards and crags that tore at them mercilessly and made any footing impossible. Sepp held onto the sled in a desperate attempt to hold onto the dogs. They were all hitched together, and he meant to stay with them. Blood spurted from his arm inside his clothes. He could feel the cold finger of death strike again and again. The dogs had to be suffering the same as he.

The team of six cried out against their pain. The ice storm muffled their howls and muzzled their call to the wild. Frantic to find footing anywhere, their paws ripped open from the effort. The life's blood of the valiant Chukchi sled dogs drained over the snowy scape. Still they tried to claw their way back up the glassy embankment to safety. In desperation, Flowers tried to find her pup. He had been hitched behind her. She could hear him and knew how much he hurt. Helpless to help him, every instinct and reflex inside her died in that moment — when she had to let Thor go.

The lightweight sled thumped and bumped down the sloping cliffs toward the Bering Sea, but then the sled stopped short, miraculously caught on a jutted ledge. Sepp managed to grab hold of one of the sled's runners and tried to hang on. Amazingly, the basket contents hadn't overturned. Sepp struggled to get a better grip on the sled and the dogs' hitch lines, worried that any moment the uncertain ledge could give way. He couldn't see through the layers of thick fog, but he could feel the hitch lines stay secure. What held them so fast? Sepp knew it wasn't his strength alone keeping the *Sibirsk hunder* from falling into the frozen sea. He didn't have time to think about who or what might be helping, so intent was he on getting the dogs back on safe ground.

"Whoa! Whoa!" he yelled at the top of his voice, at the same time pulling with all his might on the tug lines in his grip. The command might help calm the dogs into more purposeful action. In spite of their wounds, they all had to fight for their lives. Suddenly the pull on the tug lines gave . . . in Sepp's favor? He didn't believe in miracles, but he might start. Hand over fist, the frozen leather strapping slid securely through his grip until he saw the first dogs for the first time since their deadly plunge. Midnight and Midday scrambled up the icy embankment to him, then Frost, Magic, young Thor, and finally Flowers — all exhausted and all bloodied . . . and all alive. The count was good.

Sepp didn't wait for anything else to happen. He'd leave the sled and come back for it the moment the dogs cleared the deadly drop-off. He hoped that whatever had helped give them the strength and momentum to turn around would stay with them. *Sibirsk hunder* were frisky dogs that liked to keep moving. This trait served them well and helped save their lives now, Sepp believed. The dogs would keep going until they could no more. So would he.

Leonhard Seppala might be unsure, but the brave team of six Chukchi dogs knew exactly who had saved them. Their guardian Spirit had come out of nowhere and instilled within them the strength they needed to turn from death and fight for life. The magnificent, seal-brown leader dog guided them up and out of the ice storm. The shaman spirit of all the ancients fused through her to them. Generations of Chukchi dogs created a wave of howls in the heavens, and the aurora borealis flashed . . . *fast, strong, enduring.*

Spirit wasn't about to let the sled be lost, and charged beneath it to lighten the load for the third guardian — the one to save them all, for all time. Nothing must happen to the guardian, the sled, or any of the dogs. Leonhard Seppala would not see her; he was never meant to, for his own safety. The less he knew of the spirit world, the better for his peace of mind. He had an important task: to keep the pure bloodlines of the Chukchi dog alive. He must do it in the world of humans, not spirits. Nothing must cloud his efforts, especially the truth of his dangerous situation.

Strangely to Sepp, he managed to scramble to safety behind his sled dog team, and with the sled in tow. Bleeding and exhausted, he couldn't understand why they'd all made it to more sure ground. But they had. The aurora borealis flashed in the skies, and Sepp stood in wonder. It wasn't the season, yet the mystic lights of the Arctic shone down to illuminate the frigid darkness. *Another miracle,* he thought. Before he made sure of the sled and its contents, he needed to make sure of the dogs. At this point, he stood in wonder of them. Wounded, bleeding, exhausted, and anxious, they prevailed without complaint.

But something wasn't right. The dogs' watch eyes were fixed on the deadly cliff they'd just climbed. What they saw, Sepp couldn't know.

Spirit's arrival before his sent Mooglo into a worse rage. She'd come to the traitors' rescue before he could kill them. He hadn't planned on this — that he'd be outsmarted by any Chukchi at this point. His power reigned supreme, and the intruding husky dared challenge him!

Spirit didn't try to run, and had her watch eyes set on him.

This insult further enraged him.

Mooglo's anger unleashed. No sooner had he uncoiled the whip from his shoulder than he had Spirit in his knotted grip. He lashed the whip around her neck and kept it there, tightening it, then tightening it more. The whip held all his power within its grasp. *The whip always beats the dog.* He, the golem, held dominion over all. Spirit needed to know this before she died, and die she would!

Anya's dogs howled frantically. They knew what was happening. They could see it and smell it. The scent of death cloyed. Every impulse inside their battered bodies wanted to kill the demon. They knew Spirit was their guardian, *Anya.* They witnessed the life being taken from her and couldn't stop the demon. Their howls joined with those of the wolves, who answered in turn, and from all directions. An end was coming; everything in the wild knew it.

A final snap of Mooglo's whip, and the deed was done.

Spirit shut her watch eyes for the last time and sacrificed her life at the Great Crag. She never cried out. She was gone from Native Earth, and gone from the world of ancient spirits. There was no pain. There was nothing. Her ghostly death heralded the brink of extinction.

Grimy saliva spilled out the corners of Mooglo's misshapen mouth. His yellow grin poisoned the already polluted air. No one could challenge him. He held dominion. His whip killed across worlds, a secret only he held. His grin disappeared. He wasn't done. In one swift, vaporous move, Mooglo reached Leonhard Seppala and the six dogs left alive. They'd all die in one lashing. The demon sparked electric.

The first shot to Mooglo's chest stunned him. The second stopped his progress. The third killed him. The demon's existence in the world of dark spirits ended in a heart-beat — in the time it takes to give life or take it away. Mooglo's twisted body yellowed to putrid ashes and then died out, carried away on stiff arctic winds.

At once, the fog monster that lay siege rolled back out to sea, identical to a blanket turned down. The dark day cleared to soft twilight. The snowfall let up. Glacial sheets of ice groaned and melted away into the waiting sea; their cold fingers of death abruptly cut off.

All signs the ice storm was over.

Rune held onto his smoking gun, ready to reload and use it again. His feral instincts refused to calm. His breaths came in sharp pants, and his reflexes stayed taut. He'd grabbed the rifle out of Sepp's hands the moment he came on the scene. Rune needed both hands to aim the rifle and slay the serpent. War and Wisdom pulled the trigger. It all happened so fast, Rune fought for a clear grasp of what just took place.

It didn't seem real, that Mooglo was really dead. How could mere bullets kill such a powerful demon! It didn't add up . . . but it's what happened.

On the frantic race through the snow blind with Xander, Rune had no idea what he could use against Mooglo to slay him when they confronted each other. Only when he and Xander reached Sepp and the dogs, and he saw the gun in Sepp's hands, did Rune act. His feral instincts charged at the throat of the phantom predator. Rune grabbed the gun and followed his instincts to go at the enemy with his best shot. Rune hadn't even seen Mooglo before he fired. But he could hear him, and smell him, and feel his evil. Then he knew exactly where to aim. It was instantaneous.

Xander stood next to Rune. They'd banded together with Spirit in this fight. But Spirit was nowhere to be seen. Where was she? The seal-brown husky had to be here.

"Spirit!" Rune called out.

Xander barked.

"Spirit!" Rune yelled louder. His heart thudded for an altogether different reason than having just killed the demon ice storm. If something had happened to Spirit, then Anya . . . what of Anya?

The rest of Anya's dogs kept silent, not even a whimper. They knew it wouldn't do any good. Despondency set deep in their bones, yet they remained standing, no matter that their legs were torn and their paws bled.

"Rune." Sepp hurried over to him and to Xander. The movement reopened Sepp's wounds. "What were you shooting at? There was nothing there." Sepp sounded incredulous. "And who is Spirit? There's no one here but us, Rune." Never in all his time on the frontier had Sepp experienced such a confounding series of events. He wanted to be of some help, but how?

"Anya," Rune muttered into the stillness. His voice cracked.

"Who?" Sepp couldn't make out what the boy said.

"Anya is dea—" Rune started to say, but when he turned to face Leonhard Seppala, he faced *Anya,* instead.

"Rune, you look like you've seen a ghost," Sepp told him.

"I have," Rune said before he handed the rifle to Sepp and stepped past him to take Anya in his arms.

The pair clung to each other. Both shed tears and neither cared who might see.

All the Chukchi dogs, Xander included, barked and howled in celebration at seeing their guardian come back to them. Thor butted up against his mother, and howled with everything in him; so loud and so forcefully, he almost lost his footing when he did. Magic, Midday, Midnight, and Frost formed an unstoppable chorus. Despite their injuries, the huskies all danced to the same song of life.

Sepp didn't have any words for the sight in front of him. He didn't have words for any of this, actually. Maybe there were none, and maybe he shouldn't worry about finding any. This day held too many questions to answer. Sepp decided then and there he wouldn't ask for an explanation. That they all survived was good enough for him. He could return home to Constance with all the *Sibirsk hunder* that had started out with him from home. It was the code of sled dog racing, to cross the finish with the same dogs as had begun. Sepp was satisfied they survived, so no, he wouldn't ask any more questions about today's events.

Some things are best left alone and to the Almighty.

But there was one part of the code of sled dog racing Sepp would avoid at all costs. To have any dog put in harm's way, led onto treacherous ground where life-threatening injuries could be sustained, was unforgivable. As it was, Sepp would have trouble

468

forgiving himself for the injuries to Anya's dogs on this day. Their paws were torn and bleeding, and their bodies badly battered by their fall down the craggy cliffs to the Bering Sea. For the rest of his life, this lesson was well-learned. No, he didn't have much control over events today, but he would make sure to watch ever his *Sibirsk hunder* and keep them out of harm's way in all his days to come.

Anya's arms fell from Rune's.

It took every ounce of her strength to hold her human shape and not turn to useless vapor. Spirits clamored inside her, fighting for her attention and making her nauseated to the point of pain. The full effect of what had just happened at the Great Crag — that Spirit had sacrificed her life for all of theirs — sent shock waves throughout the world of spirits. Shamans came from every corner of Chukchi existence to console Anya and, at the same time, advise her. They were in a hurry to speak, since she would soon lose contact with them. Her time in the world of spirits had come to an end with her husky counterpart's death.

It is all right, the shamans whispered to her. *You can let go of our world now. Your burden is lifted. You have fulfilled the destiny for which you were born. Our lines will survive because of you and your Spirit. The demon is dead here, but not everywhere. You cannot destroy the fanatic demon, whose human rule means to crush us. This is a fight that will go on in our native land, and you must trust our people to fight from this point forward.*

Anya tried to pay attention to the shamans, but her tears got in the way. Her body flooded with the agony of losing Spirit. She, Anya, should have been the one sacrificed at the Great Crag! She should have done *something* to prevent Spirit's death! She'd failed Spirit, just like she'd failed Nanatasha and Zellie! And Mushroom and Little Wolf! And Chinook and Zeke and Homer!

It would be easy for Anya to slip into total unconsciousness now, she was so upset over her misdeeds, but she refused. She must face the shamans and her fate. The shamans were wrong. She'd failed in her purpose and needed to pay the price. She must strike a bargain with the shaman spirits. The Gatekeepers must stay on their guard. When her time was up on Native Earth, Anya did not think she deserved to have her sled pulled through to heaven. None of her dogs should wait to pull her across. This would be the right punishment. She should not come to any final sleep with the people. She should be forever banned from such a sleep of peace.

Tidal waves of emotion caught her up, and she let them pass her into oblivion. The darkness was a fitting punishment, she faintly reasoned before all went blank.

"Anya! Anya!" Rune cried out, at the same time collecting her frail body and placing her in the bed of Sepp's sled.

"Here, son." Sepp stood close and handed Rune the caribou blanket used before to protect the rifle. Anya needed all of their protection and prayers now. She didn't look good. Something had gotten to her, and to her throat. Sepp saw the red marks and cuts to her neck especially. Nothing human would have done such a thing to the girl, he thought. But then, what kind of animal could make such marks . . . like whip lashes?

This time Xander stayed with the rest of his pack and watched their guardians, on alert for what might happen next. It was an uncertain time for all the dogs. *Some will live. Many will die.* Generations of Chukchi canine instinct and intelligent breeding messaged this cruel reality. One of their own had been taken, and soon another might be. The call in the wild suddenly quieted, and not a sound penetrated the atmosphere. No wolves. No bear. No sea birds. Only one sound carried over arctic winds: Rune's cries to the heavens to save Anya.

Sepp stepped back and let Rune have his time with Anya. The girl might not live, and he could see how Rune cared for her and how he suffered. Even so, he couldn't give Rune more than a minute or two. He meant to help Rune get Anya to Nome and to the doctor. There might be something someone could do. Maybe her wounds weren't fatal. But for the moment, Sepp gave Rune and Anya their privacy.

"Anya, Anya," Rune cried against her chest. "Please don't leave me. I need you. Please," he wept on.

On some level Anya could hear him. She didn't want to leave Rune, but she didn't know any way other way than to die with Spirit. Her time on Native Earth was ending sooner than she'd thought. When Rune's tears mixed with her own, she bathed in the sunshine of such a sensation. It would have to warm her unto eternity, the distant memory of Rune Johansson's love. Would she even have any memory after the end?

An odd sensation struck, like someone was shaking her, and it wasn't Rune. What was prickling at her senses at such a time — her time of dying. Who? Then she knew . . . *Nana-tasha.* Her grandmother whispered close. Anya could hear her.

"There, there, my child. Have no fear. I am always with you. When you lie down, and when you rise up, I am with you. I have never left you. The Gatekeepers have never left you. You carried a great burden for the people. You became master over the Darkness after us. You did not fail in anything. The war of ghosts is won. Our bloodlines remain pure and steadfast. I have never been more proud of my beautiful and brave granddaughter, in Spirit and on Native Earth. It is time to let Spirit go, and take up Rune Johansson's hand. Your lives are destined."

Anya's eyes flew open at the sound of Nana-tasha's voice. In that instant she saw her beloved grandmother before her, outlined in a vision of mist and magic. The vision held for only a moment — a life-giving moment — before vanishing into the crisp, clean air.

"Thank God," Rune whispered prayerfully, as soon as he realized Anya hadn't died. His tear-filled, watch eyes were for Anya, only her.

"All right, you two." Leonhard Seppala stepped over to the sled, relieved Anya had come to. "We must get to Nome and to the doctor. Come on, both of you," he ordered like a father might. If he felt any emotion over the scene, Sepp kept it to himself.

"Wait, Sepp." Anya strained to talk. "Give me a moment with Rune, just one before we leave."

"*Ja,* I will, but only one," he said and winked at the young couple. He walked over to the waiting team to tend their wounds and make good use of his time.

"Anya, you must res—"

"No," she interrupted. "You must tell me what happened. I know Spirit is gone. I know that. Is Mooglo?" she demanded of Rune.

"Yes."

"After . . . he killed her?"

"Yes," Rune said again.

"How did you get to him? I know you must have killed him."

"I used Sepp's rifle. I shot him three times and the bullets killed him."

"But Rune, how could a gun kill such a demon?"

Rune wiped away his tears and smiled at Anya with all the love he felt within him. Then he ran a finger over her quizzical brow and down her cheek.

"Three guardians stood against him. He was no match. I think our combined force was too much for him. That is how a mere gun could kill such a demon, my Anya," Rune said.

"You, Sepp, and me," she softly spelled out.

"Exactly."

"The human spirit must prevail, Rune . . . and we did." Anya turned her cheek enough to place a gentle kiss on Rune's palm, and then raised her hand to cover his.

Xander broke ranks with his pack and ran over to the sled, wanting to comfort, and in desperate need of comfort himself. Anya reached out and scratched behind his ears. Rune stroked his back, ruffling Xander's thick fur.

A distant cry across the wild caught the attention of all three.

Xander answered the call.

Rune wondered where it came from.

Anya knew. *There's my good girl,* she thought. Zellie had made it home to the Gatekeepers after all.

HISTORICAL NOTE

Throughout this trilogy the evil-spirited golem is a representation of Joseph Stalin.

The demonic spark instilled in him at birth knew no bounds. The horror he visited upon mankind when he held power in Russia is well documented. What is not well known, I believe, is the horror he visited upon the Chukchi of far northeast Siberia and their beloved dogs. The moment I came across the cold fact Joseph Stalin ordered the mass execution of all Chukchi dogs and their breeders in the wake of communist collectivization and industrialization, essentially erasing thousands of years of careful breeding and wiping out the Siberian husky in Russia for the next eighty years, I couldn't find my PC fast enough to begin this story!

In addition to killing an estimated forty million people, Joseph Stalin tried to kill off the Siberian husky breed and wipe them from history. It didn't work, thanks to the importations of the Chukchi dog to Alaska in the early decades of the twentieth century and to the quintessential sled dog driver, the great Leonhard Seppala.

A Russian fur trader brought the first group of ten Siberian huskies to the District of Alaska in 1908, the year before the Nome Kennel Club founded and put in place the All Alaska Sweepstakes, to run every year in April at the end of the winter season. Focus from near and far turned to this prestigious, moneyed race. The next importation of approximately seventy Siberian huskies was in 1909. Then in 1911, fourteen more came. In 1914, eight more were brought to the Alaska Territory, to be followed by four more huskies in 1927. The last recorded importation of the Chukchi dog to America's last frontier took place in 1930, with an addition of eight dogs.

The total number of Siberian huskies imported to Alaska from 1908 through 1930 roughly equaled one hundred fourteen purebred Chukchi dogs. In 1930 trade with Russia was shut down, thereby preventing exports of any goods to the West, including Siberian huskies. This is the same year the breed was officially recognized by the American Kennel Club — serendipity, perhaps.

Why do these numbers and dates matter?

One source I found, *Salazka Siberian Huskies,* cites, "The development of our breed can only be attributed to the 42 dogs that Seppala took from Alaska to Maine in October 1926 and the 20 in October 1927. . . . Of all these dogs, only eight are foundation dogs represented in today's registered Siberian husky. They are: Togo (M), Harry (M), Smoky (M), Kolyma (F), Nome (F), Pearl (F), Dushka (F) and Sonia (F). Added to these . . . were the two surviving 1930 imports: Kreevanka (M) and Tserko (M), and two other dogs having a significant impact on the breed . . . 'Tuck' and 'Duke.' Therefore all of today's stock of registered Siberians are direct descendants of the above twelve dogs."

Now you know why numbers and dates matter. Not only did the original one hundred fourteen Chukchi dogs imported to Alaska register as important to sled dog racing, but these dogs — at the expert-dog-driving hand and careful-attention-to-breeding hand of Leonhard Seppala — formed the foundation for today's stock of registered Siberians.

One might argue the betting odds were "114 to 12" in our favor. We in America have reaped the benefits of such a win by saving the *Watch Eyes* of the Siberian husky, and in so doing, exposing Joseph Stalin for the demonic golem he was!

GLOSSARY

Ah — I
Anquallat village — coastal village
Ar gammel — years old
Awrite — hello
Aye — yes
Blether — long talk, chat
Bra — good
Braw — good
Cannae — cannot
Cheerio — goodbye
Dampskip — steamship
Dinnaeken — I do not know.
Dod — dead
Dodsfall — death
Doon — down
Dotter — daughter
Drukket — drunk
Dug — dog
Dutch socks — wool socks
Eskaleut — native Eskimo languages
Far — father

Farval — farewell

Fru — wife

Glass — ice

Golem — an artificial creature created by magic; an animated personified being created entirely from inanimate matter; attribution of human form to anything other than a human being

Gronlandshund — husky

Hakapik — heavy wooden club with hammerhead and metal hook on end

Hallo — hello

Haud — hold

Heid — head

Ice floe — flat expanse of floating ice

Isen — ice

Jente — girl

Ja — yes

Ken — know

Kerker — Chukchi outer fur coverall

Kin — understand

Kulak — wealthy peasant (Russia)

Lighter boat — takes passengers and supplies ashore from a large ship

Mah-ma — mama

Mener — mean

Mor — mother

Mukluks — knee-high fur boots

Naw — no

Nayiq — seal

Nee — not

Nej — no

Nio ar gammal — nine years old

Noo — now

Oot — out

Polog — fur-lined sleeping box inside tented yaranga of the Chukchi, large enough for family

Profeti — prophecy

Shaman — communicates with native spirits; a healer; a holy man or woman

Sibir — Siberia

Sibirsk hunder — Siberian huskies

Siwash socks — socks cut out of Hudson's Bay blankets for wearing inside moccasins

Sjorya — sailor's blanket; wool sailcloth

Skepp — ship

Slede — sled

Takk — thank you

Tatties — potatoes

Yaranga — Chukchi home; walrus-hide covered tent with large center pole

ABOUT THE AUTHOR

I've raised and loved Siberian huskies for over forty years. My last husky, Xander, died at the age of fourteen. His death prompted me to research Siberian huskies to find their story. When I did, I began the Watch Eyes Trilogy. Before this YA/Frontier Fantasy Fiction series, I wrote historical romance set in the Old West. My eight published novels to date are with Five Star, Gale/Cengage.

Arctic Storm, Arctic Shadow, and *Arctic Will* are set in the Arctic West.

I live between Colorado and California, my husband and I ever chasing down our children and grandchildren scattered therein. Though retired from nursing, the time I have to write is precious little. I've taken the coveted 4 a.m. slot. Sorry, folks.

My best to you, readers all,
Joanne Sundell